Also by Daniel Silva

DANIEL SILVA

A GABRIEL ALLON THRILLER

AN
INSIDE JOB

HarperCollins*Publishers*

HarperCollins*Publishers*
Australia • Brazil • Canada • France • Germany • Holland • India
Italy • Japan • Mexico • New Zealand • Poland • Spain • Sweden
Switzerland • United Kingdom • United States of America

HarperCollins acknowledges the Traditional Custodians
of the lands upon which we live and work, and pays respect
to Elders past and present.

First published in the United States of America in 2025
by HarperCollins*Publishers*
First published on Gadigal Country in Australia in 2025
by HarperCollins*Publishers* Australia Pty Limited
ABN 36 009 913 517
harpercollins.com.au

HarperCollins*Publishers*
Macken House, 39/40 Mayor Street Upper
Dublin 1, D01 C9W8, Ireland

A catalogue record for this book is available from the National Library of Australia

ISBN 978 1 4607 6628 6 (paperback)
ISBN 978 1 4607 1772 1 (ebook)
ISBN 978 1 4607 3682 1 (audiobook)

Cover design by HarperCollins Design Studio
Cover image by Adobe Stock
Author photograph by Marco Grob
Typeset in Garamond Premier Pro
Printed and bound in Australia by McPherson's Printing Group

MIX
Paper | Supporting
responsible forestry
FSC
www.fsc.org   FSC® C001695

*As always, for my wife, Jamie, and
my children, Lily and Nicholas*

Beauty perishes in life but is immortal in art.

—Leonardo da Vinci

Cast of Characters

GABRIEL ALLON	Art conservator, retired spy
CHIARA ZOLLI	Tiepolo Restoration Company
IRENE AND RAPHAEL ALLON	Children of Gabriel Allon and Chiara Zolli
ELENORA SAVIANO	Principal, Scuola Primaria Bernardo Canal
CESARE FERRARI	Commander, Art Squad
LUCA ROSSETTI	Art Squad officer
COLONEL BAGGIO	Carabinieri officer, Venice
COLONEL MANCINI	Carabinieri officer, Florence
MASSIMO RAVELLO	Medical examiner, Venice
LUIGI DONATI	Supreme pontiff, Roman Catholic Church
FATHER MARK KEEGAN	Papal private secretary
ALOIS METZLER	Commandant, Pontifical Swiss Guard
CARDINAL MATTEO BERTOLI	*Sostituto*, Vatican Secretariat of State
ANTONIO CALVESI	Chief conservator, Vatican Museums

PENELOPE RADCLIFF	Apprentice conservator, Vatican Museums
DONATELLA RICCI	Conservator, Vatican Museums
ALESSIO TOMASSINI	Head of security, Vatican Museums
OTTAVIO POZZI	Security guard, Vatican Museums
ESTEBAN RODRÍGUEZ	Director, Vatican Press Office
VERONICA MARCHESE	Director, National Etruscan Museum
GIORGIO MONTEFIORE	Leonardo scholar, Uffizi Gallery
MARTIN LANDESMANN	Swiss financier
INGRID JOHANSEN	Professional thief, computer hacker
AMELIA MARCH	*ARTnews* magazine
JULIAN ISHERWOOD	London art dealer
SARAH BANCROFT	London art dealer, former CIA operative
CHRISTOPHER KELLER	Field agent, Secret Intelligence Service
OLIVER DIMBLEBY	London art dealer
NICHOLAS LOVEGROVE	British art consultant

NILES DUNHAM	Curator, National Gallery
JEREMY CRABBE	Bonhams, London
SIMON MENDENHALL	Christie's, London
GEOFFREY HOLLAND	Director, Courtauld Gallery
PETER VAN DE VELDE	Dutch art dealer
STÉPHANE TREMBLAY	French art consultant
JACQUES MÉNARD	French art crime detective
FRANCO TEDESCHI	SBL PrivatBank, Lugano
NICO AMBROSI	Piedmont Global Capital, Milan
MARKUS VOGEL	Executive Jet Services, Zurich
ALEXANDER PROKHOROV	Russian oligarch, art collector
TERESSA SIMONETTI	Florentine noblewoman
SALVATORE ALVARO	Camorra assassin

Preface

L uigi Donati was introduced in *The Confessor*, the third book of the Gabriel Allon series. He was then the private secretary of Pietro Lucchesi, who chose the pontifical name Paul VII. Donati was elected pope in the dramatic conclave that followed Lucchesi's death. In my fictitious version of the Vatican, the papacies of Joseph Ratzinger and Jorge Mario Bergoglio, the supreme pontiffs Benedict XVI and Francis, did not occur.

———————

PART ONE

Sfumato

1

San Polo

The straight-backed wooden chairs in Dottoressa Saviano's anteroom were instruments of torture. Chiara, try as she might, could find no arrangement of her limbs that provided even a moment of comfort. At present she sat with the erect carriage of a dancer, with her hands folded atop her knees and her feet together on the scuffed wooden floor. The *dottoressa*'s secretary had cast several admiring glances at Chiara's stylish pumps—and at her stylish husband as well. She was used to women staring at Gabriel; he was still impossibly handsome. He also happened to be one of the world's finest art conservators, which conferred upon him an unwelcome local celebrity. Chiara managed the restoration company that employed him. For better or worse, they were among the most prominent couples in Venice.

Their young twins, a boy named for the painter Raphael and a girl called Irene, attended a public *scuola primaria* a few minutes' walk from the family's apartment overlooking the Grand Canal. Dottoressa Elenora Saviano, the school's principal, had asked Chiara to drop by her office at 2:00 p.m. to address a matter of the utmost urgency, the nature of which she had refused to discuss over the *telefonino*. The *dottoressa* had insisted, however, that Gabriel attend the meeting as well, for what reason she declined to say. The implication was that the undisclosed problem was serious. Chiara was confident she knew the identity of the culprit.

The secretary stole another glance at Gabriel, who pretended not to notice. He was scrolling through the headlines on his new iPhone, a replacement for the device that was damaged during a recent visit to the west of England. His chair was identical to Chiara's, and yet he looked the very picture of contentment.

"What's your secret?" she asked.

"I spend all day on my feet in front of paintings. This is a welcome change of pace."

"What about your back?"

"I swallowed a few of my little green friends before I left the apartment."

Chiara turned her head toward the anteroom's only window. It overlooked the school's central courtyard, which was deserted and darkened by shadow. There was a climbing apparatus and a space for games involving balls, but otherwise the students were left to their own devices during recess. Such was the existence of children in Venice. They played in the *calle* or the *campo* and afterward went to the *pasticceria* for a sweet. It had never occurred to Chiara, a Venetian by birth, that children might live any other way. When she was a young girl, she had loved her enchanted city of canals and bridges and ancient churches filled with art. Occasionally she went to the Giardini Pubblici for a bit of peace and quiet. But for the most part the only flora she saw were the six trees in the Campo di Ghetto Nuovo, the broad square in Cannaregio where her ancestors had lived for centuries.

She awakened her phone and discreetly checked the time. The ever-vigilant secretary noticed nevertheless.

"I'm sure it won't be much longer, Signora Zolli."

"We were told—"

The secretary's phone rang before Chiara could finish the thought. It seemed the *dottoressa* would see them now. And only fifteen minutes later than promised.

She received them with a doge-like solemnity while seated behind her desk. She was a short woman of perhaps fifty with the figure of a wine barrel. Her hair was pulled back severely from her face. Oversize spectacles magnified a pair of unblinking eyes.

They settled first on Gabriel. "Is it true, Signore Allon?"

"Is what true, Dottoressa Saviano?"

"That you have received a commission to restore the Titian in Santa Maria della Salute."

The painting, *The Descent of the Holy Spirit*, hung above one of the basilica's chapels. The Tiepolo Restoration Company, under Chiara's capable leadership, had been awarded the contract to conduct a long-overdue cleaning of the canvas—with the proviso that the work be carried out by none other than the renowned director of the firm's paintings department. A story to that effect had appeared the previous week in *Il Gazzettino*. Of course it was true, thought Chiara. Everyone in Venice knew it was true.

Gabriel's reply was more diplomatic. "As a matter of fact, I began work on it yesterday."

"Is it your first Titian?"

Chiara counted slowly to ten while her husband, with admirable forbearance, explained that he had restored numerous paintings by Titian and his workshop. He might have added that he had restored the Bellini altarpieces in San Zaccaria and San Giovanni Crisostomo, one of the Veroneses in San Sebastiano, and a Tintoretto in dell'Orte. And then, of course, there was Caravaggio's magisterial *Deposition of Christ*, one of several paintings he had cleaned clandestinely for the Vatican Museums. As it happened, his old friend was now the supreme pontiff. Not surprisingly, Gabriel neglected to mention that as well.

"Might I impose on you for a small favor?" inquired the *dottoressa*.

"How small?"

"I was wondering whether you might agree to show the children how you go about restoring a painting. We won't stay for long. Perhaps an hour or two."

Gabriel, with a glance, requested Chiara's assistance.

"I'm sorry, Dottoressa Saviano, but my husband never allows anyone to observe him while he works."

"And why is that, Signore Allon?"

Once again it was Chiara who supplied the answer. "He believes the great artists of the Venetian Renaissance deserve to have their work presented in the best possible light. He opposes any public display of paintings in a damaged state."

"He doesn't want to spoil the illusion?"

Chiara frowned. "Surely this isn't the reason you wanted to see us."

"I wish it were so."

Copies of the children's files lay on Dottoressa Saviano's desk. She set aside Raphael's—the boy was a math prodigy who was now studying with a tutor at the university—and opened Irene's instead. Chiara steeled herself for the worst.

"Your daughter is a remarkable child, Signora Zolli. I have been most impressed by her academic performance, not to mention the speed of her assimilation."

Chiara raised an eyebrow.

"I was just pointing out that Irene is somewhat new to Venice."

"But her mother is not. The Zolli family has been living here since the fifteenth century."

"But your children were born abroad."

"They are as Italian as their classmates."

The *dottoressa* sighed. They had reached an impasse. "Perhaps we should begin again."

"Yes, let's. What seems to be the issue?"

"Irene is a natural leader. Even the older students look up to her. But I'm afraid she holds rather strident political opinions for one so young."

"Since when is having an opinion a problem?"

Dottoressa Saviano opened Irene's file and extracted a single sheet of paper. "Copies of this were posted throughout the school three days ago. We have reason to believe that Irene was responsible."

"What is it?"

"See for yourself," said Dottoressa Saviano, and handed over the document. It was a call for a one-day student strike to protest the Italian government's inaction on the issue of climate change. "I have to admit, it's extremely well written for a child of her age. Or perhaps you had a hand in its drafting."

"I didn't."

"Does Irene have a computer at home?"

"Yes, of course."

"Perhaps you should monitor it more carefully."

Chiara handed the document to Gabriel. He smiled as he read it.

"You find it amusing, Signore Allon?"

"Quite."

"I don't. Not in the least. Evidently your daughter has managed to convince nearly the entire student body to boycott their classes next Wednesday. They plan to march through all six *sestieri* and stage a rally in the Piazza San Marco."

"What would be the harm? In fact, it might actually do some good. The young have a right to be worried about their future."

"The current government does not see it that way. The education minister is of the opinion that global warming is a hoax perpetrated by the political left."

"There's a lot of that going around."

"If the boycott goes forward, there will be serious consequences."

"For whom?"

"Your daughter, for one."

Gabriel returned the document. "And what if we were able to find an elegant solution to the problem?"

"What did you have in mind?"

"I prefer not to negotiate with myself."

"That's where we're different, you and I."

"How so?"

The *dottoressa* smiled. "I never negotiate."

Gabriel's opening position was that the protest march would take place on a Saturday rather than a weekday, that there would be no disruption of classes and no further posting of flyers on school property, and that none of the participants, including the organizer, would be punished in any way. In exchange, the organizer's father would agree to allow a small delegation of students to observe him carrying out one of the most important restorations undertaken in Venice in many years.

"The delegation," countered Dottoressa Saviano, "will consist of the entire *scuola primaria*."

"Out of the question."

"And the visit will be two hours in duration, giving you sufficient time to deliver a lecture on the Renaissance in Venice before commencing your demonstration."

Gabriel sighed. "Done."

"Not quite."

"What now?"

"A number of our students have shown artistic promise. I feel that with the proper instruction . . ."

Chiara began to object, but Gabriel placed a hand on her forearm. "I'd love nothing more. How soon can we start?"

"I'll leave that to your discretion, Signore Allon." The *dottoressa* returned the flyer to Irene's academic file, then, upon further reflection, consigned it to the rubbish bin. "I know you're terribly busy."

Chiara managed to smile as she bade the *dottoressa* a pleasant afternoon, but her anger boiled over downstairs as she followed Gabriel into the street.

"The nerve of that woman."

"She was a worthy opponent, I have to admit."

"She's an extortionist. And you, for some inexplicable reason, surrendered without a fight."

"There was a method to my madness."

"You were trying to protect your daughter?"

"I suppose I was."

"Talk about madness," murmured Chiara.

"She's spirited. There's a difference."

Thirty minutes remained until the end of the school day, so they walked to Bar Dogale in the Campo dei Frari and ordered coffee. The counterman served Gabriel's with *un'ombra*, a small glass of white wine. Chiara requested one as well.

"What are we going to do with her?" she asked.

"The *dottoressa*?"

"Your daughter."

"Enjoy every minute we have with her."

"That's easy for you to say."

"What's that supposed to mean?"

"It means that, for understandable reasons, Irene has you wrapped around her finger. Therefore, despite her frequent misbehavior, you have never once disciplined her."

"Why would I want to do a thing like that?"

"Tell me something, Gabriel. Do you think your daughter is a *normal* child?"

"Of course not. But neither is her brother."

"Or her father, for that matter," added Chiara quietly.

"Let's hope Dottoressa Saviano doesn't find out. Otherwise she might have second thoughts about taking me on as a part-time art instructor."

"Have you taken leave of your senses?"

"It's something I've wanted to do for a long time."

"Teach?"

Gabriel nodded.

"Why not teach at the university?"

"They won't have me. Unlike you, I don't possess an advanced degree from an esteemed institution of higher learning."

The truth was, Gabriel had no degree at all; he had abandoned his formal study of art to undertake a mission of vengeance for his country's secret intelligence service. Chiara, after completing her graduate studies at the University of Padua, had worked for the same service.

"Perhaps I should begin referring to myself as Dottoressa Zolli," she said.

"It does have a nice ring to it."

"But how will your students address you?"

"Signore Allon, I suppose."

"What about Maestro Allon?"

"Can you imagine?"

"I can, actually. You're looking more and more like a maestro every day." Chiara trailed the tip of her forefinger through Gabriel's platinum-colored hair. Then she turned to the barman and asked, "Wouldn't you agree, Paolo?"

"By all means, Dottoressa Zolli. I shall refer to him by no other name from this day forward." The barman winked at Gabriel. "Another glass of wine, Maestro?"

"A fine idea. And one for Dottoressa Zolli as well."

"I couldn't possibly," she protested.

"I must obey the maestro," said the barman, and placed two more glasses of wine on the counter.

Chiara nudged hers toward Gabriel. "Have you decided what you're going to say to your daughter?"

"I was planning to leave that in your capable hands."

"Not this time, darling. It's your turn."

"Shall I read her the riot act?"

"You will explain that what she did was wrong. Then you will suggest she find a new hobby. Saving the world from the coming climate apocalypse is exhausting her mother."

Gabriel eyed the barman. "What say you, Paolo? Do you think I should discipline my daughter for trying to organize a march about climate change?"

"Please don't, Maestro Allon. Irene is a perfect child. Perhaps the most perfect child in the entire *sestiere* of San Polo."

"That settles it, then."

Gabriel laid a pair of banknotes on the counter and escorted Chiara back to the school. The first children were spilling from the doorway when they arrived. Irene and Raphael, as always, emerged simultaneously. They were surprised to see both of their parents waiting in the street. Irene, an unusually perceptive child, instinctively took Gabriel's hand rather than her mother's.

"Do you know why we're here?" he asked as they walked along the Calle dei Saoneri.

The child nodded, then began to sob. Gabriel glanced helplessly at Chiara. With a circular gesture of her hand, she implored him to press his advantage.

"What were you thinking?" he asked.

"I thought it was the right thing to do."

"That's all well and good, but you went about it entirely the wrong way."

"How?"

"The flyer, for one. It was a terrible mistake." Gabriel brushed the tears from his daughter's face. "You must never allow your adversary to know what you're thinking."

2

Dorsoduro

It arrived in the summer of 1630, having made its way eastward from Milan, which had tried and failed to contain its spread. The Republic, with its busy port and humid air, proved a gracious host, as it had several times in the past. The fleas killed the rats first, then the people. Nearly twenty-one thousand perished between September and December alone. By the time it was finally over, a third of the population was gone. Though the doge and the Council of Ten did not know it then, Venice would never be the same.

The Venetian Senate, while the plague was still raging, decreed that a new basilica should be built on the Punta della Dogana in Dorsoduro, that it should be dedicated to the Virgin Mary, and that once each year, on the feast day celebrating her presentation at the Temple in Jerusalem, the senators and the doge would convene there after processing across the Grand Canal over a pontoon bridge. Gabriel arrived at the basilica early the following morning in a far less conspicuous manner—aboard a Number 1 vaporetto. He made his way across the deserted quay to a seldom-used side entrance crowned by a stone Venetian lion. Two knocks on the heavy wooden door summoned an elderly priest in a black cassock.

"*Buongiorno*, Signore Allon. And how are you this day?"

"Not well, I'm afraid."

"Are you under the weather?"

"No, Father Giovanni. It seems my wife is angry with me."

"Again?" The priest gave a sigh of resignation. "What have you done now, my son?"

"It's cumulative at this point, Father. Therefore, I have no hope of forgiveness."

"Perhaps I might have a word with her."

"I'd leave well enough alone, if I were you. Chances are it will only make matters worse."

The old priest escorted Gabriel into the murky half-light of the basilica. Eight radiating chapels ringed the soaring octagonal central nave. The view of one of the chapels was obstructed by a shrouded scaffold.

"I'll leave you to your work," said the priest, and vanished into the gloom.

Gabriel slipped through a gap in the tarpaulin and climbed the scaffolding to his work platform. For now, his supplies were limited to a flask of carefully calibrated solvent, a package of wooden dowels, and four bags of cotton wool—enough cotton wool, he reckoned, to remove the dirty varnish from approximately half of the enormous canvas. Three months was the estimate he had given the Venetian cultural authorities, with another three months to execute the required retouching. He might have managed to complete the restoration in a timelier fashion were it not for the fact that the basilica, one of Venice's most prominent tourist attractions, would remain open to the public for the duration of the project. It was not, for any number of reasons, Gabriel's preferred method of working.

He switched on a pair of standing halogen lamps, casting a harsh white light over the surface of the painting, then wound a swatch of cotton wool around the end of a dowel. It was his habit to listen to opera or classical music while he worked—with an old portable CD player, a faithful companion during countless restorations past—but present circumstances forbade it. He dipped his first cotton swab in solvent and twirled it gently over the wing of the radiant white dove near the top of the canvas. The soiled varnish dissolved at once, exposing Titian's masterly brushwork.

"*Buongiorno*, Signore Vecellio," said Gabriel quietly. "And how are you on this fine morning? Not well? I'm so sorry to hear that. Is your wife the problem, or has your child incurred the wrath of the doge by attempting to organize a march to protest the combustion of fossil fuels? What are fossil fuels, you ask? Perhaps another time, my old friend. It's a long story."

Gabriel discarded the soiled swath of cotton wool and fashioned another. He fell into the familiar rhythm of his craft—*dip, twirl, discard . . . dip, twirl, discard*—and by 9:00 a.m., when the doors of the basilica were thrown open, he had managed to clean a rectangle of canvas measuring about twenty by thirty centimeters. Before long he heard the squeak and shuffle of shoes over the marble floor, and by ten o'clock there was a persistent multilingual din of conversation. He persevered until ten thirty before switching off the lamps and descending the scaffold. As he emerged from behind the tarpaulin, a woman who spoke English with a British accent attempted to engage him in conversation. He feigned an inability to speak her language and, smiling apologetically, set off across the nave.

Outside, he stood on the steps of the basilica and inhaled the first cool, dry air of the season. On the opposite side of the Grand Canal, hidden away amid the luxury shops lining the Calle Larga XXII Marzo, were the business offices of the Tiepolo Restoration Company. He rang the firm's general manager and asked if she was free for coffee.

"Sorry, darling. But I'm unavailable."

"For how long?"

"The foreseeable future."

"And what if I were to grovel?"

"I might consent to having a drink with you later."

Gabriel crossed the wooden bridge spanning the Rio della Salute and set off toward Caffè Poggi, a quaint little bar near the Accademia. It was his second visit to the establishment, but the proprietor greeted him as though he had been coming there every morning for years. They exchanged pleasantries and banalities about the state of the world while Gabriel drank two coffees and devoured a cornetto filled with sweet almond paste.

"How goes the Titian?" the proprietor asked suddenly.

"How did you know?"

The proprietor indicated the display of Italian newspapers. "I read about it in *Il Gazzettino*, Signore Allon."

"The Titian goes quite well."

"Will I see you tomorrow?"

"I imagine so," said Gabriel, and went into the street. He took his time walking back to the basilica and arrived to find a line of tourists stretching from the doorway. It was the late-morning rush, the busiest part of the day. Fortunately the doors would close at noon and remain shuttered for three blessed hours, during which time Gabriel would have the place to himself. Better to delay his return by a few minutes, he thought, than to deal with the disruptive noise of the crowds.

And so he continued along the *fondamenta* to the observation point at the tip of the Punta della Dogana. Perhaps a half kilometer to the east, across an expanse of sparkling water, was the magnificent church of San Giorgio Maggiore. Even Gabriel, a jaded Venetian, never tired of the view.

For several minutes it was his alone to enjoy. Eventually two tourists appeared—Americans, newlyweds apparently—and prevailed upon him to take their photograph. He posed them with Maggiore in the background and snapped the picture. The woman was on the left side of the image, her husband the right. Gabriel thought the photo rather good, though it was marred slightly by a dark mass floating on the surface of the water near the man's outer shoulder.

He reframed the image, tapped the shutter icon, and surrendered the phone. The young Americans stayed another minute and then departed. Alone once more, Gabriel searched the white-flecked waters of the *laguna* for the object he had seen a moment ago. The dark floating mass, whatever it was, was gone.

———

There was a water taxi idling along the quay outside the basilica. Gabriel told the pilot about the object he had seen in the *laguna*, and the pilot, who spent fourteen hours a day navigating the waters of Venice, assured him it was probably nothing.

Gabriel handed the pilot a hundred euros. "Why don't we have a look, just to be sure?"

"If you wish, Signore. It's your money."

Gabriel stood at the pilot's shoulder as he eased away from the quay and headed toward Maggiore. "Here," he said after a moment. "This is where I saw it."

"There's nothing, Signore."

"Put your engine in neutral, please."

Frowning, the pilot did as Gabriel asked, and the sleek wooden vessel slowed to a stop. The pilot searched the waters off the port side,

Gabriel the starboard. Seeing no sign of the object, he ducked into the passenger cabin and headed aft.

"There!" he shouted. "There it is."

It had resurfaced about thirty meters from the taxi's stern. Gabriel rejoined the pilot as he engaged the inboard engines and came slowly about. But the object, visible a moment earlier, had once again disappeared from view.

"It's probably just a plastic rubbish bag, Signore. The *laguna* is full of them."

"Do you have a boat hook on board?"

It was a retractable model, four meters in length when fully extended, with a scratch-resistant plastic hook. Gabriel probed the waters off the starboard side of the vessel until he made contact with something heavy and sodden. After several failed attempts, he managed to snare the object and guide it gently toward the surface. The pilot fumbled for the handset of his radio as a human corpse, bloated and partially decomposed, floated into view.

"Don't," said Gabriel as he drew the phone from his pocket. "I'll take care of everything."

3

San Zaccaria

The regional headquarters of the Arma dei Carabinieri, one of Italy's two national police forces, were located in the Campo San Zaccaria. Capitano Luca Rossetti was attached to the Division for the Defense of Cultural Patrimony, better known as the Art Squad. Gabriel occasionally served as a consultant to the unit and had worked with Rossetti on a major international forgery investigation. Despite a regrettable case of mistaken identity in a darkened *corte* in San Polo—one that left Rossetti with a broken jaw and Gabriel with several fractured bones in his right hand—they remained the best of friends.

"Where?" asked the Italian policeman.

"Walk through the *sotoportego*. You can't miss me."

Rossetti hurried downstairs to the *campo* and, phone in hand, sprinted through the passageway that led to the Riva degli Schiavoni, the monumental waterfront promenade stretching along the Grand Canal. There were the usual tourists and vendors, but Rossetti saw no evidence of a dead body.

"I'm sorry, but I don't see you."

"I'm in the water taxi about a hundred meters due west of Maggiore."

Rossetti spotted the vessel at once. Gabriel was hanging over the starboard side, a phone in one hand, a rescue pole in the other.

"Whatever you do," said Rossetti, "don't let it go."

Because this was Venice, the Carabinieri maintained a substantial fleet of vessels, the first of which arrived just three minutes after Gabriel's call. Five more craft appeared soon after, along with waterborne units of the Polizia di Stato, the Guardia di Finanza, and even the Coast Guard. The armada quickly established a blockade around the crime scene, temporarily halting traffic on both the Grand and Giudecca Canals. Gabriel grimly maintained control of the corpse for several more minutes before surrendering it to a pair of Carabinieri crime scene technicians. As they hauled the body into a flat-bottomed pontoon boat, the pilot of the water taxi turned away and was violently sick over the port gunwale.

"Shall I take us back to the basilica?" asked Gabriel.

"It's against regulations."

"I think they'll make an exception in this case."

Gabriel started the taxi's engines and crept forward, breaching the blockade between two of the police craft. The traffic on the Grand Canal was at a standstill. He guided the taxi past motionless barges and vaporetti and slid into an empty spot along the quay.

"Are you feeling any better?" he asked the pilot.

"A little. But I'm not sure I'll ever forget what I saw this morning."

Neither would Gabriel. He had once discovered the body of a notorious Italian tomb raider in a vat of acid. This was worse.

He stepped onto the quay and headed up the steps of the basilica. The nave was teeming with tourists, seemingly unaware of the commotion outside. Gabriel was glad of their company. He climbed the scaffolding to his work platform and switched on the halogen lamps, flooding the Titian with dazzling white light.

"Sorry for the delay, Signore Vecellio," he said quietly as he prepared his first swab. "But you'll never guess what I just discovered in the Canal Grande."

———————

The doors of the basilica closed promptly at noon, and a heavy silence fell over the nave. Gabriel worked without a break until half past one, when he received a call from Luca Rossetti.

"We need a statement."

"On what particular subject?"

"This morning's discovery. The lead detective would like you to drop by the *stazione*."

"I'm sure he would, but I'm rather busy at the moment."

"In that case, we'll come to you."

They arrived twenty minutes later and, as instructed, knocked on the side door. The detective was a tall, gaunt figure called Baggio who wore on his shoulders the three silver stars of a *colonnello*. Gabriel explained that he had spotted something floating on the surface of the *laguna* at approximately 11:00 a.m., that he had hired a water taxi to investigate the matter, and that the object in the water, as he had feared, turned out to be a human corpse. The advanced state of decomposition made it impossible to say with any certainty whether the decedent was a man or a woman, but it appeared to Gabriel as though it was the latter.

"That is indeed the case," replied Baggio.

"It looked as though she had been in the water for a while."

"Perhaps, Signore Allon. But in my experience, the *laguna* is most unkind to the dead."

"Is there any evidence of trauma?"

"Our investigation has just begun. But you needn't concern yourself with such questions. As of this moment, your role in this unfortunate matter is officially over."

"I would appreciate it if you kept my name out of the papers."

Colonel Baggio shrugged his shoulders noncommittally. "Leaks happen, Signore Allon. But I assure you, the press won't hear anything from me."

Gabriel showed the two Carabinieri officers out and resumed work on the Titian. The crowds returned at three o'clock and remained until five, when the attendants herded them out the door. Gabriel waited until the nave was empty before switching off the lamps and descending the scaffolding.

Outside, he crossed the quay to the vaporetto stop. A Number 1 was traversing the Grand Canal diagonally from the direction of San Marco. He boarded it a moment later and went into the passenger cabin. Chiara was seated in the first row, her eyes on her mobile phone.

Gabriel sat down next to her. "I was promised a drink."

"Tough day at the office?"

"Eventful."

"So I heard," said Chiara, and handed over her phone. The lead item in *Il Gazzettino* concerned a grisly discovery in the waters near the church of San Giorgio Maggiore. The story was accompanied by a photograph of a man with platinum-colored hair leaning over the side of a water taxi, a retractable pole in his hands. The object pinned against the side of the hull was faintly visible. "Care to explain?"

"I invited you to have coffee with me. And you, of course, refused." Gabriel returned Chiara's phone. "Do the children know?"

"Irene was the one who told me."

Gabriel sighed. "You really should limit the amount of time she spends on the computer."

———————

The palazzo stood on the northern bank of the Grand Canal not far from the San Tomà vaporetto stop. From the broad loggia of its *piano nobile*, the Rialto Bridge was visible in the east. The furnishings in the spacious adjoining drawing rooms were contemporary and comfortable, and the walls were hung with an eclectic collection of paintings, including works by Gabriel's mother and grandfather, a noted German Expressionist and disciple of Max Beckmann. In the master bedroom suite were a pair of Modigliani nudes that Gabriel had painted on something of a dare. Propped on the easel in his studio was a canvas by Sebastiano Florigerio, a pro bono favor for the director of the Courtauld Gallery in London.

Gabriel was supposed to be chipping away at the painting in his spare time, but tonight he hadn't the strength, so he sat atop a stool at the kitchen counter, drinking from a large glass of Brunello, while Chiara prepared dinner. The menu, at Gabriel's request, was vegetarian. Nothing with bones and flesh, nothing from the sea.

His phone lay face down before him. He turned it over and looked again at the photograph displayed on the screen. It had been snapped, according to *Il Gazzettino*, by a passenger on a Maggiore-bound vaporetto. Precisely how the newspaper managed to identify the man holding the rescue pole was unclear, though the level of detail suggested a leak from a well-placed official source, probably Colonel Baggio of the Carabinieri. Gabriel shared his suspicions with his wife but received no reply. She was typing on her phone.

"Who is it now?"

"Bianca Locatelli from *La Repubblica*."

"Please give her the same answer that you gave the reporters from *Il Gazzettino* and *Corriere della Sera*."

"We should at least issue a statement."

"Why?"

"If nothing else, it might be good for our business."

"Only if our business was finding dead bodies. Besides, I'm not the story."

Chiara placed an assortment of antipasti on the dining room table and summoned Irene and Raphael. Gabriel was suddenly ravenously hungry, but his appetite faded when the children began to question him about the awful events of the morning. The account he gave was nearly identical to the one he had provided to Colonel Baggio, though he left out any description of the condition of the body.

"Where is she now?" asked Irene.

"In the morgue, I imagine."

"What's a morgue?" inquired Raphael.

"It's a place where the dead are kept until they can be buried. A specialist known as a forensic pathologist will try to determine what happened to her."

"Who was she?"

"The police don't know yet."

"Did someone kill her?" asked Irene.

"They don't know that either. It's quite possible she simply had an accident of some sort."

It was also possible that the woman had taken her own life, but Gabriel had no wish to spoil the meal further with talk of suicide. Chiara, sensing his discomfort, deftly shifted the topic of conversation to Saturday's protest march. It had been Gabriel's brilliant idea, but he had wisely left the planning in his wife's hands. The march would begin, she explained, in the Campo Santi Giovanni e Paolo in Castello and conclude—three hours later, provided the children maintained a steady pace—in the Piazza San Marco.

Eight other parents had agreed to help supervise the affair. Venetian social etiquette dictated that the arduous trek be followed by a celebratory lunch. Chiara had yet to settle on a venue.

"How many marchers are you expecting?"

"It could be as many as a hundred."

"In that case, we'll need outdoor seating."

"Unless we hold the luncheon here."

"Where?" asked Gabriel.

"In our apartment, darling. We have more than enough room, and I'm sure the other mothers will help me prepare the food. This is Venice, after all. It's what we do."

Chiara slipped into the kitchen and returned a few minutes later with a steaming bowl of *risotto alla Milanese*. Gabriel devoured two portions of the saffron-colored rice while Irene and Raphael excitedly worked out the details of hosting a luncheon for one hundred of their schoolmates. The sound of their voices chased the nightmarish vision of the corpse from his thoughts, but it returned later that evening as he stood at the balustrade of his loggia, watching a water taxi beating its way up the Grand Canal. The *laguna*, he thought, had indeed been unkind to her. Now she lay on a tray of cold metal in the Venice municipal morgue, alone and in darkness. A woman without a name. A woman without a face.

4

Terraferma

For the next two days, life in Venice moved at more or less a normal rhythm. The tourists tramped and traipsed, the stalls of the Rialto Market filled and emptied, the tides rose and receded, leaving no new horrors in their wake. A lengthy story about the grisly discovery in the *laguna* appeared on the front page of *Il Gazzettino*'s print edition on Thursday morning, but by Friday the coverage had been relegated to the Venezia section. Police were acting under the assumption there was foul play involved, though they had yet to determine the identity of the decedent. A request for assistance from the public had so far turned up nothing.

Gabriel passed those two otherwise tranquil autumn days atop his work platform in the Basilica di Santa Maria della Salute. The Titian proved a welcome distraction, as did the noisy patrons who filled the nave for five hours each day. He had no wish to discuss his dubious heroics with the barman at Caffè Poggi, so he brought along a thermos flask of coffee each morning and forwent his usual midday break. He worked late on Thursday, but on Friday afternoon he had drinks with Chiara on the terrace of the Monaco. She informed him that the number of marchers for tomorrow's climate demonstration had risen to one hundred and twenty-five.

"How are we possibly going to feed them?"

"Don't worry, darling. The caterers will take care of everything."

"What caterers?"

They arrived at eight the following morning and began erecting circular tables throughout the apartment. Gabriel, after locking the door of his studio, accompanied Chiara and the children to the Campo Santi Giovanni e Paolo, where no fewer than eighty young schoolchildren had already gathered. By nine o'clock, the scheduled start time of the march, their number had swelled to one hundred and fifty. Irene somehow organized them into two orderly columns. Then a loud cheer went up, and they were off.

Twelve parents kept watch over the marchers, with Chiara at the sharp end of the noisy procession and Gabriel, who knew a thing or two about surveillance and protection techniques, in a trailing position. Their route took them westward along the busy Strada Nova, where, with the exception of a few cross words from a Fratelli-supporting shopkeeper, they were well received. They paused briefly in the Campo Santa Fosca for a protective head count, then set off along the Rio Terà San Leonardo toward Santa Lucia. They arrived only fifteen minutes behind schedule. Another quick count, this one conducted by Gabriel, confirmed that they had suffered no losses.

Next they filed over the Ponte degli Scalzi and followed a circuitous route to the Accademia, where they chanted a slogan at the museum's entrance before crossing the Grand Canal a second time. After a final head count, they marched past the luxury boutiques lining the Calle Larga XXII Marzo and entered the Piazza San Marco as the giant bell atop the campanile tolled midday.

Confident they had spared the planet a climate apocalypse, they traveled in a succession of vaporetti from San Marco to San Tomà. The luncheon, like the march before it, proceeded without incident, and by four o'clock the children and the caterers had departed, and a deep and abiding silence settled once more over the rooms of the Allon family's *piano nobile*. They were in agreement that the entire enterprise, despite the unfortunate circumstances that brought it about, had been a resounding success.

Gabriel spent the remainder of the afternoon working on the Florigerio, and the next morning, after consulting the forecast, he coaxed Chiara and the children onto his Bavaria 42 sailboat for a daylong cruise on the Adriatic. They returned to the marina at sunset by the same route they had left it—through the busy Lido Inlet. If the woman's body had arrived in Venice on a morning tide, it would have traveled the same route. Gabriel, as he surveyed his surroundings, thought it improbable. The woman, he reckoned, had died a Venetian death, probably within the city's six historic *sestieri*.

By Monday morning she had vanished from the pages of Venice's daily newspaper, but the terrible image of her faceless corpse remained lodged in Gabriel's memory. He was not at all displeased, therefore, when Dottoressa Saviano suggested that the children drop by the Salute on Thursday for the promised demonstration and lecture. Gabriel arranged for the visit to begin at noon, when the basilica was closed to the public. His audience was attentive throughout the presentation, though Gabriel was distracted by the persistent vibration of his phone. He waited until the children had departed before returning the call.

"What took you so long?" asked Luca Rossetti.

"I was in the middle of something. What's so urgent?"

"The Arma dei Carabinieri requires your assistance."

"I'd love to help, Luca. But I'm unavailable."

"Great," said Rossetti before killing the connection. "Colonel Baggio and I will pick you up in front of the Salute in twenty minutes."

The patrol boat was configured like a typical Venetian water taxi, low and sleek, with an open forward helm station and a cabin aft. Gabriel sat next to Rossetti on one of the upholstered benches, and Colonel Baggio sat opposite. After leaving the Salute, the vessel had rounded the Punta della Dogana and turned into the Giudecca Canal. They were now headed westward across the *laguna* toward the mainland.

"Would you mind telling me where we're going?" asked Gabriel.

"*Terraferma*," replied Baggio.

"I gathered that. But why?"

"It is my understanding that Capitano Rossetti explained the situation."

"He said you required my assistance."

"That about covers it," said Baggio.

They put in at a small marina near the airport and climbed into a waiting unmarked Alfa Romeo, which ferried them at high speed across Mestre, the largest of Venice's four mainland boroughs. Eventually it delivered them to a drab official building above which hung a limp Italian tricolor. Inside, Gabriel followed Rossetti and Baggio into a small conference room. They were soon joined by a man clad in pale blue scrubs who carried with him a case file and the smell of death. Baggio introduced him as Dottore Massimo Ravello, the Veneto's top medical examiner.

The pathologist opened the case file and addressed Gabriel with courtroom formality. "The woman you discovered in the *laguna* was probably in her late twenties, thirty at most. She was 170 centimeters in height and wore a size thirty-eight shoe. At some point during her brief life, she suffered a fracture to her left wrist. The shape of her skull indicates that she was of Northern European ethnicity."

"Cause of death?"

"Determining the manner of death is always difficult in cases where the body is discovered in water. But in my opinion, she died by drowning."

"When?"

"A week ago, I'd say. Perhaps a day or two earlier."

"Was it an accident?"

"Unlikely." Ravello removed a photograph from the file and placed it before Gabriel. It showed the lower portion of the woman's right leg—or what remained of it. "It appears as though someone tied a line around her ankle. Whether it was before or after her death I cannot say. It was undoubtedly attached to something heavy."

Gabriel returned the photograph to Ravello. "What does any of this have to do with me?"

The medical examiner deferred to Colonel Baggio. "As you probably know, Signore Allon, we have been unable to identify the woman, in part because no one seems to realize that she is missing. We were hoping you might agree to help us discover who she was and why she was killed."

"How?"

"By giving her a face."

"A forensic sketch?" Gabriel shook his head. "I'm sorry, Colonel Baggio, but I have no training in that sort of thing. You require a professional."

"We have one on retainer. She feeds precise measurements of the skull in question into a computer program, and the program produces digital sketches. None of which," Baggio added pointedly, "has ever led to the identification of a set of human remains."

"What makes you think I would have any better luck?"

Baggio exchanged a look with Rossetti before answering. "My colleague tells me that you are an unusually gifted painter, especially when it comes to human anatomy."

"That might explain why I was hired to restore the Titian."

"From what I hear, you could paint a copy of that Titian, and no one would ever be able to tell the difference." Baggio shot another glance in Rossetti's direction. "Isn't that right, Capitano?"

Rossetti delivered his reply to Gabriel. "Would you at least try?"

Gabriel looked at Ravello and asked, "May I see the X-rays of the skull?"

The pathologist extracted three images from the file—one frontal, two lateral—and handed them over. Gabriel examined them at length with a practiced eye. As a young art student he had spent countless hours drawing human skeletons. Later he had learned how to draw skeletons inside his nudes or, conversely, nudes *around* his skeletons. He was more than confident in his ability to produce a portrait that bore at least a passing resemblance to the woman of Northern European ethnicity whom he had found in the waters off Dorsoduro. It would, however, require him to spend a few moments with his subject.

"You mentioned something about a broken wrist."

Dottore Ravello handed Gabriel another X-ray image. The fracture was clearly visible in the left radius. "How old was she when it happened?"

"Eight or nine, I'd say."

The same age as Irene. "Is there anything else you can tell me about her?"

"She was wearing no jewelry other than a pendant."

"What sort of pendant?"

"It's in the pathology lab," said Ravello. "Perhaps we should have a look at it."

——————

Gabriel followed the medical examiner down a flight of stairs to the basement level of the building. The lab was located behind a pair of locked doors. Only one of the three stainless-steel postmortem tables was occupied. The body was shrouded in white.

Ravello gently drew back the sheet, exposing the head and shoulders of the corpse. Gabriel was slow in looking down. The first thing he noticed was the significant gap between the two front teeth. She would have smiled, he thought, without parting her lips. Her remaining hair was shoulder length and the color of flax. Gabriel reckoned that her eyes had been pale blue.

"You had a look inside her lungs, I take it?"

"I'm afraid the sea scavengers didn't leave me much to work with."

"Was she a smoker?"

"I'd say not."

"Pregnant?"

"No."

"Health problems? Nasty habits?"

"Drugs or alcohol, you mean?" Ravello shook his head. "The remaining tissue of her liver looked normal. She was a good girl, this one. She didn't deserve to end up like this."

No one did, thought Gabriel, least of all the young woman stretched out before him. "May I see the pendant?" he asked.

It was zipped into a plastic evidence bag, a circular, gold-plated rendering of a male hand reaching toward an outstretched finger. Gabriel recognized it at once. It was the iconic image from Michelangelo's ceiling fresco in the Sistine Chapel, the instant that God imparted the spark of life into Adam. The engraving on the back of the pendant indicated that it had been purchased at a gift shop in the Vatican Museums.

Gabriel photographed both sides of the pendant before returning it to Ravello. "I need to touch her."

The pathologist opened a cabinet and removed a pair of flesh-colored autopsy gloves. Gabriel pulled them on, then said, "Please leave the room, Dottore."

"That body is evidence in a criminal investigation. I must remain with you at all times."

"Five minutes," said Gabriel.

The pathologist emitted a sigh of resignation, then started toward the door.

"Dottore Ravello?"

He paused.

"Turn off the lights on your way out."

The snap of a switch extinguished the overhead fluorescent lights. Then the door closed, and the darkness was absolute. They were alone now, just the two of them. Five minutes was all the time they would have together. It was all the time Gabriel required.

He reached down and laid his gloved hand on the portion of exposed bone and ligature where a face should have been. His examination was thorough but gentle, as though his subject could feel his every touch. The bones of the forehead and nose, the orbital bones of the eyes, the zygomatic bones of the cheeks, the mandible bone of the lower jaw. She appeared to him at once and with photographic clarity, a plain and pale girl in her late twenties with shoulder-length blond hair, deeply set blue eyes, an upturned nose, and a pronounced dimple in her chin. She was sitting alone at a café in Venice, a circular gold pendant around her neck. The café was Bar Dogale in the Campo dei Frari. Gabriel and the children had been sitting at the next table.

5

The Rialto

During the return trip from the mainland, Gabriel managed to convince himself that he was mistaken. Yes, there had been a young woman at Bar Dogale on the afternoon in question—an afternoon approximately two weeks earlier—and, yes, Gabriel and the children had been sitting at an adjoining table. It was half past three, the weather was warm and sultry. Irene and Raphael were snacking on *tramezzini* and discussing their day at school. The young woman, who had arrived before them, was drinking a cappuccino. She wore jeans, a sleeveless cotton sweater, and canvas trainers. Her pale blue eyes were searching the *campo* as though she were expecting someone. She seemed anxious, not at all like someone who was enjoying her visit to Venice. Several times she consulted her phone, which she held in her long-fingered right hand.

Gabriel made no mention of the woman at Bar Dogale during the ride across the *laguna*. Indeed, he spoke not a word. Colonel Baggio finally asked how long it might take him to produce a sketch. Gabriel replied, inaccurately, that he required a week at least.

"The sooner, the better."

"I'll do my best."

They dropped him at the San Tomà vaporetto stop, and he headed straight for the palazzo. Upstairs, he found the apartment deserted. Then he remembered it was Thursday, the day Raphael met with his tutor at the university. Gabriel would have the apartment to himself until nearly six.

He went into his studio and closed the door. The pathologist had allowed him to keep the three X-ray images of the woman's skull, along with a single photograph of the head and shoulders of the corpse. He consulted them only briefly before taking up a Strathmore Series 300 pad and a Faber-Castell pencil. His method was rudimentary, a simple oval bisected by faint horizontal lines for the eyes and mouth. Contrary to what he had told Colonel Baggio, it was only a few minutes before he had a finished sketch in hand.

It was the young woman from Bar Dogale.

He tore the sketch from the pad and laid it on his worktable. Surely, he told himself, it was not possible. He had simply given the dead woman the face of a woman who had caught his attention. With his near-perfect recall for visual images, it was entirely understandable. Besides, what were the chances that the two women were actually one and the same? It was a question, he thought, only his son could answer.

Somehow he had to clear the anxious young woman from Bar Dogale from his memory. He did so by concealing her beneath a layer of imaginary obliterating paint. Next he scrutinized the four photographs at considerable length. He even laid his hand on the frontal X-ray of the skull and probed the fourteen bones of the face as though he were reading a page of braille. Finally he reached for the Strathmore pad and began to sketch, the tip of his pencil moving swiftly over the smooth surface of the Bristol paper. The result was a near-perfect copy of the first sketch.

To produce his third and final sketch he used an assortment of colored pencils. He gave his subject a simple shoulder-length hair-style, a spray of freckles across her nose, a beauty mark above her lip, and a circular gold pendant bearing Michelangelo's image of God imparting the spark of life to his creation. The expression the woman wore was unsmiling, guarded. The gap between her two front teeth was hidden from view.

Gabriel photographed the finished sketch with his iPhone, then digitally cropped and darkened the image. No, he thought as he stared at the screen, he was not mistaken. Exactly nine days before he fished a woman in her late twenties from the waters of the *laguna*, the very same woman had been sitting next to him in the Campo dei Frari, waiting anxiously for someone who was running late.

———

Chiara rang a few minutes before six to say that she and the children were leaving the university. She then declared that she was too exhausted to cook and that they were going out. Gabriel suggested Vini da Arturo, a trattoria on the opposite side of the Grand Canal in San Marco. They traveled there by *traghetto* and feasted on anti-pasti and veal cutlets. Irene and Raphael spent the entire meal raving about their father's bravura performance at the Salute. His lecture, it seemed, was the talk of the *scuola primaria*.

Leaving the restaurant, they decided to walk home over the Rialto Bridge rather than utilize the time-saving convenience of a *traghetto*. Gabriel encouraged Irene and Raphael to lead the way. Then, quietly, he told Chiara about his involuntary visit to the mainland, his brief reunion with the corpse he had discovered in the *laguna*, and the conclusion he had reached regarding the young woman he had seen nine days earlier at Bar Dogale.

"Impossible," said Chiara.

"Unlikely. But not impossible." Gabriel handed over his phone. "Have a look at her."

"Pretty girl," remarked Chiara.

"Not really. Most people wouldn't have noticed her."

"But you did."

"That's because I notice everything."

"Including a beauty mark on her upper lip?"

"And the freckles," added Gabriel. "I remembered she had a few freckles."

"What about the pendant?"

Gabriel instructed Chiara to enlarge the image.

"That might be the world's smallest copy of *The Creation of Adam*."

"She was wearing it when she was murdered."

"Was the woman from Bar Dogale wearing a similar pendant?"

"No," replied Gabriel. "She was wearing the exact *same* pendant."

They had reached the Campo San Bartolomeo. The children paused to take their bearings, then disappeared around a corner. Chiara returned the phone and asked, "What makes you think that she was waiting for someone?"

"Professional instinct."

"And which profession is that, Maestro Allon?"

"Forensic sketch artist, it seems." They rounded the corner into the Salizzada Pio X. Gabriel searched the crowds for Irene and Raphael. "It appears we've lost our children."

"This is Venice, darling. It's impossible to get lost. Besides, they know the way."

"Where are they going?"

"Venchi, I imagine."

It was a gourmet chocolate shop and gelateria in the Rialto. "Since when do our children carry money?"

"The children of Maestro Allon don't need money. The shopkeepers know that you'll settle their debts."

"Some life."

"Yours or theirs?" Chiara held his hand as they walked past the stalls lining the Rialto Bridge. "Let's say for argument's sake that you're right about the woman from Bar Dogale."

"I am."

"In that case, it shouldn't be too difficult to determine who she was. Who knows? We might even be able to learn the name of the person she was planning to meet there."

"Not to put too fine a point on it, but isn't that the job of the authorities?"

"They were the ones who came to you for help."

"They asked me to produce a forensic sketch, not to solve the case."

"Who said anything about solving the case? All I'm suggesting is that we have coffee at Dogale tomorrow morning after we drop the children at school."

They had reached the San Polo side of the bridge. Irene and Raphael were nowhere in sight.

"Speaking of the children," said Gabriel.

"Follow me."

They made their way through the Rialto Market to the Ruga dei Spezieri, where they found Irene and Raphael eating chocolate gelato outside the entrance of Venchi. Chiara pulled a banknote from her bag and handed it to Gabriel.

"And a chocolate gelato for me as well, Maestro Allon."

The laughter of the children echoed along the narrow street. "And butter cookies, Maestro!" shouted Irene. "Bring us butter cookies for the walk home."

6

———

Bar Dogale

Shortly after three o'clock the next morning the apartment shook with an explosive clap of thunder. Gabriel lay in bed for another hour, listening to the rain lashing against the windows overlooking the Grand Canal, until the first stirrings of a caffeine headache sent him into the kitchen in search of coffee. He carried his first cup to his studio and drank it while working on the Florigerio. Chiara poked her head through the doorway a few minutes after six.

"You're supposed to be wearing a mask when working with those awful solvents."

"I forgot."

"That's because you have no brain cells left."

Chiara walked over to Gabriel's worktable. The three sketches lay side by side, arranged in order of execution. She reached for the un-marked manila envelope instead.

"I wouldn't, if I were you."

"What's inside?"

"Three X-rays and a photograph you don't want to see."

Chiara removed only the frontal X-ray and placed it next to the sketches. "With all due respect," she said after a moment, "I don't see the resemblance."

"You're obviously not looking at it the right way."

"It could be anyone."

"It isn't."

By eight o'clock the streets and squares of San Polo were awash with the floodwaters of a minor *acqua alta*. Clad in oilskin coats and rubber boots, Gabriel and Chiara escorted the children to school, then waded over to the Campo dei Frari. As they walked through the door of Bar Dogale, Paolo automatically placed two cappuccinos on the counter along with a basket of warm *cornetti*. Gabriel reciprocated by handing the barman his *telefonino*.

"Do you recognize her?"

"Should I?"

"She was here about two and a half weeks ago. It was a Monday afternoon. You waited on her."

"If you say so, Signore Allon."

Gabriel glanced at the security camera above the bar. "Does that thing work?"

"When it feels like it."

"What about the camera outside?"

Paolo shrugged. "Sometimes."

"Can we check the memory?"

"Is it important?"

"It might be."

The barman led Gabriel and Chiara through a cluttered storage room to an office the size of a closet. Gabriel recited the exact time and date that he had seen the young woman, and Paolo entered the information into the computer. The shot from the interior camera appeared instantly on the screen.

"We were sitting outside," said Gabriel.

Paolo clicked the mouse once, and the shot changed to the exterior view. The arrangement of the figures was as Gabriel remembered. He was seated, as usual, with his back to the front of the café. Irene was seated to his left, and Raphael was directly opposite. The young woman occupied the table to Gabriel's right. She, too, was facing the *campo*, which meant that her back was turned to the camera.

"Can you rewind it ten minutes, please?"

Paolo did as Gabriel asked, then set the scene into motion. Both tables were now unoccupied. Three minutes went by before the first of the four figures entered the shot.

"Pause it, please."

The mouse clicked, the image froze.

"Dear God," whispered Chiara.

Gabriel held his phone next to the computer screen. The resemblance between the subject of his sketch and the woman in the surveillance video was uncanny.

Chiara played devil's advocate. "It still doesn't prove—"

"I agree," replied Gabriel, cutting her off. Then he asked Paolo to advance the recording to 3:45 p.m. Gabriel and the children had left by then, but the woman remained at her table until four fifteen, when she laid a few coins atop the bill and departed. Paolo appeared a moment later to collect the empty coffee cup and the money.

"Now do you remember her?" asked Gabriel.

"Vaguely."

"Did she say anything to you?"

"She bade me a pleasant day and asked for a cappuccino."

"In Italian?"

Paolo nodded.

"What was her accent like?"

"It might have been British."

At Gabriel's request, Paolo increased the playback speed of the video. Four customers hurried out of the café like characters in a silent movie, then three more arrived. One was a tall woman with short dark hair. She wore white Capri-length trousers, flat-soled shoes, and a dark blue cotton blazer. Her handbag and single piece of carry-on luggage were matching and costly. Her sunglasses were large and fashionable. She removed them before lowering herself into the same chair where Gabriel had been sitting earlier. Paolo took the woman's order and delivered it in record time.

"British?" asked Gabriel.

"Definitely."

"It looks to me as though she came directly from the airport."

"She said she was meeting someone."

"Did anyone join her?"

"I don't think so. But we should probably watch the video, just to be sure."

They reviewed it at the maximum playback speed. Paolo's recollection proved accurate.

"Back it up to four twenty-eight," said Gabriel. "And play it at the normal speed."

Paolo did as Gabriel asked, and they watched as the woman approached Bar Dogale, towing her carry-on luggage over the paving stones of the *campo*. At the instant she removed her sunglasses, Gabriel said, "Pause it, please."

The mouse clicked, the image froze.

Gabriel looked at Chiara and asked, "Do you recognize her?"

"Should I?"

Gabriel found a photograph of the woman online. Then he enlarged the image and held his phone next to the computer screen. "How about now?"

"Impossible," whispered Chiara.

"Unlikely," said Gabriel. "But not impossible."

Admittedly Gabriel should have phoned Luca Rossetti and Colonel Baggio and told them of his suspicions. Instead he tossed a change of clothing into an overnight bag and headed for the airport. As luck would have it, there was a business-class seat available on the eleven o'clock British Airways flight to London. He waited until he had cleared passport control at Heathrow before ringing Amelia March of *ARTnews* magazine. His call went straight to voicemail. He left a brief message, and she called him back straightaway.

"When and where?" she asked.

"You tell me."

"There's a little coffeehouse on the Portobello Road near George Orwell's old cottage."

"Half past two?"

"See you then."

The small terrace house at 22 Portobello Road had not in fact been Orwell's; he had lodged there during the winter of 1927 after re-signing his position with the Indian Imperial Police. Gabriel arrived at the coffeehouse on the opposite side of the road fifteen minutes early and sat down at a table in the garden. Amelia appeared at the stroke of two thirty. She was clutching the same designer handbag and, despite the gray English skies overhead, wearing the same pair of sunglasses. She placed them on the tabletop and regarded Gabriel with a mixture of curiosity and apprehension.

"Are you angry with me?" she asked at last.

"Why on earth would I be angry with you?"

"The article."

"Oh, that," replied Gabriel.

The article in question had been occasioned by Gabriel's role in the recovery and restoration of *Self-Portrait with Bandaged Ear* by

Vincent van Gogh, which had been stolen from the Courtauld Gallery in a daring smash-and-grab robbery more than a decade earlier. Laudatory in tone, the story had referred to him as one of the most accomplished and sought-after art conservators in the world. It had also confirmed what many in the gossipy art trade already suspected—that he had spent nearly the entirety of his remarkable career living under an assumed identity forged by a clandestine division of Israel's secret intelligence service. He had retired from the service after spending five tumultuous years as its director-general. With the exception of a single operation against the Russians, he had managed to make a clean break with his past. Amelia March, though she did not know it, had played a supporting role in one of his better operations.

"Should I have asked you for a comment?" she asked.

"Isn't that the way it usually works in your business?"

"Would you have spoken to me?"

"Don't be ridiculous."

She smiled. "Once a spy, always a spy. Isn't that what they say?"

"I'm not a spy, Amelia. I am the director of the paintings department at the Tiepolo Restoration Company in Venice."

"Is that all?"

"In my spare time, I sometimes help the police solve art-related crimes."

"Are you working on anything interesting now?"

"A murder investigation, actually." Gabriel handed over his phone. On the screen was a photograph of his forensic sketch. "I found her in the waters near San Giorgio Maggiore. Thus far, the Italian police haven't been able to identify her. I was hoping you might know who she was."

Amelia looked up from the phone. "Why me?"

"Because you were supposed to meet her two weeks ago at a little place called Bar Dogale in the Campo dei Frari. And by the time you finally arrived, she was gone."

"How do you know that?"

"Swipe to the next image."

Amelia did as he asked, then frowned. "Once a spy, always a spy. Isn't that what they say, Mr. Allon?"

"I'm not a spy, Amelia. I'm an art restorer, and I just happen to live in the neighborhood."

7

Portobello Road

H ow did she make contact with you?"
　　"Email."

"Your *ARTnews* address?"

"Proton Mail. Her address was total gibberish."

They had left the coffeehouse and were walking along the Portobello Road. Amelia's step was slow and pensive, as though she were
wrestling with the implications of what she had just been told. Most
of her work dealt with sales and acquisitions and gallery openings
and other assorted art world gossip. Gabriel was all but certain she
had never once lost a source to murder.

"The exact gibberish, please."

"LDV followed by eight numbers. I assumed they were her initials."

"And the content?"

Amelia dug her phone from her handbag and, after retrieving
the email in question, handed it over. The sender's address was
LDV14521519@protonmail.com. The text was three sentences in
length, formal in language, and accurately punctuated. The anonymous author wished to make Amelia aware of a startling artistic
discovery she had made, the nature of which she could not disclose
in an email, not even an encrypted one. It was her wish to discuss

the matter in person at the earliest possible juncture. If Amelia was amenable to such a meeting, a time and place could be arranged, provided the location was somewhere in Italy.

Gabriel returned the phone. "And your reply?"

"I asked for additional information, didn't I?"

"Did she provide it?"

"She said the matter in question involved a painting. There was a suggestion of criminality."

"What sort of criminality?"

"She declined to go into the details."

"Could it have been theft?"

"Haven't the foggiest."

"Forgery?"

"Your guess is as good as mine, Mr. Allon. But as far as I was concerned, it wasn't enough to justify a plane ride to Italy. I told her so in no uncertain terms."

"How did she reply?"

"She assured me that I was making the biggest mistake of my career."

"Second biggest." Gabriel dropped his half-drunk coffee into a rubbish bin. "Who was the one to reestablish contact?"

"She was."

"Was she any more forthcoming?"

"Only about herself. Her education, to be specific. She was obviously trying to impress me."

"What was it like?"

"She did her undergraduate work at Cambridge and then picked up a graduate degree at the Courtauld Institute. Needless to say, I was unmoved."

"What made you change your mind?"

"She sent me another email. Time and place, one last chance. Otherwise she was going to give the story to a reporter from the *New York Times*."

"Bar Dogale, three o'clock?"

"Half past, actually."

"What were the ground rules?"

"She said she would recognize me."

"Why were you late?"

"My flight was delayed at Heathrow by a mechanical problem. I sent her an email explaining the situation, and she assured me that she would wait. But by the time I arrived, there was no sign of her. I spent the night in a little hotel near the Piazza San Marco and returned to London the next morning, certain that I had been the target of an elaborate practical joke."

"Did you try to make contact with her again?"

"Several times."

"And?"

"Radio silence."

"Now we know why," said Gabriel. "If I had to guess, she was murdered a few hours after she left that café."

"By whom?"

"First things first, Amelia."

"Her identity?" Amelia thumbed through the contacts on her phone. "It shouldn't be too hard to figure out who she was. After all, we know what she looked like and where she earned her graduate degree."

"May I ask who you're calling?"

"The director of the Courtauld Gallery. He's one of my better sources."

"Please don't," said Gabriel.

"Why not?"

"Because good things come to those who wait."

She slid the phone into her handbag. "Don't forget about me, Mr. Allon. Otherwise I'm going to write a very long profile about you. It will include all the material that came over the transom after my original story appeared. You have quite a track record in the art world. Especially here in London."

"Trust me, Amelia. You don't know the half of it."

"Can I quote you on that?"

Gabriel rang Dr. Geoffrey Holland, the esteemed director of the Courtauld Gallery, while hurtling along Bayswater Road in the back of a taxi. He explained that he had popped into London on short notice and was wondering whether Holland had a spare moment or two. The director assumed it had something to with the painting propped on the easel in Gabriel's studio in Venice. Gabriel did nothing to disabuse him of the notion.

"I'll meet you in the café at half past four," said Holland before ringing off. "I believe you know where to find it."

The prestigious Courtauld Institute of Art and its affiliated gallery were located in Somerset House, a palatial Renaissance complex located along a recently pedestrianized portion of the Strand. Gabriel spent a pleasant forty-five minutes roaming the exhibition rooms before making his way downstairs to the café. Geoffrey Holland, in a Savile Row suit and necktie, arrived at the stroke of four thirty. He was nothing if not punctual.

They ordered tea at the counter and sat down at a table near the window. Gabriel showed Holland a photograph depicting the current condition of the Florigerio. The director was clearly displeased by the rate of Gabriel's progress.

"You assured me that the restoration would take no more than three months."

"I'm sorry, Geoffrey, but I received a better offer. One that actually pays."

"The Titian?"

Gabriel nodded.

"We had a deal," said Holland. "I allowed you to see that surveillance video, and you agreed to clean my Florigerio. Free of charge, I might add, and in a timely fashion."

The video in question had been shot in this very room and had implicated the wife of the British home secretary in the murder of an art historian from Oxford. The resulting scandal had been one of the worst in British political history. The minor role in the affair played by the esteemed director of the Courtauld Gallery had never come to light. Neither had Gabriel's.

"Don't worry, Geoffrey. I intend to keep my end of the bargain. In the meantime, however, I require your assistance on an unrelated matter."

Holland sighed. "What is it this time?"

Gabriel handed over his phone. "Do you recognize her?"

"Yes, of course. That's Penelope Radcliff. She was a graduate student at the institute. A real superstar."

"Art history?"

"Conservation, actually. She specialized in the painters of the Florentine School."

"Where is she now?"

"I believe she's in Rome."

"Doing what?"

"Serving an apprenticeship."

"The Borghese Gallery? The Doria Pamphili?"

"Neither."

"Where, Geoffrey?"

Holland returned Gabriel's phone. "The Vatican."

8

London–Rome

Penelope Radcliff had served her first apprenticeship in the restoration lab of the Courtauld Gallery, and her mobile phone number was still on file. Gabriel dialed it for the first time while standing on the busy pavement of the Strand. The call went straight to voicemail, as did the next three. It was possible she had switched off the device or allowed the battery to expire. The more likely explanation, he thought, was that the phone was resting on the bottom of the Venetian Lagoon.

He placed his next call to Chiara and gave her an update on his findings.

"Small world," she observed. "Where do you suppose she made this startling discovery of hers?"

"She refused to say in her emails to Amelia. But we should assume it was made at the Vatican."

"And now she's dead?"

"That's a matter for Colonel Baggio to determine."

"When are you planning to tell him?"

"The minute we hang up."

"Might I suggest an alternative course of action?"

"By all means."

"You should go to Rome and warn your friend that the Vatican is about to be engulfed in yet another scandal."

"What makes you think I can get to him?"

"You're one of his most trusted friends in the world. Besides, he wouldn't be pope if it wasn't for you."

"All the more reason why he might refuse to see me."

"Be that as it may, you need to tell him that he has yet another problem on his hands."

"His problems have a way of becoming my problems."

"And vice versa," said Chiara.

Gabriel spent the night at the Sloane Square Hotel and in the morning caught an early flight to Rome. As he was stepping off the jetway at Fiumicino he spotted Luca Rossetti, in a dark suit and open-necked dress shirt, waiting at the arrival gate.

"When were you planning to tell us?" he asked.

"Tell you what?"

"About the girl from Bar Dogale."

"I see you've been talking to my friend Paolo Caruso."

"I popped into the Salute yesterday afternoon to see if you had made any progress on the sketch. And when you weren't there . . ."

"You headed straight to my usual hangout in the Campo dei Frari."

Rossetti nodded. "Paolo told me about the sketch of the young Englishwoman who had been sitting next to you and the children."

"And you put two and two together."

"Math was always my best subject."

"How did you know I was in London?"

Rossetti made a typing motion with the fingers of one hand, indicating that he had searched the manifests of flights departing from Venice. "Needless to say," he added, "I was rather surprised by the second leg of your itinerary."

"Does Baggio know you're here?"

Luca Rossetti shook his head.

"In that case, who sent you?"

"Who do you think?"

The headquarters of the Art Squad were located in an ornate yellow palazzo in Rome's tranquil Piazza di Sant'Ignazio. On the second floor was the large, high-ceilinged office of the unit's longtime commander, General Cesare Ferrari. Seated behind his desk in his blue-and-gold Carabinieri finery, he contemplated the forensic sketch displayed on Gabriel's mobile phone. The general held the device in his left hand, for his right was missing the third and fourth fingers, the result of a parcel bomb he received while serving as chief of the Carabinieri's Naples division. The assassination attempt, mounted by elements of the ultraviolent criminal organization known as the Camorra, had claimed his right eye as well. His ocular prosthesis, with its immobile pupil and unyielding gaze, unnerved underlings and adversaries alike. Even Gabriel, who had worked with General Ferrari on several high-profile cases, found his gaze difficult to bear.

"When did you realize it was her?" the general asked at last.

"The instant I laid my hand on the bones of her face. The surveillance video from Bar Dogale confirmed my suspicions."

"And yet you failed to report your findings to Colonel Baggio."

"Is that a crime?"

"A rather serious one." The general turned to Rossetti. "Wouldn't you agree, Luca?"

"At the very least, he interfered with an official investigation. I'm afraid we have no choice but to haul him before a magistrate and press charges."

Ferrari nodded his head solemnly in agreement. "Regrettably I must concur. Still, there *are* extenuating circumstances. After all, our mutual friend's conduct, as deplorable as it is, has resulted in a windfall of valuable information."

"Information," added Gabriel, "that might very well allow the Art Squad to assume control of the investigation." With a smile he added, "Wouldn't you agree, General Ferrari?"

Ferrari laid a hand piously over his heart. "The thought never entered my mind. That said, you've raised a valid point. A sensitive case involving the Vatican couldn't possibly be handled by the Venice office. It requires someone of my expertise." He paused, then added, "And yours as well."

"Might I make another observation?" inquired Gabriel.

"Please."

"We still don't know whether the woman I found in the *laguna* is Penelope Radcliff."

The general trained his monocular gaze on Rossetti. "Perhaps you should find out where she was staying."

"Shall I call the Vatican?"

"No, Luca. Not yet."

———————

It took Luca Rossetti only a few minutes to determine that Penelope Anne Radcliff, twenty-seven years of age, born in the western British city of Bristol, had been living in a rented apartment in Prati, a fashionable art nouveau quarter of Rome located on the northern fringes of the Vatican. General Ferrari, with the forefinger of his ruined right hand, pressed random buttons on the intercom panel of her building until a startled tenant finally admitted them. Upstairs, Rossetti pounded on the door of her apartment and, receiving no answer, tried the latch. It was locked.

"Allow me," said Gabriel, and drew two slender metallic tools he carried habitually in the breast pocket of his sport coat. Crouching, he inserted them into the barrel of the lock and began expertly manipulating the pins.

"Is there anything you *can't* do?" asked Ferrari.

"I can't pick this lock if you insist on talking." Gabriel twisted the lock to the right, and the latch gave way. Then he looked at Luca Rossetti and said, "After you."

Rossetti drew a stubby Beretta Cougar from his shoulder holster and headed inside, with Gabriel and General Ferrari a step behind. The sitting room was in semidarkness. Rossetti, alert to danger, swung the Beretta to the left and right with a tactical two-handed grip. The general observed his movements with a faintly bemused expression.

"That's quite enough, Luca. Put that thing away before you hurt someone."

Rossetti holstered the Beretta while Gabriel moved about the room, switching on lights. The search had been thorough but unprofessional, a ransacking. The couch cushions were askew, a chair was overturned, the top drawer of the writing desk was ajar. An Apple power cord was plugged into a nearby wall socket, but there was no trace of a computer. A small collection of monographs lay atop the coffee table. Giotto, Botticelli, Michelangelo, Raphael—four giants of the Florentine School.

"Interesting," observed General Ferrari.

"How so?"

"No books about Leonardo."

In the galley kitchen the cupboard doors hung ajar, and the contents of two drawers lay scattered across the countertop. Gabriel tore a sheet from a roll of paper towels and used it to open the refrigerator. General Ferrari contemplated the spoiled food lining the shelves.

"Perhaps we should have a look at the rest of the apartment."

They entered the bedroom to find Luca Rossetti, hands on his hips, surveying the disorder around him. The mattress had been stripped bare, and the floor was littered with clothing and personal effects, including a collection of Winsor & Newton sable-hair brushes and several vials of pigment and medium. The items had been purchased at L. Cornelissen & Son, an artists' supply shop located in London's Great Russell Street. Gabriel was a frequent customer.

"Seen enough?" he asked.

"Yes," replied the general. "I believe I have."

The official record of the case would later assert that General Ferrari rang the commander of the Carabinieri at twelve fifteen that afternoon and provided him with the name and Rome address of the unfortunate young woman whose body had been fished from the waters of the Venetian Lagoon by none other than the noted art conservator and erstwhile spy Gabriel Allon. Precisely how the general had come upon this information he neglected to say, though he intimated it had been supplied by a trusted source. This source, he added, had also informed him that the young woman had been serving an apprenticeship in the restoration lab of the Vatican Museums.

"Am I to assume," asked the commander, "that the Art Squad wishes to take control of the investigation?"

"We think it's for the best."

As did the commander of the Carabinieri. "How do you intend to handle things with the Vatican?" he asked.

"As quietly as possible. Otherwise they'll close ranks and refuse to cooperate."

"The chief of the Vatican Gendarmerie is an old friend. I'd be happy to call him on your behalf."

"In my experience it's better to start at the top."

"The secretary of state?"

"The man in white."

"His Holiness? I wish you luck, Cesare."

"I don't need luck," replied the general. "I have Gabriel Allon."

9

Arch of Bells

Ordinarily Gabriel entered the restricted quarters of the Vatican through St. Anne's Gate or the Bronze Doors, the main entrance of the Apostolic Palace. On that afternoon, however, he headed to the Arch of Bells, located on the southern flank of St. Peter's Basilica, directly beneath the statues of the apostles Thaddeus and Matthew. Two Swiss Guards in their Renaissance-era dress uniforms stood watch in the shadowed passageway, one bearing a two-meter-long halberd, the other with his hands clasped and his feet shoulder width apart at a precise sixty-degree angle. Their bearing was more rigid than usual, doubtless because their commanding officer, Colonel Alois Metzler, was standing between them, dressed in a dark business suit and tie. Colonel Metzler was the only officer in the four-hundred-year history of the Pontifical Swiss Guard to have fatally shot a Roman Catholic priest. He had committed this unthinkable act to spare Gabriel the indignity of having to pull the trigger himself.

Their greeting was businesslike and brief. In the impenetrable Swiss German of those native to Canton Uri, Metzler asked Gabriel if he was carrying a firearm. Gabriel, in the Berlin-accented Hochdeutsch of his mother, replied truthfully that he was not. Metzler nevertheless laid a hand discreetly on the small of Gabriel's back, just to make sure.

"What are you worried about, Alois? It's not as if I haven't carried a weapon around the Holy Father before. I'm practically an honorary member of the Swiss Guard."

"Membership in the Guard is restricted to single Catholic males from Switzerland who have served in the Swiss Army and are of irreproachable character. You, Gabriel, meet none of those qualifications."

"Does a fondness for fondue and Chasselas count for anything?"

Metzler treated Gabriel to a rare smile. "Let's go. The private secretary is expecting you."

They set off along the facade of the Basilica. Gabriel quickly adjusted the necktie he had purchased after leaving Penelope Radcliff's apartment.

"Nervous?" asked Metzler.

"About what?"

"Seeing the Holy Father again."

"Should I be?"

"He's the supreme pontiff of the Roman Catholic Church and the Vicar of Christ."

"He also happens to be my friend."

"Not anymore." They passed beneath a pair of archways near the Basilica's left transept. "I assume this isn't a social call."

"I'm afraid not."

"Is the Holy Father in any danger?"

Gabriel shook his head. "It's a public relations problem."

"What is it this time?"

"You'll know soon enough."

"That doesn't sound encouraging."

"Sorry to be the bearer of bad news, Alois."

"Why break with tradition?"

They turned to the left and headed across a small piazza toward the Casa Santa Marta, the Vatican's five-story clerical guesthouse. Another Swiss Guard stood watch outside the glass doorway, and Father Mark Keegan, the Holy Father's private secretary, waited in the lobby. Father Keegan was an Irishman from Philadelphia and, like his master, a member of the Society of Jesus. He had the face of an altar boy and the eyes of someone who never lost at cards. Gabriel knew the papal private secretary to be efficient, ruthless, and most of all humorless.

The priest's inscrutable gaze settled briefly on the commandant of the Swiss Guard. "Thank you, Colonel Metzler. I'll show Signore Allon out after his audience with the Holy Father."

Metzler went into the sunlit piazza, and Gabriel followed Father Keegan to the lifts. An empty carriage awaited. The priest pressed the call button for the second floor, and the doors closed.

"This had better be important."

"I wouldn't be here if it wasn't."

"I can give you ten minutes at most."

"I'd consider rearranging the Holy Father's schedule, if I were you."

"It's carved in stone."

"If you say so, Father Keegan."

The carriage doors opened to reveal a Swiss Guard in plain clothes standing in the foyer. Two more sentries in simple blue tunics flanked the doorway of Room 201. Father Keegan turned the latch without knocking and led Gabriel inside.

His first appearance on the balcony of St. Peter's had electrified the world's one billion Catholics, not least because he was the first non-cardinal to be elected pope since the fourteenth century. Gabriel, in an unprecedented break with Canon Law and Church tradition, had been present in the Sistine Chapel when the dean of the College of Cardinals asked the new supreme pontiff to state the name by which he wished to be called. His initial response, that he hadn't a clue, had provoked good-spirited laughter among the men in red. With his second, though, he sent a not-so-subtle signal to the princes of the Church that change was in the air.

He spent that first night of his papacy—and every night since—not in the spacious *appartamento pontificio* in the Apostolic Palace but in a two-room suite in the Casa Santa Marta. The Vatican Press Office, after much deliberation and Curial consultation, had declared that it was seventy-five square meters. But Gabriel, with his unfailing eye for linear dimensions, thought the actual number was closer to fifty. An arrangement of velveteen-covered couches and chairs, too heavy for the cramped space, stood near the windows, which over-looked the Basilica. The enormous Renaissance papal bed, the same bed upon which several previous popes had breathed their last, con-sumed most of the second room. The dark wooden floors shone with fresh polish. The cream-colored walls were bare.

The Holy Father sat at the small desk, the receiver of a landline phone pressed to his ear. He wore a simple white cassock and an unadorned silver pectoral cross rather than the ornate crosses of gold worn by popes down through the ages. His shoes were ordinary leather oxfords—not the traditional red slippers—and the heavy gold Ring of the Fisherman was nowhere in sight. Like his predeces-sor, he found it cumbersome and uncomfortable to wear.

At length he raised a forefinger to indicate he would be another moment longer. Father Keegan, in a stage whisper, explained the de-lay. "Cardinal Doyle." Then, for Gabriel's benefit, he added, "The archbishop of New York."

"Yes, I know."

"His Holiness is making his first visit to America next month."

With an arid smile, Gabriel indicated he knew about the Holy Father's travel plans as well. The much-publicized itinerary for the trip included an Oval Office meeting with the American president and historic addresses to both the Congress and UN General Assembly. American conservatives were apoplectic over the pontiff's plans to visit communist Cuba as well, in no small part because His Holiness had recently issued a biting apostolic exhortation decrying what he called "the invisible tyranny" of capitalism and the market. He had also condemned the global rise of far-right extremism, expressed support for the rights of migrants, and issued a clarion call for immediate action to combat climate change—positions that led one American conservative journalist to christen him "His Holiness Pope Che Guevara." His decision to reside in two small rooms in the Casa Santa Marta was viewed by most traditionalists as an affront to the majesty of the papacy. Gabriel's objections to the Holy Father's accommodations were more practical in nature. He had been in the tiny papal apartment only two minutes and already the walls were closing in on him.

The Holy Father bade the American cardinal farewell, then replaced the receiver and exhaled heavily.

"That bad?" asked Father Keegan.

"His Eminence is concerned that I might not fully appreciate the depths of America's current political divisions. He advised me to tread carefully during my remarks to Congress."

"What did you tell him?"

"I made it clear that I intend to speak my mind in Washington."

"I see," said Father Keegan warily.

The Holy Father turned to Gabriel and said, "My private secretary is concerned that I needlessly antagonized the most powerful Roman Catholic prelate in the United States."

"Did you?"

"Probably, yes."

"In that case, perhaps Father Keegan should ring His Eminence and ask him to jot down a few ideas for your remarks. Nothing too detailed, mind you. Just broad-brush themes."

"Humor him, you mean?"

"Exactly."

The Holy Father nodded toward Father Keegan, who went wordlessly into the corridor, iPhone in hand. Gabriel, alone with the successor to St. Peter, cast his eyes deliberately around the confines of the modest sitting room.

"I know what you're thinking," said the Holy Father.

"I imagine you do."

"It's all the space I need."

"It's the size of a confessional."

"Have you ever set foot in one?"

"Not lately."

"If you would like to unburden yourself . . ."

"We'd be here all day. Besides, according to your private secretary, our time is limited."

"Don't worry about Father Keegan. Believe it or not, I have a little pull around here."

The Holy Father rose from his chair and stretched his tall frame to its full, imposing height. The pious white cassock did nothing to diminish his striking Umbrian good looks. Even Hollywood never would have dared to cast him in the role of the supreme pontiff.

He extended a hand. "Don't even think about kissing it."

"I wasn't planning to," replied Gabriel, and grasped the proffered papal appendage.

The Holy Father, laughing, pulled him into a tight embrace. "I was beginning to think that you had forgotten about me."

"Not for a minute."

"Why haven't you visited?"

"One doesn't just *visit* the supreme pontiff, Holiness."

"Whyever not? And please drop the Holiness nonsense. I insist that you address me by my real name."

"Do you even remember it?"

"Luigi Donati," he replied. "I was once a humble street priest, a missionary who preached the Gospels and built schools and hospitals for the wretched of the earth. And now, thanks to you, I am trapped in this gilded cage wearing a white cassock."

"A cage, yes. But it could definitely use a touch of gold trim."

"My sources in Venice tell me that you're living in a palazzo overlooking the Grand Canal."

"We live on one floor of the palazzo, Holiness."

"Luigi," said the Holy Father. "My name is Luigi Donati."

"I'll try, Holiness."

"Try harder." Donati indicated the ornate seating arrangement. "Won't you sit down?"

"Is that allowed?"

"Not generally. But in your case, I'm prepared to make an exception."

Donati dropped onto the couch and placed his feet on the coffee table. Gabriel, after a moment's hesitation, lowered himself onto the edge of the throne-like chair opposite.

"There's no need to clasp your hands in my presence, Gabriel. I'm not an object of veneration." Donati frowned. "Quite the opposite, actually."

"You are beloved by people around the world, Luigi. Catholic and non-Catholic alike."

"My enemies refer to me as the rock star pope. Needless to say, they don't mean it as a compliment."

"They're envious."

"But determined," said Donati. "They handed me the papacy in a moment of crisis. And now they are doing everything in their power to make certain I stay in line. If I speak warmly about members of the gay and lesbian community, they scream heresy. If I suggest that divorced Catholics be allowed to receive the sacrament of the Eucharist, they accuse me of apostasy. And if I even dare mention the word *women*, well, it's as if the heavens have fallen."

"You're not actually thinking—"

"It doesn't matter what I think," interjected Donati. "The Church has no authority whatsoever to confer priestly ordination on women. It is doctrinally off the table."

"Rome has spoken, the case is closed?"

"Now and forever."

"What about celibacy and married priests?"

"All I'll say on the matter is that our current situation is unsustainable. At last count there were more than fifty thousand parishes globally without a priest. Thousands more have a part-time priest or an immigrant priest whose command of the local language and culture is shaky at best. At the risk of sounding like His Holiness Pope Obvious, Catholicism cannot thrive without a dedicated, energetic clergy to preach the Gospels and administer the sacraments. Something has to change. But if I push too far or move too quickly, the world's oldest institution could tear itself to pieces."

"What's a reformist supreme pontiff to do?"

"He moves cautiously and bides his time. After all, it is on his side. I'm quite young by historical standards, which means, barring a sudden health crisis, I'm likely to outlive the traditionalist dinosaurs who are currently standing in my way."

"And in the meantime?"

"The reformist supreme pontiff plays the role of a pastoral pope, a global street priest who tends to the needs of the poor and the sick. And because he has made it clear that he wants the Roman Catholic Church to be poor as well, he leads by example."

"By confining yourself to a cell measuring fifty square meters."

"The Vatican Press Office says it's seventy-five."

"The Press Office misspoke."

"Not for the first time," said Donati.

"Or the last, I'm afraid."

Donati frowned. "Why did you come to Rome, *mio amico*?"

"I discovered the body of a young woman in the Venetian Lagoon."

"And?"

Gabriel glanced at his wristwatch. "It seems my time has expired, Holiness."

"Take all the time you need. But if you call me Holiness one more time, I'm going to lose my temper."

"Forgive me, Luigi."

"*Ego te absolvo*," he replied. "Now start talking."

10

Casa Santa Marta

When Gabriel's briefing reached its end, Donati rose and went slowly to one of the windows. It should have been the window in the study of the *appartamento pontificio*, the same window where each Sunday at noon he prayed the Angelus to the multitude gathered below in St. Peter's Square. But this was not the third floor of the Apostolic Palace, it was a humble little room in the Casa Santa Marta, and Gabriel thought his old friend had never looked so alone.

He addressed his first words to the dome of the Basilica. "Do you know what will happen after your friend General Ferrari reveals the identity of that woman?"

"In point of fact, the announcement will be made by a certain Colonel Baggio in Venice."

"How long do we have?"

"Colonel Baggio is at this moment making contact with his counterparts at the Metropolitan Police in London. It will take some time for the formalities to play out."

"You didn't answer my question."

"Seventy-two hours. Perhaps a bit more."

"Or a bit less?"

"Could be," admitted Gabriel.

"Does this Colonel Baggio know where the deceased was working?"

"He does now."

"Will he tell the British authorities?"

"Actually he intends to let the British tell *him*."

Donati shot Gabriel a glance of papal reproach. "That doesn't sound terribly ethical to me."

"With good reason. But it will buy the Vatican some much-needed time."

"To get our story straight?"

"To gather the facts."

"The first thing I'd like to know," said Donati, "is why no one at the conservation lab informed the police that she was missing."

"I'm sure there's a perfectly reasonable explanation."

"Well, there's certainly one way to find out." Donati went to his desk and lifted the receiver of the telephone.

"May I ask what you're doing?" inquired Gabriel.

"Gathering facts."

"Put the phone down, Holiness."

Frowning, Donati returned the receiver to its cradle. "You are a member of a very small club, Gabriel Allon."

"The only non-Catholic to have witnessed the election of a pope?"

"Or to have addressed one in so insolent a manner," added Donati.

"It was for his own good."

"Was it really?"

"It is essential that you play no role in this matter whatsoever, Luigi. Otherwise you will expose yourself to criticism if there are credible allegations of wrongdoing by someone associated with the Vatican."

"Plausible deniability?"

"*Ignorantia affectata*."

"Aquinas? You're beginning to sound like a member of the Roman Curia, *mio amico*. But all the willful ignorance in the world won't protect me if there is yet another Vatican scandal. Especially a scandal involving a dead young woman." Donati lowered himself dejectedly onto the couch. "By the time the press is finished, I'll be accused of personally ordering her murder. I must know the facts."

"Allow me to gather them for you."

"What could she have found?"

"At the Vatican? You can't be serious, Luigi."

"Point taken," he replied. "In fact, I have fond memories of the morning we made a rather startling discovery in the Secret Archives. You were wearing an ill-fitting clerical suit, as I recall. I'm afraid the name on your Vatican ID badge escapes me."

"I believe it was Father Benedetti. And I never breathed a word to anyone about what we found that day."

"Or what really happened to my predecessor." Donati was silent for a moment. "If you must know, it's the real reason why I live here rather than the Apostolic Palace. As far as I'm concerned, the *appartamento* will always be Lucchesi's home."

"You needn't punish yourself for what happened, Luigi. It wasn't your fault."

"Wasn't it? If I had been there that night . . ." Donati changed the subject. "In case you were wondering, the last thing I need before my first trip to America as pope is a messy scandal."

"There won't be one if I can help it."

"Where do you intend to start?"

"I was thinking about paying a visit to my old friends in the conservation lab."

"Father Keegan will escort you."

"That won't be necessary, Holiness. I believe I remember the way."

"A very small club, indeed," said Donati, and showed Gabriel to the door.

———————

He slipped past the Swiss Guard standing outside the Casa Santa Marta and made his way around the back of the Basilica to a small courtyard at the foot of a rather ordinary-looking structure with walls the color of dun. The door, as was frequently the case, was unlocked and unattended. Inside, he scaled a flight of narrow stairs to the Sala Regia, the glorious antechamber of the Sistine Chapel.

During his last visit to the Sistina, it had been occupied by 116 cardinal-electors, and white smoke was pouring from the chimney, much to the delight of the enormous crowd waiting anxiously in St. Peter's Square. Now the chapel was filled with tourists, necks craned, eyes on Michelangelo's ceiling frescoes. Gabriel briefly joined a group of Latin American pilgrims gathered beneath *The Creation of Adam*, then set off along a treasure-laden loggia overlooking the Belvedere Courtyard. When he finally reached the Picture Gallery, he spent a few minutes communing with the paintings in Room XII, three of which he had restored, before making his way downstairs to the conservation lab.

This time the door he encountered was locked tight. The numerical passcode he entered into the keypad was no longer valid, so he laid a thumb on the intercom button. He recognized the voice that answered. It belonged to Donatella Ricci, an Early Renaissance expert who whispered soothingly to the paintings in her care.

"Who goes there?" she demanded to know.

"It's me, Donatella."

"Me who?"

"Gabriel."

"The only Gabriel I know never bothers to knock on a door, even if the door happens to be locked." A buzzer sounded and the dead bolt opened with a thud. "Welcome home."

He went inside the laboratory, and the door locked automatically behind him. He found Donatella perched atop a tall stool, palette in one hand, brush in the other. Secured to her studio easel was Bellini's *Lament over the Dead Christ*. Gabriel felt an unwelcome tug of professional envy.

"How dare you touch my Bellini," he murmured.

"It's not yours, Gabriel. It belongs to me now." Donatella swiveled round on her stool and regarded him through a pair of magnifying visors. "Is that really you?"

"Who else would it be?"

"A rather delicious-looking Italian gentleman of a certain age who resides in an enormous palazzo in Venice with one of the world's most beautiful women."

"Only that last part is true."

"The lovely Chiara hasn't thrown you out yet?"

"I'm hanging by a thread." Gabriel plucked the brush from Donatella's hand. "May I?"

"Absolutely not."

He loaded the brush and then retouched a small abrasion on the left cheek of the Magdalene.

"Not bad, Gabriel." Donatella reclaimed her brush. "What brings you to the Vatican?"

"I'm looking for someone."

"Who is it this time? A terrorist or a Russian assassin?"

"One of your apprentices, actually. A young Englishwoman named Penelope Radcliff."

"Penny," said Donatella. "She hates to be called Penelope."

Gabriel took note of Donatella's use of the present tense. "Is she around?"

"She completed her apprenticeship about a month ago. Last I heard, she was looking for work."

"Where?"

"Why all the questions, Gabriel?"

"I might be interested in hiring her," he lied, though not without considerable regret. He had always been fond of Donatella Ricci.

"You could do worse," she answered.

"The director of the Courtauld tells me she's a superstar."

"She's very talented. But she has a lot to learn."

"Was there a problem?"

"Define the word *problem*."

"A question raised for inquiry, consideration, or solution. A source of perplexity, distress, or vexation."

"You should probably talk to Antonio," said Donatella, and loaded her brush.

———————

Antonio Calvesi, the Vatican's chief conservator, was relaxing in his office, having just returned to the lab from Da Fortunato, where he lunched at least three times a week, nearly always at the expense of others.

"What are you doing here?" he asked when Gabriel strode unannounced through the door.

"I'm well, Antonio. How are you?"

"That depends on why you're back at the Vatican."

Gabriel thought it was best to continue with the fiction he had spun for Donatella—that the Tiepolo Restoration Company of

Venice was looking to expand its stable of staff conservators. Penelope Radcliff, he said, had come highly recommended.

"How did you hear about her?"

"Geoffrey Holland was raving about her the last time I was in London."

"She needs another year or two of training. But, yes, she's quite gifted."

"No problems?"

"A bit of intrigue," said Calvesi. "But no problems."

"What kind of intrigue?"

Calvesi nibbled thoughtfully on the stem of his eyeglasses before answering. "I took her under my wing when she arrived, and she made an extraordinary amount of progress."

Gabriel decided to add a touch of false flattery to his fiction. "I'm not surprised, Antonio. I learned a great deal from you."

"If memory serves, you rejected every suggestion I ever gave you. As for Signorina Radcliff, she was a far more receptive student. So much so that I agreed to let her carry out a restoration of her own."

"On what?"

"A painting, Gabriel. What else?"

"Not a painting from the main collection?"

"Goodness, no. We found something down in the storerooms for her to work on. A Madonna and Child with John the Baptist."

"Italian?"

"Florentine School."

"Support?"

"Walnut panel."

"Unusual for Florence," Gabriel pointed out.

"Quite."

"And the attribution?"

Calvesi gave a noncommittal shrug. "Manner of Raphael."

It was one of the weakest of all possible attributions, implying that the work had been made in the style of a prominent artist sometime after the artist had passed from the scene. In the case of Raffaello Sanzio da Urbino, that would have been in 1520.

"When was it painted?"

"Probably sometime in the eighteenth century."

Two centuries after Raphael's death. "Probably?" asked Gabriel.

"The provenance is rather thin. In fact, we're not quite certain how the painting even ended up in the papal collection. If it were put up for auction in London, it would be lucky to fetch a thousand pounds."

"Which made it the perfect picture for a novice conservator to take out for a test drive."

"With me sitting in the passenger seat," added Calvesi.

"How did it go?"

"After successfully calibrating the strength of her solvent, she began to remove the dirty varnish. That was when she discovered the pentimento."

Pentimento was the reappearance of imagery or discarded material that the artist had painted over—a different version of a hand, for example.

"Was the pentimento from the Madonna and Child?"

"We thought so until we examined it with infrared."

"And?"

"It was an entirely different painting. And a rather good one at that."

"How good?"

"My young apprentice was convinced that she had made one of the greatest artistic discoveries in history."

And then Gabriel understood.

LDV14521519 . . .

Penny Radcliff, twenty-seven years old, graduate of Cambridge University and the Courtauld Institute of Art, was convinced she had found a lost Leonardo.

11

Pinacoteca

In the more than seven thousand surviving pages of his notebooks—which he filled with mathematical equations, mundane daily to-do lists, seemingly random observations and riddles, and meticulous sketches of subjects ranging from the human aorta to fantastic flying machines and weapons of war—he made no mention of the circumstances surrounding his birth. The date was April 15, 1452, sometime around ten in the evening, perhaps in the tiny Tuscan hill town of Vinci, perhaps in the nearby hamlet of Anchiano. His father was a successful Florentine notary, his mother a peasant girl of sixteen. Though his parents were unwed and would never marry, his baptism was nevertheless well attended, for *non legittimo* births were commonplace in fifteenth-century Italy, especially among the nobility and upper classes. Indeed, owing to the scheming of a Florentine diplomat named Machiavelli, he would one day find himself in the employ of the ruthless Cesare Borgia, one of ten children fathered out of wedlock by His Holiness Pope Alexander VI.

He would remain in Vinci, living mainly on the estate of his paternal grandparents, until the age of twelve, when he moved into the home of his father in Florence. Having no formal education other than a bit of rudimentary mathematical training at an abacus school, he was in need of a trade to support himself. Left-handed, he taught himself to write in mirror script, from right to left across the page. He executed his first drawings in the same manner, with a distinctive right-to-left upward cross-hatching. His father showed some of the drawings to Andrea del Verrocchio, a friend and client who operated one of Florence's most highly regarded workshops, and Verrocchio agreed to take the boy on as an apprentice.

The Republic of Florence was then the epicenter of a great artistic and intellectual reawakening—a movement that would later be referred to as the Renaissance—and Verrocchio's busy workshop churned out paintings and other works of art for the city-state's increasingly wealthy elite. His apprentices, including young Leonardo da Vinci, lived in rooms upstairs and received rigorous artistic training in return for their services. The exercises included countless hours of drapery studies, which the pupils executed on linen, with only black and white paint. Leonardo, through his use of chiaroscuro, mastered the ability to create the illusion of three-dimensionality. His most revolutionary achievement, though, was *sfumato*, the hazy blurring of edges and transitions in color that would become the defining trait of his art. "Your shadows and light should be blended," he would later write, "in the manner of smoke losing itself on the air."

Leonardo made four paintings while a member of Verrocchio's workshop—three religious works and a portrait of the daughter of a Florentine banker—and in 1477, with the help of his father, he opened a workshop of his own. It would receive only three known commissions, none of which were completed. It was a failing that would persist for the remainder of his career, his seeming inability to complete his work in a timely fashion, if at all. The noblewoman Isabella d'Este, after convincing Leonardo to paint her portrait, pleaded with him to get on with it. An emissary explained the delay. Leonardo, he wrote, "cannot bear the sight of a paintbrush."

He much preferred his feather quill and his notebooks, carrying a small one with him always as he walked the streets of Florence. Muscular in build and fine in appearance, he was a witty and charming conversationalist and by all accounts generous to a fault. His clothing was colorful, usually a combination of dusty rose and dark purple, and unlike most Florentine men of his day, the hem of his gowns reached only his knee. It was no secret in Florence that, like his rival Botticelli, he was sexually attracted to men. He was once accused of engaging in sodomy with a male prostitute—a charge that might have landed him in prison had the case not been dismissed—and several boys of unsettling beauty served as apprentices in his workshop.

His favorite was Gian Giacomo Caprotti, a curly-haired peasant boy whom he referred to as Salaì, or Little Devil. The child entered Leonardo's household at the age of ten—not in Florence but in Milan, where Leonardo settled in 1482 at the invitation of Ludovico Sforza, the city-state's ruthless de facto ruler. During his seventeen-year stay in Milan, Leonardo would paint the portraits of two of Ludovico's mistresses—on walnut panels fashioned from the same tree—and a fresco for the dining hall of a monastery where Ludovico planned to create a mausoleum for his family. Having no training in fresco painting, Leonardo worked mainly in tempera and oil on dry plaster rather than the preferred method of applying water-soluble paints to a wet surface. Consequently the fresco, a depiction of the final meal shared by Jesus and his apostles, was soon beginning to flake. Giorgio Vasari, chronicler of the Italian Renaissance, wrote in 1550 that the painting was ruined.

A looming war with France forced Leonardo to leave Milan in the autumn of 1499. In the chaotic years that followed, he would serve as a military adviser to both the Venetians and the bloodthirsty Cesare Borgia. When he finally returned to Milan in April 1508, it was at the behest of the French royal governor. He resided in a house in the parish of Santa Babila, accompanied by Salaì, now in his late twenties, and a young boy named Francesco Melzi, an aspiring artist of moderate talent who was the son of a Milanese nobleman. Leonardo, intellectually restless as usual, undertook no new commissions during this period save for a mechanical lion for a pageant celebrating the arrival of France's King Louis XII. It is possible, likely even, that he spent at least some of his time adding final touches to still another undelivered painting, a portrait of a Florentine noblewoman called Lisa del Giocondo.

The portrait, which would one day be the most famous in the world, would accompany Leonardo for the remainder of his life. So, too, would Salaì and Francesco Melzi—first to Rome, where Leonardo worked briefly for the Medici pope Leo X, and finally to France, where he spent his final years in a redbrick château in the Loire Valley town of Amboise. He died there on May 2, 1519—in the arms of King François I, or so Vasari would have us believe—and was buried in the church at the royal Château d'Amboise.

Eight days before his death, with the help of a local notary, he drew up his last will and testament. To Francesco Melzi, whom he regarded as his adopted son and rightful heir, he left most of his possessions, including his money, notebooks, and "all the instruments and portraits pertaining to his art and calling as a painter." His lover and longtime assistant Salaì received only a share of a vineyard near Milan, which Ludovico Sforza had given to Leonardo as payment for the fresco that was by then falling into disrepair. Salaì, who was no doubt jealous over the affection shown to his rival Melzi, helped himself to several of his master's paintings.

Just five years later Salaì would be dead too, killed by a crossbow during still another French siege of Milan. An inventory of his estate would record that he had twelve paintings in his possession, including the portrait of the Florentine noblewoman Lisa del Giocondo. A seventeenth-century inventory of the French royal collection would reveal that King François I paid four thousand gold crowns for it, though neither the date of the transaction nor the other party to the sale was recorded.

His Majesty was so enthralled with his new acquisition that he hung it in his extravagant bathroom in the Palace of Fontainebleau, where it suffered the ravages of steam and heat. In a misguided attempt to undo the damage, a royal restorer—perhaps the Dutch artist Jean de Hoey, perhaps his son Claude—covered the painting with a thick coat of lacquer, which destroyed Leonardo's original colors and created a spider's web of distinctive surface cracks. Placed on public display in the Louvre in 1797, the painting was admired mainly by members of the intelligentsia. It was not until its shocking theft in August 1911 that Leonardo's masterpiece, the *Mona Lisa*, would achieve worldwide fame.

But what about the other paintings that devilish Salaì removed from the château at Amboise during the twilight of Leonardo's life? Or the works bequeathed to Francesco Melzi? Or the works that doubtless slipped from Leonardo's studios in Florence and Milan? Were they all accounted for, or had a handful of paintings—perhaps as many as five—been lost to the mists of time? A legion of so-called Leonardists believed that to be the case and were scouring the globe in search of them. Gabriel, for his part, had never come across a painting he believed to be a lost Leonardo. Nor, he had to admit, had he ever given the matter much thought. Until half past two that same afternoon, when Antonio Calvesi, chief of painting conservation at the Vatican Museums, showed him a photograph of *Madonna and Child with John the Baptist*, oil on walnut panel, 78 by 56 centimeters, perhaps eighteenth century, perhaps by an imitator of Raphael.

12

Pinacoteca

The photograph was displayed on the large computer monitor in Antonio Calvesi's office. It had been taken the day that he and Penelope Radcliff removed the painting from the Pinacoteca's store-rooms. The surface was covered with dust and grime, and the varnish had turned the color of a nicotine stain, dulling the colors. The next photograph, however, depicted the painting in a fully restored state, with the colors bright and vibrant. Gabriel, with his experienced eye, could easily spot the places where there had been significant retouching. It was a bit heavy-handed for his taste, but then he was known throughout the art world for the gentleness of his touch. His ambition was to come and go without being seen, to leave the painting as he had found it but restored to its original glory.

"Well?" asked Calvesi.

"I'm impressed. But how much of the work was done by you?"

"Can't you tell?"

Gabriel pointed out two instances of inpainting, one in the face of Mary, the other in the torso of the infant Jesus.

"Is it that obvious?"

"I know your work."

Calvesi pointed out a section of retouching in the pale blue stream flowing through the background. "That's Penny."

"She's rather good for one so young," said Gabriel, again using the present tense in reference to a woman he knew to be dead.

"Her father was a painter. She was born with a brush in her hand." Calvesi smiled. "Like you, Gabriel."

He ignored the compliment. "May I see the pentimento, please."

Calvesi clicked the mouse, and a new image appeared on the screen—the ghostly outline of another female lurking directly beneath the Madonna. It had been hidden by the thick layer of surface grime and tobacco-colored varnish. But Penelope Radcliff, with nothing but solvent and a swab of cotton wool, had revealed its existence.

"As you can see," said Calvesi, "it looks to be an earlier version of Mary. But when we examined the painting with infrared reflectography, this is what we found."

He clicked the mouse again, and a black-and-white infrared image appeared on the screen. It was a portrait of a fair-haired young woman gazing directly at the viewer over her left shoulder. Her eyes were large and heavy-lidded. Her left pupil was smaller than her right—considerably so.

Gabriel felt a faint queasiness in the pit of his stomach. It afflicted him whenever he was presented with a painting that, for whatever reason, wasn't quite right. In the lexicon of the art world, poor souls such as himself were sometimes referred to as "fake busters" for their uncanny ability to instantly spot forgeries or inflated attributions. But the inverse was true as well. On more than one occasion, Gabriel had authenticated autograph works of great masters that were wrongly attributed to imitators or later followers. None of his opinions, he was not ashamed to admit, had ever been called into question by higher authority.

He allowed a moment to pass before calmly posing his first question. "Do you recognize her?"

"She bears a passing resemblance to the girl who—"

"It's not a passing resemblance, Antonio. It's her."

"You can't say that with any certainty."

Gabriel dug his phone from his pocket and found an online photograph of Leonardo's *Head of a Young Woman*. It was widely accepted by scholars that the exquisite silverpoint drawing, now on display at the Biblioteca Reale in Turin, was a preparatory sketch for *Virgin of the Rocks*. The young woman had served as the model for the figure of the archangel Gabriel. Leonardo, as was often the case, had blurred the angel's gender.

Gabriel held the phone next to Calvesi's computer screen. "Look at her eyes. The pupils, to be exact. They're different sizes. Leonardo mistakenly believed that human pupils dilated separately when they were exposed to light."

"Penny noticed it too. But it doesn't prove anything."

Gabriel returned the phone to his pocket. "I don't suppose there's an underdrawing?"

Calvesi clicked on the appropriate icon, and another infrared image appeared. It was a finely rendered version of the painting itself. Some Italian Renaissance artists—Titian, for one—sketched directly onto their gesso. But Leonardo typically laid a perforated preparatory sketch on his panel and covered it with fine charcoal dust. The dust would then seep through the holes—the Italians called them *spolveri*—and thus the sketch would be transferred to the painting surface.

"Recognize her?" asked Gabriel once again.

"I will admit that the underdrawing looks a great deal like *Head of a Young Woman*."

"With good reason."

Calvesi treated Gabriel to a condescending smile. "Ever restored him?"

"Can't say that I have."

"Spent much time around him? Ever held one in your hands? A *real* Leonardo?"

"Your point, Antonio?"

"Once or twice each decade, some dealer or scholar convinces himself that he's stumbled upon a lost Leonardo. But only two new Leonardo oils have been accepted as autograph works by the hand of the master since 1909. The *Benois Madonna* and the *Salvator Mundi.*"

"That doesn't mean there aren't more."

"Do you really think our anonymous Florentine artist painted over a Leonardo?"

"Stranger things have happened, Antonio. By the eighteenth century, Leonardo's surviving oils were hidden away in private collections, and the *Last Supper* was in such terrible condition that the monks at Santa Maria delle Grazie put a door through the middle of it. It's quite possible that our anonymous Florentine painter had never heard of Leonardo da Vinci, let alone seen his work."

"But there is nothing in the historical record to suggest that he made a portrait of this woman, whoever she might be."

"There was no commission for *Portrait of a Musician* either. But Leonardo liked the way he looked, so he painted him."

"But he didn't paint this one."

"Says who?"

"Me."

"Based on what?"

"The preponderance of available evidence."

"There would have been considerably more evidence," said Gabriel, "if you had removed the painting on the surface and exposed the portrait to the light of day."

"Penny suggested the same thing."

"And?"

"I denied her request."

"Did you at least get a second opinion?"

"From God himself."

"Montefiore?"

"But of course."

Giorgio Montefiore was universally regarded as the world's foremost expert on the life and work of Leonardo da Vinci. He had a fancy title and a grand office at the Uffizi Gallery but spent most of his time writing and lecturing and rubbing elbows with art world glitterati. He was considered the last word when it came to Leonardo and the other Florentine masters. His favorable opinion of the *Salvator Mundi* had contributed greatly to its widespread if controversial acceptance as an autograph Leonardo.

"And what did God have to say about your picture?"

"He wasn't impressed."

"He might have been if it hadn't been covered by another painting."

"Giorgio was vehemently opposed to the needless destruction of the Madonna and Child."

"I didn't realize the two of you were on a first-name basis." Receiving no reply, Gabriel asked, "What happened next?"

"Penny completed the restoration of the painting, and I wrote her a glowing letter of recommendation and sent her on her way. And that," said Calvesi, "is the end of the story."

"Where is the painting now?"

"Back in the storeroom."

"I'd like to see it."

"Why?"

"Because I'm afraid there's more to the story, Antonio. Much more."

13

Pinacoteca

You misled me."

"Not true."

"How would you describe it?"

"I lied to your face."

Calvesi swiped his card through a reader, and a door opened before them. "Why?"

"The unusual nature of my inquiry required a modicum of deception."

"Your specialty."

"Forgive me, Antonio. But I needed to know what she found while she was working here."

"And you were afraid that I wouldn't tell you if I knew she was dead?"

"Would you have answered my questions if I had told you the truth?"

"Not without a lawyer present." They passed through the doorway and headed down a flight of steps. "Who are you working for this time? General Ferrari or your friend the Holy Father?"

"Both, I suppose."

"In that case, I'll light a candle for you."

"Light one for Penelope Radcliff instead."

"Do you really think she was killed because of that painting?"

"Someone turned over her apartment not long after she was murdered. I have a feeling they were looking for copies of those infrared images."

"She had a complete set of printouts. The last time I saw them, they were tucked inside her copy of Giorgio Montefiore's Leonardo monograph."

The indispensable *Complete Paintings and Drawings of Leonardo da Vinci*. "That would explain why the book wasn't in her apartment," said Gabriel.

"Could she have taken it with her to Venice?"

"Unlikely. That thing weighs about a ton and a half."

At the bottom of the stairwell they were confronted with another locked door. Calvesi opened it with his keycard and together they set off along a brightly lit corridor. By Gabriel's calculation they were now two levels beneath the Picture Gallery. The public exhibition rooms held only a small percentage of the vast papal collection of paintings, sculptures, and other objets d'art, the fair market value of which was so incalculable the Vatican listed it as a symbolic single euro. Gabriel reckoned it was about to increase substantially.

Antonio Calvesi slowed to a stop at a door labeled CAMERA IV. He unlocked it with his keycard and led Gabriel inside. Overhead fluorescent lights flickered automatically to life.

"Motion detectors," explained Antonio. Then he pointed to a surveillance camera and added, "Say hello to the boys in the control room."

"Since I'm not actually here, I'd rather not."

"Your inquiry is of an unofficial nature?"

"Is there any other kind?"

"Not at the Vatican."

The room was approximately the size of the Sistine Chapel. Arrayed along the walls were pullout storage racks. Gabriel grasped the handle of one of the racks and wheeled it into view. It was hung on both sides with paintings, all of Italian origin, most in need of conservation. The best of the lot was a picture of the resurrected Jesus.

"If I'm not mistaken," said Gabriel, "that's a Botticelli."

"You're not."

"Why is it down here?"

"Long story."

Gabriel rolled the rack back into place. "Where's my Leonardo?"

"Our only Leonardo is upstairs in the Picture Gallery," replied Calvesi, and set off toward the back of the room. With Gabriel looking on, he seized the handle of a rack labeled 27 and rolled it away from the wall. There were eight paintings on one side of the wire mesh and six on the other. There was more than sufficient space, thought Gabriel, for a seventh picture measuring, say, 78 by 56 centimeters.

"Perhaps this is the wrong rack."

"It isn't."

"You're sure?"

"I placed it here myself."

"Could someone have moved it?"

"Only someone with no sense of self-preservation."

Calvesi rolled the rack back into place and pulled its neighbor into view. Nine paintings on one side, seven on the other. None bore any resemblance—in size, support, or subject matter—to the painting they had come to see. The same was true of the adjacent rack and every other rack in the storage room. At which point Gabriel reached the unsettling conclusion that Penelope Radcliff, twenty-seven years old, graduate of Cambridge University and the Courtauld Institute of Art, had discovered a lost portrait by Leonardo da Vinci. And now the Leonardo was gone.

———————

Gabriel returned to the conservation lab long enough to collect hard copies of the photographs and infrared images of the painting, then slipped out of the Picture Gallery through a seldom-used rear door beneath the Sala della Biga. He rang Father Mark Keegan while crossing the Belvedere Courtyard.

"We need to talk."

"I'm listening," said the priest.

"Not on the phone."

"That bad?"

"Ten on the Richter scale."

They met five minutes later on the steps of the Basilica.

"A *real* Leonardo?" asked Father Keegan.

"A perhaps Leonardo at this point."

"Where is it now?"

"Gone."

The usually unflappable papal private secretary looked suddenly unwell. "It was stolen? Is that what you're saying?"

"It didn't grow a pair of legs and walk out of that storage room on its own. Someone carried it out. Someone who knew it was there in the first place."

"Someone who works for the museum?"

"Undoubtedly."

"Is that why Penelope Radcliff was murdered?"

Gabriel nodded. "She knew the painting had been pinched and took it upon herself to try to warn the art world."

"But why didn't she simply tell Antonio Calvesi that the painting was missing?"

"You're a sneaky little Jesuit. You tell me."

"Because she thought Antonio might be in on the job?"

"Correct."

"Do you think—"

"That Antonio Calvesi is involved?" Gabriel shook his head.

"What a trusting soul you are." They set off together across St. Peter's Square. Father Keegan's black cassock billowed and snapped in the gusty afternoon wind. "What now?" he asked.

"The Holy See shall bide its time and say nothing."

"We're rather good at that around here."

"So I've noticed."

"And when the authorities in Venice release the identity of the young woman whose body was discovered in the *laguna*?"

"The Vatican Press Office will express deep sadness over her death. It will remain silent, however, on the issue of the missing painting, which will allow me to continue my investigation unhindered by the glare of publicity."

"Fact-finding mission," said Father Keegan. "Since no crime has been committed, there can be no investigation."

"Well played."

"I'm a sneaky little Jesuit, remember?" Father Keegan slowed to a stop at the foot of the Egyptian obelisk. "Are you free for dinner, by any chance?"

"Why do you ask?"

"The Holy Father was wondering whether you might like to join his table at the Casa."

"As tempting as that sounds, I think I'll dine elsewhere."

"Allow me to suggest a quiet little place off the Via Veneto." The priest handed Gabriel a slip of paper. "The food is quite magnificent. And best of all, it's very discreet."

Gabriel looked down. He recognized the address. "What time am I expected?"

"Eight o'clock."

"Table for two?"

"I couldn't say."

"Dress code?"

Father Keegan smiled. "No cassocks."

14

Villa Marchese

Gabriel prevailed upon Chiara to acquire accommodations for him at the luxurious Hotel Hassler, though he declined to provide an estimate as to the length of his stay or divulge the reason he was in need of Roman lodging in the first place. Upstairs in his suite, he shaved and showered and changed into clean clothing. He briefly considered locking the photographs and infrared images in his room safe but slipped them into his attaché case instead. His dinner companion, a woman named Veronica Marchese, had a rather good eye for Italian Renaissance paintings—and a finely tuned ear for salacious art world gossip. Gabriel had not seen her since the night their mutual friend stepped onto the balcony of St. Peter's Basilica as the new supreme pontiff. He therefore feared a chilly reception. Priests were compelled by Catholic doctrine to forgive those who wronged them, but Veronica always struck Gabriel as the sort to hold a grudge.

They had met for the first time in the garden café of Italy's National Etruscan Museum. Veronica, one of the world's foremost authorities on Etruscan civilization and antiquities, was then a senior curator and an occasional consultant to the Art Squad. She was now the museum's director and its largest private benefactor, having inherited a substantial fortune from her late husband, Carlo, a member of Rome's Black Nobility. Unbeknownst to Veronica, he was also the leader of an antiquities smuggling network with connections in violent corners of the Middle East. Gabriel, in his first collaboration with General Ferrari, had smashed the network to pieces. Then, late one evening in St. Peter's Basilica, he had done the same to Carlo Marchese.

But Veronica had kept a secret from her husband as well—that many years earlier, while working on an archaeological dig near the Umbrian village of Monte Cucco, she had fallen desperately in love with a wayward Jesuit priest who had lost his faith while serving as a missionary in the Morazán province of El Salvador. Their affair had ended abruptly when the priest returned to the Church. Twenty-five years later, after one of the shortest conclaves in modern history, he was elected pope. Veronica had wept at the sight of the man she loved standing on the Loggia of the Blessings with his arms spread wide. They were not tears of joy.

The luxurious palazzo left to Veronica Marchese by her late husband was a pleasant five-minute walk from the Hassler. Gabriel rang the bell at the stroke of eight o'clock, and a sultry voice over the intercom informed him that the door was unlocked. It opened onto a long gallery hung with Italian School paintings. Veronica, in a stunning emerald-green pantsuit, waited at the opposite end. The second of her two *baci sulla guancia* lingered on his right cheek a moment longer than was customary in Roman social settings.

"I've missed you terribly, Gabriel Allon. Where on earth have you been?"

"In Venice."

"A scant two hours by train. And yet never once have you come to see me."

"I wasn't at all sure I would be welcome."

Veronica drew away and regarded him playfully through a pair of fashionable cat-eyed glasses. "Whyever not?"

"Because I made a mess of your life."

"Not for the first time," she pointed out.

"And yet here I am."

She smiled but said nothing.

"How did you know that I was in Rome?"

"Father Keegan mentioned it."

"Do the two of you speak often?"

"Now and again," she replied. "He told me that you dropped by the Vatican today to see the Holy Father and suggested I invite you to dinner."

"Any particular reason?"

"He was merely concerned with your well-being."

"He loathes me."

"He resents the closeness of your relationship with his master, but he admires you greatly. And why shouldn't he? If it wasn't for you, he would be teaching history at a Jesuit high school somewhere in America."

"What would be wrong with that?"

"For a cleric like Father Keegan, it would be intolerable. He wears his ambition on the sleeve of his black cassock, just like the rest of the Roman Curia. His one saving grace is that he is fiercely protective of the Holy Father."

"We have that in common, he and I."

"In that case, His Holiness has nothing to fear."

"I'm not so sure about that."

Veronica arched an eyebrow. "What is it this time?"

"Another scandal, I'm afraid."

"Is there a woman involved?"

"How did you guess?"

"Not me, I hope."

"No, Veronica. Not you."

She led Gabriel into an elegantly furnished sitting room and lifted a bottle of vintage Krug champagne from a crystal bucket. "It's the last bottle from Carlo's collection. I've been saving it for a special occasion." She filled two flutes, then raised hers in salutation. "To what shall we drink?"

"Old friends," suggested Gabriel.

"Lately I've become allergic to the word *old*. It springs to mind each time I look in the mirror. You, however, haven't aged a bit since I saw you last." Veronica sat down and crossed one leg over the other. "It was the day of the conclave, if I remember correctly. We watched the opening procession on television with the other Jesuits at their residence on the Borgo Santo Spirito. Then you and Luigi headed off to the Sistine Chapel, and he was gone forever."

"Can you ever forgive me?"

"The Church took Luigi away from me many years ago, Gabriel. You merely placed him permanently beyond my reach."

"You never see him?"

"The Vicar of Christ?"

"Luigi," said Gabriel.

"I've been known to attend the Wednesday General Audience. And on Sunday mornings I sometimes wander over to St. Peter's Square to hear His Holiness pray the Angelus. I believe he saw me standing beneath his window once, but I've had no contact with him other than the occasional phone call from his private secretary. We engage in an elaborate pantomime. He asks how I'm getting on, and I assure him that I've never been better. Today he told me that a dear friend had popped into Rome unexpectedly. It was the best news I've had in a very long time."

"You should find someone else, Veronica."

"I tried that once before. And look how that turned out." She drank some of her late husband's wine. "Besides, I'm too old to lose my heart to another man. I am, however, considering taking a lover. Someone young and beautiful and wildly inappropriate. The whole of Rome will be talking about nothing else."

"Have you anyone in mind?"

She waved a hand dismissively. "Enough about me, Gabriel. Tell me about the woman at the center of this brewing Vatican scandal."

"There's not much to tell, really."

"Does she have a name?"

"I would assume so. But there's no record of it."

"She's from Rome, this girl?"

"Milan, I'd say."

"What does she look like?"

"Pale hair, large eyes, quite pretty."

"Sounds like trouble. And how old is this fair-haired girl from Milan?"

Gabriel smiled. "Five centuries, at least."

———

It could be the work of one of his pupils or followers."

"The *Leonardeschi*?"

"Exactly."

"Possible," conceded Gabriel. "But the fact that it is now missing would suggest that someone thought it was a real Leonardo."

"Why wasn't it reported stolen?"

"No one knew it had vanished."

"An inside job?"

"Most museum thefts are."

They were seated on opposite sides of the table in Veronica's formal dining room, partaking of a first course of *vitello tonnato*. The photos and infrared images lay between them, along with Veronica's copy of Giorgio Montefiore's Leonardo monograph.

"Have I ever told you about my recurring nightmare?" she asked.

"Which one?"

"The one where I arrive at the Villa Giulia early one morning to find that the entire collection of the Museo Nazionale Etrusco has been stolen and all my security guards have fled the scene of the crime."

"Talk about a scandal," remarked Gabriel.

Veronica took up her knife and fork. "Let us say for argument's sake that the missing painting is an actual Leonardo."

"Let's," agreed Gabriel, and helped himself to more of the veal.

"What do you suppose the thieves intend to do with it?"

"That depends on the identity of the thieves."

"Your point?"

"It's possible the painting might end up in the hands of a wealthy collector who wants to possess the unpossessable. But the more likely scenario is that the thieves will attempt to cash in on their score by bringing the painting to market."

"Can it be done?"

"Quite easily."

"How?"

"The first thing they would need to do is remove the Madonna and Child and alter the appearance of the panel itself. If I were doing the work, I would adhere a second panel to the back of the original panel. Then I would restore the Leonardo and invent a convincing story to explain its reappearance."

"Like the cover story of a spy?"

"The concept is rather the same."

"And where do you suppose our girl will resurface?"

"Somewhere we least expect it."

"The *Salvator Mundi* was discovered at a gallery in New Orleans."

"A likely place for a Leonardo," said Gabriel.

"And twelve years later it sold for four hundred and fifty million dollars at Christie's."

"Four hundred million plus fees and commissions. But who's counting?"

"How much is *your* Leonardo worth?"

"The art historian Kenneth Clark described *Head of a Young Woman* as one of the most beautiful sketches in the world. If Leonardo in fact made an oil painting of the woman, it would be worth considerably more than the *Salvator Mundi*."

"A half billion?"

"Easily."

"But there's just one problem," said Veronica. "*Your* Leonardo was stolen from the Vatican Museums."

"Do you know how many versions of the *Salvator Mundi* there are? At least thirty. And there are scores of versions of the *Mona Lisa*. It would be quite easy to explain away two different versions of the same portrait. Besides, you know what they say about possession being nine-tenths of the law. That's doubly true in the art world."

"Won't serious collectors be reluctant to acquire it if they suspect it's somehow tainted?"

"Surely you jest."

A maid in a starched uniform appeared with the pasta course.

"*Amatriciana*," explained Veronica. "I hope you like it hot."

"The hotter, the better."

Veronica filled his bowl. "It seems to me that we have no choice but to go public."

"If we do, the Leonardo will vanish forever."

"What's the alternative?"

"We allow the thieves to think they've gotten away with the greatest art heist since the theft of the *Mona Lisa*."

Veronica took a first bite of the pasta. "He was an Italian, you know."

"Who?"

"The man who stole the *Mona Lisa* from the Louvre."

"It was an inside job."

"They always are," said Veronica. "But an inside job at the Vatican, well, that could be quite messy indeed."

15

Musei Vaticani

Antonio Calvesi met Gabriel at the public entrance of the Vatican Museums at ten the following morning. Inside, they headed down the corkscrew Bramante Staircase and through a locked doorway, into a half-lit room where four earnest-looking technicians sat staring at a wall of video screens. The stampede had commenced. On average, more than twenty thousand people visited the museum each day. Only the Louvre was busier.

The man responsible for protecting the priceless treasures of the papacy was a former corporate security specialist named Alessio Tomassini. He extended a hand warily toward Gabriel.

"Welcome back to the Vatican Museums, Signore Allon. It's been a while."

"Did you miss me, Alessio?"

"I'll let you know in a few minutes." The security chief escorted Gabriel and Calvesi into a side office and sat down behind a desktop computer. "Storage room number four?"

"How did you know?" asked Calvesi.

"I saw you and Signore Allon in there yesterday afternoon." Tomassini tapped a few keys, and a shot of the room appeared on the screen. "Are you looking for something in particular?"

"You might say that," remarked Gabriel.

"Is something missing?"

"Misplaced," interjected Calvesi.

"When was the last time it was removed from storage?"

Calvesi recited a date, and Alessio Tomassini entered it into the computer.

"Approximate time?"

"I believe it was about eleven thirty."

Tomassini started the playback at eleven, at three times the normal speed. He hit PAUSE at 11:42 a.m., when Antonio Calvesi entered the room, accompanied by a young woman.

"Signorina Radcliff?"

Greeted by silence, Tomassini set the scene in motion with a click of his mouse. Antonio Calvesi and the promising young art conservator searching for a painting in need of restoration. Something of little monetary value. Something long forgotten. The pullout rack labeled 27 had fifteen works from which to choose. Eight on one side of the wire mesh, seven on the other. They chose *Madonna and Child with John the Baptist*, oil on walnut panel, 78 by 56 centimeters, perhaps eighteenth century, perhaps by an imitator of Raphael.

Tomassini clicked PAUSE and looked at Calvesi. "I assume you and Signorina Radcliff transported the painting to the lab?"

"We did."

"Shall we watch the video?"

"That won't be necessary."

"When was it returned to storage?"

Calvesi recited another date, three months later than the first.

"The time?"

"Late afternoon. Five o'clock or so."

In point of fact, it was closer to half past. This time Calvesi was alone. He returned the newly restored painting to its original place on rack 27 and left.

The chief of security once again paused the recording. "Is that the painting that is now missing?"

"Misplaced," said Calvesi again.

"Perhaps someone moved it."

"We searched all four of the storage rooms."

"Yes, I know. I saw that too."

Tomassini clicked the play icon and increased the speed to its highest setting. Storage room 4 was off the beaten path. Days went by without a visitor, sometimes a week or two. Each time someone entered, they triggered the motion detectors, and the overhead lights flickered to life. And when they left again, the darkness returned. One of the visitors arrived at four fifteen on a Friday afternoon and made straight for rack 27.

Alessio Tomassini hit PAUSE. "Signorina Radcliff?"

Calvesi nodded, then checked the date. "It was the final day of her apprenticeship. I suppose she wanted to see the painting one last time."

Tomassini clicked PLAY, and Penelope Radcliff rolled the rack away from the wall. It held fourteen paintings. Eight on one side of the wire mesh. Six on the other. *Madonna and Child with John the Baptist*, oil on walnut panel, 78 by 56 centimeters, was gone.

"Pause it," said Gabriel.

Tomassini clicked the mouse.

"How is it possible that we missed the theft?"

"It isn't."

"Play it in reverse."

Tomassini complied with Gabriel's request. The same visitors came and went, though this time they were walking backward.

"Pause it again," said Gabriel. Then he asked, "What was that glitch in the playback?"

"I'm afraid I didn't notice one."

"Forward, Alessio. Normal speed."

Tomassini clicked PLAY. The timestamp read 11:23 p.m. The glitch occurred four minutes later, a wave that moved from the top of the screen to the bottom.

"I see it now," said Tomassini. "That was the night of the blackout."

"What blackout?"

"The entire Vatican lost power that night."

"What about the backup generators?"

"They failed. The night crew was completely in the dark for about fifteen minutes. When the lights came back on, they searched the entire museum from end to end. There was no sign of a break-in, and nothing was missing."

"How many guards on a typical night shift?"

"Five."

"Do you have a record of who was working that night?"

"Yes, of course."

"I need their names, Alessio. Their personnel files as well."

"I'm sorry, but those files are confidential."

"Shall we call the Holy Father?"

"No, Signore Allon. That won't be necessary."

16

Ostiense

The five names and their accompanying personnel files were by eleven thirty that morning in the hands of Luca Rossetti. He subjected each of the names to an invasive background check—the same check the Art Squad conducted on all applicants seeking employment at one of Italy's many national museums, especially security guards. At half past two, as Gabriel and General Ferrari were enjoying a late lunch in the Campo de' Fiori, Rossetti found his man. He collected Gabriel fifteen minutes later in an unmarked Alfa Romeo. They headed south on the Corso Vittorio.

"It's Pozzi," said Rossetti. "Ottavio Pozzi."

"What's he hiding?"

"His older brother Sandro."

"A troubled soul, is he?"

"That's one way of putting it." Rossetti inclined his head in the general direction of Trastevere. "Sandro is currently residing at Regina Coeli."

"How long is his lease?"

"He's doing twenty-five to thirty years for armed robbery, the sale and distribution of illegal narcotics, and murder. None of which Ottavio mentioned when he applied to work at the Vatican."

"How is it possible that no one noticed?"

"You know how the Vatican operates. As long as someone says he's a practicing Catholic, he's in. Even the Swiss Guards receive almost no vetting."

"Tell me about it," murmured Gabriel.

Luca Rossetti rounded the Colosseum, practically on two wheels, then raced past the Circus Maximus. His destination was an apartment block in the working-class district of Ostiense. The ground floor was covered in graffiti. Thick metal bars defended the windows and the street-level entrance.

"How shall we handle it?" asked Rossetti.

"Good cop, bad cop?"

"Which one am I?"

"Since you're the one with the badge, Luca, I suggest you play the role of bad cop."

Rossetti had two files in his possession. One was the Vatican personnel file. The other, the thicker of the two, was Sandro Pozzi's extensive criminal file. He carried them over to the entrance of the apartment block and jabbed at the weather-beaten intercom panel. A woman answered at once.

"*Buongiorno.*"

"Signora Pozzi?"

"Who wants to know?"

"Capitano Luca Rossetti of the Carabinieri. I'm here to see your husband."

"Can you come back later? Ottavio is sleeping now."

"I'm afraid it can't wait. Please open the door."

Several seconds elapsed before the buzzer sounded and the lock snapped open. Gabriel followed Rossetti into the foyer and up the stairs to the fourth floor. Giada Pozzi, wife of Ottavio Pozzi, waited in the doorway of apartment 408. She was a thin, sinewy woman of perhaps thirty-five, pierced and heavily tattooed. She ignored the Carabinieri identification that Rossetti held before her nearly black eyes.

"Why do you want to talk to him?"

"Move aside, Signora Pozzi."

"He's done nothing wrong."

"In that case, he has nothing to worry about."

The woman held her ground for a moment longer before finally yielding. Rossetti brushed past her, with Gabriel at his heels. Two children, a boy and a girl, were staring at the television in the sitting room. The boy looked to be about eight or nine. The girl was a year or two younger.

"Where's Ottavio?" asked Rossetti.

"I told you, he's sleeping."

"Wake him up. We haven't got all day."

The woman disappeared down a hallway and returned a moment later with her husband. He wore a wrinkled cotton pullover and a pair of jeans. His eyes were red-rimmed, his skin was pale, his dark hair was uncombed.

He looked at Rossetti and asked, "What do you want?"

"Is there somewhere we can speak in private? I wouldn't want to upset the children."

They all four went into the kitchen. Pozzi joined Gabriel and Rossetti at the linoleum table while his wife filled a Bialetti stovetop with Illy and San Benedetto.

Rossetti laid one of the files on the tabletop and lifted the cover. "Your Vatican personnel file, along with a copy of your original application and security questionnaire."

Ottavio Pozzi regarded the material with the blank expression of the sleep-deprived. "Where did you get that?"

"It was given to us by your boss." Rossetti placed the second file on the table. "This one we found all on our own."

Pozzi was silent.

"Why did you lie on your application?" asked Rossetti.

"I needed a job. And I knew they would never hire me if I told them my brother was a criminal."

"You could have found a job somewhere else."

"I wanted to work at the Vatican."

"Why?"

"To be close to the Holy Father."

"You admire His Holiness?"

"I love all the popes."

"You're a devout Catholic?"

"Very."

Rossetti looked at the pierced, tattooed woman. "And what about you, Signora Pozzi?"

She placed a cup of coffee before her husband but said nothing.

"Giada left the Church because of the sex abuse scandal," explained Ottavio Pozzi. "She refuses to set foot in the Vatican."

"And yet her husband spends every night there," said Rossetti. "Never the day shift. Always the night."

"I prefer it."

"And why is that?"

Pozzi gave a dreamy smile. "Have you ever been in the Sistina alone? Or the Raphael Rooms?"

"What about the storage rooms?" asked Gabriel.

Pozzi's smile faded. "I rarely go there, Signore."

"But you went there on the night of the power failure, didn't you? And while you were there, you removed this." Gabriel laid a photograph of the painting on the tabletop. "The person who hired you for the job assured you that no one would ever notice the painting was missing. And you foolishly believed him."

Pozzi glanced at the painting, then looked away. "You are mistaken, Signore."

Rossetti sighed heavily. "I would advise you to choose another path, Ottavio. Otherwise I will have no choice but to arrest you in front of your children and lock you away in Regina Coeli with that brother of yours."

"But I've done nothing wrong."

Rossetti ignored the denial. "If, however, you help us recover the painting, I might be able to persuade my commanding officer to overlook your conduct. Oh, you'll lose your job, of course. But your children won't have to visit their father in prison."

Pozzi exchanged a long look with his wife before answering. "I'm sorry, Capitano, but I'm afraid I can't help you."

"Why not?"

"Because if I do, they'll kill him."

"Kill who?"

"My brother Sandro."

"Is that why you agreed to steal the painting? Because they threatened your brother?"

Pozzi hesitated, then nodded once.

"But that's not the only reason, is it? Surely they must have paid you *some*thing."

"A hundred thousand."

"Is that all?" Luca Rossetti smiled. "Try again, Ottavio."

17

Ostiense

M̲ost evenings Ottavio Pozzi stopped at Caffè Roma, a popular neighborhood bar on the Via Casati, for a *doppio* before boarding the first of two Metro trains that took him from Ostiense to the Vatican. It was on one such evening, not long after the Feast of the Assumption, that he made the acquaintance of the man who referred to himself only as Signore Bianchi. He insisted on paying for Pozzi's coffee. Then he suggested they have a word in private.

"Describe him," said Luca Rossetti, a pen hovering over his open detective's notebook.

"Forty or so, nice jacket, gold watch. Not the sort of man you would ever want to cross."

"Italian?"

"Sure."

"Roman?"

"If he was, he wasn't born here."

"He had an accent?"

Pozzi nodded. "It was like yours, Capitano."

Rossetti had been raised in Naples, in the working-class neighborhood of Secondigliano. He spoke Italian with a distinct Neapolitan accent.

"How did Signore Bianchi know about Sandro?" he asked.

"He said the information had come from one of his associates."

"Associates?"

"He didn't go into detail. But he made it clear that these associates could get to Sandro inside Regina Coeli if I didn't do what he wanted."

"And you, of course, went straight to your boss and told him everything."

"If I had done that, they would have killed my brother. And then they would have killed me. Or maybe they would have killed Giada or one of the children. What would you have done if you were in my position?"

Rossetti turned to a fresh page in his notebook without answering. "And how, exactly, did Signore Bianchi suggest that you steal the painting and smuggle it out of the museum without anyone noticing?"

"He said there would be a power failure that would disable the museum's security system."

"Did he give you the time and date of this promised power failure?"

"Not then."

"When, Ottavio?"

"He met me at Caffè Roma two weeks later. He said the power failure would happen the next night."

"Where were you when the lights went out?"

"The Picture Gallery. Room Twelve."

"Why Room Twelve?" asked Gabriel.

"That's where the Caravaggio hangs. *The Deposition* is my favorite painting. I pray there often."

"You were having second thoughts?"

Pozzi nodded.

"Why didn't you listen to your conscience?" asked Rossetti.

"My brother."

"And when the power failed?"

The darkness in Room XII was so complete, said Pozzi, that he could scarcely see his hand in front of his face. He immediately raised the control room on his radio and was instructed to commence a museum-wide search for evidence of a break-in. He checked the main public entrance, knowing full well it was secure, then headed downstairs to the storage rooms. Because the cameras and motion detectors were disabled, his four colleagues were unaware of his whereabouts.

"How did you open the door?" asked Rossetti.

"The locks have a battery backup. All I had to do was enter the proper emergency override code. The painting was exactly where Signore Bianchi told me it would be."

"Rack twenty-seven?" asked Gabriel.

Pozzi nodded.

"How did you get it out of the Vatican?"

"I didn't."

"Who did?"

"The priest."

"What priest?" asked Gabriel.

"I don't know his name."

"Where did you give it to him?"

"The doorway that leads to the staff car park. He placed the painting in a nylon case and carried it out of the Vatican."

"Do you remember what he looked like?"

"It was quite dark. I really didn't get a good look at his face."

"Surely you must remember something about him."

"His hair was black."

"How did he wear it?"

"Neatly combed."

Gabriel drew a pen from his pocket and pulled a sheet of paper from Pozzi's Vatican personnel file. His method was rudimentary, a simple oval bisected by faint horizontal lines for the eyes and mouth.

"On what side did he part his hair, Ottavio? The left or the right?"

"The left, I believe."

"Did he wear a beard?"

"No."

"And what about his cheekbones?" asked Gabriel. "Were they rounded or angular?"

———————

Naturally ambidextrous, Gabriel worked with his left hand, with upward cross-hatching pen strokes. The finished sketch depicted a man of perhaps thirty-five with deeply set eyes, broad cheekbones, a straight nose, and a wide mouth. Gabriel dressed his subject in a clerical suit and a Roman collar, then showed his handiwork to Ottavio Pozzi, the penniless museum security guard who had unwittingly stolen a lost portrait by Leonardo da Vinci.

"That's him, Signore. That's the man."

"Did he say anything to you?"

"Not a word. He just handed me a slip of paper and walked away."

"The location of the money?"

Pozzi nodded. "It was in a luggage storage place near the Termini station."

"A hundred thousand?"

"A quarter million."

"Where is it now?"

The museum guard glanced at his wife, then said, "Hidden under our bed."

"How much is left?"

"All of it. We didn't spend a single euro."

A careful count of the newly minted banknotes, conducted by Luca Rossetti at the kitchen table, confirmed that to be the case. Some twenty minutes later the money was in the trunk of Rossetti's unmarked Alfa Romeo, bound for central Rome. Ottavio Pozzi, however, was still in his apartment. In a few hours' time he would stop at Caffè Roma for a *doppio*, then board the first of two Metro trains that would deliver him to the Vatican Museums.

"I'd feel better if he were locked inside Regina Coeli with his brother," said Rossetti.

"So would I," replied Gabriel. "But if we arrest him, it will alert Signore Bianchi and his associates in Naples that we're on to them."

"You noticed that too?"

"Rather hard to miss."

"It seems we're dealing with the Camorra."

"Yes," said Gabriel. "Lucky us."

"It would explain how Signore Bianchi knew about Sandro. The Camorra has the prison system wired."

"But it wouldn't explain how Father Bagman managed to get inside the Vatican."

"How do you suppose he did it?"

"Either he scaled the walls," said Gabriel, "or someone let him in. I'm betting it was the latter."

———

It took Rossetti nearly an hour to battle his way through the rush-hour traffic to St. Anne's Gate. A halberdier in a simple blue night uniform stood on the Vatican side of the frontier, his white-gloved hands clasped behind his back. To his immediate right was the main entrance to the Swiss Guard barracks. In the reception area, a duty officer sat ramrod-straight behind a half-moon desk. Before him was a bank of closed-circuit video monitors. On the wall behind him were a crucifix and the flags of Switzerland's twenty-six cantons.

"Where's your boss?" asked Gabriel.

"In his office."

"I need a word."

"Do you remember the way?"

"First door after the suit of armor."

The duty officer smiled and reached for his phone. "I'll let him know you're coming."

Gabriel made his way along a narrow corridor to an internal courtyard where two fresh-faced halberdiers were hacking old dress uniforms to pieces with heavy axes, the Guard's most common form of punishment. The building on the opposite side of the court was dull brown in color and contained the comfortable living quarters of senior officers, including Commandant Alois Metzler. His office was on the ground floor.

Gabriel removed the sketch from his attaché case and laid it on Metzler's desk.

"Who is he?" asked the commandant.

"I was hoping you might be able to tell me."

Metzler picked up the sketch and examined it at length. "I'm sorry, but I don't recognize him."

"I have a feeling that at least one of your men might."

"Why?"

"Because our priestly friend walked out of the Vatican a few weeks ago with a painting under his arm."

Metzler looked up from the sketch. "I assume this has something to do with the English woman."

Gabriel nodded.

"When was the theft?"

"The night of the power failure."

"It happened around eleven, if memory serves."

"Eleven twenty-seven," said Gabriel. "Leaving our priestly friend plenty of time to slip out of the Vatican before the gates closed at midnight. But someone had to have cleared him into the Vatican earlier that evening."

"He could have come through the Arch of Bells, the Bronze Doors, or St. Anne's Gate."

"Can you find out which halberdiers were working that night?"

Metzler consulted the old duty rosters on his computer, then placed a series of terse phone calls. Three youthful Swiss Guards were soon standing at attention in his office. One wore a dress uniform, one wore a simple blue night uniform, and the third, having been roused from sleep, was clad in jeans and a Swiss Army fleece pullover.

Metzler held up the sketch. "Did any of you see this man leave the Vatican the night of the power outage?"

"I did, Colonel Metzler."

It was the halberdier in the colorful dress uniform. He had been stationed at St. Anne's Gate.

"Was he carrying anything?"

"A large nylon satchel."

"You didn't think it odd?"

"No, Colonel Metzler. I did not."

"Did he speak to you?"

"Not a word."

Metzler gritted his teeth. "And who was the idiot who allowed him to enter the Vatican?"

"It was me," said the halberdier dressed in jeans and a fleece. He had been working that night at the Arch of Bells.

"Do you remember the time?"

"Around eight thirty."

"You spoke to him, I hope."

"Yes, Colonel."

"What was his name?"

"Father Spada."

"First name?"

"Giuseppe."

"Did he have a Vatican identification?"

"No, Colonel."

"Who cleared him into the Vatican?"

"It was Father Keegan."

"You're sure?"

"Yes, Colonel."

With a wave of his hand, Metzler sent the three halberdiers filing out of his office. Then he looked at Gabriel and said, "A rather unexpected development."

"That's one way of putting it." Gabriel drew his phone and dialed the Holy Father's private secretary. "We have a problem."

"The Pantheon," said Father Keegan. "Eight o'clock."

18

Osteria Lucrezia

The four-car motorcade arrived at the Pantheon, the ancient pagan temple turned Roman Catholic basilica, at the stroke of eight o'clock. Three of the vehicles were unmarked sedans, and the fourth was a Mercedes saloon model with opaque curtains drawn over the rear windows. As Gabriel approached the car, the rear passenger-side door opened to reveal a darkly handsome man dressed in chinos and a plaid sport jacket.

"Don't just stand there," said Luigi Donati. "Get in."

Gabriel slid into the back seat, and the motorcade shot forward. "Did you run out of clean cassocks, Holiness?"

"I have twelve, if you must know. But it's rather hard to go unnoticed when one is draped head-to-toe in white."

"You don't say."

"It is a verifiable fact. We can look it up, if you like."

"You're one of the most recognizable public figures in the world, Luigi, regardless of how you're dressed."

"I beg to differ. In the words of the theologian Erasmus of Rotterdam, *vestis virum facit*."

"Clothes make the man?"

"Absolutely."

The secret papal motorcade turned onto the Via del Tritone. The pedestrians filing along the pavements paid it no heed. They were Romans, after all.

"Where are we going?" asked Gabriel.

"I wouldn't want to spoil the surprise."

"Private residence?"

"Public restaurant."

"You can't be serious."

"Wait until you taste the *trippa alla Romana*. Your life will never be the same."

It was a traditional Roman dish of entrails stewed in tomatoes and aromatics. "I'd sooner eat my shoe than the digestive organs of a bovine," said Gabriel.

"But you're quite fond of *fegato alla Veneziana*, if I remember correctly."

"Calf's liver is different, Holiness."

"I shall rule on the matter in my next encyclical." Donati peered round the edge of the curtain covering his window. "This is my diocese, you know."

"That would explain why they call you the Bishop of Rome."

Donati gave him a withering sidelong look. "Something bothering you?"

"As an occasional consultant to the Vatican on matters related to papal security, I can say with confidence that this is a terrible idea."

"It's not the first time I've slipped out of the Vatican in civilian dress. And yet no one seems to have noticed, mainly because I never travel in my official car."

"What about your security detail?"

"It's a smaller version of my usual team. The two men in the front seat are plainclothes Swiss Guards. The officers in the escort cars are Polizia di Stato. Rest assured, I am very well protected."

The restaurant, Osteria Lucrezia, was located on a quiet street not far from the train station. They arrived there to find the neon sign extinguished and the window shades tightly drawn. The placard on the door read CHIUSO.

"Too bad," said Gabriel. "I suppose we have no choice but to return to the Vatican."

"The restaurant is closed for a small private party."

"How many guests will be in attendance?"

"Just two."

Donati stepped from the car and, surrounded by his security detail, walked calmly into the restaurant. Gabriel followed a moment later. The dining room he entered was small and cramped, not unlike Vini da Arturo in Venice. The Bishop of Rome, in his sport jacket and chinos, was chatting amiably with the proprietor and the chef. There was no bowing or scraping or pressing of lips to a proffered ring, just three Italian men exchanging pleasantries. The rest of the staff, it seemed, had been given the night off.

Donati introduced his dinner companion without divulging his name or occupation, and they sat down at a table covered in white paper. The proprietor removed the cork from a bottle of the house white and poured two glasses. Donati, with a glance, instructed the members of his security detail to make themselves scarce. The Polizia di Stato officers withdrew to the exterior of the restaurant. A Swiss Guard stood just inside the door.

"I hope you're hungry."

"Famished," replied Gabriel.

"Busy day?"

"Quite."

"Is it going to spoil my appetite?"

"Probably."

"In that case, let's have some antipasti first."

The onslaught commenced with a plate of fried Roman artichokes and zucchini flowers, followed by an assortment of crostini and cured meats. Then came the vegetables drenched in olive oil and the balls of fresh mozzarella. During the brief lull before the pasta course, Gabriel placed the composite sketch on the table. Donati, dabbing at the corners of his mouth with a paper napkin, regarded it with interest.

"I have a feeling I've seen this man before."

"Could it have been the evening of the recent power outage?"

Donati looked up. "Yes, that's it. His name was Father Spada, as I recall."

"Don't tell me you actually met him."

"Briefly."

"Where?"

"In my apartment at the Casa."

"And the purpose of this meeting?"

"Father Spada works for Caritas Internationalis at a migrant house in Mali. Caritas provides aid and comfort to the migrants before they embark on their journey across the Sahara toward Europe."

"A noble endeavor on the Church's part, Luigi. But Father Spada doesn't work for Caritas. In fact, I doubt he's an actual priest."

"He certainly looked like a priest."

"*Vestis virum facit*," said Gabriel, and told Donati the rest of the story.

————————

His Holiness took up a fork and spoon and laid siege to his spaghetti carbonara. "But why didn't the security guard simply remove the painting from the museum himself?"

"The public entrance on the Viale Vaticano is sealed tight after the museum closes. The painting had to be given to someone who could carry it past the Swiss Guard at St. Anne's Gate."

"Someone wearing the clerical suit and Roman collar of a Catholic priest?"

Gabriel nodded. "And carrying a nylon satchel large enough to hold a walnut panel measuring seventy-eight by fifty-six centimeters."

"That would explain the framed photograph he presented to me. A group of Caritas workers feeding weary refugees."

"How clever of him." Gabriel sampled his tagliatelle with mushrooms. "But how was he able to get in the same room with you in the first place?"

"If I recall correctly, the visit was arranged by someone at Caritas headquarters here in Rome."

"Was anyone else present?"

"Father Keegan, of course. And Bertoli was there as well."

"Bertoli?"

"Cardinal Matteo Bertoli is the Substitute for General Affairs of the Secretariat of State."

"The *sostituto*?"

Donati nodded. "He's essentially the chief of staff of the Roman Catholic Church. He manages the Curia, handles the flow of all papal documents, and oversees the operations of our diplomatic nuncios abroad. He even maintains control of the Fisherman's Ring when I'm not wearing it."

"How does he feel about the current pope?"

"My master was the one who appointed Bertoli, with my blessing, of course. I have no doubt that he's more doctrinally conservative than I am. But he has been loyal to a fault, and the machinery of the Curia is functioning smoothly."

"With the exception of security around the Holy Father," said Gabriel.

"Father Spada was never a threat to me. In fact, he was quite charming."

"Most thieves are."

"I wouldn't know," said Donati.

"How long were you with him?"

"Less than five minutes. We exchanged a few words. Then Father Keegan showed him out."

"He somehow managed to remain behind the walls until the power failure."

"It probably didn't hurt that he was dressed as a priest."

"Or that he's an extremely competent professional criminal," added Gabriel.

"Mafia?"

"Camorra."

"The worst of the worst," remarked Donati. "But how did they know about the painting's existence?"

"Obviously someone told them."

"Any suspects?"

"Your private secretary seems to think I should march Antonio Calvesi down to the Castel Sant'Angelo and attach him to the rack."

"Do you think he's behind it?"

"Antonio is not without faults," said Gabriel. "But he's no thief."

"Who else knew?"

"Besides Penelope Radcliff? Everyone in the conservation lab, I suppose. And then, of course, there's the esteemed Giorgio Montefiore from the Uffizi."

"Have you ever met him?"

"He once remarked favorably on one of my restorations. But, no, I have never had the pleasure."

"He has an ego the size of St. Peter's." Donati lowered his voice. "Or so I'm told."

"Told by whom?"

"A friend of mine who knows him well. She once attended a party at Montefiore's villa in Florence. He lives like a Medici, does our Giorgio. And he owes it all to his claim of being the world's foremost Leonardist."

"Do you think he would agree to see your friend on short notice?"

"I don't see why not. But I'd keep your name out of it. Giorgio might get suspicious."

Gabriel inserted his fork into the tagliatelle and twirled. "Not bad, Holiness."

"I'm a Jesuit," said Donati. "I'm conspiratorial by nature."

19

Galleria degli Uffizi

Gabriel was standing outside the entrance of the Hassler the following morning when Veronica Marchese pulled up in her flashy open-top Mercedes Cabriolet. She wore a pair of movie-starlet sunglasses and an Hermès scarf over her dark hair. All that was missing, he thought, was a devilishly handsome leading man at her side. He supposed he would have to do.

He dropped into the passenger seat and placed his lips against the proffered cheek. It smelled of jasmine and vanilla. "Is that intoxicating French perfume for me or your friend Giorgio?"

"A little of both." Veronica pressed the throttle and the car lurched away from the curb. "Did you enjoy Osteria Lucrezia?"

"I don't believe my text message made any mention of where I dined last evening."

"How else could I have possibly known?"

"Good question." They shot past the church of Trinità dei Monti in a blur and a moment later careened around the Piazza del Popolo. "Do the brakes work on this thing?"

"I don't often use them, if you must know."

"They can be quite useful at controlling your forward momentum."

"Venetians," she said with mock contempt.

"Admittedly we do move at a slower pace."

"But when in Rome, speed is of the essence. Besides, we don't want to keep Giorgio waiting."

They raced along the Tiber for a time, then wound their way through the northern districts of Rome to the Autostrada. Soon they were blazing along at nearly twice the posted speed limit.

"Did you have the *trippa* last evening?"

"I passed."

"What was the occasion?"

"A problem regarding security at the Vatican."

"Father Spada, you mean?" She took her eyes from the road long enough to give him a knowing sidelong look. "Father Keegan told me all about your rather embarrassing discovery."

"What other details of my investigation did he divulge?"

"That the inside connection was a security guard named Ottavio Pozzi."

"There had to be another."

"Someone who knew about the portrait?"

"Exactly."

"Who do you suppose she was?" asked Veronica.

"The woman you just ran over with your motorcar? I believe it was Myrtle Wilson."

"The girl in the Leonardo."

"We haven't a clue."

"Perhaps Giorgio will be able to shed some light on the matter."

"I believe his Leonardo monograph is silent on that issue."

"It is," said Veronica. "I reread his notes on the *Virgin of the Rocks* last night."

"I did some reading as well," said Gabriel.

"Anything interesting?"

"Montefiore's memoirs. He wrote at length about the one dis-appointment of his otherwise glittering career."

"And what was that?"

"His failure to find a lost Leonardo." Gabriel pointed out a speed limit sign. "Don't you think you should slow down a bit, Signora Buchanan?"

Veronica smiled and put her foot to the floor.

Ordinarily it was a drive of three hours from Rome to Florence, but Veronica managed to cover the distance in just under two and a half. She deposited her car in a garage outside the *zona a traffico limitato*, and they walked along the Arno to the Uffizi. Montefiore had promised to meet Veronica at Door 3, the museum's main visitor entrance, at eleven o'clock. But at eleven fifteen there was still no sign of him.

"Perhaps you should call him," said Gabriel.

Veronica sent a text message instead. There was no response.

"He must be in a meeting," she said.

"Why didn't he tell you that he was running late?"

"Because he's Giorgio Montefiore."

They led themselves on an unhurried tour of the Piazzale degli Uffizi, pausing briefly to ponder the statue of Leonardo, and returned to Door 3 at eleven thirty. Montefiore was nowhere to be seen.

This time Veronica dialed his number. The call went straight to voicemail.

"Try his office," suggested Gabriel.

She found a number online. A secretary informed her that Monte-fiore had not yet arrived at the museum.

"We had an appointment at eleven."

"I wouldn't worry, Dottoressa Marchese. He's almost never on time."

Veronica rang off and dialed his mobile a second time. Once again her call went directly to voicemail.

"Do you remember where he lives?" asked Gabriel.

Veronica pointed toward the opposite bank of the Arno.

"Inside the *zona* or outside?"

"The latter."

"Let's take the car," said Gabriel. "And never mind the brakes."

The villa stood atop a low hill on the southern fringes of the city, behind a stone wall approximately three meters in height. The metal gate was tightly locked. Gabriel pressed the call button on the intercom and received no response. Veronica rang Montefiore's mobile phone a final time, with the same result.

"What now?" she asked.

"I suppose one of us should climb over the gate."

"I nominate you for the job."

"My back is killing me."

"You'll manage somehow, I'm sure."

Gabriel considered his options for a moment, then clambered onto the bonnet of Veronica's Mercedes. Even with the added elevation, he was scarcely able to grasp the top of the gate. The bars were vertical, thus robbing him of a toehold to ease his ascent. Nevertheless, after several seconds of sustained effort, he managed to hoist a leg over the barrier. With a simple rotation of his shoulders, the rest of him soon followed. He dangled there a moment, calculating the distance between his feet and the gravel drive, and then released his grip. The landing was excruciating but for the most part dignified.

"Bravo," declared Veronica through the bars of the gate. "You were magnificent."

"Now you."

"I'll wait here, if you don't mind."

Gabriel brushed the dust from his gabardine trousers and headed up the drive to the entrance of the villa. He didn't bother with the bell push, placing a hand on the latch instead. Like the gate, the door was locked. Breaching it, however, required nothing more arduous than a few seconds of gentle work with the slender tools in the breast pocket of his jacket.

He opened the door and stepped into the cool shadows of the entrance hall. Which was where he discovered Giorgio Montefiore lying in a crimson pool of recently shed blood, with three tightly spaced bullet holes in the center of his forehead. His life's ambition had finally been realized, thought Gabriel. He had found his lost Leonardo. And now he was dead.

20

Hotel Hassler

It was Contessa Teressa Simonetti, a faded Florentine noblewoman with midnight-blue blood flowing through her veins, who sounded the alarm. She did so at 12:17 p.m., with a call to the Florence headquarters of the Carabinieri. The dispatcher was justifiably dubious, for the contessa was getting on in years and was a frequent if unreliable observer of crimes and misdeeds of every sort.

"An intruder, you say?"

"I saw him with my own eyes."

"When?"

"As he was climbing over the gate."

The dispatcher asked the contessa for a description of the suspect and dutifully jotted down her answer. It was hardly the portrait of a typical Tuscan criminal, but then the contessa was blind as a bat.

"Was there anyone with him?"

"A woman."

"Where is she now?"

"Sitting in her car."

None of which sounded to the dispatcher like the elements of a crime in progress. Still, the purported incident warranted further investigation, if only because the property in question was the art-filled residence of Giorgio Montefiore, the world's foremost expert on Leonardo da Vinci. As it happened, a Carabinieri patrol car was in the vicinity and arrived on the scene less than two minutes later. There the officers discovered an attractive woman sitting behind the wheel of a Mercedes-Benz Cabriolet convertible. They found her companion in the entrance hall of the villa, crouched casually next to a man who had been shot three times at close range.

In short order the officers determined that the woman was the director of the Museo Nazionale Etrusco, that her companion was a prominent art conservator from Venice, and that the victim was the owner of the property, the aforementioned Giorgio Montefiore. The condition of the blood suggested that he had been dead for approximately four hours, long before the prominent Venetian art conservator made entry into the villa.

"How did you get inside?" asked one of the officers.

"The front door. How else?"

"It was unlocked?"

"Not exactly."

By one o'clock the villa was crawling with crime scene technicians, and the museum director and art conservator, having been relieved of their mobile devices and other personal effects, were seated in separate interview rooms at the Carabinieri *stazione* in the Piazza dei Giudici. The questioning was polite in tone but thorough enough to reveal significant discrepancies in their explanations as to why they had traveled to Florence to meet with Giorgio Montefiore in the first place. The museum director said the visit was personal in nature. The art conservator, however, insisted it was professional.

"Can you be more specific?" asked his interrogator, a *colonnello* called Manzini.

"I required his assistance on a restoration."

"That would explain the photographs in your attaché case."

"It would indeed."

"Perhaps there's a connection between this painting of yours and Montefiore's murder?"

"You've been reading too many thrillers, Colonel Manzini."

The *colonnello*, knowing a little of the art conservator's past, was certain there was more to the story. He was likewise confident that a few hours in a holding cell might serve to loosen the conservator's tongue. The powers that be in Rome, however, had other ideas. Manzini, after making his objections known, reluctantly destroyed his interview notes and escorted the two subjects downstairs. The Mercedes convertible was parked in the piazza. The conservator slid into the passenger seat, the museum director behind the wheel. The engine roared, the tires chirped, and then they were gone.

———————

They arrived at the Hassler shortly after seven o'clock. Veronica left her car with the valet and accompanied Gabriel upstairs to the hotel's Michelin-starred restaurant. General Ferrari, in a charcoal-gray business suit, sat at a table near the window. He directed Gabriel to the chair at his right, where there was no hiding from the unforgiving gaze of his ocular prosthesis.

"We had an agreement," he said without preamble.

"Did we?"

"Your mandate to look into this matter did not extend beyond the territory of the Holy See. The last time I checked, Florence is part of the Italian Republic."

"My inquiry took an unexpected turn."

"To put it mildly," replied Ferrari with a frown. "Imagine my surprise when the commander of the Carabinieri in Tuscany informed me that you had been detained for questioning in Giorgio Montefiore's murder. Fortunately you were accompanied by the director of the Museo Nazionale Etrusco, which allowed me to secure your release without too much difficulty."

Veronica opened the wine list, one of the finest in Rome. "And you shall be richly rewarded."

"That would be unethical."

"Red or white?"

"Perhaps we should start with white," suggested the general.

"How about a lovely chardonnay from Alto Adige?"

"If you insist."

Veronica gave their order to the sommelier, who went in search of the bottle. General Ferrari admired the view of Rome for a moment before turning once more to Gabriel.

"Perhaps you should start from the beginning."

"An apprentice restorer at the Vatican Museums discovers a lost portrait by Leonardo da Vinci hidden beneath a worthless Madonna and Child. The head of the Vatican conservation lab asks the world's leading Leonardist to have a look at the painting. The world's leading Leonardist assures him that it is not a Leonardo, though he suspects the opposite is true."

"Why would he do a thing like that?" asked General Ferrari.

"The most logical explanation is that he wanted the painting for himself. Or a piece of it, at least."

"Are you suggesting he entered into a conspiracy?"

Gabriel gave a noncommittal shrug of his shoulders. "Let's call it a partnership."

"With whom?"

"An organization with the wherewithal to steal the painting from the storage rooms of the Vatican Picture Gallery."

"The Camorra?"

"So it would appear."

"But why did they kill him?"

"It's possible that he had outlived his usefulness."

"At what point?"

"The minute he told his partners that the painting was an autograph work by Leonardo da Vinci."

General Ferrari considered this for a moment. "Forgive me, but I have a hard time picturing Giorgio Montefiore hammering out a deal to steal a lost Leonardo with some Camorra chieftain in Secondigliano or Scampia."

"So do I," replied Gabriel. "There has to be more to the story."

"Such as?"

"A Vatican connection."

"Beyond the museum guard?"

Gabriel nodded.

"I was afraid you were going to say that." General Ferrari opened his attaché case and removed Gabriel's composite sketch of Father Spada, the priest who was not a priest. "How on earth did he get past the Swiss Guards?"

"Someone arranged for him to have a private audience with His Holiness."

"Surely you're joking."

"I wish I was. It was an unforgivable lapse in papal security."

"Imagine for a moment that he had come to the Vatican for a different reason. You might well be investigating the assassination of a pope."

"Not for the first time," replied Gabriel. "But back to the matter at hand."

"The Leonardo?"

Gabriel nodded.

"What do you suppose they intend to do with it?"

"Sell it to the highest bidder."

"If that happens, it will disappear forever."

"Which is why we need to recover it as quickly as possible."

Ferrari held up the sketch. "I'd like to show this to some of my informants in Naples."

"Why would you want to do a thing like that?"

"Find the thief, find the painting."

"None of your informants will betray the Camorra, Cesare. Not unless they have a death wish."

"What would you suggest?"

"We forget about the thief and patiently bide our time until the painting resurfaces."

"And then what?"

Gabriel smiled. "We steal it back."

PART TWO

———

Contrapposto

21

Dorsoduro

At some point—perhaps in 1496, though the exact date is not known—the prior from Santa Maria delle Grazie lost all patience with the Florentine artist who had been commissioned to paint a mural of the Last Supper on the wall of the convent's refectory. The project was running hopelessly behind schedule, and the Florentine, as usual, was solely to blame. Some days he would apply a single brushstroke to the work and then abruptly depart. Other days he would appear not at all. The prior, having nowhere else to turn, appealed to the ruler of Milan, Duke Ludovico Sforza, who summoned the Florentine for a meeting. What followed was a lengthy lecture, painter to patron, on the nature of creativity. "Men of lofty genius," the artist declared, "sometimes accomplish the most when they work least, for their minds are occupied with their ideas and the perfection of their conceptions, to which they afterwards give form."

There were days, too, when the Florentine mounted his scaffolding at dawn and remained there, brush in hand, forsaking food and drink, until sunset. Gabriel, after his return to Venice, adhered to a similar schedule, though unlike the Florentine, who allowed spectators to watch him at work, he remained hidden from view behind his tarpaulin shroud. It was not a brush he wielded but hand-fashioned swabs dipped in foul-smelling solvent. Chiara, during an inspection visit to the basilica, pleaded with him yet again to wear a protective mask while he worked. Smiling, he dropped a soiled wad of cotton wool onto his platform and suggested she take her complaints to the doge.

"But I shouldn't expect a favorable ruling, Dottoressa Zolli. You see, His Serenity the Doge agrees with me that masks are uncomfortable and will delay the completion of my commission."

His smartphone, a contraption even the Florentine never fathomed, was distraction enough, for it shivered each time the name Giorgio Montefiore appeared in print anywhere on the Internet, be it in a reputable publication or in the truthless precincts of social media. In death, the Leonardist was eulogized in Olympian terms. "A monumental intellect," declared the president of the Louvre. "Irreplaceable," seconded the director of the National Gallery of Art in Washington, a noted scholar of Leonardo himself. Still, there was uncomfortable speculation, some of it whispered, as to the motive behind Montefiore's execution-style murder. The authorities in Florence suggested it was robbery, though they declined to say whether anything in Montefiore's villa was missing.

The intense media coverage largely overshadowed a statement from the regional headquarters of the Carabinieri in Venice regarding the identity of the woman whose body had been found floating in the waters near the church of San Giorgio Maggiore. Hours later, police in Britain revealed that she had recently completed an apprenticeship at the conservation lab at the Vatican Museums. The Vatican Press Office expressed the profound sorrow of the Holy See and offered condolences to the family, though it made no mention of a missing walnut panel measuring 78 by 56 centimeters. Some in the press wondered whether the two art world deaths, one in Venice, the other in Florence, might be related. General Cesare Ferrari, the highly regarded commander of the Art Squad, declared unequivocally that they were not.

In truth, there were numerous connections, including the identity of the man who had discovered both bodies. He mounted his scaffolding at the Salute each morning at dawn and remained there, forsaking food and drink, shunning a protective mask, until the sun had set. Consequently he completed the first phase of the restoration—the removal of the surface grime and previous overpainting—several weeks earlier than anticipated. He photographed the altarpiece in its cleaned and damaged state and then commenced the final stage of the project, the retouching of those portions of the painting that had flaked away or faded with age. His palette was Titian's palette, as were his brushstrokes, though occasionally, when the mood struck him, he employed the left-handed technique of the procrastinatory Florentine. The one who had painted a lost portrait of a girl from Milan. She had no name, he thought. But she had the face of an angel.

Over dinner one evening at Al Covo, a quiet little restaurant in the *sestiere* of Castello, Chiara suggested that Gabriel paint an approximate copy of the missing Leonardo. He reminded her that he was rather busy at the moment.

"The Titian?" She waved her hand dismissively. "You're miles ahead of schedule."

"Apparently the director of the Courtauld Gallery would like his Florigerio back."

"It's nearly finished."

Which was true. "I'll need a panel," said Gabriel. "Preferably walnut."

"Why can't you simply paint it on canvas?"

He gave Chiara a despairing look.

"There's a lovely man called Marco on the mainland who does custom woodworking. I'm sure he can make you a walnut panel."

Gabriel leaned toward his daughter and asked confidingly, "Do you suppose they're having an affair?"

"Torrid," replied the child, and laughed hysterically.

It took the lovely Marco a week to find an appropriate plank of walnut and another week to fashion it into a panel worthy of the eminent Maestro Allon. Gabriel, for his part, required only three nocturnal sessions at his easel to produce his first version of the portrait. His wife was not impressed.

"You overdid the *sfumato*. She looks out of focus."

He buried her beneath a layer of obliterating paint and made a second version of the portrait, which was more to Chiara's liking. "Do you know how much that would be worth on the open market?" she asked.

"Two or three hundred euros. But if it were an autograph Leonardo, well, that's another story."

"What shall we do with this one?"

Gabriel carried the panel into the apartment's main sitting room and placed it atop a pile of kindling on the grate. Chiara watched sadly as the funeral pyre consumed the girl from Milan.

"Dottoressa Saviano rang today."

"What has your daughter done now?"

"Nothing, thank goodness. The *dottoressa* was merely wondering when you would like to begin your new career."

"And what did you tell her?"

"That you had to finish the Titian first."

"I finished it two days ago."

"Freak," whispered Chiara, and warmed her hands against the flames.

———————

The *dottoressa* thought Wednesdays were best—Wednesdays at half past three, in a light-filled activity room on the school's upper floor. Twelve students, equally divided by gender and ranging in age from seven to ten, had been selected for the program. Gabriel gave them each a Strathmore sketchpad and a packet of Faber-Castell pencils, and informed them that their artistic training, while enjoyable, would be rigorous in nature. Indeed, on that first Wednesday they spent the entire hour doing nothing more than learning how to draw a proper tapered line. The following week they drew circles and squares, and the week after that they turned their circles and squares into spheres and cubes, with appropriate shading to create the illusion of three-dimensionality.

The culmination of their first month of art school was a simple still life with a vase and pear. Gabriel was impressed by the quality of the work, as was Dottoressa Saviano. She asked whether he might be willing to take on an additional student or two. He confessed that he was surprised that his son, whose artistic gifts were glaringly obvious, had not been on the original list.

"He was, Signore Allon."

"And?"

"He declined to take part."

Gabriel made no effort to conceal his disappointment. "Perhaps I can convince him to change his mind."

The *dottoressa* smiled tenderly. "It can't be easy having someone like you as a father. My advice is that you remain patient."

The following week Gabriel took his students, now fourteen in number, to the Campo San Polo, where he explained perspective and the concept of a vanishing point. They put the lesson into practice a week later by sketching the exterior of the enormous Frari Church. Chiara and Irene observed the proceedings from their table at Bar Dogale, but Raphael was scratching away at something in one of his notebooks. Gabriel assumed it was a complex mathematics equation, but a surreptitious search of the boy's book bag, conducted later that evening, revealed that not to be the case.

He showed the sketch to Chiara and asked, "Why didn't you tell me?"

"Patience," was all she said.

But by then Gabriel was beginning to lose faith, not in his son but in his prediction that the Leonardo would soon resurface. The case, such as it was, had gone cold. The Carabinieri in Florence had officially categorized the murder of Giorgio Montefiore as unsolved, and their brethren in Venice were still not certain how Penelope Radcliff had ended up in the waters of the *laguna*. Both deaths had slipped from the pages of the Italian papers by the time His Holiness Luigi Donati departed for America. He dazzled at the United Nations and ruffled a few conservative feathers in Washington, but otherwise his first visit to the New World as pope was undiminished by any hint of Vatican scandal. It was, thought Gabriel, the only bright spot in the entire sordid affair.

If there was another, it was the overwhelmingly positive reaction to his restoration of the Titian. Tourists flocked to Santa Maria della Salute to see the altarpiece, as did curators, connoisseurs, and dealers from the four corners of the art world. Among those who made the pilgrimage to Venice was Julian Isherwood, owner of a respected gallery in London that specialized in Italian and Dutch Old Master paintings. He arrived the following Wednesday and was wondering whether Gabriel was free for a drink at, say, three o'clock. Gabriel informed his old friend that he had a prior commitment.

"Break it," demanded Julian.

"Can't," replied Gabriel. "But I might be free at five."

"Harry's Bar?"

"See you then, Julian."

22

Harry's Bar

He was bivouacked at a table in the back corner of the room, behind an empty glass and a depleted bowl of oily green olives. Spotting Gabriel coming through the door, he thrust an arm aloft and waved, as though he were in need of rescue. With his chalk stripe suit, lavender necktie, and plentiful gray locks, he cut a rather elegant if dubious figure, a look he described as dignified depravity. As was often the case, he looked slightly hungover.

Gabriel approached the table through the cocktail-hour din and sat down. A white-jacketed waiter appeared at once with two Bellinis and a fresh bowl of olives.

"It seems your reputation precedes you," said Julian.

"What reputation is that?"

"World's finest restorer of Italian Old Master paintings. Perhaps the greatest who ever lived."

"I take it you approve of the Titian."

"I would genuflect, my dear boy, but I wouldn't want to cause a scene."

"We're at Harry's Bar, Julian. It's always a scene."

He cast his eyes around the crowded room and smiled wistfully. "I fell in love in this bar once."

"Where *haven't* you fallen in love?"

"This was different."

"You always say that."

"But in her case, it was true."

"A Venetian girl, was she?"

Julian nodded. "The daughter of a viscount who lived in a palazzo not far from yours. She was far too young, of course, and dangerously beautiful. I begged her to marry me within an hour of meeting her. Much to my surprise, she turned me down."

"I thought you were opposed to the very idea of marriage."

"As a general principle, yes. But in her case, I was prepared to make an exception." He took a long draft of his Bellini. "It pains me to say this, but I was never the same after she broke my heart."

"You managed quite well, as I recall."

"All those beautiful women, you mean?" He emitted an overwrought sigh. "What I wouldn't give for one last fling. With any luck it will end disastrously. Those are the best kind of flings, wouldn't you agree?"

"These days, I try to keep the disasters to a minimum."

"Not me, petal. I specialize in them."

Julian was regarded as one of the most learned and influential Old Masters dealers in the world, with a gold-plated client list and a matchless talent for finding misattributed paintings known as "sleepers" and bringing them to market. And yet time and time again he had flirted with financial ruin, in large part because he preferred to possess art rather than sell it, a near-fatal affliction for someone in his line of work. His unusually close relationship with Gabriel was for many years a source of considerable speculation among the incestuous inhabitants of the London art world. Amelia March's story in *ARTnews*, while entirely accurate, had only scratched the surface.

It was Julian Isherwood, the only child of a noted German-Jewish art dealer who was murdered at the Sobibor death camp, who had helped to build and maintain Gabriel's cover identity during his long career as an intelligence operative.

At Gabriel's suggestion, Julian had recently agreed to take on a partner, an American art historian named Sarah Bancroft who had spent several years working as a clandestine operative for the Central Intelligence Agency. Beautiful, brilliant, and ruthlessly efficient, she had succeeded in putting Isherwood Fine Arts on a firm financial footing. Julian, having been relieved of nearly all responsibility, now dwelled in the nether region between retirement and emeritus status. He rarely set foot in the gallery before noon, leaving him just enough time to make a general nuisance of himself before embarking on the three-hour period of his day he reserved for his luncheon. Gabriel was pleased that his old friend had decided to parachute unannounced into Venice. Julian was one of those rare souls who made life a bit less tedious.

He plucked a fat green olive from the bowl and devoured it. "I heard a terrible rumor about you recently."

"Really? Where?"

"The bar at Wiltons. Where else?"

The celebrated Jermyn Street restaurant was an art world watering hole. Julian made a nuisance of himself there as well. "And the nature of this rumor?" asked Gabriel.

"That you were the one who discovered the body of that poor girl from the Courtauld floating in the Venetian Lagoon."

"It wasn't exactly a secret, Julian. It was in all the Italian papers."

"These days I only read the *Guardian*." Another olive disappeared. "I suppose you heard about poor Giorgio Montefiore."

"Giorgio's murder made the papers too."

"You didn't find the body, did you?"

Gabriel smiled but said nothing.

"Montefiore thought quite highly of himself," Julian continued. "Even by the lofty standards of the art world. But in my humble opinion, his reputation was entirely undeserved."

"And why was that?"

"That would require me to speak ill of the dead, something I try to avoid at my age."

"It will never leave this table."

Julian lifted his gaze toward the ceiling, as though searching his memory. "About a hundred years ago, I popped into Italy on one of my hunting expeditions. It was before the Italian government got serious about protecting the country's cultural heritage. We dealers used to buy paintings by the ton and cart them back to London. Only a small percentage were autograph works by great masters. The rest were workshop pieces or later copies. Manner of so-and-so, circle of what's-his-name—that sort of thing."

"You, however, could always tell the difference."

"I wasn't half bad," said Julian with false modesty. "But less erudite dealers often sought the advice of an Italian art historian. One who was known to be rather charitable with his opinions. If the price was right, of course."

"Montefiore?"

Julian nodded. "During the aforementioned hunting expedition, I stumbled on a lovely portrait that looked to me as though it had been painted by Perugino. I took the picture to Montefiore, who was inclined to agree, provided I hand over the requisite sum of money."

"And your reaction?"

"I was appalled and told him so. It was the last time we ever spoke."

"Well done, Julian."

"Accepting money in exchange for a favorable attribution is unconscionable. You would never do such a thing. And you have one of the best pair of eyes in the business."

"It's a bright red line," agreed Gabriel. "A definite no-no."

"The late Giorgio Montefiore didn't agree. I have it on the highest authority that he continued the practice throughout his career."

"Anything in particular?"

"In these litigious times, I shall say no more."

They finished their first round of Bellinis and a second appeared, compliments of the house.

"Come here often?" asked Julian.

"Only when you're in town."

"I wish I could stay longer. Venice is lovely this time of year."

"Where are you off to?"

"Your friend Sarah Bancroft has graciously allowed me to see a painting in Amsterdam. An old contact of mine stumbled upon something interesting in one of the flea markets. Or so he says. He's convinced he has a sleeper on his hands."

"Genre?"

"Portraiture."

"Subject?"

"A young woman."

Gabriel felt a sudden queasiness in his stomach. "I don't suppose he sent you a photograph."

"I asked for one, but he refused. Said he doesn't want one floating around in the ether yet."

"Does your old contact have a name?"

"Peter van de Velde. He's a bit of a slippery character, but over the years he's unearthed some lovely pictures from old Dutch collections."

"What time is he expecting you?"

"Ten o'clock tomorrow morning." Julian raised his Bellini to his lips. "Why do you ask?"

———

Gabriel waited until they had left Harry's Bar before delivering his answer. It was ten minutes in duration and included an admission that, yes, he was the one who had found Giorgio Montefiore's body at his villa in Florence.

"Why am I not surprised?" asked Julian.

"Imagine how I felt."

They were walking in the Piazza San Marco. The enormous square was in darkness and empty of tourists and pigeons. Julian's face was awash in the light of Gabriel's mobile phone. Displayed on the screen was the ghostly infrared image of the missing portrait.

"I fell in love with her once too. It happened the first time I ever saw that sketch in the Biblioteca Reale. It is one of the greatest ever made." Julian surrendered the phone. "But will you allow me to point out the obvious?"

"If you insist."

"We don't know whether Peter van de Velde's flea market sleeper is your perhaps Leonardo."

"We will the minute you walk into his gallery tomorrow morning."

"And if it is your Leonardo? What then?"

"One step at a time, Julian."

"I tell myself the same thing each time I descend a flight of stairs." He paused at the foot of the campanile and lifted his gaze skyward. "But why do you suppose Peter decided to show the painting to me, of all people?"

"Your reputation precedes you as well."

"Not-so-secret accomplice of the world's most famous retired spy?"

"Respected London Old Masters dealer with a track record for finding misattributed works. And if you were to declare the painting a Leonardo, others will undoubtedly concur."

"At least *some*one still appreciates me." They set off toward the Grand Canal. Julian's gait was loose-limbed and precarious. "I don't need to remind you, petal, that two people have been murdered because of this painting. Needless to say, I'd rather not be the third."

"Don't worry, you'll have me looking over your shoulder. And Sarah, of course. We can't possibly run an operation in Amsterdam without a skilled field agent like Sarah."

"Your dear friend Sarah is still in the prime of her life. I, however, have entered the autumn of my years. And I would feel better if you accompanied me to the meeting with Van de Velde tomorrow."

"I wasn't invited. And if I walk into that gallery, you can be sure the painting will magically disappear."

Julian slowed to a stop at the edge of the Riva degli Schiavoni. A flotilla of gondolas swayed on the evening tide. "Where exactly did you find her?"

Gabriel pointed to the moonlit waters between the Punta della Dogana and the church of San Giorgio Maggiore.

"The poor girl," said Julian quietly. "The poor, poor girl."

"She was murdered because she tried to warn the art world about the Leonardo. The least we can do is finish what she started."

"One last fling in Amsterdam?"

"Why not?"

"It might end disastrously, you know."

Gabriel smiled sadly. "The good ones always do."

23

Galerie Van de Velde

Gabriel had saved few reminders of his decades-long career in the secret world, only a pair of false German passports, a Beretta pistol, and a copy of the world's most formidable cell phone hacking malware. The passports and the gun were locked in the safe in his dressing room. The malware, which was known as Proteus, was hidden beneath a deceptive icon on his laptop computer. Its most insidious feature was that it required no blunder on the part of the target, no unwise software update or click of an innocent-looking photograph or advertisement. All Gabriel had to do was enter the target's phone number into the application, and within minutes the device would be under his complete control. He could read the target's emails and text messages, review the target's browsing history and telephone metadata, and monitor the target's physical movements with the GPS location services. Perhaps most important, he could activate the phone's microphone and camera and thus turn the device into a full-time instrument of surveillance.

He unleashed Proteus on Peter van de Velde's mobile phone when he returned to the apartment, and at nine o'clock that evening, after a pleasant dinner with Chiara and the children, he settled onto the loggia with his laptop to review the art dealer's digital debris.

He began with the emails. There were more than thirty thousand, divided equally between incoming and outgoing. Most were in English, the semiofficial language of the international art trade, and the rest were in Dutch, German, or French. Gabriel spotted the names of a few noteworthy dealers and collectors but found no correspondence with one Giorgio Montefiore or any reference to a lost portrait by Leonardo da Vinci.

The same was true of the text messages, which included a lengthy thread with Julian. Their last exchange had occurred at 3:42 p.m. that afternoon. It seemed that Van de Velde had taken the liberty of hiring a car to collect Julian at Amsterdam's Schiphol Airport, no minor expense for a small independent dealer. Julian had once again requested a photograph of the painting. Van de Velde, in declining the request, had promised that it would be well worth the wait.

The only direct air link between Venice and Amsterdam was a KLM flight that departed Marco Polo at the dreadful hour of seven. Gabriel and Julian traveled to the airport in separate water taxis and boarded the plane as though they were strangers. Their seats were on opposite sides of the first-class cabin. Gabriel spent the nearly two-hour flight working his way through the remaining data on Peter van de Velde's phone. Julian sipped champagne and flirted with his neighbor, an attractive Dutch woman of perhaps forty who seemed to find him utterly charming.

Upon arrival in Amsterdam, Gabriel's travel document received additional scrutiny at passport control, delaying his admission to the Netherlands by several minutes. He hastened to ground transportation in time to see a dark-suited man helping Julian into the back of a luxurious Mercedes sedan. Gabriel had a car waiting as well, though it was an economical Renault hatchback. The woman behind the wheel had shoulder-length blond hair, skin the color of alabaster, and eyes like a cloudless summer sky. They regarded Gabriel coolly as he dropped into the passenger seat.

"Long time no see," she said, smothering a yawn. "Now, please tell me why we're back in Amsterdam."

––––––––––––

It was Gabriel, not the Central Intelligence Agency, who had schooled Sarah Bancroft in the basics of tradecraft. He had taught her how to lie, how to steal, how to fight, and how to use a gun—a skill she put to good use one cold winter's afternoon in Zurich when she fired two bullets into a Moscow Center assassin. She had received no training, however, in vehicular surveillance, an oversight Gabriel always regretted, never more so than at that moment.

"You're too damn close. We might as well be sitting in the back seat next to Julian."

"I don't want to lose him."

"We know where he's going. Therefore, we cannot possibly lose him."

Sarah reduced her speed and allowed a gap to open between the Renault and the black Mercedes. They were hurtling northward along the A10, Amsterdam's circular motorway. Their destination, Galerie Van de Velde, was located in the historic Canal District. The gallery's owner and namesake was sipping coffee at the café next door, scrolling through the morning headlines on his compromised phone. Gabriel was monitoring the feed from the device on his laptop computer, which was connected to the Internet via a mobile hot spot.

"I assume you had a look at the photos stored on his phone," said Sarah.

"Only the ones he's taken since the painting was stolen from the Vatican."

"And?"

"There were no photos of the Leonardo."

"And nothing in his texts or emails either?"

"No."

Sarah followed the Mercedes off the motorway. "And what, pray tell, do you deduce from this?"

"That Van de Velde and his associates are careful."

"The other possibility is that Van de Velde intends to show Julian a worthless Dutch or Flemish portrait that he found in an Amsterdam flea market. Which would mean that you've dragged me here for no good reason."

"You had big plans today?"

"I was thinking about taking my luncheon at the Wolseley. And then, of course, there's my usual après-work Belvedere martini at Wiltons. Three olives, Saharan dry, painfully cold."

Sarah had a voice and manner from a different age. As always, Gabriel felt as though he were conversing with a character from a Fitzgerald novel. "I'm sure we can find you a decent martini in Amsterdam," he said.

"I wish we could say the same for your perhaps Leonardo. But the chances that the painting is in the hands of Peter van de Velde are slim to none."

"I happen to think the odds are a bit more favorable."

"And if it is your Leonardo?"

"I shall make entry into the gallery and reclaim it. And then I will ask Van de Velde to provide me with the names of his associates."

"What happens if Van de Velde decides to ring the authorities?"

"You don't know much about criminals, do you?"

"Thanks to you, I know a great deal about criminals. And Peter van de Velde never struck me as one."

"You don't seem to know much about art dealers either."

"We're not all corrupt, you know. Some of us actually have standards."

"You'll get over that, I'm sure." They were headed east along the Overtoom, one of Amsterdam's busiest boulevards. The black Mercedes sedan was nowhere in sight. "It appears as though you've managed to lose him."

"I'll pretend I didn't hear that."

They crossed the Singelgracht and entered the Canal District. Bicycles lined the bridges and leaned against the brickwork of the gabled houses. Galerie Van de Velde occupied two floors of a commercial building on the Prinsengracht. They arrived there in time to see Julian teetering through the front door.

"The eagle has landed," said Gabriel.

"In all his glory," added Sarah.

She rolled slowly past the gallery and guided the Renault into a parking space along the embankment of the canal. Gabriel increased the volume on the feed from Van de Velde's compromised mobile phone. "Julie!" the art dealer exclaimed. "Tell me all about Venice. Is the Titian as glorious as they say?"

"Is it?" inquired Sarah.

"Julian seems to think I'm the greatest restorer who ever lived."

"I might have something for you, if you can spare the time."

"I have a feeling I'll soon be working on a lost portrait of a young woman."

Sarah smothered another yawn. "Slim to none, darling."

———

The paintings hanging in the gallery's quaint exhibition rooms were mainly nineteenth-century Dutch landscapes, still lifes, and floral arrangements, the kind of pictures that high-end London dealers like

Julian referred to derisively as "chocolate box." Peter van de Velde was a touch chocolate box himself. The formfitting suit, the too-long leather loafers, the gelled and coiffed head of gray-blond hair, the pricey Swiss timepiece—everything was just so.

Seated in Van de Velde's comfortable office, they engaged in the polite conversational foreplay that precedes any art world transaction. The current slump in the market, the bleak outlook for the global economy, the dreadful state of Europe's politics. Van de Velde was looking forward to the upcoming Fine Art Fair in Maastricht. Julian, who had grown weary of the annual gathering, indicated that his partner would be attending on his behalf.

"American, is she?"

"Not so you'd know it." Frowning, Julian shot a glance at his wristwatch. "Do you think we might have a look at your painting now, Peter. I'd love to be on the two o'clock flight back to London."

Van de Velde slid a single-page document across the desk and laid a pen atop it.

"A nondisclosure agreement?" Julian shook his head. "I've never signed one and never will."

"This situation is different."

Julian thrust on his reading glasses and reviewed the document with exaggerated care. Then, after a final expression of righteous indignation, all of it counterfeit, he added his illegible signature where indicated. Van de Velde slipped the document into a desk drawer. Julian pocketed the pen.

"The painting," he said with genuine impatience.

"As I told you, it was discovered here in Amsterdam."

Julian took note of Van de Velde's use of the passive voice. "You led me to believe that *you* were the one who found it, Peter."

"The truth is, the painting was brought to me by another individual.

It was in terrible condition, but I agreed there was something special about it. You know the feeling, Julian. The funny feeling at the back of your neck."

He knew it all too well. "How much did you pay for it?"

"Five thousand euros. The money was given to me by one of my investors, a connoisseur and collector with an extraordinary eye. He, too, is convinced the painting is a sleeper."

"He's your partner, this connoisseur and collector?"

"More or less."

"In that case, what do you want from me?"

"Your opinion."

"I'm a dealer, Peter. I only authenticate paintings that I'm interested in acquiring for myself or a client."

"My partner and I would be more than happy to sell it to you. But I'm afraid it's going to cost you."

"What did you have in mind?"

"If I'm right about this painting, it will sell for several hundred million."

"What did you find, Peter? A lost Vermeer?"

"Something better than a Vermeer."

"There's only one other Old Master painter who could fetch that kind of money."

Van de Velde smiled. "Shall we have a look now?"

"I thought you would never ask."

Van de Velde stood and reached for his overcoat. "Right this way."

The best laid plans of mice and men," said Sarah.

"And crooked Dutch art dealers," replied Gabriel.

"So it would appear." Sarah started the engine of the Renault. "Can you ever forgive me for doubting you?"

"That depends on your performance behind the wheel during the next few minutes." Gabriel watched the Mercedes sedan roll past his window. In the back seat were Julian and Peter van de Velde. "This is the part where you follow them."

Sarah waited a few seconds before easing away from the curb. The Mercedes made a quick left turn and headed out of the Canal District. A moment later it was speeding in the opposite direction along the Overtoom.

Sarah settled in fifty meters behind it. "Where do you suppose they're going?"

"I'm sure Julian is wondering the same thing."

"Perhaps I should ring him. Just checking in, that sort of thing."

"Perhaps you should concentrate on your driving. Otherwise you're going to lose them at the next light."

Sarah put her foot to the floor and followed the Mercedes across the busy intersection. It continued west on the Overtoom, then headed south on the A10 toward Schiphol Airport.

"You don't think . . ."

"It's beginning to look that way," replied Gabriel.

"But why the airport?"

"What better way to view a stolen Leonardo?"

Schiphol's general aviation terminal was located in a remote corner of the airfield. From a car park along the edge of the tarmac, Gabriel watched helplessly as Julian followed Peter van de Velde up the forward airstair of a Dassault Falcon 900LX. The feed from the Dutch art dealer's phone died a few seconds after the cabin door closed.

Sarah snapped a photograph of the Dassault as it rolled slowly across the tarmac toward the runway. "Who do you suppose is on that plane?"

"A member of the Camorra," replied Gabriel. "Or at least a reasonable facsimile."

"Is Julian in any danger?"

"A little."

"Let's hope they don't kill him," said Sarah. "We'll never hear the end of it."

24

Wiltons

Julian Isherwood had examined paintings in cellars and salesrooms, in bank vaults and bonded warehouses, and on one occasion while engaged in the act of love with the widow of a wealthy collector. But never once during his storied career had he assessed a work of art while airborne. He supposed there was a first time for everything, even at his advanced age.

There were five other passengers aboard the Dassault—four security goons and a well-dressed man in his late fifties with a sharp-featured face, olive-complected skin, and thinning hair combed closely to his scalp. Julian extended his hand in greeting, but the man demanded his mobile phone instead. He did so in Italian-accented English. Julian surrendered the device under protest, then watched it disappear into a black nylon pouch. A pretty cabin attendant presented him with a glass of prosecco. From Peter van de Velde he received a muted apology.

"Sorry, Julian. My partner is a careful man."

"Does he have a name, your partner?"

"Not one he wishes to divulge at this time."

Van de Velde waited until the plane had leveled off somewhere over the Netherlands before finally fetching a shallow art transport case from the cabin's aft compartment. Inside, covered by two sheets of protective glassine paper, was a portrait of a beautiful fair-haired woman gazing directly at the viewer over her left shoulder—78 by 56 centimeters, or thereabouts. Van de Velde, after first pulling on a pair of protective white gloves, removed the panel from the case and laid it carefully on the cabin's table.

"Do you recognize her, Julian?"

"Yes, of course."

Van de Velde offered him a pair of gloves. "Have a closer look. I think you'll see something special."

Julian pulled on the gloves and, grasping the painting with both hands, turned it over and had a look at the back. The original walnut panel had been adhered to an oak panel, perhaps nineteenth century, with three scratched and dented horizontal supports—one along the top edge of the painting, one across the center, and one at the bottom. There were no stamps or markings of any kind, nothing that might identify a previous owner. Julian, inhaling deeply, thought he detected the faintest aroma of fresh rabbit skin glue.

He laid the panel on the table and examined the image in the sunlight streaming through the Dassault's windows. Typically he used a handheld ultraviolet torch to expose the overpainting of previous restorations, but in this case it wasn't necessary; a large portion of the panel's surface was covered in recently applied inpainting. The woman's heavy-lidded left eye, however, had received no retouching. When Julian viewed the iris and pupil through a magnifying glass, he feared for an instant that his heart had ceased to beat.

"What do you think?" asked Van de Velde.

Julian didn't dare answer truthfully, for his anger was at that moment incandescent. Instead he lowered the magnifying glass and waited for the painting to speak to him. It was quite talkative indeed.

"It's a lovely picture of obvious quality, Peter. But one wonders how it ended up in an Amsterdam flea market."

"You should have seen it before it was restored. There were several layers of old overpaint and a gloppy coat of brown varnish. At first I thought it was Dutch or Flemish. But I no longer believe that's the case."

"Nor do I," said Julian.

"Is it Italian?"

"Almost certainly."

"Florentine School?"

"Could be, Peter. But where are we going with this?"

"My partner and I were wondering . . ." He left the thought unfinished.

"Whether I thought it was a Leonardo?"

Van de Velde nodded.

"Come now, Peter. You don't really expect me to answer that question after spending less than five minutes with the picture."

"But you were clearly impressed by it. I saw it in your eyes."

"I agree that the brushwork resembles Leonardo's, but that does not mean it is his. Furthermore, there is nothing in the historical record to suggest he ever used the silverpoint preparatory sketch of the young woman to produce an oil painting."

"There's nothing about the *Salvator Mundi* either."

Julian, with his silence, conceded the point. He had yet to look up from the painting. She had been horribly mistreated, the beautiful young woman with mismatched pupils. Julian, at that instant, resolved to rescue her. But how? Personal heroics were not his calling card, especially at thirty thousand feet. The occasional act of professional duplicity in service of a noble cause was more his style.

"There's a simple solution, you know."

"What's that?" asked Van de Velde.

"Let me take the picture back to London. I'll show it to the curators at the National Gallery and subject it to rigorous scientific analysis. I'll also hire someone to research the painting's provenance."

"Who's going to pay for all this?"

"Isherwood Fine Arts."

"And what would Isherwood Fine Arts expect in return?"

"If my work results in the discovery of a lost painting by Leonardo, it will be well worth the money."

Van de Velde turned to his nameless partner, who shook his head slowly. "Sorry, Mr. Isherwood, but the painting stays with us."

"In that case, you leave me no choice but to buy it."

The man smiled. "The bidding starts at two hundred and fifty million."

"If it's a Leonardo, it's a steal at that price." Julian checked the time. "Mind taking me back to Schiphol now? With a bit of luck, I can still make my flight to London."

———————

The Dassault Falcon deposited Julian not at Amsterdam's Schiphol Airport but at Le Bourget in Paris. His hosts had been good enough to arrange another chauffeured car. He rang Sarah during the drive to the Gare du Nord. She seemed genuinely relieved to hear the sound of his voice.

"I was beginning to think you'd fallen off a cliff."

"There are no cliffs in Holland, petal. That said, my day took a most unexpected turn."

"I'm afraid to ask where you are."

"The Eighteenth Arrondissement of Paris."

"Could be worse."

"Much," he agreed.

"Did you see it?"

"I did indeed."

"And?"

"We should talk when I get back to London."

"You know where to find me," she said, and rang off.

He arrived at the Gare du Nord in time to catch the two thirty Eurostar and strode through the door of Wiltons a few minutes before five o'clock. As misfortune would have it, he collided with tubby Oliver Dimbleby, a thoroughly disreputable Old Masters dealer from Bury Street.

"Julie!" he purred. "Haven't seen you in days. Where in God's name have you been?"

"A sanatorium, if you must know."

"Nothing serious, I hope."

"Emotional exhaustion."

"I hear it's fatal."

"They've given me three weeks to live."

The usual crowd was arrayed along the bar. Tweedy Jeremy Crabbe from Bonhams, suntanned Simon Mendenhall from Christie's, the learned Niles Dunham of the National Gallery. Roddy Hutchinson, universally regarded as the most unscrupulous dealer in all of St. James's, was baring his soul to the impossibly beautiful former fashion model who now owned a successful contemporary art gallery in King Street. Nicky Lovegrove, art adviser to the vastly rich, was whispering sweet nothings into the ear of Amelia March, who was scribbling furiously in her reporter's notebook.

Julian peered over her shoulder. "What are you working on?"

"Your obituary."

"Please treat me kindly."

"Don't I always?"

Sarah and Gabriel were seated at the bar's corner table. Sarah was drinking her usual three-olive Belvedere martini, Gabriel a glass of white wine. Julian lifted the bottle from the ice bucket and scrutinized the label.

"Domaine Laroche Grand Cru Chablis."

"Sarah's treat," said Gabriel. "A little something to celebrate the successful completion of your mission."

Julian pulled up a chair and settled wearily into it. "My mission, as you call it, was far more harrowing than previously advertised. Especially the unscheduled private flight from Amsterdam to Paris. Don't get me wrong, the plane was lovely. But I didn't much care for the other passengers."

"How many were there?"

"Five," replied Julian while pouring himself a glass of the Chablis. "Including Peter van de Velde's so-called partner. Looked like a perfectly presentable businessman, but I doubt that was the case."

"Italian, was he?"

"Definitely."

"And the others?"

"They were the businessman's bodyguards. Or perhaps the painting's."

"Is it a Leonardo?"

"Many careers have been ruined by mistaken attributions to Leonardo . . ."

"But?"

"I believe it's him."

"What sort of condition is it in?"

"Dreadful. I have a right mind to go back to Amsterdam and wring Peter van de Velde's neck."

"In all likelihood, Van de Velde had very little to do with it. He's merely fronting the deal for the men who stole it from the Vatican."

"But he knows the other players, though."

"Some of them," Gabriel admitted. "But he doesn't have posses-sion of the painting. And if we confront him, we will lose our greatest advantage."

"Which is?"

"The men who stole the Leonardo are under the impression that they've gotten away with the greatest art heist in history. And their overconfidence has led them to make two critical mistakes."

"The first?"

"Inviting you to Amsterdam."

"And the second?"

It was Sarah, martini glass to her lips, who answered. "Putting you on that airplane."

———

It was a mistake, Sarah continued, because international convention requires all civilian aircraft to have a unique alphanumeric identifica-tion code prominently displayed on their exterior. These codes allow air traffic controllers and airport authorities to track and record the movement of individual planes around the globe. But private citizens likewise have access to the data, as the CIA discovered when investi-gative reporters revealed that the Agency was using a fleet of private jets to secretly transfer captured members of al-Qaeda to so-called black sites for enhanced interrogation. The multibillionaire chairman of a French luxury goods conglomerate had recently unloaded his Bombardier 7500 because he had grown weary of climate activists posting his carbon emissions on social media.

"I should have such problems," muttered Julian. "But who owns the plane that I was on this morning?"

"Eiger Air Transport," replied Sarah.

"A shell company, I assume."

"But of course. It's Swiss registered, as is the plane itself. In fact, it headed to Switzerland after dropping you at Le Bourget."

"Somewhere nice?"

"Lugano," answered Gabriel. "Your perfectly presentable Italian businessman and his bodyguards then made their way by car to a bank in the Piazza della Riforma, Lugano's main square."

"How do you know that?"

"Because they foolishly took Peter van de Velde with him, and I was monitoring his phone."

"And the name of this bank?"

"SBL PrivatBank SA."

"Is the Leonardo now hidden in that bank?"

"It might be," replied Gabriel. "But I have a feeling it's been on the move of late."

"Why?"

"The plane's flight records," interjected Sarah. "It was in Dubai for three days last week. And the week before, it made stops in Tokyo and Hong Kong."

"It sounds to me as if they're showing the painting to prospective buyers. There are any number of extremely wealthy people in the world who would think nothing about plunking down a few hundred million for an authentic Leonardo, regardless of where it came from."

"Don't worry," said Gabriel. "We won't let that happen."

"What are we going to do? Break into that bank in Lugano?"

"We're going to wait for them to make another mistake."

"And then?"

Gabriel looked at the cast of art world characters lining the bar. "We'll make our move."

25

Lac Léman

At the time of its founding in 1873, it was known as Società Bancaria Lugano. It shortened its name a century later after acquiring several competitors and embarking on a rapid international expansion, one that left its balance sheet laden with debt. A series of scandals followed, including a costly scrape with the US Department of Justice for helping thousands of American citizens conceal their wealth from the Internal Revenue Service. Years of management chaos and heavy losses finally caught up with SBL, pushing the bank to the brink of insolvency. It was saved from collapse, though, by an eleventh-hour infusion of capital, the source of which remained a mystery.

This much about SBL's history Gabriel was able to glean from nothing more painstaking than a simple search of the Internet. But having tangled with Swiss banks in the past, he was confident there was more to the story. Fortunately he had a trusted source at the pinnacle of the Swiss financial services industry, an ethically challenged billionaire venture capitalist named Martin Landesmann. Some years earlier they had worked together on an operation to smuggle dozens of explosive-filled centrifuges into Iran's secret nuclear facilities. Martin's participation in the affair, while pivotal, had not been voluntary.

Though he was a Züricher by birth, Martin dwelled in a palatial villa on the leafy northern shore of Lake Geneva. Gabriel arrived there in a taxi and was admitted by Martin's beautiful French-born wife, Monique. Her greeting was formal but decidedly cool. Given the complexity of their history, it was the best Gabriel could have hoped for.

Her husband was outside on the villa's terrace, a phone to his ear. He was dressed, as was his custom, like the lower half of a gray scale: slate-gray cashmere pullover, charcoal-gray trousers, black loafers. The attire paired nicely with his glossy silver hair and trendy silver spectacles. Spotting Gabriel, he raised a marble-white hand toward a circular table upon which a porcelain coffee service had been placed. Gabriel sat down and admired the view of the Mont Blanc massif, which had received a dusting of snow overnight. A passing motorboat opened a wound in the flat waters of the blue lake.

Several more minutes elapsed before Martin was finally able to extract himself from the phone call. "You must forgive me," he said as he sat down. "But I'm afraid we have a rather serious crisis on our hands at One World."

One World was Martin's charitable foundation. It funneled billions in aid to developing nations, promoted democracy, protected the rights of journalists and political activists, and warned of the dangers posed by a warming climate. Mainly it provided Martin with a shimmering patina of corporate conscientiousness that blinded the press and Swiss regulators to the true nature of his business. Still, one had to hand it to Martin. He was one of the most fascinating criminals that Gabriel had ever met.

"And the nature of this crisis?"

"It involves our efforts to care for those displaced by the fighting in Sudan. Needless to say, it's a dangerous place to operate."

"Almost as dangerous as Geneva," remarked Gabriel.

"Have you been causing trouble in our fair city again?"

"A minor incident at the Freeport not long ago."

Martin poured coffee. "Not *l'affaire Edmond Ricard*?"

"*Oui*."

"And what about the so-called Picasso Papers scandal? Were you involved in that as well?"

"It's possible."

"Those documents caused quite a sensation. A number of my less scrupulous colleagues lost a great deal of sleep."

"But not you?"

"Global Vision Investments is entirely legitimate now. Which is to say I'm only mildly corrupt. Indeed, by Swiss standards, I am a paragon of virtue."

"You don't expect me to believe that, do you?"

He smiled over the rim of his coffee cup. "Believe what you will, Gabriel."

"I think I liked the old Martin better. The one who tried his very best to have me killed."

"I thought we'd put that behind us."

"It rankles from time to time."

"Did we not steal several billion dollars from the Russian president together?"

"It was great fun, wasn't it?"

"And do I not allow you to use my airplanes and my apartment in Paris whenever you need them?"

"You've been very generous."

"And what about all that cash and jewelry I lent you? Monique is still miffed about that one."

"She's not terribly fond of me either."

Martin laughed. The ice was well and truly broken. "What brings you back to Geneva this time?" he asked. "Business or pleasure?"

"Business, I'm afraid."

Martin sighed. "How much do you need now?"

"I don't need your money. Only some information."

"How refreshing. And the topic?"

"SBL PrivatBank of Lugano."

Martin's expression turned serious. "I know it well."

"And?"

"Definitely not a paragon of virtue. Quite the other thing, in fact."

––––––––––

Among the far-flung constellation of enterprises controlled by Martin Landesmann was a small but wildly profitable financial services company located in the principality of Liechtenstein. This unethical house of finance, which was known as Meisner PrivatBank, had once served as the portal of a sophisticated laundromat that turned dirty money into clean cash and then buried it in the legitimate economy. His clientele was a rogues' gallery of tax evaders, kleptocrats, and criminals of every stripe—including a sprawling organization based in the southern Italian region of Campania that derived most of its income through the sale and distribution of narcotics, especially South American cocaine.

"The Camorra," said Gabriel.

"They generally refer to themselves as the *Sistema*. Still, a rose by any other name . . ."

"Stinks to high heaven, Martin."

He made no reply.

"How much do you suppose you made looking after their money?"

"If the truth be told, I made much more from the Colombians. But they were ill-mannered hotheads. The Camorra were all business."

"You didn't answer my question."

"I made a great deal," said Martin. "And so has every other banker or financier in this country who handles hot Italian money. Do you know how much the three main Italian criminal organizations earn each year?"

"More than Deutsche Bank and McDonald's combined."

"Correct. That amount of money can't be hidden beneath a mattress. It has to go somewhere. And the truth is, it's *every*where."

"What's the current state of your relationship?"

"With the Camorra? Nonexistent."

"Who ended it?"

"They did."

"Were they unhappy with you?"

"If that were the case, I would be dead. They simply decided to take their business elsewhere."

"SBL PrivatBank of Lugano?"

Martin nodded. "But they're not ordinary clients. The Camorra was the source of the investment capital that saved SBL from collapse. The current chairman is nothing but a figurehead. The bank's board of directors reside in Naples."

"Surely they must have someone on the senior management team."

"His name is Franco Tedeschi. He's the head of SBL's asset management division. But the assets he manages belong to the Camorra."

Gabriel awakened his phone and found a photograph of Tedeschi on the bank's website. Late fifties, angular features, thinning hair— the man Julian had seen on the Dassault Falcon.

"That's Franco, all right," said Martin. "The CFO of Camorra Incorporated. But why the sudden interest in a dirty bank from Lugano?"

"The dirty bank has something of great value that belongs to a friend of mine."

"Who's the friend?"

"The supreme pontiff of the Roman Catholic Church."

"Is there anyone you *don't* know?"

"I don't know anyone from the Camorra."

"Consider yourself lucky," said Martin. "And the object of great value?"

"A lost portrait by Leonardo da Vinci."

Martin, an astute collector himself, raised an eyebrow. "You have my full attention. Please continue."

Gabriel delivered an abbreviated but accurate account of the case thus far. Martin sat spellbound throughout, a forefinger pressed thoughtfully to his lips.

"Those two murders reek of the Camorra," he said. "They're very good at what they do, and that includes killing those who threaten their business interests. Which is why I would advise you to end your investigation as quickly as possible and forget about that painting. Otherwise the next dead body that turns up in the Venetian Lagoon is likely to be yours."

"I can look after myself, Martin."

He placed a hand on Gabriel's arm. "Listen carefully, my friend. The Camorra can kill anyone, anywhere, at any time. And that includes the likes of you."

"I find your sudden concern about my safety touching. But I have no intention of leaving that painting in the hands of your former clients from Naples."

"I thought that would be your answer. Therefore, you leave me no choice but to help you recover it."

"What sort of assistance are you offering?"

"Financial advice, of course. The first thing I'll need is access to SBL's balance sheet, along with all its underlying assets, liabilities, loans, and the accounts of its major clients."

"Why?"

"Art is money, Gabriel. Never forget that."

26

Kandestederne

At the tip of Denmark's Jutland peninsula lies a slender, sandy spit of land formed by the ceaseless clash between the North Sea and its smaller rival, the Baltic. Ingrid Johansen lived a few kilometers to the south in the bleak, windswept dunes of Kandestederne. Though it was one of Scandinavia's most popular summer resorts, she much preferred the winter months, when she had the place largely to herself. Yes, the weather was dreadful and the days were short, but her cottage was fully winterized and filled with distractions, including an enormous collection of books, a high-end Norwegian-made audio system, and her computers. She did not mind the solitude; indeed, she actively sought it. The director-general of the Danish security and intelligence service was one of the handful of people in the world who knew how to reach her. The ground rules of their relationship required Ingrid to notify the director each time she returned to the country. She had done so a fortnight earlier, having spent most of the autumn lying low at her villa on Mykonos.

She had purchased her Greek hideaway with the proceeds of a summerlong crime spree in Saint-Tropez. A number of large scores in Switzerland, including a cash-stuffed briefcase she snatched one afternoon in the elegant lobby bar of the Hôtel Métropole in Geneva,

had financed the wholesale renovation of her cottage in Kandestederne. The director of Danish intelligence was well aware of Ingrid's
criminal past, as were his colleagues in the Ministry of Justice. They
had nevertheless granted her official absolution when, at the behest of
a legendary spy named Gabriel Allon, she agreed to slip into Russia
and steal a secret Kremlin plan to wage nuclear war in Ukraine. The
operation had ended violently at the Finnish border. Ingrid had only
a vague memory of how she had managed to survive. Eleven officers
of the Russian Border Force had not been so fortunate.

Under her arrangement with the Danish government, she had
been allowed to keep her sizable personal fortune, much of which
was hidden at Banca Privada d'Andorra, and all of her property and
assets. She was also permitted to carry a firearm, though the Danish
National Police insisted she surrender the Glock 26 subcompact she
had purchased from the Black Cobras street gang in Malmö. Her
new weapon was a Heckler & Koch USP9. It was not as concealable
as her old Glock, but it was highly accurate and packed enough of
a punch to stop even the most determined Moscow Center assassin.

At present the weapon was tucked into the rear pocket of her
fleece-lined winter cycling jacket. She was headed westward across
the peninsula on the Skagensvej, sailing along at just under forty
kilometers an hour. According to her onboard computer, her cadence
was a brisk ninety-seven pedal strokes per minute. Her heart rate was
only slightly higher.

She stopped for coffee at a café near the ferry terminal in Hirts-
hals, then started toward the Baltic port town of Frederikshavn. By
the time she arrived, the clouds had moved in, and a light rain was
beginning to fall. She headed north to Hulsig, then turned directly
into a fierce headwind for the five-kilometer stretch run back to
Kandestederne.

Her cottage stood at the northernmost edge of the settlement, at the end of a narrow lane. She arrived there to find a petrol-powered Audi sedan parked next to her all-electric Volvo EX90. The ground rules of her relationship with the director of Danish intelligence required her to report any and all suspicious activity around her place of residence. Instead she flung open the front door and hurried inside.

Nothing?" asked Gabriel.

"Zilch."

"Surely you've picked a pocket or two."

"Only one, Mr. Allon."

He patted the front of his cashmere sport jacket and realized that his billfold was missing. Ingrid must have stolen it during their brief embrace. "You certainly haven't lost your touch."

"But I've definitely lost the craving to steal." She returned the plundered booty with a frown. "That crazy Corsican witch doctor is to blame. She's ruined me."

The Corsican woman in question would have been appalled to hear herself described in so disparaging a manner. She was not a witch doctor, she was a *signadora*, a healer of those afflicted with the *occhju*, the evil eye. She also possessed the power to see the past and foretell the future, as Ingrid had discovered during a visit to the old woman's parlor.

She pulled the cork from a bottle of Sancerre and poured two glasses. Rain was hurling itself against the soaring windows of her sitting room, blurring the remarkable view of the North Sea. The furnishings were modern and Scandinavian, as was the artwork adorning her walls. One of the canvases, a winter seascape with two distant figures walking along the water's edge, looked curiously out of place. Gabriel had made the painting on the beach below Ingrid's terrace and given it to her as a peace offering. Seeing it hanging on her wall, he regretted not having burned it.

"And what about your other pastime?" he asked, accepting a glass of the wine.

"My charitable endeavors, you mean?"

"No," he answered. "Click, click, click."

It was how Ingrid referred to her uncanny ability to penetrate even the most sophisticated computer network as though she were walking through an open door.

"My last hack was that bank in the British Virgin Islands."

"If memory serves, you didn't break much of a sweat."

She smiled. "Candy from a baby."

"Do you think you can hack SBL PrivatBank of Lugano?"

She rolled her pale blue eyes. Her hair was the color of toffee and streaked with blond. Parted in the middle, it framed a face of straight, even features. There was nothing out of place, not a line or mark.

"I'm insulted that you would even bother to ask. But why SBL?"

Gabriel explained.

"Never a dull moment," observed Ingrid. "You really need to find a new hobby, Mr. Allon."

"Be that as it may, can it be done?"

"If a computer network can be accessed via the Internet, it can be penetrated and manipulated. There is, however, a downside when it comes to SBL."

"You're referring to the fact that it's controlled by the Camorra?"

She nodded. "Rule number one in the criminal world, Mr. Allon. Never steal from the Italians. And don't even *think* about stealing from the Camorra."

"We stole from the Russians."

"And they weren't terribly happy about it, were they? Still, it would be a shame to leave the painting in the hands of the Mafia, especially if it's a Leonardo."

"It *is* a Leonardo."

"With all due respect, the odds are it isn't."

"When did you become a connoisseur of the Italian High Renaissance?"

"I did steal a Vermeer once."

"Vermeer was Dutch," said Gabriel. "And the painting you stole is still missing."

"What better way to atone for my sins than to help you recover what might be the last Leonardo?" She watched the rain beating against her windows. "I only wish that Corsican witch hadn't cast a spell on me."

"Nothing?" asked Gabriel.

"No," she said with a sigh. "The thrill is gone."

———————

That evening they drove to Skagen and had dinner at the Brøndums Hotel. In the nineteenth century it had been a gathering spot for a circle of Scandinavian artists who came to the fishing village each summer, drawn by the unusual quality of the light. Having little in the way of money, they oftentimes handed over finished canvases to the proprietor in lieu of payment. Ingrid, at the conclusion of a delicious meal, suggested that Gabriel settle their bill in the same manner.

"With what?"

"You'll paint something tomorrow."

"I was hoping to spend the day reviewing the balance sheet of a dubious Lugano-based financial services company."

"I'm fast, Mr. Allon, but not that fast."

"How long will it take?"

"You should count on an extended stay here in northernmost Denmark." She placed a stack of banknotes atop the bill. "A month or two, at least."

On the second floor of the cottage in Kandestederne was a spacious guest suite with a private bath and a fine view of the sea. Regrettably it was located adjacent to the computer-crammed lair where Ingrid locked herself away a few minutes after their return from Skagen. Gabriel, having endured two previous hacks, braced himself for a long night of keyboard clatter and experimental Nordic jazz, and was richly rewarded with both. He finally headed downstairs at five fifteen and brewed a pot of coffee. Another four hours went by before the sky turned from black to iron gray. Ingrid appeared shortly thereafter, in leggings and a workout tank. Her bare arms were toned and inkless. Her eyes were shot with red.

"Sleep well?" she asked.

"Never better."

"What are your plans for the day?"

Gabriel gazed out the window at the raw, damp morning unfurling itself over the sand dunes. "A bit of sunbathing and a swim in the North Sea."

"A fine idea, Mr. Allon. We'll make a Dane out of you yet."

And with that, she headed upstairs and vanished once more behind the closed door of her lair. Gabriel drove to Frederikshavn and purchased two changes of warm clothing, a pair of waterproof hiking boots, and a consignment of painting supplies, including four pre-stretched canvases and a French plein air easel. He erected the easel on the beach during a sudden burst of fair weather and, brush and palette in hand, raced to capture the extraordinary interplay between light and sea. The finished canvas was leaning against the wall in the sitting room when Ingrid, in the same clothing, her hair in disarray, wandered downstairs a few minutes after 7:00 p.m.

"Sign it," she insisted.

Gabriel shook his head.

"You're like Leonardo. He never signed his work either."

"And he never would have made a painting as dreadful as that one."

"He did produce the first landscape in the history of Western art, though. It was a sketch of the countryside near Florence."

"Is that so?" asked Gabriel archly.

"I did a bit of research last night."

"You were supposed to be hacking SBL PrivatBank of Lugano."

"I did that too."

"Am I allowed to ask how it's going?"

"I've breached the outer perimeter. Now I'm just waiting for someone to grant me access to the inner ring."

"Any candidates?"

"Don't worry, Mr. Allon. It won't be much longer."

She made them a simple dinner of mushroom omelets and a green salad and then returned to work, leaving the dirty dishes in Gabriel's hands. He listened to the four Brahms symphonies on Ingrid's audio system and at midnight crawled into bed. There he endured the clatter of keyboards until 2:00 a.m., when the racket in the next room suddenly fell silent. The respite was brief, three hours at most, then it started up again. Gabriel, his head throbbing, went downstairs and made the coffee. Ingrid showed her flawless face shortly after eight.

"Not a word," she muttered, and was gone.

Alone once more, Gabriel stared mystified at a Danish morning television program until ten o'clock. Then he pulled on his warms and his waterproof boots and made the fifteen-kilometer hike along the beach to Grenen, where the incoming waters of the North Sea collide with the outgoing current of the Baltic. He lunched at a coffeehouse near the Skagens Museum and was back in Kandestederne in time to make a painting of the sun setting over the gorse-covered dunes.

It was a few minutes after five when he returned to the cottage. On the low table in the sitting room he found a chilled bottle of Sancerre, two wineglasses, a portable hard drive, and a handwritten note. The hard drive contained the current balance sheet of SBL PrivatBank of Lugano, along with several hundred thousand pages of supporting documents. The note concerned their dinner plans. They had a reservation at the Brøndums Hotel at 8:00 p.m. The proprietor had agreed to accept two unsigned landscapes in lieu of payment.

27

———

Kandestederne

Swiss financial authorities, while forgiving of many sins, have always frowned upon corporate espionage, especially when directed against a member of the family. Martin Landesmann, therefore, thought it wise for him to travel from Geneva to Denmark to review the hacked material from SBL PrivatBank. His Gulfstream G550 landed at Aalborg International Airport shortly after eleven o'clock the following morning. Gabriel collected the environmentally mindful Swiss financier in Ingrid's electric Volvo.

"I applaud your decision to go green," he declared as the vehicle slid silently away from the terminal.

"Says the man who just stepped off one of his two private jets."

"The Gulfstream is far more fuel-efficient than my Boeing Business Jet," said Martin without a trace of irony.

"I suppose we all have to make sacrifices."

"I couldn't have said it better myself."

"Feel free to use it at Davos."

"I just might."

Gabriel made his way to the E39 and headed north. Martin gazed at the tabletop-flat landscape beyond his window.

"Why Denmark?" he asked.

"My associate is Danish."

"Your hacker, you mean?"

"She has other skills as well."

"Such as?"

"I'd remove that Patek Philippe Perpetual from your wrist, if I were you. And hide your billfold as well."

"A pickpocket, is she?"

"The best I've ever seen."

"How did you meet her?"

"She stole a Vermeer from a villa on the Amalfi Coast. And then she stole your wife's jewelry."

"Well," said Martin. "That explains everything."

————————

The woman who admitted Martin Landesmann into her beachfront home in Kandestederne one hour later did not live up to advance billing. Indeed, in dress and aspect she was by all appearances a model citizen who had never once put a foot wrong. Martin was so taken by her that he failed to notice the admiring glance she cast toward his costly Swiss timepiece—or the subtle brush of her hand that located the billfold in the breast pocket of his gray sport jacket. Perhaps he recognized in her a kindred spirit. They were, thought Gabriel, two sides of the same coin.

The pleasantries complete, they filed into the sitting room, where a printed copy of SBL's most recent balance sheet waited on the coffee table. It was a detailed version, some three hundred pages in length. Martin reviewed the document line by line, pausing occasionally to circle an entry with his fat Montblanc pen or to make a margin note. His survey complete, he looked up from the document and announced his preliminary findings.

"It won't surprise you to learn that SBL PrivatBank SA of Lugano has emerged from its recent period of turbulence with flying colors. Its turnaround is nothing short of miraculous. It is the very picture of financial and moral health."

"Do you believe it?" asked Gabriel.

"Not for a minute. It is a wholly owned subsidiary of Camorra Incorporated. And it's being propped up by dirty Camorra money."

To prove his thesis, Martin required real-time access to SBL's most sensitive internal data—its deposits, its trading book, its portfolio of loans, the compensation paid to senior executives, even the bank's insurance records. He was granted that access by Ingrid, who was logged into SBL's internal network. He spent an hour in the private banking division, perusing the accounts of high-net-worth individuals at will, and another hour rummaging through the files in the asset management division. With the exception of the occasional raised eyebrow, he offered no commentary on the nature of his findings.

He reviewed the bank's trading book next and then conducted a loan-by-loan survey of the lending division. His last stop was the email inbox of Franco Tedeschi, the Camorra's man on SBL's senior management team. Tedeschi's correspondence included a lengthy exchange with an executive vice president from the Zurich Insurance Group, Switzerland's largest insurer.

"I found it," Martin announced.

"Found what?" asked Gabriel.

"Your Leonardo."

"Where is it?"

"Locked in an underground vault at SBL headquarters. But the more important question is, how did it get there and why?"

"And the answer?"

"Someone lost a great deal of the Camorra's money. And someone had to pay."

"Who?"

"I haven't the faintest idea."

————————

But there were important clues, added Martin, scattered throughout the bank's records, especially in the asset management division. The firm's clients included individuals, institutions, and businesses, many of which were anonymous shell corporations or holding companies. It bought, sold, and managed investments on behalf of those clients with the goal of increasing their wealth over time. It also lent the clients' money, in some cases extremely large sums of money. To manage its risk, the bank then sold portions of those loans to other investors, oftentimes to its own clients—sometimes, even, to the client who had taken the loan in the first place.

"Why would it do a thing like that?" asked Gabriel.

"Because much of the bank's lending isn't actual lending. And many of its clients aren't actual clients. They're merely fronts for our friends from Naples."

"How does it work?"

"You did a bit of mischievous banking in your past life. You tell me."

"A company called Mafia Limitato opens an account at SBL."

"We should probably do something about the name. But please continue."

"Mafia Limitato then retains the services of the bank's asset management division to invest its money wisely. The asset manager plows some of the money into bonds and equities and uses the rest to purchase real estate."

"Incorrect."

"Where did I go wrong?"

"Mafia Limitato actually *borrows* the money from SBL to purchase the real estate."

"Why?"

"The tax advantages, of course. Mobsters hate to pay taxes."

"So Mafia Limitato takes a loan it doesn't need and then buys the loan from the bank?"

Martin nodded. "Which launders still more dirty money and removes nonexistent risk from the bank's balance sheet."

"Why is the risk nonexistent?"

"Because there is absolutely no chance Mafia Limitato will default on a loan it took from a bank it controls." Martin sighed. "Do I have to explain everything?"

"It's a shell game? Is that what you're saying?"

"In a manner of speaking, yes. But it also provides SBL with additional capital to lend to other clients. One of those clients borrowed four hundred million dollars from SBL to purchase a piece of commercial real estate in London. And SBL, of course, immediately sold the loan to Mafia Limitato."

"Who was the unlucky client?"

"Something called the Mayfair Group. It looks as though it might be a real estate holding company. It was represented in the deal by a Milanese financial adviser, a certain Nico Ambrosi. His firm is called Piedmont Global Capital."

"And the property?"

"A retail-and-office block on New Bond Street. Which is the interesting part."

"How so?"

"I know the property well. In fact, my firm took a hard look at it when it came on the market."

"And?"

"I wouldn't have paid more than two hundred million for it. But the Mayfair Group, whatever it is, paid twice that. Not surprisingly, it defaulted on the loan two years after it was issued."

"And Mafia Limitato was left holding the bag?"

Martin nodded slowly. "As you can imagine, they were *molto* angry."

"What does any of this have to do with my Leonardo?"

"Your Leonardo was used to repay the loan. At least that is my strong suspicion."

"Based on what?"

"The timing of certain moves by one Franco Tedeschi, chief of SBL's asset management division, beginning with his purchase of a small portrait of a woman, artist unknown, from Galerie Van de Velde in Amsterdam for the sum of five thousand euros. Signore Tedeschi then contacted his man at Zurich Insurance Group and requested a policy on his new acquisition. The man from ZIG insisted on seeing the painting for himself and brought along an expert from the Kunsthaus museum. The expert had a look at the painting in SBL's vault. And guess what he had to say?"

"That my Leonardo is a Leonardo."

Martin nodded. "ZIG issued a half-billion-dollar policy. And just two days later, SBL PrivatBank of Lugano magically forgave the four-hundred-million-dollar loan it had given to the Mayfair Group for the building on New Bond Street."

"The painting was used as collateral after the fact?"

"It certainly looks that way. If nothing else, we can now say with some degree of certainty that your Leonardo is in that bank vault. And it must remain there until it is sold."

"Says who?"

"The Zurich Insurance Group spelled out the provision in granular detail in the policy."

"I don't suppose there are photographs."

"Yes, of course. Front and back." Martin handed over Ingrid's laptop. "See for yourself."

There were eight images in all. The high resolution suggested they had been taken by a professional art photographer. "So the only scenario that would require ZIG to pay out the policy is a theft from the bank vault?"

"That's correct."

"And if the painting was stolen, say, while it was in transit?"

"Mafia Limitato would be left holding the bag." Martin sighed. "Good heavens, Gabriel. Do I have to explain *everything*?"

28

Piazza della Riforma

A handsome promenade, shaded by plane trees and lined with small marinas, stretched along the gentle curve of the blue bay. Luxury motorcars moved at a stately pace along the lakefront boulevard, but much of the town's ancient center was closed to traffic, including the Via Nassa, a cobbled arcade lined with exclusive retailers. Ingrid slowed to a stop outside a Bulgari boutique and scrutinized the costly gold-and-diamond trinkets displayed in the window.

"Nothing?" asked Gabriel.

"Not yet, I'm afraid." She paused again outside the Hermès boutique, then wandered across the street to Cartier. "But I'm definitely getting warmer."

They continued along the Via Nassa to the Piazza della Riforma. In the northwest corner of the square was the Lugano office of Credit Suisse. UBS, Switzerland's largest financial services company, was on the eastern flank. In the building next door was the global headquarters of SBL PrivatBank SA.

"It looks so respectable," said Ingrid.

"So do you," replied Gabriel. "But looks can be deceiving."

There was a restaurant a few paces from the bank's main entrance. Gabriel and Ingrid requested a table in the square and were seated at once. Their waiter spoke the Swiss dialect of Italian. Ingrid plucked the corkscrew from the pocket of his apron as he was taking their order.

"If only it were that easy to steal your Leonardo," she said, and slid the corkscrew into her handbag.

"What happens when he delivers our bottle of pinot grigio and discovers his corkscrew is missing?"

"He will assume he misplaced it."

"And why is that?"

"Because never in a million years would he think that I was skilled or brazen enough to steal it. That is the secret of my success, Mr. Allon."

"Your charm and demure looks?"

"And the best pair of hands in the business," she added.

"But what if the corkscrew was worth a half billion dollars? And what if our waiter was a member of the Campanian criminal organization known as the Camorra?"

"He still wouldn't suspect me."

"We'll see about that."

Just then the waiter stepped from the doorway of the restaurant, bottle in hand. He displayed the label to Gabriel, then reached into the pocket of his apron. "Forgive me, Signore," he said with a frown, and went in search of the missing corkscrew, leaving the bottle behind on the table. Ingrid raised an eyebrow.

"Don't even think about it," warned Gabriel.

"You're afraid he might notice?"

"I'm certain he would. Especially if the bottle of wine was worth a half billion dollars."

The waiter reappeared with a new corkscrew. Gabriel forwent the usual approval process and instructed him to pour two glasses. When he was gone, Ingrid added a second corkscrew to her handbag. Then she directed her gaze toward the exterior of SBL's headquarters.

"And what if we were trying to steal a painting hidden in a vault beneath that building? How would we pull it off without the bank managers knowing?"

"You're the professional. You tell me."

"I would steal the painting the same way they stole it."

"An inside job?"

"Of course."

"And where are we supposed to find this helpful insider?"

"At SBL PrivatBank, Mr. Allon. Where else? It would have to be someone quite senior. Someone who has access to the vault at any time, day or night."

"It would be easier to tunnel into that vault than to find someone who would be willing to help us. But that's not the only problem with your plan."

"What's the other?"

"The ZIG insurance policy. I refuse to allow Camorra Incorporated to profit from their crime."

"In that case," said Ingrid, "we have to steal the painting while it's out of the vault."

She turned her head to watch a Mercedes-Maybach sedan drawing up at the side entrance of the bank. A fit-looking specimen emerged from the passenger seat and opened the rear door. Franco Tedeschi, head of SBL's asset management division, climbed out of the car and went swiftly inside.

"Is it my imagination," asked Ingrid, "or are the windows of that lovely Mercedes limousine bulletproof?"

"They are," replied Gabriel. "And the armor could stop a rocket-propelled grenade."

"Why does a mere asset manager need a car like that?"

"Lugano is a dangerous town."

"I never realized." Ingrid slipped on a pair of sunglasses and smiled. "But then looks can be deceiving."

———

Of their father's beautiful young friend from Denmark, Irene and Raphael knew little but suspected much. They knew, for example, that she had worked with their father on two of his secret projects— the ones they were never to discuss with their friends from school— and that she was good with computers. They also knew that she could perform card and magic tricks, that she was unusually strong for someone so small in stature, and that she was lethal with a pool cue in her hands. This they had witnessed firsthand one afternoon at an Irish pub in Cannaregio, where she won a thousand euros shooting billiards against four Englishmen from Manchester.

She shared Irene's passion about the dangers of climate change and Raphael's facility with numbers. After dinner that evening she helped the boy untangle a complex advanced geometry concept while Gabriel and his daughter saw to the dishes. Chiara was perched atop a stool at the kitchen island, scrutinizing the photographs of the Leonardo panel attached to the $500 million policy issued by the Zurich Insurance Group.

"Do you know how many crimes you've already committed, darling?"

"None, actually."

"Did you or did you not steal a copy of an insurance policy from SBL PrivatBank of Lugano?"

"And thousands of other confidential documents as well. But it was all Ingrid's doing."

"She's incorrigible," chirped Irene.

"A hopeless reprobate," agreed Gabriel, and handed the child a pot to dry.

Her mother was not amused. "And what were you doing while Ingrid was hacking a Swiss bank?"

"I was painting, if you must know."

"Anything good?"

"A couple of seascapes that are now in the possession of the Brøndums Hotel in Skagen."

Chiara seemed not to hear his answer. "The photographs are extremely high resolution. If you look carefully, you can see the work of the conservator."

"Yes," said Gabriel dryly.

"You disapprove of the job he did?"

"I hate to admit it, but he gave a rather good accounting of himself."

"Did you happen to take a look at the back of the panel?" Chiara turned the computer screen in Gabriel's direction. "He's adhered a supporting panel to the original."

"As I predicted he would. Thus making it next to impossible to prove that the painting was the one stolen from the Vatican."

"The provenance is a joke," observed Chiara.

"But the attribution to Leonardo by the Kunsthaus is worth at least a hundred million dollars. Julian is certain it's an autograph Leonardo as well, which means others will follow. It's only a matter of time before they find a buyer."

"What do you intend to do about it?"

Gabriel smiled. "I'm going to help them."

29

Hotel Danieli

The children insisted that Ingrid walk them to school the following morning. She held their hands tightly, fearful she might lose them in the labyrinthine streets, and breathed a small sigh of relief when they reached their destination safely. She grew disoriented herself during the short walk back to the San Tomà vaporetto stop. Gabriel waited on the platform, a manila envelope beneath one arm.

"I demand to know where you're taking me," she said.

"The Hotel Danieli."

"Why?"

"To have breakfast with the commander of the Art Squad."

"This might come as a surprise, Mr. Allon, but I do my best to avoid police officers."

"You have nothing to fear. Besides, it's time the two of you became better acquainted."

They boarded a Number 1 and rode down the gentle sweep of the Grand Canal to San Zaccaria. A good-looking man in a dark suit met them outside the Danieli. Gabriel made the introductions.

"Capitano Luca Rossetti, meet Ingrid Johansen."

Ingrid reluctantly grasped the outstretched hand. Then Rossetti spoke a few words in Italian to Gabriel, and they all three entered the hotel. General Cesare Ferrari, the legendary commander of the Art Squad, was seated upstairs in the terrace restaurant. Unlike the young captain, he was dressed in a blue uniform with gold trim.

His smile was brief. "If it isn't the sticky-fingered Signorina Johansen. A pleasure to finally meet you."

"The pleasure is all mine," said Ingrid, and sat down. A waiter brought them four cappuccinos and a basket of warm Italian pastries. The view of the Venetian Lagoon looked as though it had been painted by the hand of Turner. General Ferrari, however, had eyes only for Ingrid. His right, she realized suddenly, was a prosthetic. His left shone with unexpected kindness.

"Please try to relax, Signorina Johansen. I am well aware of the dangerous mission you undertook in Moscow and have no interest in your previous work." He turned to Gabriel. "Or yours, for that matter. I am, however, quite eager to hear all about your more recent endeavors. Especially your visit to Amsterdam with your old friend Julian Isherwood."

"An art dealer named Peter van de Velde asked Julian to have a look at a painting he supposedly found in an Amsterdam flea market. A portrait of a young woman, oil on walnut panel. The viewing took place aboard a private aircraft."

"How novel."

"Julian thought so too."

"And what did he think of the painting?"

"He's convinced it's an autograph work by Leonardo da Vinci."

"Is it the painting that was stolen from the Vatican?"

"Without question."

"And where is it now?"

"A bank in Lugano."

"Not SBL PrivatBank?"

"How did you know?"

The general shrugged. "Because SBL is the Banca di Camorra."

————————

Not surprisingly, General Ferrari was eager to know how Gabriel had determined the painting's whereabouts—and why he had renewed his partnership with the beautiful Danish thief who had once stolen a priceless painting by Johannes Vermeer. Gabriel's answer included an admission that a crime had occurred, a data breach from a Swiss financial services firm. Because no aspect of this crime had taken place on Italian soil, the general felt free to review some of the illicitly acquired material, including a $500 million insurance policy and documents related to the forgiveness of a troubled $400 million loan made by SBL PrivatBank to a real estate holding company known as the Mayfair Group.

"Your friend Martin Landesmann has put forward an intriguing theory," the general admitted. "But it's entirely speculative."

"He speaks with considerable authority where the Camorra is concerned."

General Ferrari displayed his ruined right hand. "As do I. But are you telling me that Saint Martin, he of the glittering international reputation, has laundered the Camorra's money?"

"Hard to believe, I know. But they went their separate ways after the Camorra secretly acquired SBL."

"Thus solving their money laundering problems once and for all. My colleagues in the Guardia di Finanza alerted Swiss regulators about the source of the investment capital that saved SBL from collapse, but they refused to listen." The general indicated the stack of documents. "Perhaps they'll listen now."

"Our first priority," said Gabriel, "is the painting."

General Ferrari nodded thoughtfully. "If we were to play it strictly by the book, I would approach the Swiss Federal Police and ask them to intervene."

"With evidence gathered in an illicit hack? I wish you luck, Cesare. Besides, even if the Swiss agree to look into the matter, it will take years to get that painting back."

"What's the alternative?"

"We put the painting in play. And then, when the opportunity presents itself, we acquire it."

"Steal it, you mean?"

"Think of it as an extrajudicial seizure."

"The Art Squad cannot be party to a theft," Ferrari protested. "After all, we are in the business of investigating art crime and prosecuting the perpetrators." He looked at Ingrid and added, "Present company excluded, of course. And then there is the issue of the insurance policy. If you were to *acquire* the painting, ZIG would be on the hook for a half billion dollars."

"But only if the painting is stolen from the vault. And only if SBL PrivatBank of Lugano were to submit a claim."

"Why wouldn't it?"

"Because SBL won't realize its Leonardo is missing."

"Impossible," scoffed the general.

Gabriel looked at Ingrid, who returned Luca Rossetti's wristwatch. "Difficult," she said with a beguiling smile. "But by no means impossible."

30

San Tomà

Gabriel caught an early train to Milan the following morning and from a reputable Old Masters gallery near the Duomo purchased a midsize devotional painting, oil on walnut panel, perhaps sixteenth century, by an unknown artist from the Northern Italian School. The price was ten thousand euros, more than he had hoped to spend, but the panel itself was in remarkably good condition, with no fractures or supporting structures and only a slight convex warping. The dealer insisted the dimensions were 80 by 58 centimeters, though Gabriel suspected the actual width was closer to sixty. He remeasured the panel with his iPhone and, as expected, was proven correct. The dealer, embarrassed, revised the dimensions in the final sales contract.

With the painting tucked into a nylon case, Gabriel walked to the convent of the Santa Maria delle Grazie to have a look at *The Last Supper*. Then he took a taxi to Milano Centrale and caught the 1:20 back to Venice. It was a few minutes after five when he arrived at the apartment. He laid the panel on the worktable in his studio and with a razor-sharp scraper and a heavy heart did violence to the work of the anonymous sixteenth-century Northern Italian artist.

Next morning he carried his ten-thousand-euro plank of walnut to the mainland woodworking shop of one Marco Amato. He instructed Marco to shave two centimeters off the panel's height and four from its width—and to do it in a way that the alterations were not visible. He then informed Marco that he required still another panel, of oak rather than walnut, and provided the woodworker with a high-resolution photograph of how he wanted it to look.

"The same size?"

"The same everything. I want you to make an exact duplicate of that supporting panel."

"May I ask why, Maestro Allon?"

"No, you may not. And if you call me maestro one more time I'm going to shave two or three centimeters off you."

Gabriel returned to San Polo and spent the remainder of the day in his studio working on a preparatory study of a nameless young girl who had lived in Milan more than five hundred years ago. He based his composition on two sources—Leonardo's original silverpoint sketch and the Zurich Insurance Group photograph of the painting in its current condition. He made four sketches in all, then, with Chiara looking over his shoulder, chose one. With a steel-tipped scratch awl, he pierced the sketch with hundreds of tiny holes, or *spolveri*. The three remaining sketches he burned.

He returned to Marco Amato's workshop late the following morning to collect his costly piece of walnut, which was now 78 by 56 centimeters. Back in his studio, he prepared the panel as Leonardo's studio assistants would have prepared his—with layers of wood oil and lead white paint mixed with finely ground soda-lime glass. Three days later, when the preparation was sufficiently dry, he laid the sketch atop it and sprinkled the paper with powdery wood ash he had gathered from the hearth in the sitting room. The ash seeped through the tiny *spolveri*, leaving a dotted outline of the sketch on the surface of the panel. Using a Winsor & Newton Series 7 brush loaded with pale gray paint, he connected the dots and commenced work on a complete monochromatic version of the painting. It was long past sunset by the time he finished. He had eaten nothing all day.

––––––––––

Ingrid took a place of her own, a charming one-bedroom overlooking the Rio de la Frescada for a hundred and fifty a night. Her cyber-activity now included full-time surveillance of a Swiss bank, a Dutch art dealer, and a Dassault Falcon 900LX owned by the offshore shell company Eiger Air Transport. Nevertheless she collected Irene and Raphael from school each afternoon and, after a visit to the *pasticceria* or *gelateria* of their choice, delivered them to the Allon family apartment. Invariably she slipped into Gabriel's studio and briefed him on any developments, such as an overnight flight by the Dassault from Lugano to Singapore, home of a billionaire shipping magnate who was in the market for a newly discovered masterpiece by Leonardo da Vinci. Most afternoons, though, she sat silently atop a stool and watched Gabriel work.

By the end of the first week he had laid down the first earth-toned base layers of paint. Next he began building color and contour with thin glazes. There were no discernible lines anywhere in the image, for Leonardo insisted they did not exist in nature. There were only scarcely perceptible transitions, the technique he called *sfumato*. This, Gabriel explained to Ingrid one afternoon, was how they were going to steal the painting. They would make it disappear in the manner of smoke losing itself on the air.

The *sfumato* stratagem, as Gabriel referred to it, required a perfect copy of the painting. The hand of the master clearly had to be in evidence, thus Gabriel's decision to make the entire picture using only his left. It could not be rushed, this copy. There could be no cutting of corners, no forcing of the issue. Layer by layer, no discernible lines, smoke vanishing into thin air.

The finely ground glass that Gabriel added to his preparation not only brightened the painting but helped to speed the drying as well. Still, each new layer of paint and glaze had to dry thoroughly before he could add the next, a process that typically took several hours. On days when the sun was shining he would place the painting on the loggia and expose it to the southern sky. But when the weather was cloudy and damp he had no recourse other than a powerful fan.

During one daily intermission he took Ingrid sailing aboard his Bavaria 42. Franco Tedeschi and Peter van de Velde spent that same afternoon aboard the Dassault Falcon, bound for Abu Dhabi. The viewing took place late that evening on an airport tarmac. The prospective buyer was a hotheaded young sheikh with more money than sense. He offered a hundred million for the painting. Franco turned him down flat.

On Wednesdays, Gabriel made certain to schedule the drying period so that he could keep his weekly appointment with his fourteen young art students. During one lesson they made simple still lifes using no lines, only faint edges and subtle gradations of shading. The week after that they produced their first drapery studies—again without lines.

Each Thursday, Gabriel escorted Raphael to the university for his weekly session with his mathematics tutor. While walking home one evening, the boy asked Gabriel why his friend Ingrid was staying in Venice—and why he was spending so much time working on the painting in his studio. The explanation Gabriel concocted might have worked once, but not that evening. His son was far too intelligent to be deceived by a half-baked cover story spun by his father.

"It's a Leonardo, isn't it?"

"Since I'm the one painting it, it cannot possibly be a Leonardo."

"Of course it can."

Gabriel smiled. "You're a very sophisticated young man, Raffi. But what makes you think I'm painting a Leonardo?"

"The sketch," answered the boy.

"What sketch?"

"The one I saw in the book lying on your worktable. It's called *Head of a Woman* or *Study for an Angel*. Leonardo drew it when he was working on a painting called *Virgin of the Rocks*."

Gabriel received this revelation with mixed emotions. He was encouraged that Raphael had shown an interest in something other than advanced mathematics. He was less pleased to hear that the boy had flouted his father's long-standing edict that no one enter his studio when he was not present.

"How many times have I told you—"

"Mama said it was all right."

"Did she?"

The child nodded his head vigorously.

"And what do you do when you visit my studio, Raffi?"

"Sometimes I do my schoolwork. It's very quiet."

"And when you're not doing your schoolwork?"

"I draw."

That would explain the missing pages in Gabriel's sketchpad and the foreshortened pencils. He had suspected that someone had been using his supplies without authorization but had not wished to sound like a mentally unbalanced madman by confronting his wife and young children.

"What sort of drawings?" he asked.

"Still lifes, mainly. Mama arranges them for me."

The plot thickens. "How many still lifes have you made, Raffi?"

He shrugged in reply.

"Anything else?"

"I drew a copy of the Leonardo sketch. The one of the girl."

"Where is it now?"

All of Raphael's drawings, Gabriel discovered when they returned home, were carefully dated and stored in a handsome leather art portfolio, a gift from the child's mother. The still lifes were far more advanced than anything made by Gabriel's students. The copy of *Head of a Young Woman*, also known as *Study for an Angel*, was near photographic. Gabriel asked his son whether he had traced the picture. The boy swore he had not.

Unconvinced, Gabriel led Raphael into his studio and asked him to draw a copy of his copy. The boy scarcely glanced at his source material. The young woman, it seemed, had been culled from his prodigious memory.

Gabriel dated the sketch and placed it in Raphael's portfolio. "Will you come to my class next Wednesday?" he asked.

"No," replied the child, and walked out.

31

San Tomà

By eleven o'clock the following morning they had a bidding war on their hands. The competitors were five in number and scattered around the globe—the Singaporean shipping magnate, the hotheaded sheikh from Abu Dhabi, a Swedish steel baron, the third-richest man in China, and a mystery buyer represented by a French art consultant named Stéphane Tremblay. Monsieur Tremblay, Gabriel explained to Ingrid, was the former director of the paintings department at the Louvre. A very serious player indeed.

"He rang Peter van de Velde last night. Said his client has the hots for the painting."

"How hot?"

"A hundred and twenty-five million. When the Swedish steel baron bid a hundred and thirty, Tremblay and his client immediately went to one fifty."

With Gabriel's permission, Ingrid unleashed the hacking malware Proteus on the art consultant's phone, and by early afternoon she was sifting through his emails, text messages, and telephone metadata. His clients included some of the wealthiest and most prominent collectors in France, none of whom appeared interested in acquiring a newly discovered Leonardo being offered for sale by a third-tier dealer in Amsterdam. Tremblay's mystery client was listed in his contacts only as Archimedes. Their most recent exchange of text messages made it clear that Archimedes was in it for the long haul.

All this Ingrid explained to Gabriel after walking Irene and Raphael home from school. They spoke outside on the loggia, where the panel was drying in the tangerine light of the declining sun. The beautiful girl from Milan appeared to be eavesdropping on their conversation. Her heavy-lidded eyes, with their mismatched pupils, tracked Ingrid's every move.

"How much longer?" she asked.

"Two weeks, maybe three."

"She looks nearly finished to me."

"I'm sure she does," said Gabriel. "But I still have a great deal of work to do."

"Such as?"

"Several more layers of paint and glaze on her face. Then I have to make the painting appear as though it's undergone a recent restoration."

"What about the surface cracks?"

"I will apply a special varnish that promotes craquelure and hope for the best."

"Hope?"

"I prefer to induce craquelure by baking a forgery for three hours at two hundred and twenty degrees Fahrenheit. But that only works for canvases, not walnut panels."

"What happens if the auction ends before your painting is finished?"

"We will have a serious problem on our hands."

"Surely there's something you can do to speed up the process."

"What do you suggest?"

"You're the professional," quipped Ingrid. "You tell me."

Gabriel blew on the surface of the panel. Ingrid doubled over with laughter.

———————

That evening the third-richest man in China raised his offer to $175 million. The bidder known only as Archimedes waited only twelve hours before instructing his French art consultant, via a supposedly encrypted text message, to increase his bid to $180 million. In an effort to determine Archimedes's identity, Ingrid hacked his phone. She reported her findings to Gabriel that afternoon. She had to raise her voice to be heard over the whirring of the large fan in his studio.

"It's clean as a whistle. Professionally clean, if you ask me. I can't even figure out where he is."

Whoever Archimedes was, he quickly found himself in a shootout with four determined adversaries. Indeed, in the span of just forty-eight hours, a flurry of bids pushed the offer on the table past the $200 million mark. By the week's end, the third-richest man in China was in the pole position with a bid of $250 million. Gabriel, as he labored to complete his version of the painting, feared the Leonardo might slip beyond his reach. He had plenty of friends in high places in western Europe and the Middle East, but none in China. If the painting ended up in the hands of a billionaire from Shanghai, it would likely be lost forever.

He was pleased, therefore, when the Swedish steel baron raised his offer to $275 million, which set off another round of furious bidding. It was the hotheaded young sheikh from Abu Dhabi, scion of the world's wealthiest family, who broke the $300 million barrier, only to be outdone when the buyer known as Archimedes bid

$325 million. If the deal were concluded at that price, it would make the Leonardo the second-most expensive painting ever sold, eclipsed only by the price paid at auction for the *Salvator Mundi*.

Archimedes's art adviser, Stéphane Tremblay, made this very point in an indiscreet text message sent to his mistress, a curator of French School paintings at the Louvre. As luck would have it, he also disclosed the identity of his client. Ingrid delivered the news to Gabriel as he was standing before the painting, a hand to his chin, his head tilted slightly to one side.

"You're absolutely certain it's him?" he asked at length.

"Would you like to see the text message? The only thing missing was his patronymic."

"It's my understanding that he owns the largest villa in Antibes."

"The most expensive too."

"The perfect place to hang the world's most expensive painting, don't you think?"

"Second most expensive," she corrected him.

"For the moment, at least."

Gabriel said nothing more. He was staring at the portrait, his pose unchanged. The girl from Milan was staring at Ingrid.

"Is she finished?"

"Yes," replied Gabriel. "I believe she is."

32

Queen's Gate Terrace

Christopher Keller, officer of His Majesty's Secret Intelligence Service, husband of Old Masters art dealer Sarah Bancroft, was waiting curbside behind the wheel of his Bentley Continental when Gabriel stepped from Heathrow's Terminal 5 at half past four the following afternoon. He wore a Burberry Camden car coat atop a suit by Richard Anderson of Savile Row. His hair was sun-bleached, his skin was taut and dark, his eyes were bright blue. The notch in the center of his chin looked as though it had been cleaved with a chisel. His mouth seemed permanently fixed in an ironic half smile.

He cast a ponderous glance at his wristwatch as Gabriel settled into the passenger seat. It was the kind of sporting timepiece worn by men who scaled mountain peaks, dived to great ocean depths, and leapt from perfectly good airplanes. Christopher had made his first jump while serving in the elite 22 Special Air Service Regiment of the British Army. He was now employed by a clandestine department of the SIS that carried out politically sensitive black operations. He had spent much of the last two years in Ukraine. Gabriel had only the vaguest idea what he was doing there. His art dealer wife, a former CIA officer, had no clue at all.

"Your flight landed more than an hour ago," he informed Gabriel in a lazy West End drawl. "Where in God's name have you been?"

"I had a devil of a time getting through customs, if you must know."

"They gave you a good going-over, did they?"

"It was touch and go."

"What seemed to be the problem?"

"It might have been the newly discovered Leonardo in my carry-on luggage."

Christopher looked at the solander museum case resting upright on Gabriel's knees. "Would you mind terribly if we put your Leonardo in the boot?"

"I'd rather put you in the boot, Christopher."

He slipped the Bentley into gear and eased slowly from the curb. "The damn thing is blocking my peripheral vision."

"Try looking straight ahead," said Gabriel. "That's where the road is."

———

In the northeastern corner of Kensington, a short walk from Hyde Park and the Royal Albert Hall, lies Queen's Gate Terrace. Only eight hundred feet in length, it is lined with several hundred million pounds' worth of prime London real estate, much of it foreign owned. Christopher dwelled in a luxury maisonette in the Georgian town house at Number 18. His neighbors were under the impression that his name was Peter Marlowe and that he was a wildly successful international business consultant, thus the flashy motorcar, the constant overseas travel, and the glamorous American-born wife.

"Astonishing," said Sarah. "It's an absolutely perfect copy."

She was looking down at Gabriel's Leonardo, which was lying on the kitchen island. In one hand was a high-resolution photograph of the real Leonardo, in the other a Belvedere martini. Christopher, after giving the painting no more than a passing glance, was pouring Johnnie Walker Black Label into a crystal tumbler. Gabriel, for his part, was pulling the cork from a bottle of Sancerre.

Sarah placed the photograph and her drink on the countertop and took up the painting with both hands. "Walnut?"

"What do you think?" asked Gabriel.

"I think you murdered a sixteenth-century Milanese School picture and painted this one in its place."

"It was Northern Italian School. And it needed to be put out of its misery."

"How much did you pay for it?"

"Ten thousand euros."

"Ouch."

"I'm accepting donations."

"Sorry, darling. But I gave at the office." Sarah returned the panel to the countertop. "But what are you going to do with it?"

"I'm going to sell it, of course."

"To whom?"

"At present there are five collectors attempting to acquire the real Leonardo. The current offer on the table is three hundred and twenty-five million dollars. The bid was made by the French art consultant Stéphane Tremblay on behalf of his client."

"I showed a painting to Stéphane not long ago. But who's the client?"

"A Russian oligarch named Alexander Prokhorov."

Sarah frowned. "He prefers to be called Proko. No first name, just Proko."

"Do you know him?"

"When Proko came to London, he bought a big mansion up in Highgate and filled it with paintings. I used to bump into him at auctions and gallery openings. He was quite the man about town." She made a show of thought. "I forget how he made his money."

It was Christopher who supplied the answer. "Proko was the largest supplier of pipes for the Russian oil-and-gas industry. At last check, he's worth in excess of twenty-five billion dollars."

"Most of it earned corruptly through his Kremlin connections," Gabriel pointed out.

"Which is why His Majesty's Government froze all of Proko's British-based assets after the invasion of Ukraine. He left London in a snit and settled in Antibes with his twenty-seven-year-old girlfriend. Yuliana is her name, if I'm not mistaken. Apparently she was a flight attendant."

"They usually are," said Gabriel. "But why haven't the French seized Proko's assets?"

"Because for some unfathomable reason, they decided to give him a French passport."

"And if he were to plunk down several hundred million dollars for an autograph work by Gabriel Allon?"

"His Majesty's Government would not shed a tear. Provided, of course, there was no fallout from our occasional allies the French."

"Let me worry about the French," said Gabriel. "The more important question is, what do we do with the money?"

"The money that Proko is about to pay for your painting?"

"Yes, Christopher. That money."

"I'm not *actually* an international business consultant. But won't that money be paid to the Banca di Camorra?"

"I assume so."

"Then the money would remain there, would it not?"

"Under no circumstances."

"You're going to steal the money *and* the painting?"

"I'm going to recover the painting. As for the money," added Gabriel, "I intend to reroute it."

"How?"

"My associate will see to that. You remember Ingrid, don't you?"

"With considerable fondness," said Christopher. "But can she really pull it off?"

"She seems to think so."

"In that case, we should probably put the money to good use."

"Widows and orphans?"

"How about something a bit more pressing?"

"Such as?"

"The Ukrainians," suggested Sarah.

Christopher smiled. "What a fine idea. Three hundred and twenty-five million dollars would buy a lot of badly needed bullets and antitank weapons."

"But four hundred million would buy more," said Gabriel.

"So would five hundred million," added Sarah.

"A half bloody billion?" asked Christopher. "How are you going to do that?"

Sarah sipped her martini. "Watch me."

33

Mason's Yard

Isherwood Fine Arts, purveyors of museum-quality Italian and Dutch Old Master paintings since 1968, occupied three floors of a sagging Victorian warehouse in a quiet quadrangle of commerce known as Mason's Yard. Julian pressed the call button on the intercom at half past eleven the following morning, and Sarah buzzed him inside. She was seated at her desk in the gallery's business office, a phone to her ear. She pointed toward the ceiling with the tip of her fountain pen and mouthed the words *You have a visitor*.

Julian hung his mackintosh on the coat tree and rode the tiny lift up to the gallery's glorious exhibition room. The twelve paintings hanging on the walls were the finest in the gallery's inventory. A thirteenth was propped upon the baize-covered display pedestal. Gabriel stood before it, hand to chin, head tilted slightly to one side. Julian adopted an identical pose.

At length he asked, "What am I looking at?"

"You tell me, Julian."

He leaned close to the panel and examined the brushwork on the woman's face. There were no lines, only subtle transitions achieved with thin layers of paint and glaze.

"I'm inclined to make a firm attribution to Leonardo."

"What's stopping you?"

"The fact that the painting is currently in my gallery."

"Is that the only reason?"

"Absolutely. It's breathtaking."

"But is it the painting you saw on that airplane?"

"For an instant, I thought it was."

"Do me a favor and pick it up."

Julian grasped the panel by the vertical edges and lifted it from the pedestal.

"How's the weight?"

"Just right."

"Have a look at the back, if you wouldn't mind."

Julian turned the painting over. "Good heavens. How on earth were you able to do that?"

"I can only take credit for the front of the painting. But you're to blame for what's going to happen next."

"What have I done now?"

"Do you remember that nondisclosure agreement you signed at Peter van de Velde's gallery in Amsterdam?"

"It wasn't worth the paper it was written on."

"Still, you *did* sign it, Julian. And yet, regrettably, it appears as though you've violated the terms."

"Is that so? And just who did I tell about the painting?"

Gabriel smiled. "Everyone."

———————

They arrived at the gallery one by one, at five-minute intervals. Jeremy Crabbe from Bonhams, Simon Mendenhall from Christie's, Niles Dunham from the National Gallery, Nicky Lovegrove, art adviser to the vastly rich. Sarah gave them no reason for the summons, though she implied it was a matter of great importance. Naturally they wondered whether it concerned the imminent demise of her partner. No, she assured them, Julian had made a full recovery from his recent bout of emotional exhaustion.

The last to arrive was tubby Oliver Dimbleby. He squeezed into the lift with Sarah and rode it up to the exhibition room, where Julian and the other invited guests were gazing in astonishment at the painting propped on the display easel. It was a portrait of a young woman who bore a striking resemblance to the girl whom Leonardo da Vinci had used as his model for the archangel Gabriel in *Virgin of the Rocks*. But that was not possible, Oliver told himself, because nowhere in the mountain of scholarship dedicated to Leonardo and his maddeningly small oeuvre was there any indication he had ever made such a painting.

The presence of the noted art restorer and retired spy Gabriel Allon suggested that something devious was afoot. Oliver had played a supporting role in several of Gabriel's capers, most recently on a case involving a forgery ring that was flooding the art market with fake Old Masters. Having witnessed firsthand Gabriel's uncanny ability to mimic the brushwork of the greatest painters who ever lived, Oliver was skeptical as to the authenticity of the portrait. Nicky Lovegrove, for reasons Oliver could not possibly fathom, appeared equally dubious.

"All right," said Nicky finally, gaveling the proceedings to order. "What's the bloody story?"

The story, as recounted by Gabriel, involved a dead body in the Venetian Lagoon, an unreported theft from the Vatican Museums, a Swiss bank controlled by the Italian Mafia, and a Russian oligarch living grandly in the south of France. It was Gabriel's ambition to recover the stolen painting by simultaneously deceiving the Swiss bank and the Russian oligarch—and to transfer the proceeds of this deception to the Ukrainian government. He required the help, it seemed, of the London art world figures assembled in the room. He offered anyone who did not wish to participate in the scheme a chance to leave. Not surprisingly, there were no takers.

But who among them would be the first to dip his toe into the water? It would have to be someone possessed of immense charm and charisma and yet utterly devoid of morals or scruples. They were all in agreement that there was only one man for the job. Smiling, Gabriel placed the portrait in a solander case and was gone.

———————

He gave the same presentation four hours later in Paris, this time to Jacques Ménard, chief of the art crime unit of the French Police Nationale. The meeting took place not in a gallery or in Ménard's office on the Quai des Orfèvres, but in a dreary hotel room near the Gare du Nord. It was Gabriel, who had worked with Ménard in the past, who chose the venue. The French art sleuth, after examining the portrait in the hotel room's dim light, declared it worthy of the Musée du Louvre. But he made it clear that neither he nor his under-lings would take part in the scheme Gabriel had in mind.

"Absolutely not, *mon ami*. Never in a million years."

"Will you allow me to restate three important facts?"

"Be my guest."

"The painting is stolen, the seller is a Swiss bank controlled by the Camorra, and the buyer is a corrupt Russian oligarch."

"Who happens to be a naturalized citizen of France," added Ménard. "Therefore, I cannot possibly defraud him."

"Leave the fraud to me, Jacques. I just need you to avert your gaze for a few seconds."

"And what will happen during this brief interlude?"

"*Contrapposto*," said Gabriel.

"I beg your pardon?"

Gabriel lowered his eyes toward the painting. "Look at the way she's posed. She's turned to the right but looking to the left, as though she's been taken by surprise. That's the essence of *contrapposto*. Never a static pose, always opposing directions. We're going to create the same effect."

"And then?"

"*Sfumato*," replied Gabriel. "Like smoke losing itself on the air."

The French policeman, intrigued, lit a cigarette and the bargaining commenced. After thirty minutes they had an operational plan in place, one that achieved the desired result while at the same time protecting Ménard's political and legal flank. Gabriel settled the bill for the room and then took a taxi to Le Bourget, where he carried the painting aboard a waiting Gulfstream G550. The aircraft's owner, the Swiss financier and philanthropist Martin Landesmann, was enjoying a preflight glass of Dom Pérignon. The cabin attendant, an attractive German-speaking woman of perhaps thirty-five, poured a glass for Gabriel as well. She expressed no interest at all in the contents of the rectangular case. In fact, she scarcely looked at it—or at Gabriel, for that matter.

"She's rather discreet, isn't she?"

"Sabine? Very," said Martin. "And she's quite good at her job. It's harder than it looks, you know."

"Pouring Dom Pérignon?"

Martin smiled. "Looking after globetrotting businessmen such as myself. Some of us have rather large egos. And we're not always on our best behavior."

"You pay her well, I take it."

"Sabine works for the company that manages my planes."

"Executive Jet Services of Zurich?"

"Correct."

"It's the same company that manages SBL's Dassault Falcon."

"I'm not surprised," said Martin. "They handle most of the Swiss banking industry's private aircraft."

"Do you always have the same cabin attendant?"

"Usually. I'm rather close to the man who runs the company. Whenever possible, he gives me the same cockpit and cabin crew."

"Does he do the same for SBL?"

"I would imagine so."

The Gulfstream eased away from the terminal.

"And what if I wanted to make a change to SBL's cabin crew for a single flight?" asked Gabriel.

"Why would you want to do a thing like that?"

"Eyes and ears only."

"Nothing illegal?"

"You have my word, Martin."

"I think it can be arranged. Provided, of course, you have a presentable candidate in mind."

"More than presentable."

"Your friend the computer hacker?"

Gabriel nodded.

"She certainly looks the part. But she'll have to undergo training before the flight."

"How hard can it be to pour a glass of Dom Pérignon?"

"For a mobster banker and his heavily armed bodyguards? Harder than it looks."

The flying time from Paris to Venice was one hour and forty-five minutes. Luca Rossetti whisked Gabriel through the arrivals process and gave him a ride home to San Polo in a Carabinieri patrol boat. He placed the painting in his studio and went into the kitchen, where he found Ingrid and his wife singing along to Eros Ramazzotti's "Parla con me" at the top of their lungs. Receiving no greeting or acknowledgment of his arrival, he poured a glass of Barbaresco and helped himself to a crostini smeared with artichokes and creamy ricotta cheese.

"Is there any news?" he asked of no one in particular.

"It seems we have a new bidder for the Leonardo," Ingrid shouted over the music.

"Really? Who?"

Ingrid smiled and sang, *"Parla con me . . ."*

34

London–Zurich–Venice

Oliver Dimbleby waddled into Galerie van de Velde promptly at half past ten the following morning and, like Julian Isherwood before him, was presented with a pen and a nondisclosure agreement, which he signed without complaint. The viewing took place an hour later aboard the Dassault Falcon, though this time the aircraft never left the tarmac at Schiphol Airport. Oliver intimated that he had two clients, both Americans of eleven-figure wealth, who might be interested in acquiring a trophy painting like the Leonardo. He also implied, not without justification, that he was on firm footing with a well-endowed museum in Los Angeles. He was confident, therefore, that he could assemble a deal in as little as seventy-two hours. Peter van de Velde informed Oliver that the offer on the table was $325 million and sent him on his way. Oliver rang Gabriel while waiting to board his flight back to London and gave him a condition report.

"It's a perfect match, my boy. You've outdone yourself."

"Who else was on the plane?"

"Four security guards and a little Italian banker with a face like a ferret. Van de Velde did all the talking. If I had to guess, he's eagerly awaiting my next call."

"How quickly can you get an offer on the table?"

"That's entirely up to you."

"Close of business feels right to me. And make sure you shoot your mouth off at Wiltons tonight."

"That would be a violation of the nondisclosure agreement."

"These things happen, Ollie. Especially where you're concerned."

He transmitted the bid to Peter van de Velde at four o'clock that afternoon. His email was appropriately weighty in tone, for the offer was $350 million. Oliver being Oliver, he let it slip to Nicky Lovegrove at Wiltons, and Nicky quietly resolved to throw his hat in the ring. At least that was the version of events he imparted into the ear of Julian Isherwood, who was in on the entire charade.

None of which Nicky mentioned to Peter van de Velde when they spoke by telephone. He claimed to have heard about the new Leonardo from a "highly placed art world source." This source, whom he refused to further characterize, had informed him that the numbers being thrown around were already stratospheric, which was music to Nicky's ears. He represented some of the world's wealthiest collectors. The higher the altitude, the higher his commission.

"You would be well advised, Peter, to show me the picture at your earliest convenience."

"How about tomorrow?"

The viewing took place not in Amsterdam but in a suite at the Hotel Splendide Royal in Lugano. Twenty-four hours later Nicky Lovegrove submitted a bid of $375 million on behalf of a phantom client. When informed of the offer, Oliver Dimbleby raised the price of the deal to $390 million. The Russian oligarch Alexander Prokhorov waited two full days before getting back in the game. He did so with an astonishing offer of $400 million, equaling the price paid at auction for the *Salvator Mundi*.

It was at this point that Simon Mendenhall informed Peter van de Velde that Christie's stood ready to dispose of the painting, either at auction or through a private sale. Not surprisingly, Jeremy Crabbe of Bonhams got wind of Simon's gambit and rang Van de Velde with an offer of his own. Poor Niles Dunham, a mere curator at the National Gallery, had nothing to offer other than his infallible eye and unquestioned integrity. Like Nicky Lovegrove, he was shown the painting in Lugano, in a suite at the Hotel Splendide. "It's him," was all he said.

Niles delivered the same message to Gabriel later that evening—and to the other members of the conspiracy gathered at the bar at Wiltons. Oliver Dimbleby's imaginary client, after giving the situation some imaginary thought, immediately raised his offer to $410 million. Not to be outdone, Nicky Lovegrove's nonexistent client bid $425 million. Alexander Prokhorov, his manhood on the line, instructed his art adviser Stéphane Tremblay to put an end to the proceedings. Tremblay transmitted a bid of $450 million to Peter van de Velde. They had left the stratosphere for the mesosphere. It was time to close the deal and claim the prize.

───────────

The headquarters of Executive Jet Services were located in a squat gray building on the eastern fringes of Zurich's Kloten Airport. From his office on the fourth floor, Markus Vogel had a fine view of the airfield's flightline. At present, though, his eyes were fixed on the resumé lying on his desk. It had been forwarded to him by a billionaire financier who owned not one but two private aircraft, both of which were maintained and crewed by Executive Jet Services at a cost of several million Swiss francs annually. This financier, whose name was Martin Landesmann, had asked Markus Vogel to grant him an unusual favor. Under normal circumstances, Vogel would not have given it a second thought; it was a violation of the company's pledge to provide its clients absolute privacy. But Landesmann was a fixture at Davos and Aspen and a renowned global do-gooder, and the owners of the other aircraft were in Vogel's opinion a rather shady bunch, even by the reduced standards of the Swiss financial services industry.

The head of the firm's asset management division, an Italian fellow named Franco Tedeschi, had been racking up a lot of miles of late, always with a retinue of armed security men and a flat rectangular case. According to Erika Schmidt, the plane's usual cabin attendant, the case contained a painting. Potential buyers had been viewing the work in flight or on airport tarmacs. Erika had overheard offers in the hundreds of millions.

It was Martin Landesmann's wish to replace Erika Schmidt on a future flight, for reasons he declined to disclose. He had given his solemn word, though, that the substitute cabin attendant would engage in no illicit activity and would perform her prescribed duties with the utmost professionalism. He had also implied that Vogel, if he were to grant the request, would receive a substantial gratuity in return, something in the neighborhood, say, of a hundred thousand Swiss francs. Vogel was therefore inclined to do whatever was necessary to keep his famous client happy.

Still, he was troubled by the quality of the resumé lying on his desk. It was thin gruel, to say the least. The applicant was a thirty-seven-year-old female who spoke Danish, German, and English fluently but had no experience in the hospitality industry. Indeed, as far as Markus Vogel could tell, the woman had no real work history at all. There were no references other than Martin Landesmann and no contact information. Nor was there a photograph, a requirement for those seeking employment as a cabin attendant. Vogel, for all he knew, was being asked to hire an overweight Scandinavian milkmaid.

He was therefore pleasantly surprised when, late the following morning, the woman in question strode into his office for her interview. She wore a dark pantsuit and stylish pumps that added a few centimeters to her compact, athletic frame. Her hair was the color of toffee, her eyes were pale blue. Vogel asked her the usual sort of questions, and she managed to say next to nothing, all the while sounding witty and engaging. She was highly intelligent, he thought, and dangerously manipulative. If he didn't know better, he might have suspected that Martin Landesmann had fallen under the spell of a beautiful confidence artist.

It was not a real job interview, for the outcome was a foregone conclusion. Vogel handed her over to Frau Huber, supervisor of the cabin staff, and for the next three days Frau Huber put her through her paces. The training covered everything from food and beverage preparation to personal etiquette and the unique challenges of tending to the needs of those of unlimited wealth. She proved to be a quick study, though at times she could scarcely hide her boredom, especially during Frau Huber's lecture on what was expected of her in the unlikely event of a water landing. She seemed to know her way around a wine list and mixed a mean Manhattan. Even in her pumps, she moved without a sound.

The last act of her training was a written test, which she passed with a perfect score. With her new uniform in hand, she headed across the tarmac and up the airstair of a waiting Gulfstream G550, managed and maintained by Executive Jet Services. The plane departed Zurich thirty minutes later, bound for Venice. Markus Vogel consulted the aircraft's flight logs and saw that it had made a brief stop in the Italian city ten days earlier. On that occasion there had been two passengers on board. One was the plane's owner, Martin Landesmann. The other was someone named Gabriel Allon.

———————

It was Sarah Bancroft who whispered it into the ear of Amelia March, intrepid reporter from *ARTnews* magazine. Nothing specific, mind you, just a bit of gossip she had overheard about a fight among several London art world figures over a major new piece that had come onto the market. Nicky Lovegrove, when asked for a comment that evening at Wiltons, called the rumor "pure rubbish," a sentiment shared, interestingly enough, by Simon Mendenhall, Jeremy Crabbe, Oliver Dimbleby, and Niles Dunham.

Still, it was more than enough in Amelia's estimation to justify a short item on her social media feed. It appeared at nine fifteen that evening, and by morning it was the talk of the art world. A representative of the hotheaded young sheikh from Abu Dhabi informed Peter van de Velde that His Highness wished to submit a new bid for the painting. So, too, did the third-richest man in China and the billionaire shipping magnate from Singapore. By day's end, the offer on the table was a head-spinning $475 million.

The sharp increase in price, while a welcome development, was not without its potential complications, for it appeared that Alexander Prokhorov was, in the lexicon of the auction trade, all done. Finally, after forty-eight hours of deafening silence, the Russian oligarch weighed in with an offer of $500 million. The Singaporean shipping magnate reluctantly bowed out of the contest, followed soon after by the third-richest man in China. The hotheaded sheikh waited twenty-four hours before folding his tent.

Peter van de Velde offered Nicky Lovegrove's imaginary client a chance to get back into the game, but the imaginary client tossed his cards upon the table. When Oliver Dimbleby's imaginary client followed suit a few hours later, the deal was done. At $500 million, it shattered the record price paid for the *Salvator Mundi*. And yet, with few exceptions, no one in the art world was aware that history had been made. For now, at least, the existence of the painting remained a closely guarded secret, as did the identities of both the seller and the buyer.

It just so happened that Alexander Prokhorov had yet to lay eyes on the painting for which he had agreed to pay a record-setting sum of money. He insisted on seeing the picture for himself, preferably at his villa in Antibes, before committing to the purchase. Stéphane Tremblay put the demand to Peter van de Velde, and the Dutch art dealer, after first consulting with Franco Tedeschi in Lugano, agreed to the terms without delay. He suggested the viewing take place on Friday at 2:00 p.m., but the Russian oligarch requested Wednesday at two instead. If the painting met with his approval, he would sign the sales agreement and transmit the $500 million to the seller's account.

Which left Gabriel forty-eight hours to put the final pieces of his operation in place. He did so with a rapid series of four telephone calls. The first was to General Cesare Ferrari, chief of the Art Squad, and the second was to his French counterpart, Jacques Ménard of the Police Nationale. He caught Sarah Bancroft as she was walking along Duke Street toward Wiltons and reached Martin Landesmann at his villa on Lake Geneva. Martin quickly placed a call of his own, to Markus Vogel of Executive Jet Services, and Vogel informed Frau Huber, supervisor of the cabin staff, of a crew change for a forthcoming flight between Lugano and Nice. Frau Huber found this intriguing for any number of reasons, not least because there was nothing in the computer to indicate that such a flight had been scheduled.

She penciled in the change nevertheless and informed Ingrid, via a text message to a burner phone, that she would be making her maiden voyage on Wednesday morning. Unbeknownst to Frau Huber, her new employee spent Tuesday afternoon plotting to steal a lost masterpiece by Leonardo da Vinci from the very men upon whom she would soon be waiting. Her partner in crime, for his part, informed Dottoressa Elenora Saviano that, owing to a scheduling conflict, he would not be able to keep his appointment that week with his fourteen art students.

That evening Ingrid joined the Allon family for dinner at Vini da Arturo, and at six the following morning, dressed in her new uniform and a navy blue raincoat, she boarded a train bound for Lugano. Gabriel had booked two seats on the nine o'clock flight to Nice, one for himself and the other for the solander museum case. Two plainclothes French policemen met him as he stepped from the jetway at Côte d'Azur Airport and escorted him to a windowless room near passport control where Jacques Ménard, in a sleek dark suit and tie, sat at a spotless white table.

He looked at the museum case. "What have you got there?"

"Nothing at all, Jacques."

Ménard smiled. "*Contrapposto?*"

"Poof," said Gabriel. "Like smoke losing itself on the air."

35

Hotel Splendide

It was a few minutes after ten o'clock when Sarah Bancroft stepped from the Belle Époque entrance of the Hotel Splendide. Brushing past the doorman, she set off along the lakefront through the cold gray morning. There was snow on the surrounding mountain peaks and a few gritty flakes adrift on the wind. The city around her was postcard pretty but strangely inanimate and dated. She half expected to bump into Dick and Nicole Diver walking toward her along the promenade. Perhaps they would meet up with Rosemary Hoyt and Abe North for drinks later at the Grand Café Al Porto and talk about their plans for the summer in Cannes.

Sarah laughed quietly at the thought. She had arrived in Lugano the previous evening after making a brief stop in Zurich. There she had inspected several Old Master paintings—including works by Raphael, Rembrandt, and Rubens—at the home of a world-renowned violinist. Or so went the cover story she would tell the Swiss authorities in the event today's caper went sideways. Her husband had traveled to Lugano under his SIS identity, the international business consultant Peter Marlowe. Presently he was in their suite at the Splendide making phone calls to clients, all of whom were sitting at desks at SIS headquarters in London.

Sarah had to admit it felt good to be back in the game. She had played it better than most during her brief career, but then Gabriel Allon had been whispering in her ear. She recalled the occasion of their first meeting—it had taken place in a CIA safe house in Georgetown—and the frigid winter's night in Copenhagen when, unwisely, she had confessed her love for him. The spell was finally broken when she spent a few nights holed up in a hotel in Frinton-on-Sea with Christopher, who just happened to be one of Gabriel's closest friends. They were wed in secret, with only a handful of senior SIS officers in attendance. Gabriel had given away the bride.

A gust of wind rattled the fronds of the palm trees lining the lakefront boulevard. Sarah thought they looked out of place in the mountainous setting. Then she recalled that a trick of the weather patterns had blessed Lugano with one of the warmest climates in Switzerland. But not today, she thought. The temperature was hovering around the freezing mark, and the clouds were leaden and low. She only hoped there were no weather delays at the airport. They were about to carry out one of the greatest heists in history. Timing, as the saying went, was everything.

She crossed to the other side of the boulevard and made her way to the Piazza della Riforma. Lights burned in the windows of SBL PrivatBank's global headquarters. She entered the café opposite the bank and ordered a cappuccino. Twenty minutes later, at 10:50 a.m., a convoy of three Mercedes saloon cars appeared at the bank's side entrance.

Right on schedule, she thought.

She rang Christopher and with studied indifference inquired as to his whereabouts. He informed her that he was waiting for the valet at the Splendide to deliver their car. He did so in Peter Marlowe's public school drawl in the event Switzerland's formidable signals intelligence service was monitoring the call.

"Here he comes now," said Christopher. "I won't be but a moment or two."

"Take your time, darling," replied Sarah and rang off.

Her detachment was as counterfeit as Christopher's earlier phone calls. It was imperative that her husband collect her in the Piazza della Riforma at eleven o'clock sharp. That was when Franco Tedeschi, head of SBL PrivatBank's asset management division, was scheduled to leave for the airport. Markus Vogel of Executive Flight Services had reserved a noon departure slot for the short flight to Nice. It was a drive of approximately twenty-five minutes to the home of Alexander Prokhorov in Antibes, with ground transportation arranged by Herr Vogel. If everything went according to plan, Franco Tedeschi and party would be back in Lugano by 5:00 p.m. At which point a second heist would occur. It was for that reason Sarah and Christopher were minding their manners on the phone. They would soon be accessories to a major international crime.

Sarah waited until 10:59 to settle her bill and leave the café. She paid little heed to the six men who poured from the side entrance of SBL PrivatBank a minute later. One was Franco Tedeschi, one was Peter van de Velde, and the other four were bodyguards, all officially licensed to carry firearms. It was Van de Velde who had possession of the painting. He joined Franco Tedeschi in the back seat of the second Mercedes, and the four bodyguards piled into the lead vehicle and the chase car. Several doors slammed in unison. Then the motorcade sped from the bank as though fleeing the scene of a crime.

Sarah, however, took her time making her way from the piazza to the lakefront boulevard, where Christopher, behind the wheel of a rented Audi, slowed long enough to collect her. A moment later he was directly behind the third Mercedes in the convoy.

"Slow down, darling. You're too close."

Christopher frowned. "You've obviously been hanging out with your old boyfriend again."

She squeezed the back of his powerful sun-bronzed hand. "We were never lovers. You know that."

"Not for your lack of trying."

"It was a passing phase."

"That lasted the better part of ten years, as I recall."

The motorcade entered a traffic circle. "Pay attention, darling. Otherwise you'll lose them."

"Because I know where they're going," replied Christopher, lighting a Marlboro, "that's not possible."

"Spend much time here in lovely Lugano?"

"Can't say I have. You?"

"In a past life," she replied, and helped herself to one of her husband's Marlboros.

"You really need to stop that, you know. It's a dreadful habit."

"But I do look devastating with a cigarette." She coaxed his gold Dunhill lighter into flame. "Drive faster, darling. I want to see them get on the plane."

Christopher pointedly maintained his current rate of speed as he shadowed the three-vehicle convoy toward Lugano's small airport. It was located on the western edge of the city, hard against a mountainside, which required an unusually steep approach. There was a single small terminal building and a car park adjacent to the flightline. Christopher slid into an empty space and killed the engine. The three Mercedes saloon cars were now parked on the apron next to a Dassault Falcon 900LX. Ingrid stood in the open cabin door, a plastic smile on her flawless face.

"Look familiar?" asked Christopher.

"The pretty Danish thief, or the luxurious private business jet?"

Several car doors opened at once, and six men spilled onto the tarmac. Peter van de Velde was still in possession of the painting. He hurried up the airstair, followed by Franco Tedeschi and two of the bodyguards. The other two remained on the tarmac, scanning their surroundings. They failed to notice the handsome couple sitting in a rented Audi in the car park.

"Tell me something," said Christopher. "What exactly did you and your old boyfriend do while Julian was flying around Europe with the painting?"

"We checked into a hotel near the airport, and I had my way with him."

"Funny, he didn't mention it."

"You know Gabriel, darling. He was always very discreet." Sarah watched the two bodyguards heading up the airstair. "Think she can handle them?"

"Ingrid? Without question."

"That good, is she?"

"If SIS had ten more just like her, Britain would rule the world again."

They glimpsed her one last time as she closed the cabin door. Then the plane taxied to the end of the runway. It passed directly above them at 12:05 p.m., a few minutes behind schedule. Sarah shot a text to Gabriel, informing him that the most expensive painting in the world was headed his way.

"What shall we do now?" she asked.

"Why don't we go back to the Splendide so I can have my way with you?"

"You've already had your way with me once this morning. Besides, you checked out of our room."

"In that case, I suppose we'll have to settle for a nice lunch."

"How about the Grand Café Al Porto? The Divers are meeting up with Rosemary and Abe North there. They asked if we would like to join them."

"Who?" asked Christopher.

Sarah sighed and stole another cigarette. It was good to be back in the game.

36

Lugano–Nice

The pilot informed Ingrid that the flight time to Nice would be fifty-two minutes. The caterers had nevertheless provisioned the aircraft with a full lunch service, with a choice between boeuf bourguignon and seafood risotto. For those looking for lighter fare, there was a fruit plate with an assortment of gourmet French and Swiss cheeses. There was also a selection of freshly baked artisan breads and savory snacks of every sort. The liquor was premium. The wines were vintage and grand cru.

The four hulking bodyguards were sprawled on the opposing couches at the back of the cabin. According to the manifest, two of the men were Swiss Italians and the other two were the real thing. Franco Tedeschi was reclining on the starboard side of the cabin, eyes on his phone, which was attached to the plane's Wi-Fi network. Peter van de Velde sat at the table on the port side of the cabin. The world's most expensive painting lay before him, safe inside its sarcophagus. He appraised Ingrid with an art dealer's eye as she delivered his coffee.

"You're not the usual girl."

"I'm new to the company."

"How fortunate for us." He looked her up and down. "Dutch?"

"Danish, actually."

"What's your name?"

"Rikke."

"Like the song?"

"Almost," she said, and smiled. It implied that she was there to see to his every need and desire save one. "Would you care for the risotto or the boeuf bourguignon?"

The Dutch art dealer laid a hand protectively on the case. "Nothing for me, thank you."

Ingrid expressed no interest in the contents of the case, for such questions were a violation of company policy. Instead she turned to Franco Tedeschi, who was staring at her over his half-moon reading glasses.

"Where's Erika?"

"Another flight, I'm afraid."

"I should have been told."

"I'll notify Herr Vogel about your concerns."

"Please do." He looked down at his phone. "Risotto."

Ingrid retreated to the cramped galley. The oven, when opened, exhaled the foul odor of *cuisine industrielle*. She delivered four portions of the boeuf bourguignon to the security men and presented Franco Tedeschi with his seafood risotto. Receiving no expression of gratitude or even acknowledgment, she turned to Peter van de Velde.

"Are you sure I can't bring you something?"

"I'm quite fine, thank you."

Doubtless because a moment earlier he had treated himself to a prolonged examination of Ingrid's ass. "At least let me bring you some more coffee."

"If you insist."

She fetched the pot from the galley and poured. Van de Velde added the cream himself. "Not even a little curious?"

"About what, Mr. Van de Velde?"

He looked down at the transport case. "The contents of that box."

"Not the least bit."

"Your colleague never mentioned it?"

"Erika? Never."

Ingrid started toward the rear of the cabin, but Van de Velde placed a hand on her forearm. "Do you like art?" he blurted.

"Who doesn't?"

"You'd be surprised." Another smile. "And what sort of art do you like, Rikke?"

"Twentieth century, mainly."

"The Impressionists?"

"Sure."

"Van Gogh?"

"Yes, of course."

"And what about the Old Masters?" he wondered.

"I'm quite fond of Vermeer. *Girl with a Pearl Earring* is one of my favorites."

Van de Velde tapped the case lightly with the tip of his forefinger. "This painting is quite similar. But it's much better. And much more valuable as well."

"What have you got in there? The *Mona Lisa*?"

"Not quite, but close."

"What does that mean?"

He raised an eyebrow but said nothing.

"Impossible."

"Would you care to have a look? This is your one and only chance. Because shortly after two o'clock this afternoon, it will disappear forever."

It was Franco Tedeschi, from the opposite side of the cabin, who answered on Ingrid's behalf. "No, Peter. She does not wish to see the painting."

"Actually," said Ingrid, "I'd love nothing more."

Van de Velde popped the latches and opened the case.

———————

The text message landed on Gabriel's phone at 12:52 p.m. It was vaguely worded but clear in its meaning. He showed the message to Jacques Ménard, who consulted an open notebook computer.

"They're on final approach. They should be on the ground in less than five minutes." Ménard closed the laptop. "Wait here."

"Where else would I go, Jacques? Duty-free?"

The French art sleuth frowned on his way out the door. Alone, Gabriel pictured the encounter that would soon take place on the tarmac of Cote d'Azur Airport. A check of the passports, an inspection of the cargo, a request for further information. Nothing serious, messieurs. It won't take but a moment.

37

Côte d'Azur Airport

Two uniformed French border policemen were waiting on the tarmac when the Dassault rolled to a stop near Signature Flight Support, the airport's fixed-base operator. They were accompanied by a tall man in a dark business suit who might have been mistaken for a French movie idol. Ingrid knew the handsome man to be Jacques Ménard, director of the Police Nationale's art crime unit. She opened the forward door, and the three men filed up the airstair and into the cabin. The radios of the border policemen crackled with crosstalk. Jacques Ménard, with nothing more than a glance, instructed the officers to lower the volume.

One of the border policemen carried a clipboard, the other a hand-held passport scanner. They started at the back of the cabin with the four security men and worked their way forward, concluding with Ingrid and the two members of the cockpit crew. Jacques Ménard observed the proceedings with only mild interest.

The check complete, the two border policemen inquired as to the length of the arriving party's stay in France. The pilot replied that he had reserved a 4:00 p.m. departure slot. He and his two colleagues, he added, planned to spend the down time relaxing in a crew room at Signature Flight Support.

"And the purpose of the visit?" asked one of the officers.

"Business," replied Franco Tedeschi tersely.

Jacques Ménard spoke for the first time. "What sort of business, messieurs?"

"My colleague and I are showing a painting to a potential buyer."

Ménard looked at the transport case, which was still lying on the table. "What sort of painting, please?"

"A portrait of a woman," replied Peter van de Velde.

"Date?" asked Ménard.

"Late fifteenth or early sixteenth century."

"Support?"

"Wood panel."

"What type of wood, please?"

"Does it matter?"

"It might, yes."

"Walnut."

"The painting is Northern European in origin?"

"Milan."

"I see. And the artist?"

Van de Velde exchanged a look with Franco Tedeschi before answering. "Leonardo da Vinci."

Ménard gave a skeptical smile. "I'm no expert, but I'm quite certain there are no pictures by Leonardo currently on the market."

"This is a newly discovered work."

"Is that so? And where was it discovered, please?"

"In Amsterdam."

"That's a long way from Milan."

"So is Paris, monsieur. But that's where the *Mona Lisa* ended up."

"*Touché*." Ménard looked down at the transport case. "Open it, please."

Van de Velde, after a moment's hesitation, flipped the latches and lifted the cover. Ménard contemplated the painting without expression. At length he said, "It's extraordinary. But I rather doubt it's genuine. After all, there are only nineteen known works by Leonardo in existence."

"There are now twenty," said the Dutch art dealer.

"You are no doubt aware, Monsieur Van de Velde, that we had a rather serious forgery scandal here in France a few years ago involving Old Master paintings. They were of such high quality that they fooled even the experts at the Louvre. To be honest, we're still cleaning up the mess."

"Rest assured, monsieur, this painting is no forgery."

"Are you the owner?"

It was Franco Tedeschi who answered. "The painting is owned by my bank."

"SBL PrivatBank of Lugano?"

"That's correct."

"And the potential buyer?"

"He wishes to remain anonymous."

"Is he French?"

"Yes."

"Does he intend to purchase the painting today?"

"That is our hope."

"For how much?"

"The sale is private."

"The buyer will nevertheless have to pay VAT taxes. And you and your bank, of course, will have to pay an import duty. For the full amount of the purchase price," added Ménard. "Otherwise I'm going to fall on you from a very great height." He turned to Van de Velde. "Close the case, please."

The Dutch art dealer complied with the request. Ménard grasped the handle and lifted the case from the table. Franco Tedeschi reddened with anger.

"What do you think you're doing?"

"I'm going to make some photographs of this painting for our records. And then you can be on your way."

"In that case, I'm coming with you."

"You will wait here on your beautiful private jet. Otherwise you can change your departure slot and return to Switzerland without completing the sale of the painting." Ménard shrugged. "The choice is yours, messieurs."

———————

The two border policemen waited at the foot of the airstair while Ménard headed across the tarmac and into the terminal. Every square meter of the building was covered by CCTV cameras, especially the area around passport control and customs, but the windowless interior room where Gabriel waited was free of visual surveillance. Ménard removed the Leonardo from the transport case and laid it on the table next to Gabriel's version. The two men stared at the paintings in silence for nearly a minute.

"I can't tell the difference," said Ménard at last.

"I can," answered Gabriel gloomily.

"That's because you painted it. No one else will be able to tell them apart."

"It's glaringly obvious."

"Let's have a look at the back of the paintings, shall we?"

Ménard lifted the Leonardo from the table as though he feared it might explode and gently turned it over. Gabriel handled his copy with far less care. Another moment passed while they examined the backs of the two paintings, side by side.

"Extraordinary," whispered Ménard.

"A disaster waiting to happen."

"It's your call."

"Actually it's yours, Jacques. You're the one who's going to lose his head if this goes off the rails."

Ménard placed the Leonardo in Gabriel's solander case and closed the lid. *"Au revoir, mon ami."*

Gabriel carried the world's most expensive painting through the terminal to ground transportation, where an unmarked Renault sedan idled curbside in the brilliant Provençal sunlight. Inside were three Police Nationale officers in plainclothes. He slid into the back seat, and the Renault rolled forward at once. Five minutes later they were speeding eastward on the A8 Autoroute toward the Italian border. Gabriel pressed the case against his thighs to dampen the vibration. One last journey, he thought. Then she would be home.

Ingrid was tidying up the galley when Jacques Ménard came up the airstair with the art transport case. He moved past her without a word or glance and placed it with exaggerated care on the table in the cabin. Franco Tedeschi nodded toward Peter van de Velde, who popped the latches and lifted the lid. His examination was painstaking and included a check of the supporting panel.

"What exactly are you looking for?" asked Ménard.

"Damage."

"You won't find any. Here in France we know how to handle paintings."

"But this is no ordinary painting."

"I must say, it was an honor to spend a moment or two alone with it. Imagine, a newly discovered Leonardo. As a Frenchman, I only wish you had sold it to the Musée du Louvre."

Franco Tedeschi smiled coldly. "The Louvre couldn't afford it."

"A sad state of affairs, if you ask me," said Ménard, and walked off the aircraft.

Peter van de Velde was still staring at the painting.

"Are you sure there's no damage?" asked Tedeschi.

"None at all." Van de Velde closed the transport case. "Shall we?"

Tedeschi looked at Ingrid. "Yes, I think we shall."

38

Antibes

The formalities complete, Ingrid removed her overcoat and handbag from the forward storage closet and headed down the airstair. Two S-Class Mercedes sedans waited on the tarmac, along with a courtesy van for the crew. For some reason, Ingrid's six passengers seemed in no hurry to leave the aircraft, so she stood outside in the cold blustery air and made small talk with the two French policemen. She was looking forward to a couple hours of down time in the crew room at Signature Flight Support. Bleary-eyed, she resolved to never again think an unkind thought about anyone who tended to the needs of the flying public. It was, she thought, a dreadfully difficult way to earn a living.

Another minute went by before the first two security men clambered down the airstair with the hypervigilance of commandos preparing to make a dynamic entry into a den of terrorists. Peter van de Velde, art transport case in hand, was next, followed by the other two security men. Van de Velde ducked into the back seat of the first Mercedes as though he were evading enemy gunfire, and the security men set a four-cornered defensive perimeter. The French border policemen rolled their eyes. It was all faintly ridiculous.

Franco Tedeschi, a phone to his ear, appeared last. His descent down the airstair was unhurried. When he reached the tarmac, he headed not for the Mercedes but for Ingrid.

He killed the phone call and said, "This is your lucky day, Rikke."

"Why is that, Mr. Tedeschi?"

"Because you are about to witness a historic event." The Italian banker took her by the arm. "Right this way, please. We mustn't keep our buyer waiting."

Before Ingrid could object, he was ushering her across the tarmac toward the first Mercedes. She joined Peter van de Velde in the back seat, and Tedeschi squeezed into the space next to her. The car sank as the larger of the two Italian security guards, a behemoth with a shaved head and a tattoo on the back of his thick neck, wedged himself into the passenger seat. The other three security men hurled themselves into the second Mercedes. Then the two cars shot forward in unison and raced past a line of parked private aircraft.

Franco Tedeschi, CFO of Camorra Inc., calmly lit a cigarette. "Why did that French policeman photograph my Leonardo, Rikke? Why today of all days?"

"How should I know?" replied Ingrid.

"I was wondering the same thing."

Gabriel and his three-officer escort had put ten kilometers behind them by the time his phone rang. It was Jacques Ménard calling to say that all had not gone according to plan at the airport.

"Where is she?"

"On her way to Antibes."

Gabriel killed the call and ordered the driver to reverse course.

Then he looked at the officer seated next to him and asked if he and his colleagues were carrying firearms.

"*Oui*, Monsieur Allon. Big ones."

———————

Your passport, please," said Franco Tedeschi.

"Why do you want to see my passport?"

"Don't make me ask again."

Ingrid unzipped her handbag.

"Prada," observed Tedeschi.

"It's fake."

Which wasn't the case. Ingrid had acquired the bag free of charge during a visit to Courchevel. Her passport had been provided to her by the director of the Danish intelligence service. Tedeschi opened it to the first page.

"Rikke Jorgensen?"

"That's me," said Ingrid.

"Do you happen to remember your date of birth?"

"You can't be serious."

"Humor me."

Ingrid sighed and recited the birth date listed in the passport.

"Where were you born, Rikke Jorgensen?"

"A little town west of Copenhagen."

"What's it called, this town?"

"It's quite unpronounceable."

"Are you married?"

"Happily."

"Children?"

"A boy and a girl. They're five and three, in case you were wondering."

"And what does Mr. Jorgensen do?"

"His last name is Nielsen, and he works on a drilling platform in the North Sea."

"Fossil fuels are bad for the planet."

"Rubbish."

"You're not worried about global warming?"

"I support it, if you must know. It's very cold in Denmark." Ingrid plucked the passport from Tedeschi's grasp. "Where are you taking me?"

"To the home of our buyer. He lives not far from here in Antibes."

"Lucky him."

"You've been?"

"My husband and I went on holiday in Cannes recently."

"It's changed, Cannes. And not for the better."

"I'll have to take your word for it," remarked Ingrid, and returned the passport to her handbag.

"It's real, by the way," said Franco Tedeschi.

"The passport? Of course it's real."

Tedeschi gazed out his window. "I was referring to your Prada handbag, Rikke Jorgensen."

———

The villa stood on the highest point of the cape, shielded from view by towering hedgerows and protected by security measures worthy of the Palais de l'Élysée. There were twelve bedrooms, sixteen bathrooms, eight assorted drawing rooms and parlors, two professional kitchens, a library and adjoining office suite, a wine cellar, a cinema, a discotheque, a game room, a hotel-sized spa and fitness center, a Turkish bath and sauna, indoor and outdoor swimming pools, a red clay tennis court, a caretaker's villa, a ten-car garage, and a man-made lake patrolled by a flotilla of snow-white mute swans. Upon its many walls hung a portion of the owner's collection of fine art. Some of his best pictures, however, adorned his mansion in Highgate, which had been seized, along with its contents, by the British government. He had more than a hundred paintings stashed in the Geneva Freeport and a dozen more hidden aboard *Anastasia*, his eighty-five-meter superyacht. At present the vessel was moored in Golfe-Juan, which he could see from the window of his private study on the second floor.

It was never the life Alexander Prokhorov could have imagined for himself when he was a boy in the Soviet Union, but he had come to believe it was the life he deserved. He had worked harder and been more resourceful, he assured himself, had seen opportunity where others saw only collapse and ruin. And he had become rich as a tsar in the process, a billionaire many times over. Had he cut corners and broken laws? Yes, of course. He had also resorted to violence on occasion. But so had many other men like him, men who had dared to stake their claim in the Wild East. He had nothing but contempt for those who were too stupid or lazy to make their mark in the brave new world of Russia's gangster capitalism—or in the supposedly rules-based economies in the West, for that matter. There were winners and losers in life, and Alexander Prokhorov was a winner. The needs of the homeless and the hungry, the disabled and the mentally ill, were of no concern to him. His own bottomless needs were all that mattered.

What Alexander Prokhorov craved most was respect. He wanted to be known not as a man who had made his fortune manufacturing industrial pipe but as a modern-day Medici. It was the reason he had invested more than a billion dollars in paintings—because nothing conferred a patina of elegance and sophistication faster than fine art, even upon those who possessed neither. Once word leaked that he was the owner of a newly discovered portrait by the greatest artist who ever lived, the rich and the famous would be beating down his door to have a look at it. All his many sins would soon be forgotten, absolved by the *sfumato* brushwork of a long-dead painter from the tiny Tuscan hamlet of Vinci.

But elegance and sophistication would not come cheap. For Alexander Prokhorov the price was $500 million. It was far more than he had wanted to spend for the painting, but the price had soared during the final days of the frenzied secret auction. Prokhorov's man at Société Générale was awaiting his order to initiate the wire transfer. With the press of a button, the money would flow to SBL PrivatBank, and the Leonardo would be his. Pending the results of one final examination, of course. The viewing would take place downstairs in the Gatsbyesque library. Stéphane Tremblay was waiting there now, magnifying glass and ultraviolet torch at the ready.

Prokhorov, for his part, was enjoying a few moments alone upstairs in his private study. He looked down at the single sheet of stationery—from Smythson of Bond Street—lying on the desk. On it, he had written out the number, with all its many zeros. It was, by any reckoning, an extraordinary amount of money. Still, it represented only a fraction of his immense personal wealth. Yes, he had lost the house in Highgate, and there were two hundred million or so at Barclays and HSBC that he would never see again. But when all was said and done, he had emerged from his scrape with the British in remarkably good shape. By his own calculation he was closing in on a net worth of $30 billion. For a man like Alexander Prokhorov, $500 million was pocket change.

The phone on his desk purred softly. It was the security guard at the front gate, informing him that his guests had arrived. He went to the window and glimpsed a pair of matching S-Class Mercedes sedans making their way up the long drive. They rolled to a stop in the circular forecourt and six men emerged, one of whom was in possession of the painting that soon would be Prokhorov's.

Only four of the men headed toward the entrance of the villa. The remaining two—security guards, presumably—lowered themselves into the back seat of the first car and closed the doors. Alexander Prokhorov cast a final glance at the number written on the piece of stationery lying on his desk, then headed downstairs to meet his destiny. It was, he assured himself, exactly what he deserved.

39

Antibes–Lugano

On the western side of Cap d'Antibes was a marina with a boat dealership and a dive shop and a small café. Gabriel and his three Police Nationale chaperones sat in the unmarked Renault in the car park. Gabriel's notebook computer rested atop the museum case, connected to the Internet via his mobile hot spot. With the help of the hacking malware Proteus, he was eavesdropping on an art transaction taking place in a palatial villa located approximately one hundred and fifty meters to the east. For the past fifteen minutes, four men had been engaged in a spirited discussion—a Dutch art dealer, a French art consultant, the CFO of Camorra Inc., and a Kremlin-connected Russian oligarch. There was nothing to indicate that Ingrid was in the room. Given her recent exploits in Moscow, it was probably for the best.

"Where do you suppose she is?" asked the officer sitting at his side.

"It is my profound hope that she's outside in the car with Rocco and Enzo. It is also my profound hope that Alexander Prokhorov and his art adviser don't realize that they're about to spend five hundred million dollars for an original Gabriel Allon. Otherwise things will get rather ugly."

"The heist of the century," remarked the officer, whose name was Jean-Luc.

"Not yet, it isn't."

"It sounds to me as though you've got him."

"In that case, why hasn't he signed the sales agreement?"

"Give him a few minutes, Monsieur Allon. Five hundred million is a great deal of money."

"Once upon a time it was. But not anymore."

Just then the conversation in the villa fell silent. For several minutes not one of the four men present spoke a single word.

"It's over," said Gabriel darkly.

"Almost," agreed the French policeman.

"I'm done for."

"You're just fine. And so is your friend Ingrid."

Two more minutes went by. Not a sound.

"Come on, Proko," pleaded Gabriel. "What are you waiting for?"

Ingrid was at that moment thinking the same thing, though unlike Gabriel, she had no inkling as to what was taking place inside the opulent villa. The weight of her two captors was bearing down on her. She made no attempt to address them, for she did not speak their language and they did not speak hers. Besides, they did not strike her as brilliant conversationalists. The French limousine driver seemed like a reasonable fellow, but sensing something was amiss, he had left his post to have a cigarette. Ingrid, who was only an occasional smoker, was sorely in need of one herself.

According to her wristwatch, it was seven minutes past three o'clock when Franco Tedeschi and Peter van de Velde finally emerged from the villa. They wore blank expressions on their faces. Van de Velde was carrying the art transport case with his usual care. The two security men were as vigilant as ever.

Ingrid's two captors climbed out of the Mercedes, and Tedeschi and Van de Velde took their places. Neither man spoke as the car rolled up the drive with the slowness of a hearse. But a moment after they passed through the security gate, Van de Velde let out a mighty shout and slapped his palms against the transport case.

"Don't worry, Rikke," said Franco Tedeschi. "There's nothing in it."

"I'm relieved."

"So am I. There was a slight delay with the wire transfer, but otherwise the transaction went off without a hitch." He placed a hand on her arm. "I hope you can forgive my behavior earlier."

"As far I'm concerned, it never happened."

"And you won't mention it to Herr Vogel?"

Ingrid smiled. "Why on earth would I do a thing like that?"

———

There was an excellent wine shop in the *centre ville* of Antibes near the old Marché Provençal. Tedeschi grabbed two bottles of chilled champagne, which he and Van de Velde drank during the short drive back to the airport. They polished off two more before the plane left the ground. Tedeschi insisted that Ingrid have a glass too, but she declined, citing the unbendable rules of Executive Jet Services regarding the consumption of wine and spirits with passengers. In truth, she could have used a drink, but the effervescence in champagne sent the alcohol straight to her brain, and she required a clear head to carry out her remaining duties.

The caterers had provisioned the plane with a full dinner service—

chicken cordon bleu or roasted salmon with a savory lemon cream sauce—but Tedeschi and party selected the liquid option instead, accompanied by oven-warmed nuts and other high-sodium fare. Ingrid dispensed with the collection of bottles and glasses during the steep final approach to Lugano, for she was quite certain her passengers would have refused to surrender them. Upon arrival they tripped happily down the airstair and into their waiting limousines with none of the tactical flare of their prior movements. Peter van de Velde, feeling no pain, left the empty transport case behind in the cabin.

The driving time between Lugano Airport and the Piazza della Riforma was only twenty minutes or so. Ingrid used two of those minutes to quickly put the cabin in some semblance of order. Then she fetched her carry-on bag from the cargo hold and, after bidding the flight crew a good evening, wheeled it across the tarmac toward the Gulfstream G550 owned by the Swiss financier and philanthropist Martin Landesmann. He was relaxing in the cabin, a glass of champagne at his elbow, as Ingrid came up the airstair. Christopher Keller was holding a tumbler of whisky in his sledgehammer hand. His beautiful art dealer wife was mixing a martini in the galley.

"How was your day?" she asked in that peculiar throaty voice of hers.

"A bit more exciting than planned."

"So we were told." Sarah checked the time. "By my calculation, we have approximately fifteen minutes before Franco Tedeschi arrives at his bank. Therefore, we should get on with it."

Ingrid unzipped her carry-on and removed her laptop.

"Password?" she asked Martin.

"One World."

"The name of your bloody foundation?"

"A single word with no caps," he replied sheepishly.

Ingrid entered the password and connected her computer to the Gulfstream's Wi-Fi system. After logging into SBL PrivatBank's network, she looked at Christopher and said, "Account and routing numbers, please."

He handed her a slip of paper. Ninety seconds was all it took to initiate the transfer. "Ring your man at Oschadbank, Mr. Keller. The money is on its way."

Christopher routed the call through SIS headquarters in London. It took three minutes for the president of Oschadbank to come on the line. Russian missiles, he explained, were once again falling on Kyiv.

"Has the money arrived?" asked Christopher.

"Nothing yet."

Two more minutes went by.

"Well?" asked Christopher.

"Still nothing, I'm afraid."

Christopher looked at Ingrid. "Perhaps you should send it again."

"Patience, Mr. Keller."

Another minute passed, then the Ukrainian bank executive announced, "We have the money. On behalf of the Ukrainian people, I thank you for your generous contribution to our war effort."

"Glad to be of assistance. Please spend it wisely." Christopher killed the call and raised his glass toward Ingrid. "It was a pleasure working with you again."

"The pleasure was all mine." She looked at Martin and said, "I could use a lift back to Denmark, if you wouldn't mind."

"How about Saint-Barthélemy instead? I've rented an enormous villa in Pointe Milou for the holidays."

"It sounds lovely. But I don't have a stitch of clothing."

"All the better," said Martin with a smile.

"What about Mrs. Landesmann?"

"Monique flew to the Caribbean this morning on my Boeing Business Jet."

Ingrid was apoplectic. "Separate transatlantic flights?"

Martin sipped his champagne. "We all have to make sacrifices, Ms. Johansen."

PART THREE

Sprezzatura

40

Ventimiglia

The French police officers deposited Gabriel on the other side of the border in the faded Ligurian resort town of Ventimiglia. Luca Rossetti, in gabardine trousers and a woolen pullover, was drinking coffee at a little bar along the waterfront. Gabriel sat down at Rossetti's table and placed the museum case upright on the floor. The Carabinieri officer ignored it.

"How was the drive?" he asked.

"Longer than expected."

"Those idiot French cops couldn't find Italy?"

"Franco Tedeschi moved the goalposts."

"But the sale went smoothly?"

Gabriel nodded. "And the money is now in the hands of the Ukrainian government."

"There's going to be hell to pay."

"And then some," added Gabriel.

Rossetti signaled the barman and ordered two coffees.

"Shouldn't we be leaving, Luca?"

"What's the rush?"

Gabriel lowered his eyes toward the museum case.

"Don't worry, we're safe here."

"Are you suggesting there are no mafiosi in Liguria?"

"A few, I suppose. But have a look at the other patrons in this establishment."

Gabriel glanced around the interior of the little café. Four other tables were occupied, all by plainclothes Carabinieri officers. "What about the heartthrob behind the bar?"

"His name is Angelo. He's a great kid. Everybody loves him."

"Where have I heard that before?"

Angelo the beloved barman placed two coffees on their table and withdrew. Rossetti added sugar to his and stirred it slowly. He seemed in no hurry to be on his way.

"We've been digging through those documents that your girlfriend stole from SBL PrivatBank."

"She's not my girlfriend, Luca. But please continue."

"Two names appear over and over again. Interestingly enough, these names appear frequently in our files as well, not to mention the files of our colleagues at the Guardia di Finanza."

"And they are?"

"Nico Ambrosi and Piedmont Global Capital."

"The Milan firm that was part of the London real estate deal?"

Rossetti nodded. "Ambrosi and his firm are one of SBL's biggest clients. He feeds hundreds of millions into the bank's investment funds each year and borrows hundreds of millions to finance real estate and development deals all over Europe."

"What's wrong with that?"

"Nothing. Except that everyone seems to think Nico's money is dirty."

"How dirty?"

"Camorra dirty," replied Rossetti. "And he's working hand-in-glove with his friend Franco Tedeschi to launder and invest the Camorra's money."

"Why is he still in business?"

"Regrettably the Guardia di Finanza has never been able to make a case against him. Nico has friends in high places, including at the Vatican. Or so it is said."

"By whom?"

Rossetti shrugged his shoulders but said nothing.

"What aren't you telling me, Luca?"

"That your friend Martin Landesmann knows how to spot a bad deal on a balance sheet. After reviewing all of the underlying documents, General Ferrari and I agree that there was something wrong with the purchase of that office building in London. And with SBL's decision to forgive the loan as well," added Rossetti. "We are of the opinion that the transaction warrants further investigation, as are our associates at the Guardia."

"I wish you and your associates well, Luca. But my work here is done."

"Almost."

Rossetti left a banknote on the table and they went into the street, followed closely by the other four officers. From somewhere over the Ligurian came the faint beating of a helicopter rotor. The lights appeared a moment later.

"Your chariot has arrived," said Rossetti.

"I hope the pilot knows what he's doing."

"Apparently this is his first flight."

"Just my luck."

The helicopter alighted on Ventimiglia's beachfront esplanade. Gabriel waited until the rotor had slowed nearly to a stop before carrying his fragile cargo aboard. He strapped himself into a seat and looked at the youthful pilot.

"My friend tells me this is your first flight."

"Second, actually," the pilot replied with a crooked smile.

"How did the first one go?"

"I had to ditch it in the Ligurian. I was lucky to survive."

"That's not funny."

"You're telling me."

———————

As they were approaching the northern tip of the island of Corsica, the pilot admitted that he had logged several thousand hours of flying time for the Carabinieri with no incidents other than a single hard landing in the Dolomites during a blizzard. Gabriel nevertheless breathed a small sigh of relief when he spotted the floodlit dome of St. Peter's rising over the seven hills of Rome. The Vatican's helipad was located at the eastern tip of the city-state. From there it was a walk of five minutes through the Vatican Gardens to the small courtyard at the foot of a rather ordinary-looking structure with walls the color of dun.

Gabriel slipped through the unlocked door and climbed the steps to the Sala Regia. Father Mark Keegan, a phone to his ear, nodded toward the entrance of the Sistine Chapel. Inside, His Holiness Luigi Donati, Bishop of Rome, Pontifex Maximus, successor to the Apostle Peter, knelt on a simple wooden prie-dieu before Michelangelo's *Last Judgment*. Gabriel passed through the opening in the *transenna*, the marble screen that divided the chapel in two, and approached his old friend soundlessly from behind.

"Don't skulk, Gabriel." Donati peered at him over one shoulder. "It makes me nervous when you skulk."

"I didn't want to disturb you."

"I don't require complete silence to pray. I'm rather good at it after all these years."

Gabriel went to Donati's side. "Come here often?"

"Every chance I get. It's my personal chapel, you know." Donati lifted his gaze toward the *Last Judgment*, with its swirling mass of souls rising and falling to their eternal fates. "Have you an opinion about it?"

"As a depiction of the end of days?"

"As a work of art," answered Donati.

"It is not without its shortcomings."

"The Council of Trent thought the nudity blasphemous."

"But your predecessor Pius the Sixth had the good sense to wait until Michelangelo died before adding fig leaves and garments to some of the figures."

"One of history's great artistic crimes. Fortunately it was rectified during the last restoration." Donati rose from the prie-dieu and gazed down the length of the empty chapel. "Do you remember the last time we were here together? I begged you to take me away before the cardinal-electors could place the awful burden of the papacy on my shoulders. And you, as I recall, refused."

"You're mistaken, Holiness."

"I'm infallible."

"Only when you speak ex cathedra. I, however, am never wrong."

Donati looked at the museum case hanging from Gabriel's right hand. "And what do you have there?"

"Something that belongs to you."

"Is it a painting, by any chance?"

"A rather good one."

"I'll be the judge of that."

Gabriel removed the Leonardo from the case and balanced the panel atop the armrest of the prie-dieu. Donati stared at the girl from Milan as though he had been struck mute.

"Are you certain it's a Leonardo?" he asked at last.

"He trained and employed a large number of very talented studio assistants, all of whom could mimic his style. It's possible that someone like Giovanni Boltraffio or Bernardino Luini made it. But I think it's a Leonardo, and I'm not alone."

"What now?"

"We remove all the many layers of overpaint and strip it down to the original. Then we invite the greatest Leonardo scholars in the world to examine it. I'm confident they will reach a consensus on the attribution."

"And then?"

"The painting will have to be restored."

"Is there any chance I could convince you to handle it?"

"So much for your infallibility, Holiness." Gabriel smiled. "It would be the honor of a lifetime to restore the painting. In fact, I've already made a perfect copy of it."

"Really? Where is it now?"

"It was sold to a Russian oligarch this afternoon for a half billion dollars."

"Sold by whom?" asked Donati.

"A Swiss bank controlled by the Camorra."

"But why did the bank sell your copy to the Russian?"

"They were under the impression it was the real Leonardo."

"You somehow managed to switch the paintings?"

Gabriel smiled but said nothing.

"I'm afraid to ask how the Camorra-controlled bank ended up with the Leonardo in the first place."

"It appears as though it was used to pay off a loan for a piece of commercial real estate in London."

Donati's eyes narrowed. "And the address of this property?"

"New Bond Street. The borrower was something called the May-fair Group. We haven't been able to determine who or what it is."

"You should have come to me, *mio amico*." Donati turned to face the *Last Judgment*. "I could have told you everything you needed to know."

41

Casa Santa Marta

The guests milling about the lobby of the Casa Santa Marta caught an unexpected glimpse of the Vicar of Christ five minutes later as he hastened into a waiting elevator, accompanied by his private secretary and a layman carrying a flat rectangular case. Upstairs, the pontiff and his party headed straight for Room 201 and closed the door behind them.

"All of it," demanded Donati.

"The less you know, the better, Luigi."

"You're beginning to sound like Father Keegan."

"Laws were broken," explained Gabriel. "Many laws."

"I would have expected nothing less. Now tell me the name of the bank."

"SBL PrivatBank."

"It's headquartered in Lugano, if I'm not mistaken."

"You're not. It got into trouble a few years ago when it tried to compete with the big boys. The Camorra saved SBL from collapse with an infusion of capital and took control of it."

"The year, please?"

"Does it matter?"

"Humor me."

"Approximately eight years ago."

Donati appeared to file the date away in his memory for later reference. "But how did you learn about the loan for the office building in New Bond Street?"

"For the record, I never referred to the property as an office building. I described it as an expensive piece of commercial real estate. You're the one who referred to it as an office building."

"They're rather the same thing. But please answer the question."

"An associate of mine hacked into the bank and stole its most sensitive files."

"Naughty boy," said Donati.

"Naughty girl, actually."

"And the five hundred million dollars the Russian oligarch paid for the fake painting?"

"My associate transferred the money to Ukraine."

"Does the Camorra know their money is missing?"

"I can't imagine they don't," replied Gabriel. "But you were about to tell me everything I needed to know about the Mayfair Group."

"It's a British-registered holding company that was created some time ago to manage the acquisition of several pieces of London real estate, including the building in New Bond Street."

"Created by whom?"

"A pair of London lawyers, both of whom happen to be devout Roman Catholics."

"And the beneficial owner of the British-registered holding company?"

"The short answer? Vatican Incorporated."

"What would be the long answer?"

"The building is owned by an investment fund controlled by the Secretariat of State. The purpose of this fund is to generate the revenue needed to run the Roman Curia."

"And the person in charge of the fund?"

"That would be the Substitute for General Affairs." Donati lowered his voice. "Cardinal Matteo Bertoli."

———————

The original source of the money, Donati continued, was the Lateran Treaty of 1929, which established Vatican City as an independent sovereign state controlled by the Holy See. As part of the treaty, the Italian government of Prime Minister Benito Mussolini agreed to compensate the Church for the loss of its feudal possessions known as the Papal States. The Vatican used a portion of the settlement to conduct a renovation of the city-state itself that included the construction of the walls and an expansion of the museums. The remaining funds it invested, leaving the Holy See with controlling stakes in several of Italy's largest banks and industrial enterprises.

"In retrospect," said Donati, "the original settlement with Mussolini was a terrible deal. The Church received the equivalent of only ninety-two million dollars for sixteen thousand square miles of land that included much of central Italy. But the proceeds from that original sum of money now account for nearly the entirety of the Church's wealth."

"How much is there?" asked Gabriel.

"We're getting into sensitive territory."

"We crossed that border a long time ago."

Donati lit a cigarette before answering. "One reads numbers in the less reputable press that bear no resemblance to the truth. Oh, I suppose we could dispose of all of our churches, convents, monasteries, schools, and hospitals, and it might add up to two or three hundred billion dollars. But we can't exactly sell St. Patrick's Cathedral to a property developer, now can we?"

"You're avoiding my question."

"Let's call it twenty billion, give or take. Most of the money is controlled by the Vatican Bank and something called the Administration of the Patrimony of the Apostolic See."

"How much does Cardinal Bertoli control?"

"Approximately three billion dollars."

"That's more than most professional fund managers handle."

"Cardinal Bertoli has an experienced outside adviser looking over his shoulder, a man named—"

"Nico Ambrosi."

Donati frowned. "How did you know that?"

"Ambrosi was the middleman in the purchase of the building in New Bond Street. My friends in the Carabinieri say his primary client is the Camorra."

"Nico Ambrosi is a practicing Catholic who has proven to be an effective steward of our money."

"How do you explain the New Bond Street deal?"

"That building is one of our most profitable ventures."

"In that case, why did Vatican Incorporated default on the loan?"

"It didn't. In fact, our most recent quarterly report indicates the property is generating higher-than-expected revenue."

"And who prepared the quarterly report?"

"Cardinal Bertoli, of course."

Gabriel allowed a silence to settle over the room.

"Careful," said Donati at last. "You're leveling a very serious accusation against a high-ranking prelate. All without a shred of proof."

"I am doing no such thing. I would, however, like to see all the quarterly reports prepared by Cardinal Bertoli since his elevation to the post of *sostituto*."

"I'm sure you would," said Donati.

"I'll also need to have a look at the cardinal's account at the Vatican Bank."

"Good luck with that."

"Someone is lying, Luigi. And I have a feeling I know who it is. Let me see the quarterly reports. I'm sure I'll be proven right."

"You're infallible, are you?"

"Only in matters involving my friend the supreme pontiff."

Donati looked at Father Keegan. "Get him everything he needs."

But where to stash the Leonardo? That was the question that Gabriel and the Holy Father debated while Father Keegan went in search of the documents. His Holiness was of the opinion that the painting should be returned from whence it came—namely, the underground storerooms of the Vatican Museums. Gabriel respectfully disagreed. There was little chance, he argued, that the painting's recovery would remain a secret for long if it were returned to the museum. Furthermore, there was *every* chance that the news might reach the ears of the very men who had stolen the painting in the first place, including Cardinal Bertoli.

It was at this point that His Holiness reminded Gabriel that Cardinal Bertoli, a prelate with a spotless record, was deserving of a presumption of innocence. His Holiness conceded, however, that present circumstances warranted an unusually high degree of secrecy, perhaps even a touch of deception. That was because Cardinal Bertoli was responsible for the day-to-day operations of the Curia and the city-state and had the place wired to the hilt.

"In fact, he's the only member of the Roman Curia who can see me without an appointment."

"Is there nowhere in the Vatican he can't set foot?"

His Holiness answered by escorting Gabriel into the papal bedroom and opening the doors of the ornate wooden wardrobe. Which was where, at 9:20 p.m., they hid the painting for which a Russian oligarch had just paid a half billion dollars. It was, thought Gabriel, a fitting end to a most remarkable day.

Father Keegan appeared a few minutes later with a stack of documents bound by a metal clasp—a decade's worth of quarterly reports from the Curial investment fund. Downstairs, he escorted Gabriel to the Arch of Bells, where two Swiss Guards stood watch in their blue night uniforms.

"I don't need to remind you that these documents—"

"No, Father Keegan. You don't."

"Where are you planning to review them?"

"The Hassler, if they'll have me."

"Do you have any dinner plans?"

"Room service."

"That little place off the Via Veneto is open quite late."

"Is it?"

Father Keegan turned without another word and headed back to the Casa Santa Marta. Sneaky little Jesuit, thought Gabriel, and went in search of a taxi.

42

Villa Marchese

I was hoping you would bring the Leonardo," said Veronica Marchese. "But I must admit, these documents are far more interesting. All the dirty laundry of Vatican Incorporated, right at our fingertips."

"But one wonders why the Holy Father's private secretary wanted you to see them."

"The private secretary was only the messenger, I can assure you. It was the Holy Father himself who wanted me to see the quarterly reports."

"The question still stands."

"Why, you mean?" The doorbell tolled before Veronica could answer. "Our dinner has arrived. Will you excuse me?"

Gabriel listened to the clatter of Veronica's pumps as she made the long walk from the palazzo's kitchen to its front entrance. She returned a moment later with several bags bearing the name of a seafood restaurant on the Via Sicilia.

"Is someone else joining us?" asked Gabriel.

"I didn't know what you wanted, so I ordered a little of everything. There's a bottle of Alteni di Brassica sauvignon blanc in the fridge. It should pair nicely with the seafood."

"In my experience, Alteni di Brassica pairs nicely with just about anything." Gabriel pulled the wine from the refrigerator and removed the cork. He poured two glasses and handed one to Veronica. "You were saying?"

"Why would Luigi want me to see the documents?" Veronica removed the containers of food and began arranging them on the countertop. "As you might remember, he often turned to me for advice on temporal matters while he was serving as private secretary to Pope Lucchesi. You know what it's like inside the Curia, Gabriel. The Apostolic Palace is a gilded cage filled with ruthless, sexually repressed men who know little of the world beyond the walls. I was the only person Luigi could trust. Other than you, of course."

"But you were much better connected than I was."

"At least here in Rome." Veronica opened a cabinet and took down two plates. "And despite the fact that I am an archaeologist by training, I know a thing or two about the business world and investing. But the princes of the Church know nothing of high finance. Therefore, they have no choice but to rely on the advice of experts, the so-called men of trust. Men like my late husband, Carlo. And Nico Ambrosi, of course."

"General Ferrari thinks he's connected to the Camorra."

"He's not alone. Everyone in Italian business circles knows that Nico is corrupt. And yet this is the person Cardinal Bertoli turned to for advice on how to invest the Curia's money."

"I assume you raised it with Luigi."

"On numerous occasions. And he assured me that the Church's finances were in good hands. Evidently the fund was experiencing spectacular growth, something on the order of fifteen percent annually with no losses. I told Luigi that it was too good to be true. But I was most concerned about the massive investments in high-end real estate, especially the London deal."

"Because?"

"The amount of debt Bertoli was taking on. Four hundred million for the New Bond Street building alone. And he borrowed huge sums of money to purchase other properties as well, all on the advice of Nico Ambrosi. You can be sure that Nico and his partner Franco Tedeschi earned enormous fees for each loan."

They filled their plates with food and settled atop stools at the end of the counter.

"Please forgive the informality," said Veronica. "But it was all very last-minute."

"It's perfect. I only wish Luigi could join us."

"I have to admit, I'm terribly envious that you were allowed to have dinner alone with him."

"We were hardly alone."

"How did he look in civilian clothes?"

"More handsome than ever."

"I was afraid you were going to say that. But tell me something, Gabriel. Do you think he's happy?"

"He seemed to enjoy himself for a few minutes. But I have a feeling he's incredibly lonely."

"Of course he is. I can see it every time he steps in front of the television cameras. Behind that benevolent pastoral smile that he's perfected, His Holiness is dying of loneliness."

"He doesn't like it when I call him that. He insists that I refer to him as Luigi."

"That's because he's desperately clinging to the man he was before the conclave. But I'm afraid that person is receding by the day. Soon no one will remember his real name."

"His papal name does have a certain ring to it, don't you think?"

"I'll never forget that night in St. Peter's Square when I heard it for the first time. Still, I was hoping for something with a bit more flair. Pope Alessandro would have been nice. Or perhaps Pope Gregorio. Luigi always struck me as a Gregorio."

"What about Julius?" asked Gabriel.

"Or Marcellus," suggested Veronica.

"There's never been a Pope Gabriel, has there?"

"Or a Pope Veronica. And you can be certain there never will be."

"His Holiness informed me that it's doctrinally off the table."

"The ordination of women?" Veronica turned her wineglass slowly on the countertop. "I have it on the highest authority that His Holiness personally believes that women should be allowed to serve as priests."

"It will destroy the Church."

"If anyone is going to destroy the Church, it's Cardinal Bertoli." She reached for the stack of quarterly reports. "Shall we make this a working dinner?"

"By all means."

She handed Gabriel the most recent four years' worth of reports and kept the rest for herself. Twenty minutes of silence ensued, broken only by the rustle of paper.

"Do you see what I see?" asked Veronica at last.

"I believe I do."

"Is there any chance we can get a look at Cardinal Bertoli's Vatican Bank account?"

"Yes," replied Gabriel. "I believe there is."

———————

Previous occupants of the throne of St. Peter celebrated mass each morning in the private chapel of the *appartamento pontificio*. His

Holiness Pope Donati, however, chose to attend mass in the chapel at the Casa Santa Marta instead. Sometimes he served as the celebrant, but usually he could be found sitting in the last row, as though he were an ordinary parishioner with a preference for white clothing. On the morning after he secretly took possession of a lost painting by Leonardo da Vinci, he was accompanied by several Roman sex workers whom the Church had set on the path to redemption. At the conclusion of the service, the women joined His Holiness for breakfast in the Casa's dining room, much to the dismay of a visiting delegation of American priests from the traditionalist order Opus Dei.

The pope's private secretary, Father Mark Keegan, was not at his master's side that morning, which gave rise to speculation in certain quarters of the Curia that he did not approve. In truth, he had other matters to attend to, including the collection of certain confidential documents from the Vatican Bank. The task complete, he headed to Caffè Greco, the fabled coffeehouse on the Via dei Condotti. There, in a quiet back room, he placed the documents in the hands of one of the Holy Father's closest friends and confidants.

Gabriel started with Cardinal Bertoli's most recent Vatican Bank statement. "It seems I'm in the wrong line of work."

"Yes," said Father Keegan vaguely.

"How much do Curial cardinals make?"

The priest pointed out the most recent automatic deposit of Cardinal Bertoli's salary. "Do the math."

"It's not enough to explain a balance like that."

"His Eminence has a number of wealthy benefactors who have supported him throughout his career. He caused a bit of a scandal not long ago when he undertook a major renovation of his apartment in the Palazzo San Carlo. It's several times larger than the Holy Father's suite in the Casa Santa Marta and includes a large rooftop terrace with a magnificent view of Rome. The striking contrast in their living conditions has been a source of some controversy." Father Keegan handed over another Vatican Bank statement. "The difference in the size of their accounts is even more glaring."

"Forty-two thousand euros? After all these years?"

"He's given away most of his money."

"To whom?"

"Anyone who needed it more than he did."

"Perhaps you should take away his ATM card."

"He doesn't have one. But it wouldn't stop him. The Holy Father has said on numerous occasions that he wants the Church to be poor. And he insists on leading by example."

"If Veronica and I are right, the Holy Father might soon get his wish."

"How bad?"

"Pompeii."

"Perhaps you could be a little more specific."

"The numbers Cardinal Bertoli used for his quarterly statements aren't real. And even if they were, they don't add up."

Father Keegan sipped his cappuccino. "Go on."

"Bertoli has placed nearly the entirety of the Curia's funds in the hands of a single adviser with a rather dubious reputation. And that adviser has in turn invested most of that money in financial instruments and funds managed by a Swiss bank controlled by the Camorra. According to the cardinal's quarterly statements, those investments have almost doubled in value during his tenure. But it's simply not the case."

"How can you be sure?"

"I've seen the bank's internal numbers. Furthermore, Cardinal Bertoli and his adviser have borrowed more than a billion dollars from the same bank to make a number of risky real estate invest-ments. The New Bond Street property was the first to go under. But I suspect it won't be the last."

"And your theory is that Cardinal Bertoli somehow used the painting to pay off the loan?"

"Precisely."

"But why didn't he simply dip into the Curia's cash reserves?"

"Because it's possible there are no cash reserves."

Father Keegan's face drained of color. "You can't be serious."

"I'm only drawing the logical inference."

"How could such a thing be possible?"

"I believe the word is embezzlement."

"On whose part?"

"Camorra Incorporated. But the fact Cardinal Bertoli participated in a scheme to steal a lost painting by Leonardo would suggest he's been lining his pockets too."

"Allegedly participated," said Father Keegan. "But how did he know about the painting in the first place?"

"I was hoping *you* might be able to tell me."

"He does have a number of very fine paintings in his newly ren-ovated apartment in the Piazza San Carlo. In fact, it's a bit like a private museum."

"Gifts from wealthy benefactors?" asked Gabriel.

"Actually the cardinal borrows them."

"From where?"

"The storerooms of the Vatican Museums."

43

Hotel Hassler

Gabriel left Caffè Greco five minutes after Father Keegan and set off across the Piazza di Spagna. He arrived at the top of the steps to find Luca Rossetti standing outside the church of the Trinità dei Monti. Together they repaired to Gabriel's suite at the Hassler, where General Ferrari, in a dark suit and tie, was leafing through the pages of Cardinal Bertoli's quarterly financial reports.

"Enlightening reading," he remarked without looking up. "I should break into your hotel room more often."

"Those documents are for my eyes only."

"I can imagine why. After all, I read not long ago that the Church was going bankrupt because of declining donations from the faithful and the costly financial settlements over the sexual abuse scandal." Ferrari tapped the page with his ruined right hand. "But it says here that the Vatican has been acquiring expensive commercial real estate all over Europe with the help of its financial adviser, Nico Ambrosi. He does have the Midas touch, doesn't he? My goodness, look at those returns."

"I have reason to believe the numbers aren't real."

"As do the Carabinieri and our associates at the Guardia di Finanza. But these documents all but prove it. They also suggest that Cardinal

Bertoli is engaged in activities that can only be described as embezzlement and fraud."

"How long have you known?"

"About His Eminence? Let's just say Bertoli has been on the radar
of Italian law enforcement for some time now. But because he is a
high-ranking official of a sovereign state, we have been powerless to
pursue him." The general paused, then added, "Until now."

"Which is why Luca was in no hurry to leave that beachfront bar
in Ventimiglia last night. He mentioned Nico Ambrosi's name because he wanted me to do the Carabinieri's bidding behind the walls
of the Vatican."

The general placed the quarterly statements in his attaché case.
"I'll also need the documents that Father Keegan gave you at Caffè
Greco."

"You can't have them."

Ferrari held out his hand, and Gabriel surrendered Cardinal Bertoli's Vatican Bank statements.

"Only six million? I expected more. But then I suppose the cardinal
has a few million stashed at Piedmont Global Capital in Milan." The
statements disappeared into Ferrari's attaché case. Then he looked at
Rossetti and said, "Perhaps you should tell Gabriel about his friend
Franco Tedeschi."

"His plane landed in Naples a couple of hours ago. He was met at
the airport by several known associates of Lorenzo Di Falco, leader
of the Camorra's most powerful clan."

"I wouldn't want to be in Franco's shoes," said Gabriel.

"Neither would I," said General Ferrari. "The Di Falco clan was
behind the attempt on my life when I was commander of the Naples
division. Lorenzo is the sort to kill first and ask questions later, especially when money is involved."

"How long does poor Franco have to live?"

"I suppose that depends on whether he can find the person who transferred five hundred million dollars of the Camorra's money to an account in Kyiv."

"Regrettably it was Franco himself who authorized the transfer."

"A lovely touch on Ingrid's part. But you can be sure that Di Falco isn't going to fall for it. If he feels his empire is threatened in any way, the bullets will fly. Which is why we need to move quickly."

"With what?"

"The destruction of Camorra Incorporated and the arrests of Franco Tedeschi, Nico Ambrosi, and Lorenzo Di Falco on charges of murder, theft, fraud, embezzlement, and money laundering."

"You don't have enough evidence to make arrests."

"Not yet," agreed the general. "But you're going to help me get it."

"How?"

"His Eminence Cardinal Bertoli."

It took the better part of an hour for the hacking malware Proteus to seize control of the cardinal's phone and another thirty minutes to drain the device of emails, text messages, photographs, geolocation data, and telephone metadata. In short order, Gabriel was able to establish that Cardinal Bertoli had spent more than a million euros renovating his apartment in the Palazzo San Carlo, that he was dissatisfied with his present cook, that he suffered from insomnia and migraine headaches, that he maintained a close relationship with his younger sister, that he was a frequent visitor to the storerooms of the Vatican Museums, and that he had more than ten million euros in a brokerage account at Piedmont Global Capital of Milan.

By all appearances he was a dedicated and effective manager of the Roman Curia and the Vatican city-state. Typically his day began at half past four in the morning and did not end until after midnight. The finances of the Holy See were of paramount concern, as evidenced by the frequent emails, text messages, and phone calls he exchanged with his investment adviser, Nico Ambrosi. They met face to face at least once each week, either at the Vatican or in one of Rome's better restaurants. They were circumspect in their electronic communications, but occasionally sensitive documents changed hands. One concerned a multimillion-euro loss on a complex currency play; another, a failed investment in a high-risk global growth fund. His Eminence, however, reported neither loss to the Holy Father in the corresponding quarterly report. The currency play, in Cardinal Bertoli's telling, netted the Holy See a profit of some fourteen percent. The global growth fund, despite all evidence to the contrary, was firing on all cylinders.

The building in London's New Bond Street had been troubled from the start, but the global pandemic had made a bad situation worse. Occupancy plummeted, revenue nosedived, and the debt grew burdensome. Cardinal Bertoli instructed Nico Ambrosi to request a grace period from their lender, SBL PrivatBank. And when the request was denied, the cardinal demanded a bridge loan of $100 million to tide him over. The bank wasn't interested.

Pressure was building elsewhere within the Curia's portfolio as investments failed to deliver and cash on hand dwindled. Millions went up in smoke with the collapse of Archegos Capital Management, and millions more were tied up in other money-losing ventures. SBL PrivatBank demanded additional collateral, but Bertoli had none to offer. A sale of the New Bond Street property was not an option, for it was worth less than half of what the Vatican had originally paid for it. Having no other recourse, Bertoli went hat in hand to wealthy Catholic businessmen in search of a bailout. His pleas fell on deaf ears.

Though his investment portfolio was teetering on the brink of collapse, Cardinal Bertoli, early the previous summer, had undertaken a refreshment of the paintings in his apartment in the Palazzo San Carlo. With the help of the chief conservator of the Vatican Museums, he made four visits to the underground storerooms. After one such visit, the cardinal telephoned an acquaintance who worked for the Uffizi Gallery in Florence. The acquaintance was Giorgio Montefiore, the world's foremost expert on the life and work of Leonardo da Vinci.

———————

Why can't you come to the lab?" asked Antonio Calvesi.

"It's complicated."

"It usually is where you're concerned."

"Be that as it may," said Gabriel, "I require a word with you outside the walls."

"About what?"

"Cardinal Bertoli."

There was silence on the line.

"Are you still there, Antonio?"

"Michelangelo," he said, and killed the connection.

It was the name of a little tourist bar across the street from the entrance of the Pinacoteca, the sort of place where most employees of the Vatican city-state wouldn't be caught dead. Gabriel arrived at three fifteen. Calvesi was drinking coffee at a plastic table outside.

"What about Bertoli?" he asked.

"It has come to my attention that he sometimes borrows paintings from the collection of the Musei Vaticani to adorn the walls of his rather large apartment."

"Sometimes?" Calvesi shook his head. "His Eminence treats the storerooms of the Pinacoteca as though they are his private art gallery."

"You disapprove?"

"Only the Holy Father and the Cardinal Secretary of State outrank Bertoli. Therefore, it doesn't matter whether I approve or disapprove. Bertoli picks out the paintings that catch his eye, and I arrange to have them temporarily transferred to his possession."

"Surely there's some paperwork involved."

Calvesi shrugged. "You know how this place works, Gabriel. Some things around here are handled very informally."

"When did the Madonna and Child by a follower of Raphael catch Bertoli's eye?"

"Is that what this is about?"

"When, Antonio?"

"Not long after Penny began work on it."

"Where was it at the time?"

"In the lab."

"Had she discovered the hidden painting by then?"

Calvesi nodded.

"And you, of course, told Bertoli about it."

"I might have mentioned it in passing."

"The cardinal must have been quite intrigued."

Calvesi folded his arms across his chest. "Where are we going with this?"

"The late Giorgio Montefiore."

"What about him?"

"On the day that you and I discovered the painting was missing, you left me with the impression that you were the one who had asked Montefiore to have a look at it. But that wasn't the case, was it, Antonio?"

He shook his head. "It was Bertoli who called Montefiore. Then Montefiore called me."

"He wanted to see the painting?"

"What do you think?"

"I think you should have told me the truth the first time."

"It didn't seem relevant. Besides, I didn't realize I was speaking to a police officer."

"Luckily for you, you weren't. Nevertheless I intend to tell the Holy Father that you were the one who arranged to have the painting removed from the storeroom."

"But it's not true."

"I know it isn't true, Antonio. And so does Cardinal Bertoli."

44

Osteria Lucrezia

We really have to stop meeting like this, Holiness."

"Forgive me, Gabriel. But it was the only place I could get a reservation on short notice."

They were back at Lucrezia, the little osteria near the train station. Polizia di Stato officers outside, a Swiss Guard inside, the Vicar of Christ in a plaid sport jacket and an open-necked dress shirt.

"You're not safe here," said Gabriel.

Donati nudged a plate of arancini across the tabletop. "Have one of these. You'll feel better."

"I'll feel better when you're back in your bed at the Casa Santa Marta."

"I'm safer in this restaurant than I am at the Casa."

"All the more reason you should move across town to the Apostolic Palace. I hear there's a lovely apartment available on the third floor."

"I visit it each Sunday when I pray the Angelus."

"Have you ever noticed her down there in the square?"

"Who?"

Gabriel made no reply.

"If you are referring to Veronica, I haven't seen her. But then my crowds have been rather large of late."

"The travails of the rock star pope."

"If you must know, I hate it when they call me that. It demeans the papacy."

"Enjoy it while it lasts."

Gabriel served himself one of the crispy arancini balls and ate it with a knife and fork. Donati, frowning, plucked one from the plate and popped it into his mouth.

"Venetians," he muttered with dismay.

"Veronica made the same remark not long ago when I complained about her driving."

"You should have seen the way she drove when she was young. She was an absolute madwoman behind the wheel of a car."

"Nothing has changed."

"But that's not true, *mio amico*. A great deal has changed. A papal private secretary is allowed to maintain a friendship with a woman, but a supreme pontiff is not."

"She knows that, Luigi."

"Does she?"

"Yes, of course."

"All I want is for her to be happy."

"She is," replied Gabriel. "Deliriously so."

"Is she seeing someone?"

"A devastatingly handsome younger man. All of Rome is talking about nothing else."

"It's a sin, you know."

"An affair with a younger man?"

"Lying to the pope."

"If that's the case," said Gabriel, "the Substitute for General Affairs will be reciting Hail Marys for the remainder of his earthly life."

The proprietor appeared with the pasta course, spinach ravioli with butter and sage for Gabriel and for His Holiness a mountain of *cacio e pepe*. He impaled the dish with a fork and twirled.

"Father Mark mentioned something about an ancient Roman city on the Bay of Naples that was buried under several meters of volcanic ash in 79 AD. Surely it's not as bad as all that."

"I regret to inform you that the Church of Rome will soon be engulfed in the worst financial scandal since Pope Leo the Tenth financed the construction of St. Peter's Basilica with the sale of indulgences."

"Cardinal Bertoli and Nico Ambrosi?"

Gabriel nodded.

"Can you prove it?"

"I have the cardinal's emails and text messages. I also have geolocation data and telephone metadata."

"Am I to understand that you hacked the personal cellular device of the third most powerful prelate in the Roman Catholic Church?"

"The prelate is a criminal who has been acting in league with other criminals."

"Perhaps. But the cardinal is also a highly skilled creature of the Curia who was a brilliant Vatican diplomat before I appointed him to the post of *sostituto*. You can be sure he'll have a perfectly innocent-sounding explanation for his actions."

"But we'll be able to prove he's lying."

"How?"

"*Sprezzatura*," replied Gabriel. "It's a studied nonchalance that the great painters of the Renaissance like Leonardo and Raphael used to great effect. You're going to use it too. If you think you can pull it off, that is."

"Are you asking the supreme pontiff of the Church of Rome to tell a lie?"

"A small one," said Gabriel.

Donati's expression darkened. "I'm ashamed to admit it, but I lied to you just a moment ago."

"About what?"

"I *have* seen her in the square beneath my window. I see her every time she comes."

In the immediate aftermath of his appointment to the powerful post of *sostituto*, Cardinal Matteo Bertoli allowed himself to entertain the notion that one day he might be a pope. His hopes began to fade late in the turbulent papacy of Pietro Lucchesi when his name did not appear on anyone's list of those deemed *papabile*. And they were crushed entirely when the conclave shocked the world by placing the Ring of the Fisherman on the hand of Lucchesi's liberal private secretary. His Holiness Luigi Donati was no longer a young man, but he was in remarkably good health despite a lifelong addiction to cigarettes. Bertoli had been privy to the results of the Holy Father's most recent physical. Indeed, he had retained a copy of the doctor's report for his personal files. It suggested that, barring some unforeseen health emergency, Pope Donati would sit atop the throne of St. Peter for many years to come.

There had been a round of Curial bloodletting in the days following the conclave, but His Holiness had left the Secretariat of State, the central governing bureaucracy of the Vatican, largely untouched. He regarded the Substitute for General Affairs as a trusted ally, and Bertoli had given His Holiness no reason to question his allegiance. Quietly, though, he had aligned himself with elements of the Curia who had grown weary of the Holy Father's sanctimonious quest to rid the Vatican of corruption and upend the lives of privilege led by many of the Church's most senior figures. Cardinal Bertoli himself had come under withering criticism over the size and opulence of his penthouse apartment in the Palazzo San Carlo—and the money he had accepted from benefactors to pay for its renovation. He had adopted the time-tested Vatican strategy of silence when dealing with inquiries from the press. Had he chosen candor instead, he might have said that it was not his fault that Pope Francis of Assisi had forsaken the *appartamento* in the Apostolic Palace in favor of a hotel suite the size of a broom closet. It was, in Bertoli's estimation, an affront to the majesty of the papacy itself.

If there was one consolation to the Holy Father's unorthodox living arrangements, it was that the Casa Santa Marta was located directly adjacent to the Palazzo San Carlo—which allowed Bertoli, from the comfort of his private study, to keep a close eye on the man he so faithlessly served. At present there were lights burning behind the drawn curtains of Room 201, but Bertoli knew for certain that the Holy Father was not at home. He had once again slipped the bonds of the Vatican with the help of Colonel Alois Metzler, the commandant of the Swiss Guard. As *sostituto*, Bertoli was responsible for planning all papal travel, including brief excursions across the border separating the city-state from the Republic of Italy. He did not approve of the Holy Father's clandestine forays outside the walls and had made his views known. Still, he could hardly blame His Saintliness for wanting a decent meal now and again. The nightly fare in the dining hall of the Casa Santa Marta was most uninspired.

Bertoli's cook had managed to outdo herself that evening. He had dined alone, with only a recording of Schubert's piano trios for company, and then retired to his office. A pile of Curial paperwork awaited him, including the final itinerary for the Holy Father's weekend visit to the distant Italian island of Lampedusa, where he intended to once again virtue-signal his support for the rights of the wretched of the earth to seek sanctuary and employment in the land of their choice. On the way home, he would stop in Palermo to celebrate an open-air mass with Cardinal Vincenzo Cordero, the leftist liberation theologian whom he had recently appointed the city's archbishop. Afterward he would process through the streets of Palermo to the cathedral, where he intended to pray at the tomb of Father Pino Puglisi, the anti-Mafia priest who was murdered by the Cosa Nostra in 1993.

The visit to Lampedusa was certain to generate controversy, for it would be viewed, with some justification, as a direct criticism of Italy's current anti-immigration government. Bertoli, if left to his own devices, would have preferred to spend his Saturday relaxing in his penthouse apartment. But protocol dictated that he be at the Holy Father's side, nodding approvingly at his every utterance, no matter how objectionable he found them. Such was his calling, to serve as cupbearer to His Holiness Pope Che Guevara.

His contempt for the Holy Father notwithstanding, Bertoli offered a small prayer of thanks when, at twenty minutes past ten, a Mercedes saloon car braked to a halt at a side entrance of the Casa Santa Marta. His Holiness, in a jacket and trousers, climbed out of the car and disappeared through the doorway. The lights in Room 201 burned until 11:00 p.m., then were extinguished.

Bertoli worked for another ninety minutes before retiring himself. He slept dreadfully as usual and by seven the next morning, having bathed and dressed and celebrated mass in his private chapel, was back at his desk. He remained there until 8:50 a.m., when, Curial briefcase in hand, he walked next door to the Casa Santa Marta for his regularly scheduled morning meeting with the Holy Father.

His Saintliness was standing in the lobby, bidding farewell to a group of homeless Romans whom he had invited to breakfast in the dining hall. Bertoli followed him into a waiting elevator, along with two plainclothes Swiss Guards. It was the Holy Father who pressed the call button for the second floor.

"What do you have for me today, Eminence?"

"Nothing terribly pressing, Holiness."

"Good," he said, clapping Bertoli on the shoulder. "Because I have something that I think you're going to find very interesting."

45

Casa Santa Marta

Cardinal Bertoli gazed silently at the object in the padded box as though he were a mourner paying his final respects to a distant relative. Father Keegan, seemingly oblivious to the cardinal's reverie, was reviewing the schedule for the next day's trip to Lampedusa and Palermo. His Holiness, a cigarette burning between the first two fingers of his right hand, was skimming his daily news digest. For once, it contained nothing salacious about the Vatican. The favorable press coverage, he reckoned, would likely end soon enough.

Bertoli raised a hand to his mouth and coughed gently. "And where, exactly, did the Art Squad find it, Holiness?"

Donati was slow in looking up from the news digest. "Find what, Eminence?"

Bertoli inclined his head toward the portrait of the young woman. With his angular face, aquiline nose, and hooded eyes, he looked like a figure from an El Greco painting. His gold pectoral cross dwarfed the simple cross of silver worn by Donati.

"I'm afraid, Eminence, that General Ferrari declined to answer that question."

"May I ask why?"

"Apparently only one of the suspects is in custody. The Art Squad is still trying to identify any accomplices."

"But the Art Squad has no jurisdiction in this matter. Not if the painting was really stolen from the Pinacoteca."

Donati crushed out his cigarette. "You have reason to doubt that, Cardinal Bertoli?"

"No theft was ever reported."

"Which means the thief undoubtedly had help from someone on the inside."

The El Greco face adopted a pained expression.

"Shocking, I know."

"May I point out something else, Holiness?"

"Please," said Donati amiably.

"I'm quite familiar with the paintings in the Pinacoteca's inventory."

"So I've been told."

"And I am almost certain," Bertoli continued, "that I have never seen this painting in our storerooms."

"But that's the fascinating part of the story, Eminence. You see, it was hidden beneath another painting, a rather pedestrian Madonna and Child by an imitator of Raphael."

"With all due respect, Holiness, there is no such thing as a pedestrian Madonna and Child."

"Would you like to hear the rest of the story, Cardinal?"

"Forgive me, Holiness."

"A number of art historians have examined the painting."

"And?"

"They have concluded that it might well be a lost work by Leonardo."

"Astonishing," breathed the cardinal.

Donati nodded his head slowly in agreement. "And that, of course, would explain why someone at the Vatican helped the thieves to steal it."

"Is there a suspect?"

Donati sighed heavily. "Antonio Calvesi."

"The chief conservator? Impossible, Holiness."

"General Ferrari led me to believe an arrest is imminent. I asked him to wait until I return from Palermo."

Bertoli closed the transport case and engaged the locks.

"May I ask what you're doing, Matteo?"

"I'm going to take the painting back to the museum."

"The painting will remain in my apartment until such time as we can announce its discovery."

"But it isn't safe here."

"If the painting isn't safe here, Cardinal Bertoli, then neither am I." Donati lit another cigarette. "Shall we review the itinerary for tomorrow's trip?"

The trip would be only a few hours in duration, but it was a logistical nightmare, with two flights, two helicopter rides, and a brief sea voyage aboard a Coast Guard patrol boat. Archbishop Cordero of Palermo anticipated a crowd of two hundred thousand pilgrims at the open-air mass. Donati had rejected several drafts of his homily, and the hasty rewrite that Cardinal Bertoli handed him now was Curial mush. Not for the first time, he planned to speak extemporaneously.

"The Vatican Security Office believes there are no threats beyond the usual," said Bertoli. "Nevertheless I would implore His Holiness to use the bulletproof popemobile for the procession to the cathedral."

"I shall not process through the streets of Palermo like a goldfish in a bowl. I must have physical contact with my flock."

"Palermo is a dangerous city, Holiness."

"Not for me, it isn't."

With that, the cardinal moved on to other Curial matters, including an appointment to the Council for Justice and Peace and a gathering storm at the Congregation for the Doctrine of the Faith.

"What is it now?" asked Donati wearily.

"Cardinal Byrne."

A retired archbishop emeritus from the American Midwest and a conservative thorn in Donati's side. "I've made it abundantly clear to Cardinal Byrne that he is no longer permitted to celebrate the Traditional Latin Mass."

"He believes he's being persecuted."

"And I believe that champions of the Latin rite like Cardinal Byrne are exploiting the issue in order to oppose me."

"He has supporters inside the Holy Office."

"So do I, Eminence. And if it's a showdown he wants, he shall have one."

It was on that contentious note that Cardinal Bertoli, after a final glance at the art transport case lying on the coffee table, gathered his papers and took his leave. Donati and Father Keegan repaired to the sitting room windows, which gave them an overhead view of the cardinal's departure. His Eminence had a phone to his ear.

"Who do you suppose he's calling?" asked Donati.

Father Keegan's phone pinged with an incoming text message. "He's talking to Nico Ambrosi, Holiness."

"About what?"

Another text message landed on Father Keegan's phone. "He was wondering whether Nico was free for dinner this evening."

"Is he?"

"Seems so."

"And where will they be dining?"

A few seconds passed before the answer appeared on Father Kee-gan's phone. "Pipero, Holiness."

"On a Friday evening? How do you suppose Nico was able to get a reservation?"

"He must know someone."

"Do you think that I could get a reservation at Pipero on short notice on a Friday evening?"

"No, Holiness. Not a chance."

46

Ristorante Pipero

The restaurant was located on the Corso Vittorio, directly opposite the Chiesa Nuova, the original home of Caravaggio's *Deposition of Christ*. Owing to a last-minute cancellation, the Art Squad had been able to obtain a table for two. General Ferrari decided that handsome Luca Rossetti was best suited for the assignment. At present he was sitting in the back of an unmarked Alfa Romeo parked next to the church. Gabriel sat at his side, a laptop on his knees. The winking blue light on the screen indicated that His Eminence Cardinal Bertoli was in his office on the third floor of the Apostolic Palace. His Milanese financial adviser, Nico Ambrosi, was stepping off a train at Roma Termini.

"Just the way you and your boss planned it all along," said Gabriel.

"Not even the general could have imagined it would end like this." Rossetti shook his head slowly. "This is going to be one of the biggest scandals in the history of the Church."

"Exactly what I was hoping to avoid."

"Your friend the Holy Father isn't to blame."

"I'm not sure his enemies will see it that way."

Rossetti's phone pulsed with an incoming text. "Ambrosi is five minutes away."

"Tell your colleagues to give him a wide berth."

"We know how to follow people."

"Do you remember the night you tried to follow me home from Harry's Bar?"

Rossetti rubbed his jaw. "I'm lucky you didn't kill me."

"It was an innocent mistake."

"It was an assault."

"I broke my damned hand on that granite head of yours."

"I'll have you know my head is made of the finest Italian marble."

A chauffeured Mercedes sedan slowed to a stop outside the restaurant.

"That was fast," said Rossetti.

"I believe that's your dinner date, Luca."

The driver opened the rear door and Veronica Marchese, in a shimmering black pantsuit, stepped into view. Rossetti regarded her admiringly. "She's very beautiful."

"And quite unavailable."

"Still grieving for that husband of hers?"

"She's grieving," said Gabriel. "But not for Carlo Marchese."

Rossetti opened his door. "Any advice?"

"Order the gnocchi with fontina. You'll thank me later."

Veronica was chatting with the maître d' when Luca Rossetti came through the door. He offered a hand in greeting, but she gave him an intimate kiss on each cheek instead.

"How was your day, darling?"

"Busy. Yours?"

"Perfectly dreadful." She smiled. "Until this moment, that is."

She held Rossetti's arm as the maître d' ushered them to their table.

Only one other table in the dining room was not yet occupied—the one in a semiprivate alcove. It was set for three people.

Veronica was looking at the drinks menu. "Shall we have an aperitif?"

"I'm on duty."

"No, you're not. You're having dinner with a prominent museum director at one of Rome's trendiest restaurants."

"And what is the nature of our relationship?"

She sighed. "Purely physical, I'm afraid."

"In that case, this promises to be an interesting evening."

"In more ways than one." Veronica directed her gaze toward the attractive, dark-suited man who was now being shown to the secluded table in the alcove. It was Nico Ambrosi. "Did you happen to notice the number of place settings?"

Rossetti nodded.

"I wonder who the third guest could be."

"We'll know soon enough."

Veronica checked the time. "What do you suppose is keeping His Eminence?"

"Shall we ask our mutual friend?"

"Why not?"

Rossetti shot a message to Gabriel. The reply was instant. "Cardinal Bertoli just left the Vatican with a Polizia di Stato escort."

"Tell me something, Luca. Why does a mere cardinal require a police escort every time he crosses the border and enters Italy?"

"If it were up to me, he wouldn't get one." Rossetti put away his phone. "How did you meet him?"

"Our mutual friend?"

Rossetti nodded.

"Several years ago, I helped him take down an antiquities smuggling network. Unfortunately the leader of the network turned out to be my late husband."

"I'm sorry, Dottoressa Marchese. It was before my time."

She leaned across the table and whispered, "Since we're sleeping together, Luca, you should probably refer to me by my given name."

"It's one of my favorites."

"My mother chose it. She loved the story of the young woman from Jerusalem who wiped the face of Jesus as he carried his cross to Golgotha."

"You were raised in a religious home?"

She nodded, then asked, "What about you?"

"I was a model Catholic."

"And now?"

"I'm Catholic the way most Italians are Catholic."

"Not so much?"

"I still believe," said Rossetti. "At least I think I do. But I lost my faith in the Church a long time ago."

"You're not alone."

Several heads turned as Cardinal Bertoli, resplendent in his crimson-trimmed cassock, glided across the dining room at the side of the maître d'. As he approached the alcove, Nico Ambrosi rose to greet him. They exchanged a businesslike handshake and sat down. Cardinal Bertoli placed his *telefonino* on the tablecloth, then gestured toward the third place setting.

"I could be mistaken," said Veronica, "but it looks to me as though His Eminence is wondering the same thing we are."

"Are you suggesting that Nico Ambrosi would invite someone to dinner without the cardinal's knowledge?"

"I wouldn't put anything past Nico."

A waiter appeared and Rossetti requested two glasses of prosecco.

"Are you from Naples?" asked Veronica.

"Is it that obvious?"

She smiled but said nothing.

"I grew up in a neighborhood controlled by the Camorra. When I was a boy, I saw bodies in the streets."

"Is that why you became a police officer?"

"I suppose so. My mother wept for a week when I told her."

"Why?"

"She wanted me to become a priest. Can you imagine me in a Roman collar and a clerical suit?"

"I can, actually." Just then the door of the restaurant opened, and a man with an angular face and hair combed closely to his scalp came in from the street. "Guest number three?"

"Definitely."

"Who is he?"

"A banker from Lugano who just lost a half billion dollars belonging to the Camorra."

"Franco Tedeschi?"

Rossetti nodded, then watched as Tedeschi made his way unescorted to the table in the alcove. He shook the hands of Nico Ambrosi and Cardinal Bertoli and lowered himself into the remaining chair.

"The unholy trinity," observed Veronica. Then, with a wry smile, she added, "It's a shame no one's listening in on their conversation."

The waiter delivered the prosecco.

"What should we drink to?" asked Rossetti.

"How about to us?"

"Is there any chance our relationship can become something more than physical?"

"I'm afraid not. You see, Luca, I'm hopelessly in love with someone else."

"Really? Who?"

Veronica smiled sadly. "I'll never tell."

47

Ristorante Pipero

It became apparent, even before the waiter dared to approach their table, that they had been deceived on a grand scale. But determining how it had happened and who was to blame took a bit of doing. It was beyond dispute that someone had managed to exchange the real Leonardo for a perfect copy—a copy that Franco Tedeschi had sold to the Russian oligarch Alexander "Proko" Prokhorov for the record-setting sum of $500 million. Tedeschi suspected that the swap had taken place at the airport in Nice. And he was all but certain the cabin attendant on his bank's private jet, a Danish woman who called herself Rikke Jorgensen, had been in on the heist.

But who had made the perfect copy of the Leonardo? And how had General Ferrari of the Art Squad learned that the painting had been stolen in the first place? Tedeschi was confident the general hadn't been tipped off by the young British art conservator; a gentleman from Naples had taken care of that problem up in Venice. And the same gentleman from Naples had made quick work of Giorgio Montefiore a few weeks later in Florence when greed got the better of him.

"Who else could it have been?" asked Cardinal Bertoli.

"It had to be someone inside the Vatican."

"Surely you're not suggesting that I had something to do with it."

"Of course not, Eminence."

"Who then?"

Tedeschi jotted a name on the back of one of his business cards and slid it across the table. Bertoli looked down briefly, then turned the card over.

"I thought your associates put the fear of God in him."

"Not the fear of God, Eminence. The fear of the Camorra. God forgives, but the Camorra never forgets."

"Truly inspiring, Franco." Bertoli pushed the business card across the tablecloth. "Words to live by."

The proprietor appeared and with considerable fanfare welcomed the three men to his establishment. By all appearances they were a distinguished group—two prosperous financiers and a powerful Vatican prelate. But the two financiers were in the business of laundering money for Don Lorenzo Di Falco, leader of the Camorra's richest and most powerful clan. And the Vatican prelate, through his own actions, had made the Roman Catholic Church an unwitting partner in the enterprise.

When they were alone again, Cardinal Bertoli asked, "But how did the police know that you were the one who had the painting?"

"In order to sell it, we had to show it to potential buyers."

"It was my understanding they were required to sign a nondisclosure agreement."

"They were. But someone must have managed to trace the painting to the bank."

"And the five hundred million dollars the Russian oligarch paid for it?"

"It was transferred to an account at Oschadbank in Kyiv."

"By whom?"

"A hacker who somehow managed to penetrate our computer network."

Bertoli fingered his gold pectoral cross. "And when your Russian buyer discovers that he paid a half billion dollars for a forgery?"

"Obviously he will want his money back."

"Which means you will be out a grand total of one billion dollars."

"For your sake, Eminence, let's hope it doesn't come to that."

"My sake?" Bertoli smiled coldly. "The Russian oligarch is your problem, Franco. I lived up to my end of the bargain."

"My investor doesn't see it that way."

"He's your problem too."

Tedeschi leaned across the table. "Let me make this clear, Cardinal Bertoli. You owe Don Di Falco four hundred million dollars. And you have exactly seventy-two hours to come up with the money."

"Forgive me, Franco, but I'm afraid I don't have four hundred million lying around at the moment." Bertoli looked at his financial adviser and said, "Isn't that right, Nico?"

Ambrosi allowed Tedeschi to answer on his behalf.

"The money or the building, Eminence. The choice is yours."

"New Bond Street? It's worth far less than what the Vatican originally paid for it. And if you foreclose, it will result in a scandal that will undoubtedly lead to my dismissal as the *sostituto*, which will in turn lead to your arrest on charges of embezzlement and money laundering. To avoid a lengthy prison sentence, you will be tempted to implicate your investor in Naples, Don Di Falco. Therefore, Don Di Falco will almost certainly have you both killed before you go to trial."

The two Camorra moneymen exchanged a long look but said nothing. Cardinal Bertoli used the silence to check his phone. He had two missed calls, both from the same number.

"Will you excuse me, gentlemen? I'll try to be brief." He dialed the number and lifted the phone to his ear. "Good evening, Father Keegan. What seems to be the problem? . . . Is it urgent? I was just sitting down to dinner. . . . Yes, of course. I'm on my way."

Bertoli tapped the phone irritably, severing the connection. "I'm afraid I have to return to the Vatican. It seems the Holy Father would like a word."

"We're not finished," said Franco Tedeschi.

"We are, actually." Bertoli rose solemnly to his feet and looked down his El Greco nose at the crooked little banker from Lugano. "My advice to you, Franco, is that you forget about that four hundred million dollars. Otherwise we will all go down together. And that includes your investor from Naples."

Bertoli turned without another word and, blessing hand raised, glided serenely across the dining room and out the door.

"Now you know how he got to be a cardinal," said Nico Ambrosi.

"His Eminence is playing a dangerous game."

"So are we, Franco. Never forget that."

Tedeschi drew a phone from the breast pocket of his suit jacket.

"Who are you calling?"

"Who do you think?"

"He'll kill him, you know."

Tedeschi shrugged. "God forgives, but Don Lorenzo Di Falco never forgets."

"Words to die by," said Nico Ambrosi.

48

Casa Santa Marta

The Swiss Guard standing watch outside the Casa Santa Marta knew there was going to be trouble the instant Cardinal Bertoli leapt from the back of his car. A similar thought crossed Father Keegan's mind when Bertoli presented himself at the door of Room 201. His Eminence, having been called away from dinner, was fit to be tied. Father Keegan's countenance, however, was as inscrutable as ever.

"Good evening, Cardinal Bertoli. Sorry to interrupt your evening, but I'm afraid it couldn't be helped."

"I trust it's something important."

"I'll let the Holy Father explain."

He was seated at his little writing desk, a stack of papers before him. He gave his *sostituto* no more than a cursory glance. "Please have a seat, Matteo. We need to talk."

"About what, Holiness?"

"I said sit down."

Bertoli drew away as though he were avoiding a blow. "I demand to know the meaning of this."

"Trust me, you are in no position to make demands."

Bertoli held his ground for a moment longer before settling into one of the overstuffed armchairs.

"Where were you this evening, Matteo?"

"I was at dinner."

"With whom?"

"Nico Ambrosi."

"Your investment adviser?"

"*Our* investment adviser, Holiness."

"The man who convinced you to pay four hundred million dollars for an office building in London?"

"I fail to see how that is relevant."

"You will shortly. But tell me something, Matteo. Did anyone else join you and your friend Nico Ambrosi for dinner this evening?"

"It was just the two of us."

"There wasn't a third person at your table? A banker named Franco Tedeschi? He was the one who lent you the money to purchase the New Bond Street property."

Bertoli recalibrated. "Signore Tedeschi joined us briefly, Holiness. But how did you possibly know that?"

Donati handed Bertoli a leather-bound document bearing the emblem of the Secretariat of State. "I assume you recognize this. After all, you were the one who prepared it."

"It is this year's first-quarter report on the secretariat's investment portfolio."

"Open the report to page one, please."

Bertoli complied with the request, laboriously.

"Please remind me what it says, Matteo."

"It states that the total value of the secretariat's portfolio is three point eight billion euros."

"And the cash reserves?"

"Slightly less than five hundred million."

"Very impressive," said Donati with mock admiration. "Now have a look at page twelve."

Bertoli turned to the appropriate page. "It states that the income from our property in New Bond Street is more than sufficient to cover the cost of the debt service."

"Is that an accurate statement?"

"Yes, of course."

"Then how do you explain the fact that you and your investment adviser failed to make a number of payments?"

"We didn't, Holiness."

"You're lying to me, Matteo. Not for the first time, I might add."

Donati handed over a single sheet of paper. It was an email from Franco Tedeschi of SBL PrivatBank to Nico Ambrosi of Piedmont Global Capital. Bertoli scrutinized the document without expression.

"Where did you get this?"

"Never mind where I got it. Just answer my question."

Bertoli considered his response. "Forgive me, Holiness. But I cannot explain the discrepancy."

"The only possible explanation, Matteo, is that the quarterly report was fraudulent. And every other report you've given me since I became pope has been fraudulent as well."

The cardinal was suddenly on his feet. "This is an outrage!"

"I couldn't agree more. But please have a seat. We're only just getting started." Donati turned to Father Keegan. "Perhaps you should ask our friend to join us now."

———

Gabriel entered the papal suite without waiting for a summons. Cardinal Bertoli regarded him contemptuously, then looked to Donati for an explanation.

"You remember our friend Gabriel, don't you, Matteo? He was in the Sistina the night of the conclave."

"Yes, of course, Holiness. But why is he here?"

"I'm afraid I misled you this morning. You see, it wasn't the Italian police who recovered the stolen painting. It was Gabriel. And Antonio Calvesi wasn't behind the theft."

"I'm relieved to hear that. But who could have done such a thing?"

It was Gabriel who answered. "You, Cardinal Bertoli."

Bertoli emitted a dry Curial laugh. "You've obviously taken leave of your senses, Signore Allon." Bertoli turned to Donati and added, "You both have."

Donati, with a wave of his hand, instructed Gabriel to present the evidence of Bertoli's guilt. He sat down opposite the cardinal and opened his laptop.

"The true valuation of the Secretariat of State's investment portfolio is not three point eight billion euros, and you have nowhere near five hundred million in cash reserves."

Bertoli lifted his gaze toward the ceiling and in a benedictory voice declared, "False."

"A more accurate valuation," Gabriel continued, "would be about two billion euros. But when you subtract the liabilities, namely, the money you owe SBL PrivatBank, it's less than a billion."

"Also false."

"I can show you the statement that Nico Ambrosi sent you earlier this year. It paints an accurate picture of the secretariat's investment portfolio, not the fiction you served up in your quarterly reports. To make matters worse, SBL PrivatBank was calling in its loan for the New Bond Street building, and you had almost no cash on hand. You needed money, and you needed it quickly. Otherwise your mismanagement and embezzlement of Vatican funds would come to light. You found a solution to your problems one afternoon during a visit to the conservation lab of the Vatican Museums."

"I never saw that painting until this morning."

"Antonio Calvesi was the one who showed it to you. He also told you about the hidden portrait and the suspicions of an apprentice conservator named Penelope Radcliff. You called your friend Giorgio Montefiore at the Uffizi, and Giorgio asked to see the painting. He told Antonio it wasn't a Leonardo, but he told you that it probably was. And you, in turn, informed Nico Ambrosi that you had discovered a way to repay your delinquent loan."

Bertoli feigned incredulity. "And how, Signore Allon, did I manage to steal the painting from the storerooms without anyone noticing?"

"With the help of your associates in the Camorra, of course. They're quite good at stealing things. They're also good at killing people. You had the unhappy task this evening of informing the CFO of Camorra Incorporated that the painting he sold to a Russian oligarch for five hundred million dollars was undoubtedly a copy. And then the CFO of Camorra Incorporated told you that a hacker had rerouted the money to Oschadbank in Kyiv. Which means that you are once again on the hook for a loan you cannot possibly repay."

Bertoli offered Gabriel a wintry smile. "A highly entertaining story, Signore Allon. You have a vivid imagination."

Gabriel tapped the keyboard of his laptop once.

Forgive me, Franco, but I'm afraid I don't have four hundred million lying around at the moment . . .

Gabriel paused the recording. "Shall we listen to the rest of the conversation? It leaves little to the imagination."

Donati came to the cardinal's rescue—temporarily, at least. "That won't be necessary. I think it is now abundantly clear to His Eminence that he isn't going to be able to lie his way out of this mess. Isn't that right, Matteo?"

"My conscience is clear, Holiness."

"Do you have one? I'm not so sure." Donati regarded Bertoli through the blue-gray smoke rising from the end of his cigarette. "Perhaps it would be better if you didn't accompany me to Lampedusa and Palermo tomorrow."

Bertoli absorbed this news without expression. "Is it your intention to dismiss me?"

"Two people are dead because of your actions, Matteo. What would you do if you were in my position?"

"I had nothing to do with that woman's death. She would still be alive if she hadn't . . ." His voice trailed off.

"Hadn't what, Matteo? Make a clean breast of it, for God's sake. Confess your sins before it's too late." Receiving no reply, Donati said, "As for your future, I will withhold any decision pending a thorough outside audit of the investment portfolio. If, as expected, it uncovers misconduct on your part, I will have no choice but to take disciplinary action. In the meantime, you are to have no further contact with Nico Ambrosi or Franco Tedeschi."

"But, Holiness, that's not possible. We have—"

"None," snapped Donati. "Is that clear?"

Bertoli rose to his feet, slowly this time. "You are making a grave mistake."

"The mistake," said Donati evenly, "was allowing you to oversee the Curia's investments. For whatever reason, be it greed or incompetence, you've managed to get yourself and the Church into business with some of the very worst people in the world."

"But you were the one who put me in the job—remember, Holiness? And you approved each and every one of my investments."

"You're not threatening a pope, are you, Matteo?"

"I am offering His Holiness sage advice. And he would be wise to heed it."

"I should turn a blind eye to your conduct? Sweep it under the Curial rug?"

"What I am suggesting, Holiness, is that you give me time to put our financial house in order. Otherwise there will be a scandal that will do irreparable harm to the Holy Mother Church."

"But it will be your scandal, Matteo. Not mine. And it will provide me with the leverage I need to finally institute real reform."

"Turn over the tables of the money changers? Force the princes of the Church to give up their large apartments and live in squalid little rooms like this one? The Curia will rise up in rebellion against you. You will tear this Church to pieces and destroy your papacy in the process."

"No, Matteo. I will save this Church from the likes of you before it's too late. Now get out of my sight."

Bertoli, in one final act of defiance, stood motionless for a long moment before finally leaving the papal suite. Donati, his hand shaking, crushed out his cigarette.

"My God, Gabriel, what have I done?"

"I believe you just declared war, Holiness."

"Yes," he agreed. "But against whom?"

49

Palazzo San Carlo

While crossing the Piazza Santa Marta, Cardinal Matteo Bertoli found himself thinking, quite unexpectedly, about his decision to become a priest. As recounted in the pages of his unread autobiography, he had heard a clarion call from a cloudless Abruzzian sky commanding him to forsake earthly pursuits and spread the good news of the Gospels. But that version of the story was apocryphal. In truth, he had joined the priesthood because it seemed like an attractive alternative to a life of backbreaking physical labor in his hardscrabble village. The local parish priest, Monsignor Grasso, was a man of considerable influence and lived a comfortable life, with plenty to eat and a Fiat motorcar at his disposal. It was rumored, though never proven, that not all of the money the faithful placed on the collection plate each Sunday made its way to the archdiocese. There were also whispers—again never substantiated—that the monsignor was the biological father of at least two village children. Young Matteo Bertoli, for his part, did not regard the requirement of celibacy as an impediment. He had never had much interest in women, nor they in him.

Bertoli's unhealthy interest in money would begin many years later after he was appointed the apostolic nuncio to Angola. Though

life in the former Portuguese colony was dreary and at times dangerous, he lived in a walled villa and was looked after by a large staff of
domestic servants. He quickly grew accustomed to the luxurious life
of an ambassador and to the attention of wealthy Angolan Catholics
wishing to curry favor with the pope's emissary. A great deal of cash
was thrown in his direction, always in the form of donations to the
Church. Most of the money Bertoli sent along to Rome, but a not
insignificant sum he used for personal expenses. They included the
purchase of a villa by the sea in his native Abruzzo. His sister Angelica
was the property's owner of record.

Bertoli was sent next to Nigeria, followed by the Philippines, Bue-
nos Aires, and finally Madrid, where he was much admired by the
Spanish elite. One of his patrons was a corrupt businessman who
wished to conceal a nine-figure sum of money in the Vatican Bank.
Bertoli personally opened an account for the businessman and was
rewarded with a payment of two million euros, which he deposited
in the Vatican Bank as well.

The money was a pittance, though, compared to the small fortune
he had made through his association with Nico Ambrosi. It was said
that Ambrosi was a devout Catholic, a friend of the Vatican, a man
of trust. As it turned out, Ambrosi was none of those things. He was
a criminal financier who was helping the Camorra launder its dirty
money. And so was his friend and associate, Franco Tedeschi of SBL
PrivatBank.

The two moneymen had assured Bertoli they would take good
care of the Church's finances. Instead they had weighted every
transaction in their favor and in the process embezzled hundreds of
millions in Church funds on behalf of the Camorra. A case in point
was the office building in New Bond Street. Bertoli had paid twice
what the building was worth, producing millions in fees for Ambrosi

and Tedeschi and a windfall profit for Lorenzo Di Falco, who owned the building secretly through a shell company. Nevertheless, when Bertoli fell behind on the interest payments, Tedeschi refused to renegotiate the terms of the loan. Bertoli was in no position to challenge the decision; he had accepted millions in kickbacks and was in it up to his neck. The painting had been the answer to his prayers. And no one would have known a thing if it weren't for that young British art conservator.

Bertoli slipped through the entrance of the Palazzo San Carlo and rode the lift upstairs to his apartment. The main drawing room was larger than the entire papal suite in the Casa Santa Marta, with a fine view over the rooftops of Rome. Yes, it was grand, but other princes of the Church lived better, including the traditionalist firebrand Cardinal Byrne, who dwelled rent-free in a spacious apartment across the street from the Vatican. And then there was Ortolani, better known in the Italian press as Cardinal Seven Bathrooms. Bertoli reckoned he could count on the support of both men in the event of a showdown. Otherwise it would be their heads on the block next.

For now, at least, he was alone. There was no question that an independent audit of the Vatican's finances would find substantial wrongdoing on his part. The punishment would be swift—he would be dismissed as the *sostituto* and cast out of the College of Cardinals. A humiliating trial before a Vatican tribunal was not out of the question. He supposed the best he could hope for was a lengthy stay in a remote abbey, the kind of place where the brothers wore sandpaper habits and subsisted on coarse bread and stone soup. Yes, he had made mistakes, committed grave sins, but the likes of Archbishop Paul Marcinkus had done far worse. The Polish pope had nevertheless stood by him, even after Michele Sindona was convicted of fraud and Roberto Calvi was found swinging from Blackfriars

Bridge. Bertoli could expect no such support from the pontiff he served. His Holiness Pope Sanctimonious had vowed to root out Vatican corruption once and for all. He was going to destroy the Church in order to save it.

But the fate of the Holy Mother Church, thought Matteo Bertoli, rested in his hands now. It was he who was going to save it, not the charlatan who lived in the hostel next door rather than the Apostolic Palace. His Saintliness had made his intentions clear; he wished to bankrupt the Church and return it to its roots, whatever that meant. It was long past time for Bertoli to stage an intervention. Who knew? Perhaps it was not too late for him, after all.

He extinguished the lamps in the drawing room, and the lights of Rome came into sharper relief. So, too, did his thoughts. He had a narrow window of opportunity, a few days, no more. It was by no means impossible; Bertoli knew better than anyone the vulnerabilities. He had only to make a single phone call, and the deed was as good as done. He would not issue a directive, merely a warning. His conscience would be clear, his place in God's heavenly kingdom secure. He would save himself and his Church. There was no higher calling.

A single phone call, he thought, to the very man who had got him into this mess in the first place. But not from his Vatican landline or his usual *telefonino*; it was obvious the Holy Father's clever friend had managed to hack it. He would place the call from his second cell phone, the one he used for his most private affairs. It was hidden in his dressing room, so thoroughly that not even Sister Eugenia, his meddlesome household nun, knew of its existence.

He fetched the phone now and carried it onto his rooftop terrace. A few words was all it took, a warning rather than a directive.

"You and your investor from Naples have a serious problem, Nico. Two, in fact."

Bertoli then recited a pair of names. Nico Ambrosi took note of the second.

"How is he involved in this?"

"He's the one who switched the paintings. And if I had to guess, he's the one who made five hundred million dollars disappear. He knows everything, Nico. And so does the Holy Father."

"Is there a way to make these problems go away?"

"That's entirely up to you and your investor in Naples."

And with that, the connection died, and the deed was done. Bertoli switched off the phone and watched a layman of medium height and build stepping from the entrance of the Casa Santa Marta. Speak of the devil, he thought, and went to bed.

50

Caffè Roma

An unmarked Carabinieri Alfa Romeo was parked just beyond the metal barricades separating the territory of the city-state from the Republic. Luca Rossetti was behind the wheel, and in the passenger seat was his dinner companion, Veronica Marchese. Gabriel slid into the back seat and closed the door. Rossetti swung onto the Via della Conciliazione and headed toward the Tiber.

"How did it go in there?"

"It was a Curial knife fight. Cardinal Bertoli denied everything, of course, but His Holiness was having none of it."

"What happens now?"

"His Holiness has ordered an independent audit of Vatican Incorporated. Bertoli will remain in his job for the time being."

Veronica glanced at Gabriel over one shoulder. "An independent audit of the Vatican's secret finances? The Curia will never stand for it."

"His Eminence made that very point. He's no supporter of the Holy Father, by the way. Quite the opposite."

"I tried to tell him. But he wouldn't listen."

"Who wouldn't listen?" asked Rossetti.

Gabriel changed the subject. "What happened after the cardinal left the restaurant?"

"Tedeschi made a couple of phone calls. Then he and Nico finished their dinner. In my professional opinion, it was not a pleasant meal."

"Where are they now?"

"On their way to Naples, presumably for a meeting with Don Lorenzo Di Falco. If Don Lorenzo had any sense, he would kill Nico and Franco tonight and cut his losses."

"I'm worried about Ottavio Pozzi," said Gabriel.

"Pozzi is the least of their problems."

"He accepted two hundred and fifty thousand euros to steal the painting. And then he told you everything."

"You were there too, as I recall."

"But I was the good cop. And if someone from the Di Falco clan of the Camorra shows up at his door looking for the money, Pozzi is as good as dead."

Rossetti's *telefonino* rang before he could reply. He lifted the device to his ear, listened in silence, then said, "We're on our way." A moment later they were speeding southward along the Tiber with the grille lights flashing.

"On our way where?" asked Gabriel.

"Ostiense."

"Is something wrong?"

"Pozzi."

————————

It happened at 11:22 p.m. That much, at least, was certain. The killer hadn't bothered with a suppressor, and the sound of gunfire could be heard throughout much of the neighborhood. He had approached Ottavio Pozzi from behind as he was ordering a *doppio* at Caffè Roma and had emptied his magazine into the museum guard's head and back. Then, calmly, he had walked out of the café and climbed into a waiting car. No one, it seemed, could recall the make or model.

The twenty-six-year-old barman, who had been standing directly in the line of fire, was fortunate not to have been hit as well. He was being interviewed by a pair of uniformed Polizia di Stato officers when Rossetti turned into the Via Casati. A large crowd had gathered in the street outside the café, some still in their nightclothes. Others watched from the balconies of the graffiti-spattered apartment blocks, ghostly phantoms in the flashing blue light.

Veronica waited next to the car while Gabriel and Rossetti shouldered their way through the crowd and went to the door of the café. They could proceed no further; the floor was drenched with blood and littered with shell casings. Pozzi lay where he had fallen, the arrangement of his limbs contorted by death. A crime scene technician was probing the bullet holes in the back of Pozzi's head. In all likelihood, he had never felt a thing.

Luca Rossetti swung away and raised a hand to his mouth.

"Are you okay?" asked Gabriel.

"I'm supposed to be the one asking that question."

"I wish it bothered me, Luca. But it doesn't."

"Never?"

"The first time."

"Where was it?"

"Here in Rome. I was just a kid."

"So was I when I saw my first dead body. They left him in the street outside our apartment building so everyone could see what happened if you crossed them." He stared at the body lying in a pool of blood on the dirty linoleum floor. "I've always hated them."

"You should have his brother moved into solitary confinement. Otherwise he's next."

Rossetti stepped away to make the call. The crime scene technician was searching Pozzi's clothing. In the outer pocket of his blood-soaked overcoat he found an ID badge for the Musei Vaticani. It disappeared into an evidence bag.

Rossetti returned a moment later, his face ashen. "Sandro Pozzi was stabbed to death an hour ago. It appears to have been the work of a Camorra prison executioner."

Gabriel looked at the body of Sandro Pozzi's younger brother— the brother who would still be alive if only he had told the truth on a job application.

"I'd like to have a word with the barman."

"The Polizia is in charge here, not us."

"He had to have seen the killer's face."

"If he did, he won't tell you."

"There's always a first time, Luca."

"Or a last."

Gabriel dug his phone from his pocket and retrieved a photograph of the sketch he had made with the help of Ottavio Pozzi. It was Father Spada, the priest who was not a priest. Rossetti plucked the phone from Gabriel's grasp.

"Maybe I should handle it. You're not an actual cop, you know."

Rossetti walked over to the two Polizia di Stato officers, displayed his Carabinieri ID, and requested permission to show the witness a composite sketch of a suspect in another case. The witness gave the sketch only a passing glance, then shook his head. Rossetti asked the witness to have another look. He did so reluctantly and shook his head a second time.

Rossetti returned to Gabriel's side and handed over the phone. "Did you see that?"

"He's lying."

"No doubt about it."

Gabriel stared down at Pozzi's body. "I suppose you're obligated to tell your colleagues in the Polizia everything you know."

"Everything," agreed Rossetti. "But not right away."

"How long can you wait?"

"I imagine we'll wait until after Ambrosi and Tedeschi are in custody." Rossetti put a hand on Gabriel's arm. "Let's get out of here."

Gabriel followed Rossetti back to the Alfa Romeo. Veronica was leaning against the hood. In the flashing blue light, her face appeared deathly pale. She looked at Gabriel and said, "It might be wise if you went back to Venice in the morning."

"Actually I think I'll stay in Rome for another day or two."

"Palermo is lovely this time of year."

"Yes," said Gabriel. "So is Lampedusa, I'm told."

51

St. Anne's Gate

At half past five the following morning, Gabriel slid into the back seat of a black sedan with SCV license plates. He scanned the newspapers during the short drive across the river to the Vatican. *La Repubblica* had published several hundred words about an execution-style murder in the working-class neighborhood of Ostiense. The story did not include the victim's name or place of employment. Nor did it mention the presence of a prominent art conservator at the scene of the crime—the same art conservator, as it turned out, who had found the body of a young woman floating in the Venetian Lagoon, recovered a lost painting by Leonardo da Vinci, and set in motion a financial scandal that would soon plunge the Catholic Church into a state of open warfare. His Holiness Luigi Donati was hoping to keep the scandal at bay long enough for him to complete a whirlwind visit to the Mediterranean islands of Lampedusa and Sicily. It was Gabriel's considered opinion that His Holiness would not get his wish.

The driver delivered Gabriel to St. Anne's Gate. The Swiss Guard standing watch there was expecting him, as was his commandant, Colonel Metzler. He was partaking of a traditional Swiss breakfast in the mess, surrounded by several officers in dark suits. They made a place for Gabriel at the table and fetched him coffee and something to eat.

"No tie?" asked Metzler over a spoonful of muesli.

"I didn't pack one."

Metzler shot a glance at one of his men, who abruptly left the mess in search of neckwear.

"What I need," said Gabriel, "is a weapon. And not a halberd. They're impossible to conceal."

Metzler allowed himself a brief smile. He was on edge, and so were his men. They always were when a pope was about to venture beyond the walls of the Vatican, especially a pope as divisive as Luigi Donati. The Holy Father's last-minute request to add Gabriel to his security detail didn't help matters.

"You should know this place is swirling with rumors," said Metzler. "And most of them involve you."

"What have I done this time?"

"Evidently there was some sort of confrontation last evening between the Holy Father and the *sostituto*. It is said that you were present for this meeting."

"Word travels fast around here."

"Is it true that Cardinal Bertoli is on his way out?"

"Perhaps we should discuss this in private."

Metzler rose to his feet. "I know just the place."

———

During the walk downstairs to the Swiss Guard's indoor firing range, Gabriel told the commandant as much as he could about the scandal that was about to engulf the Vatican. He implied that it was financial in nature and involved a pair of dubious Italian financiers who were connected to the Camorra. Metzler had been at the Vatican long enough to realize what that meant.

"Blood is going to flow."

"It already is."

"When?"

"Last night in Ostiense."

"The shooting in that café?"

Gabriel nodded. "The target was Ottavio Pozzi, the guard from the Vatican Museums who removed the painting from the storeroom. The killer was the fellow who carried it through St. Anne's Gate."

"Father Spada?"

"He was no priest, Alois. He's a Camorra executioner. I saw his handiwork last night. And in Florence as well," added Gabriel. "He's not one for subtlety."

"And now you're afraid the Holy Father's life might be in danger?"

"If it were up to me, His Holiness would develop a sudden case of malaria and cancel the trip."

"That's not going to happen. He has a stubborn streak, your friend. He's also rather reckless when it comes to his security. He refuses to use the bulletproof popemobile, no matter where he is. It's only a matter of time before someone takes a shot at him."

"Which is why I want to be in his hip pocket today until he's back inside the Vatican."

"With all due respect, Gabriel, my men can handle it."

"I know they can. But I'm rather good at this sort of thing myself."

"And the other thing as well." Metzler led Gabriel through the door of the firing range and removed a SIG Sauer P226 from the gun cabinet. "Do you know how to use one of these?"

"Is the pope Catholic?"

"Depends on who you ask." Metzler handed Gabriel a fully loaded magazine and then switched on the range lights.

"Is this really necessary?"

"It is if you're going to carry a gun around my men."

"I thought the range was closed in the morning because of the noise."

"Papal dispensation." Metzler ran a target ten meters down the range. "Whenever you're ready."

"What do you want me to do, Alois? Insert the bullets manually?"

Metzler increased the distance to twenty meters.

"Oh, for heaven's sake. Run the damn thing to the end of the range." Metzler did as Gabriel asked.

"Where would you like me to shoot the poor chap?"

"Center mass."

"What if he's wearing body armor?"

"He's made of recycled paper. Now get on with it already."

Gabriel rammed the magazine into the butt and racked the slide. Then his arm swung up and fifteen rounds poured from the SIG Sauer in a steady stream. The result was a single large hole in the center of the target's chest.

Metzler handed Gabriel a box of ammunition. "Do it again."

Gabriel thumbed fifteen rounds into the magazine and charged the weapon. "Where would you like me to shoot him now?"

"Center mass."

"Eyes open or eyes closed?"

Receiving no answer, Gabriel raised his arm a second time and fired fifteen shots in quick succession. Metzler reeled in the target. There was a single hole in the center of the target's forehead.

"I don't suppose you'd like to carry a spare magazine."

"No," replied Gabriel. "I've never really needed one."

The boarding of the motor coaches took place in the Piazza Papa Pio XII at the ungodly hour of 6:45 a.m. The first coach was reserved for the red-and-purple-sashed Curial traveling party and the plainclothes Swiss Guards and Polizia di Stato officers who provided close protection whenever the pope set foot in public. A delegation of important Catholic VIPs filed onto the second coach, along with the *Vaticanisti* and a couple of minders from the Press Office. Gabriel spotted a few familiar faces, including an impeccably sourced American from a respected Catholic news service. His colleague from *La Repubblica*, who made a habit of exposing Vatican scandals, boarded the coach last. He did so with a phone to his ear and a hand over his mouth, never a good sign.

By seven thirty the coaches were on final approach to Fiumicino Airport. Only then did His Holiness Luigi Donati emerge from the Casa Santa Marta, resplendent in his white cassock and a white overcoat, the large gold *Anello Piscatorio* on the third finger of his right hand. A step behind was Father Mark Keegan, who was lugging a pair of heavy papal attaché cases. A shuttle bus delivered them to the helipad, where they boarded a Boeing Grey Wolf on loan from the Italian Air Force. Gabriel ducked into the passenger cabin a moment later, unobserved by any member of the Roman Curia, and settled into the seat next to the supreme pontiff.

"That tie doesn't match your blazer," observed His Holiness as the helicopter floated over the Vatican wall.

"I suppose you never have that problem."

"No," replied Donati. "But I have plenty of others."

"Including the *Vaticanisti*. They no doubt noticed that Cardinal Bertoli wasn't part of the Curial delegation this morning. It's only a matter of time before one of them finds out about last night's meeting."

Donati sighed. "Have you any good news?"

"The Polizia di Stato just released the name and occupation of the man who was killed in Ostiense last night."

"Was that fake priest really the gunman?"

"That is my suspicion, Holiness."

Donati frowned. "Must you call me that?"

"I shall today, if you don't mind."

He squeezed Gabriel's hand. "Don't worry, *mio amico*. Everything will be fine."

"I'd feel better if you used the bulletproof popemobile."

"Too late for that," said Donati, and closed his eyes.

"Say one for me too, Holiness."

"If you must know," replied Donati irritably, "I was only trying to get a few minutes of sleep."

52

Lampedusa

The supreme pontiff of the Roman Catholic Church does not have an airplane of his own; he merely borrows one when needed from the Italian national carrier ITA Airways. His usual jetliner had a customized forward cabin with devotional pictures and a privacy door bearing the papal seal. But the short runway at Lampedusa Airport required the papal entourage to squeeze onto a smaller turboprop instead. The flight was designated AZ4000, the number reserved for the pope.

Ordinarily there were two rows of seats in the plane's first-class cabin, but the airline had removed the first row in order to give Donati, the tallest man to ever occupy the papacy, more legroom. He spent most of the flight reworking the remarks he planned to deliver at the refugee center in Lampedusa. Gabriel and Father Keegan, seated on the opposite side of the aisle, monitored the fast-breaking news on the Internet. The story of Ottavio Pozzi's brutal murder had spread beyond Italy. One of the London papers had made reference to the recent death of a young British art conservator in Venice. And then there was the still unsolved murder of the renowned Leonardo expert Giorgio Montefiore. Social media was ablaze with rumors and speculation, much of it generated by the *Vaticanisti*, who were blasting away on their feeds from the back of the airplane.

Ninety minutes into the flight, the director of the Vatican Press

Office, a slick former television reporter from Madrid named Esteban Rodríguez, poked his head into the forward cabin and looked at Father Keegan.

"We've got big trouble."

"Ottavio Pozzi?"

Rodríguez nodded. "We have to say something."

"The Holy See is shocked and outraged by this unspeakable act of violence."

"Is there anything else I should know?"

"Probably, Esteban. But now is not the time."

"What about Cardinal Bertoli?"

Donati looked up from his remarks. "Tell the *Vaticanisti* that His Eminence has a touch of the flu and regrettably was unable to make the trip."

"Is that the truth, Holiness?"

"Of course not. But when has that ever mattered to the Press Office?"

"Might I raise another matter, Holiness?"

"Quickly."

The director cast a nervous glance in Gabriel's direction before speaking. "Several reporters recognized Signore Allon when we were boarding at Fiumicino. They were wondering why he is accompanying you."

"Tell the reporters that they are mistaken."

"But, Holiness . . ."

Donati ended the conversation with a languid wave of his hand, and Rodríguez headed aft to confront the lions. It took only twenty minutes for his words to find their way into print. They had little impact on the controversy swirling beneath the papal airplane. A dead museum guard, an absent Curial cardinal—surely there had to be a connection. It was now a race among the *Vaticanisti* to see who got the story first.

By then Gabriel could see the khaki-colored coastline of Tunisia outside his window. The seething cauldron of unrest known as Libya was straight ahead. Both countries served as embarkation points for desperate African migrants trying to make their way to Europe. More often than not, the Italian island of Lampedusa was their destination of choice.

The airport was located in the southeast corner of the island. They approached from the west, seemingly a few meters above the turquoise waters of the Mediterranean. Father Keegan, a nervous flyer, made the sign of the cross as the plane thudded safely onto the runway. Gabriel privately seconded the motion. The bumpy three-hour flight had played havoc with his back.

Alois Metzler had provided him with a standard-issue Swiss Guard miniature radio with an earpiece and wrist mic. He switched it on and heard the crosstalk of the Polizia di Stato officers posted on the tarmac. A delegation of local dignitaries, both political and religious, waited in the blinding Mediterranean sunlight, and several thousand sign-waving faithful strained at the metal barricades. The anticipation was palpable. The rock star pope had arrived.

The plane rolled to a stop, and a pair of mobile stairways approached the front and rear doors. The security personnel filed off the aircraft first, followed by the Curial traveling party and the Vatican press corps. Then Alois Metzler entered the first-class cabin with two of his men.

"Ready when you are, Holiness."

Donati rose to his feet and looked at Gabriel. "I think you're going to enjoy this."

"From your mouth to God's ear."

"That can be arranged, *mio amico*."

Donati stepped into the open doorway, revealing himself to the crowd below.

It was pandemonium.

One of his predecessors had made a habit of kissing the ground upon reaching his destination, but Donati merely blessed the crowd with two regal motions of his right hand. Then the security detail encircled him, with the Polizia di Stato providing the outer ring of protection and the Swiss Guard the inner ring. Gabriel, having positioned himself in the Holy Father's proverbial hip pocket, was the last line of defense.

His Holiness greeted the assembled dignitaries first, beginning with Lampedusa's mayor, who was so starstruck that Gabriel feared the man might faint. Everyone received a moment of Donati's undivided attention, a moment they would never forget. He embraced them, he laid hands upon them. And if they insisted, he allowed them to kiss the Ring of the Fisherman, though it was widely known that he despaired of this most ancient of papal rituals. One of the dignitaries, a woman in her thirties, was confined to a wheelchair. So overwhelming was the impact of Donati's blessing that Gabriel thought she might rise to her feet and walk again.

The official schedule called for the motorcade to depart the airport immediately following the tarmac meet-and-greet. His Holiness, however, headed for the metal barricades instead. The concentric rings of security tightened as the now delirious crowd surged forward. He blessed their rosaries and their crucifixes and their children, and they tugged at the hem of his white garment and pressed their lips to the heavy ring of gold on his right hand. Gabriel's right hand rested protectively against the fascia wrapped around Donati's waist. Twice he had to retrieve the fallen papal zucchetto.

Finally, fifteen minutes behind schedule, His Holiness headed for the waiting motorcade and squeezed into the back seat of a tiny all-electric Fiat. Gabriel climbed in next to him, and Father Keegan dropped into the passenger seat. The driver was a handsome, square-shouldered Helvetian. Gabriel rapped a knuckle lightly against his window. It was ordinary vehicle glass.

"Well?" asked Donati as the motorcade jerked forward. "Was it what you expected?"

"No, Holiness. It was overwhelming."

"But this isn't your first rodeo, as our American friends like to say. You've seen the adulation that comes with the job."

"That's true. But you're different."

"Wait until we get to Palermo." Father Keegan handed him a disinfectant wipe, which he used to clean the Ring of the Fisherman. "I really wish they wouldn't kiss it."

"You can't blame them, Holiness. It's tradition."

"So was burning heretics at the stake. But we don't do that anymore."

Gabriel and Father Keegan checked their phones.

"How bad is it?" asked Donati.

"Ten on the Richter scale," said Gabriel.

"Pompeii," seconded Father Keegan.

Donati sighed. "In that case, I suppose I have no choice but to change the subject."

The rickety twenty-meter fishing trawler had set sail from the Libyan port of Misrata. On board were nearly five hundred migrants from Eritrea, Somalia, and Ghana who had each paid $3,000 to a human trafficking network to smuggle them to Europe. On the moonless night of October 3, 2013, after spending two days adrift on the Mediterranean, the trawler approached Lampedusa's southern coast.

When no one on shore spotted the vessel, a passenger set fire to a blanket, hoping it would attract notice. Instead the burning blanket ignited canisters of gasoline, and soon the ship was ablaze. Most of the migrants, many of whom could not swim, hurled themselves into the sea. The remaining passengers were cast into the water when the vessel capsized. The Italian Coast Guard, with the help of Lampedusa's fishing fleet, would eventually recover the bodies of 368 people, including a baby who had been born aboard the doomed boat. The dead were laid out dockside in Lampedusa's harbor, an image that, more than a decade after the disaster, remained seared into the memories of the island's inhabitants.

The shipwreck had occurred less than a kilometer from Lampedusa's famed Spiaggia dei Conigli, one of the world's most popular beaches. His Holiness traveled to the spot aboard a Coast Guard patrol boat, accompanied by a flotilla of fishing vessels that had taken part in the rescue and recovery efforts. He dropped a wreath of flowers into the sea and prayed for those who had perished—and for those who were all but certain to die as war and famine compelled ever-greater numbers of the world's poorest people to seek a better life in the West. Then the boats sounded their horns in unison. It sounded to Gabriel like the desperate cries of the drowning.

The survivors of the shipwreck were taken to the Lampedusa immigrant reception center, where Donati headed next. As was often the case, it was overwhelmed by new arrivals, many of whom were camped in the surrounding streets or in an adjacent field. Donati walked among them, a towering figure in white, dispensing blessings and parcels of food and clothing. Inside the overcrowded center he delivered his remarks, which bore no resemblance to the ones that had been written for him by the Curia. The message of the Gospels, he said, compelled Christians to show kindness and compassion to strangers, regardless of their religious faith or the color of their skin. Therefore, one could not possibly call oneself a Christian and behave with indifference toward the suffering of others. He reserved his harshest criticism, though, for the politicians of the far right who pursued power by stoking anti-immigrant resentment among their followers. Roundups and mass deportations, he declared, were not only inhumane, they were unchristian. Jesus would not have remained silent in the face of such cruelty, and neither would his Church. It was, thought Gabriel, yet another declaration of war.

Not far from the reception center was a barren field strewn with the carcasses of hundreds of broken and dilapidated migrant ships. Donati was moved to despair by the piles of abandoned shoes and clothing, all that remained of those whose desperate attempt to reach Europe had ended in death. Emotionally exhausted, he crawled into the back of the tiny Fiat for the short drive back to the airport. The sight of jubilant crowds lining the road temporarily lifted his spirits.

"Stop the car," he commanded. "I want to walk."

"Please don't," said Gabriel. "They haven't been screened for weapons."

"I will not ride in this car while women and children are huddled in a nearby field without adequate food or shelter."

Gabriel raised his wrist mic to his lips and informed Alois Metzler of the Holy Father's intentions. Then he looked at Donati and said, "No crowd surfing, Holiness."

"You have my word."

"And please keep things moving," added Father Keegan. "We're already behind schedule."

"Don't worry, they can't start the papal mass in Palermo without me."

And with that, Donati leapt from the back of the car and rushed headlong into the crowd's embrace. By the time Gabriel and the rest of the security detail caught up with him, His Holiness was cradling a small boy in his arms and posing for a selfie with the child's parents.

One of the Polizia di Stato officers returned the child to his mother, and Gabriel, with a firm tug at the papal fascia, managed to get His Holiness moving again. He strode past the crowds at a determined clip, his right arm raised in blessing, a soldier of God on a mission of mercy. As he was nearing the entrance of the airport, a wild-eyed man lunged toward him while clutching a long daggerlike weapon in his right hand. Or so it appeared to Gabriel, whose lightning-fast response resulted in the attacker being taken violently to the ground. Only then did Gabriel realize that the object in the man's hand was nothing more dangerous than a silver crucifix. When Donati helped the fallen pilgrim to his feet, the multitude roared its approval. For better or worse, they had managed to change the subject.

53

Palermo

During his first trip as the newly elected pope, Luigi Donati had startled the Vatican press corps by conducting an impromptu news conference in the back of his plane, a practice he continued throughout his papacy. His failure to address reporters after his emotionally charged visit to Lampedusa was viewed by most of the *Vaticanisti* as still more evidence that His Holiness was hiding something. The wily Esteban Rodríguez of the Press Office blamed it on the short duration of the flight—it was less than an hour—and on the fact that the Holy Father was still hard at work on his homily for the open-air mass in Palermo. That much, at least, was true.

There was no crowd on hand when the papal plane touched down at Palermo Airport, and only a small delegation of Sicilian VIPs waited on the tarmac. Donati greeted them cordially, then squeezed into the back seat of another all-electric Fiat for the twenty-minute drive to the site of the open-air mass. Gabriel once again sat at his side, though this time he didn't bother with an inspection of his window. The supreme pontiff of the Roman Catholic Church, spiritual leader of more than a billion souls, was riding in an unarmored vehicle through one of Western Europe's most dangerous cities.

"You disapprove?"

"Strenuously, Holiness."

"I will not travel in a bombproof saloon car like some potentate."

"But you *are* a potentate."

"I'm an absolute monarch. There's a difference."

"You are also the only hope in a world gone mad," said Gabriel. "Someone has to speak for the poorest among us. Someone has to tell those who call themselves Christians that they are behaving in ways that Jesus himself wouldn't recognize."

"Do I really make a difference? Sometimes I'm not so sure."

"You were extraordinary in Lampedusa. You changed hearts and minds."

Donati adopted a confiding tone. "I'll let you in on a little secret, *mio amico*. You haven't seen anything yet."

The grassy park known as the Foro Italico stretched for several hundred meters along Palermo's picturesque waterfront. An undulating mass of humanity, some three hundred thousand in number, filled it from stem to stern. Gabriel walked the perimeter of the esplanade and was pleased to see Italian cops with handheld mags opening backpacks and patting down pilgrims. There were sharpshooters on the rooftops of nearby buildings and Carabinieri patrol boats in the whitecapped bay. Someone, it seemed, had gotten the message.

The temporary altar was the size of a stage at an outdoor music festival and flanked by jumbotrons. Gabriel searched the underside of the platform for stray parcels or toolboxes left behind by workmen—anything that might contain a bomb. Then he headed to the small trailer behind the platform where Father Keegan was placing the pallium over Donati's gold-embroidered chasuble.

"Nervous?" he asked.

"A little, Holiness."

"If you'd like to reprise your role as Father Benedetti, I'm sure we can find some vestments for you."

"I think I'll watch from the wings with Colonel Metzler."

"That's probably for the better. But please try not to assault anyone. We wouldn't want another ugly incident."

Gabriel left Donati's trailer and found Metzler standing on the left side of the altar. The afternoon light was beginning to fade, and the massive crowd was growing restless. His Holiness, as was often the case, was running late.

Metzler checked the time. "When he was the private secretary, he was punctual as a Swiss watch. But now that he's pope . . ."

"His Tardiness?"

"We call it Donati time. It's an hour behind the rest of Rome."

"I'll be sure to let him know."

"Please do."

Just then one of the Swiss Guards posted outside Donati's trailer came on the radio to say that His Holiness was on the move. He processed onto the altar only thirty minutes behind schedule, accompanied by dozens of cardinals, bishops, monsignori, and priests. After sanctifying the table and the crucifix with incense, he took his place before a simple wooden celebrant's chair and made the sign of the cross.

"In the name of the Father, and of the Son, and of the Holy Spirit."

Three hundred thousand voices replied, "Amen."

"Watch this," said Alois Metzler.

"I'm watching," replied Gabriel.

———

It occurred to Gabriel during the recitation of the Kyrie that he had never seen his old friend celebrate a mass. Donati's own sense was that he was not terribly good at it, that he was an intellectual and a missionary at heart, better suited to the jungles and the favelas than to a parish church. He was wrong about that, though; with his towering physical presence and warm baritone voice, he commanded the enormous altar as an actor commands the stage. Even Gabriel, who had known Donati more than twenty years, could scarcely take his eyes off him. In the Foro Italico, no one stirred. The three hundred thousand Catholic faithful were in his thrall.

When it came time for him to deliver his homily, the sun was dipping below the buildings along the western side of the esplanade. He was slow in taking to the pulpit, deliberate. Father Keegan attempted to place a leather portfolio before him, but he returned it with a kindly smile. The message was unmistakable. On this perfect Saturday afternoon in Palermo, the Vicar of Christ planned to address his flock without aid of a prepared script.

"There is a hill not far from the Sea of Galilee," he began at last. "One day early in his ministry, Jesus gathered his disciples atop this hill and delivered a sermon. The words he spoke that day were considered so vital to our faith that early Christians were compelled to memorize them. And yet many of us seem to have forgotten them. And so, my brothers and sisters, if you will indulge me, I will recite a few of them now, for I can say with certainty that they were the reason I became a priest." He paused for what seemed like an eternity, then said, "Blessed are the poor in spirit, for theirs is the Kingdom of Heaven. Blessed are they who mourn, for they will be comforted. Blessed are the meek—"

Three hundred thousand voices supplied the final six words of the verse.

"For they shall inherit the earth."

Donati cast a glance in Gabriel's direction, then asked, "Where in the fifth chapter of Matthew does Jesus say that those of unimaginable wealth will be welcomed into the Kingdom of Heaven? Or those who use political power to serve their own interests rather than the interests of their people? Blessed is the oligarch? Blessed is the tyrant? Blessed is the torturer? The oppressor? The cruel of heart? Forgive me, my brothers and sisters, but my copy of Matthew omitted those lines."

He waited for a ripple of laughter to die away before continuing. "Nor did Jesus ever instruct his apostles to build a Church that acquired great wealth of its own. Or a Church that refused to adapt and change. My goodness, it wasn't until three centuries after Our Lord died on a Roman cross that we settled the most basic tenets of our faith, tenets which we will affirm in a few moments when we recite the words of the Creed. And time and time again down through the centuries, we convened councils to make additional changes to our doctrine and practice. Not all of the changes were wise, and some did profound damage to the Church. But that does not mean change is something to fear. Sometimes it is necessary. I submit to you, my brothers and sisters, that now is just such a time."

For the next twenty minutes, as the sky darkened and the air turned cold, he explained why that was the case. Because the world, he proclaimed, needed the Church now more than ever. It needed a healthy Church, a vital Church, a merciful Church, and, yes, a younger Church. A Church that did not have to go begging for priests. A Church unafraid to take sides. A Church on the barricades. A Church that looked after those in harm's way.

"A Church that follows the simple lessons that Jesus gave to his disciples on that hilltop near the Sea of Galilee." Donati spread his arms wide as though he were standing on the same hilltop. "Blessed are the poor in spirit."

"For theirs is the Kingdom of Heaven," replied the multitude.

"Blessed are they who mourn."

"For they will be comforted."

"Blessed are the meek."

"For they shall inherit the earth."

He made the sign of the cross. "In the name of the Father, and of the Son, and of the Holy Spirit."

Three hundred thousand voices thundered, "Amen."

54

Casa Santa Marta

It was a few minutes after 6:00 p.m. when His Holiness placed newly consecrated hosts on the tongues of forty young first communicants. A battalion of ciborium-wielding priests and deacons then presented the sacrament to the rest of the multitude in a remarkable display of precision and planning. Even so, it would be another hour before Donati finally delivered the Concluding Rite, commanding the faithful to go forth and serve the Lord. It sounded to Gabriel like a call to arms. The final "Amen" of the mass made the temporary altar tremble beneath his feet.

A large portion of the crowd joined Donati's procession to Palermo Cathedral, and tens of thousands of ecstatic Sicilians lined the route. His visit to the tomb of Father Pino Puglisi was private, with only Archbishop Cordero and the Curial delegation present. Then he slipped out a side door and into the back of his Fiat 500 for the high-speed ride to the airport. ITA Airways Flight AZ4000 departed Palermo at nine fifteen, and two hours later His Holiness was striding through the glass doorway of the Casa Santa Marta. Despite the lateness of the hour, he insisted that Gabriel join him for dinner.

"Forgive me, Holiness. But I've had enough excitement for one day."

"I know a little place that stays open late. I think you'll find it interesting."

Gabriel was relieved when Donati led him downstairs to the Casa's kitchen. They sat at a small table in the corner while two nuns from the Daughters of Charity warmed leftovers from the evening meal—rigatoni pomodoro, green beans with garlic and olive oil, thick slices of *vitella alla fornara*. Gabriel read the reviews of the papal trip while Donati, a napkin tucked into the collar of his white cassock, ate his first meal since breakfast. The *New York Times* had declared the homily "an earthquake" that was certain to anger traditionalists who were already wary of the liberal pope's intentions. *La Repubblica* said it was the clearest signal yet that His Holiness intended to call a Third Vatican Council to address the divisive issues confronting the Catholic Church.

"Did any of the reporters speak to Cardinal Byrne, by any chance?"

"I'm afraid so, Holiness."

"He disapproved, I take it?"

"He called it heretical rubbish."

"I expected far worse."

"He's also convinced you're preparing to call Vatican Three."

"He's wrong. Not for the first time, I might add. It's possible I'll call one at some point, but not now."

"Why wait?"

"I have other more pressing matters to attend to, including Cardinal Byrne himself. I'm afraid His Eminence is about to lose his salary and that rather palatial subsidized apartment of his."

"What is it with the apartments?" asked Gabriel.

"It's an obsession around here. Most of the younger priests live in dormitory-style religious houses or in dreadful little apartments. They spend their days plotting against one another at the office, and on the way home the children of Rome call them *bagarozzi*." It was the Italian word for black beetles. "If they're lucky enough to become a bishop, they get a modest subsidized apartment with a few sticks of furniture. The big apartments are reserved for the red-hatted princes of the Church. And yet even then, they're never satisfied. How many square meters is it? Is it within the walls or without? Are there enough rooms for household nuns and perhaps a relative or two? It never ends." Donati impaled a tube of rigatoni. "This isn't bad, you know. They've definitely raised their game."

"They must have found out about your secret visits to Osteria Lucrezia."

"We should have a drop of wine, don't you think?"

"It's late."

"My mother always said a little wine before bed was good for the blood."

"Mothers are never wrong."

"Especially Italian mothers."

"Or Jewish."

Donati asked one of the nuns to bring some wine, and she returned a moment later with a bottle of Umbrian red. Gabriel removed the cork and filled their glasses.

"What will happen to Cardinal Bertoli?"

"If I had any sense, I would take his advice and sweep the matter under the Curial rug."

"It won't stay there. The Italians are determined to go after the Camorra's money laundering operation. And they're going to start by arresting Nico Ambrosi and Franco Tedeschi."

"But they won't have much of a case against them without the cooperation of Cardinal Bertoli."

"Spoken like a canon lawyer. But you're not really thinking about letting him off the hook, are you?"

"It will be a fight to the death, *mio amico*. And even if I pre-
vail, I will undoubtedly inflict damage on my papacy in the process.
You have to understand, the Curia and the powerful cardinals run
the Catholic Church. They merely tolerate a pope. My only hope of
bringing about lasting reform is to survive."

Gabriel held up his wineglass to the light. "In that case, you should
try some of this Sagrantino. It's delicious."

"The grapes come from a village in Umbria called Montefalco. I
lived not far from there during my sabbatical from the priesthood."

In a little villa on the slopes of Monte Cucco, thought Gabriel. A
beautiful young archaeologist named Veronica Marchese had lived
there too.

"I suppose you'll be returning to Venice tomorrow," said Donati.

"If I don't, I will no longer be employed by the Tiepolo Restoration Company."

"I'm going to miss you. In spite of everything, I've enjoyed having
you around."

"With any luck, I'll be back soon."

"The Leonardo?"

Gabriel nodded.

"I suppose we should discuss your fee."

"It will be astronomical."

"Didn't you listen to my homily in Palermo? Blessed are the poor."

"I have a wife and two children who need looking after."

Donati smiled sadly. He and Veronica were going to have children
too. Lots of children.

"Which train are you taking?" he asked.

"Midmorning, I suppose."

"Is there any way I can convince you to postpone your departure
until after the Angelus?"

"I really should be leaving."

Donati sighed. "When a pope personally invites someone to attend the Angelus, the answer is yes."

"It would be my honor, Holiness."

"Perhaps our friend would like to attend as well."

"Is that an invitation?"

"I suppose it is."

"Then I'm sure the answer is yes."

55

St. Peter's Square

The video of Gabriel's encounter with the crucifix-wielding pilgrim in Lampedusa was by half past ten the following morning an Internet sensation. Nevertheless, when he checked out of the Hassler, the girl at reception handed him a copy of his bill with a vacant smile and wished him a pleasant day. He left his bag with the porter and headed across the Piazza di Spagna to Caffè Greco. Veronica Marchese and Luca Rossetti were drinking coffee at a table in the front room. Gabriel ordered a cappuccino at the counter and joined them.

Rossetti pointed to the photograph splashed across the front page of *La Repubblica*. "The fellow on the Holy Father's right reminds me of someone I know."

"He's a plainclothes Swiss Guard who happens to look a bit like me."

"The resemblance is uncanny."

"Not if you look closely."

Veronica did just that. "I'm afraid I have to agree with Luca. But since when does the Swiss Guard hire men of your age?"

"And what age is that, Dottoressa Marchese?"

"Bronze."

"She would know," said Rossetti. "After all, she's a rather prominent archaeologist."

A waiter delivered Gabriel's cappuccino. "Are the two of you quite finished?"

"Actually," answered Rossetti, "we were wondering what provoked you to assault an innocent pilgrim."

"I thought the pilgrim was about to plunge a knife into the pontiff."

"No other trouble?"

"None at all. It was an unforgettable day."

"So why are we going to the Angelus?"

"Because His Holiness insisted I come, and I wanted some company."

"You're not going to assault anyone, are you?"

"To be determined."

Rossetti rubbed his jaw. "I'm lucky you didn't kill me."

Gabriel smiled. "Double or nothing?"

Veronica devoured a cream-filled cornetto while walking between Gabriel and Luca Rossetti through the cold shadows of the Via dei Condotti. She spoke of the Holy Father's controversial homily in Palermo as though he were merely the spiritual leader of a billion Catholics and not someone she had once planned to marry. Rossetti appeared to have no sense she was dissembling. She had been hiding her true feelings about Luigi Donati for more than thirty years. She was rather good at it by now.

It became apparent when they reached the Via della Conciliazione that this would be no ordinary Sunday Angelus. Thousands of faithful were streaming westward toward the Vatican, and thousands more were queued at the magnetometers at the edge of St. Peter's Square. Veronica pointed out the unusually large number of television crews, their cameras trained on the distant window where the rock star pope would soon appear.

"I've never seen anything like this at a Sunday Angelus. It's as if they're expecting the Second Coming."

"He's made the papacy relevant again," replied Gabriel.

"The global street priest? A Church on the barricades?"

"I saw it with my own eyes yesterday in Lampedusa."

"Lucky you." Veronica looked at the long lines stretching from the magnetometers. "Is there any chance we can use the VIP entrance?"

Gabriel turned to Luca Rossetti and said, "We'll meet you in the square."

Rossetti displayed his Carabinieri badge to a Vatican gendarme, then swung a leg over the barrier and disappeared into the crowd. Gabriel and Veronica headed to St. Anne's Gate. The halberdier waved them over the border with a crisp salute, and Gabriel slipped into the Swiss Guard barracks. The duty officer at the reception desk practically leapt to his feet.

"Good morning, Herr Allon."

"My friend and I are planning to attend the Angelus. Do you mind if we take the shortcut through the palace?"

"Not a problem. I'll let the sentries know you're coming."

Gabriel stepped outside and collected Veronica. She clung to his arm as they headed up the Via Sant'Anna, two sinners in the city of saints.

"Was it my imagination," asked Gabriel, "or were you just flirting with that handsome young halberdier?"

"I was merely helping to relieve the terrible boredom of his job. They work those poor boys like slaves."

"I have a feeling my friend Luca Rossetti has fallen hopelessly under your spell."

"I know he has. But I made it clear to Luca that I was in love with someone else." She slowed to a stop outside the entrance of the Vatican Bank. Because it was a Sunday, it was tightly shuttered. "It's the belly of the beast, this so-called Institute for Religious Works. The root of all the scandals and corruption. Luigi needs to raze it and start over."

"I have it on the highest authority he intends to do just that."

"Do they know what's coming?"

"If they don't by now, they will in a few minutes."

"A poor Church? The end of Vatican Incorporated? If he isn't careful, the entire enterprise could come crashing down."

A few paces beyond the Vatican Bank was a rear entrance to the Apostolic Palace. Because the Holy Father no longer dwelled there, security inside was not what it once was. Gabriel and Veronica walked unchallenged across the San Damaso Courtyard and out the Bronze Doors, into St. Peter's Square. The crowd was nearly as large as the one that had greeted Donati on the night of his election. Gabriel dialed Rossetti's number but the call failed to connect. The thirty thousand or so mobile phones packed into the square had soaked up all the available cellular service.

Gabriel took Veronica by the hand, and they waded into the densely packed mass of humanity. After five minutes of determined effort they reached the Maderno Fountain. The upper floors of the Apostolic Palace were visible above Bernini's Colonnade. The window of the papal study, the last on the uppermost floor, was closed tight.

Veronica stood on the tips of her toes. "Do you really think he'll be able to see us when we're surrounded by all these people?"

"I'm sure he will."

She laughed at herself. "It's rather pathetic, don't you think?"

"Being madly in love with someone you can't possibly have?"

"Yes."

"I think it's the greatest love story never told."

"Like Romeo and Juliet?"

"Better."

"But shouldn't I be the one on the balcony?"

"Too cliché."

"How does it end, this story? Does the girl get the boy?"

"No, Veronica. I'm afraid not."

"So terribly tragic. But what happens to her?"

"She falls in love with someone else before it's too late."

"Talk about cliché. Besides, the girl can never love another. In the end, the boy will die surrounded by red-robed princes, and the girl will die alone." She checked the time. "The window is usually open by now."

"He must be running late."

Veronica frowned. "Donati time."

———

Previous popes had only to rise from their desk and walk two or three paces to reach the window on the eastern corner of the Apostolic Palace. His Holiness Luigi Donati, however, had to first make his way to the palace from his lesser quarters in the Casa Santa Marta. Typically he walked there with Father Keegan, which gave him a moment to gather his thoughts. On that morning, however, he made the short journey in an all-electric motorcar, for it was true he was running late.

The car delivered them to the San Damaso Courtyard, and an ornate elevator bore them slowly to the third floor. To the left were the offices of the Secretariat of State. The twenty rooms of the *appartamento pontificio* were to the right.

A Swiss Guard opened the door, and Donati followed Father Keegan inside. As usual, he found the sheer size of the place overwhelming, but he had always been fond of the private study. The window and the shades had been thrown open to the glorious Roman morning—and to the sustained roar of the immense crowd gathered in the square below. Father Keegan placed the prepared text on the plexiglass lectern, then gave Donati a serious look.

"I would advise His Holiness to deliver the address as written."

"And what if the Holy Spirit compels me to take a detour or two?"

"Resist."

"Defy the will of the Holy Spirit? Is that really your counsel, Father Keegan?" Receiving no answer, Donati checked his old Hamilton wristwatch. "Shall we?"

"Yes, Holiness. It's time."

Donati waited ten additional seconds, then stepped in front of the open window.

It was pandemonium.

———

He stood there for a long moment, his arms extended over the rapturous throng in the square, seemingly unaware of the fact that someone was shooting at him. So deafening were the cheers that Gabriel only noticed the gunfire when he spotted the wound in the palace facade about a meter to Donati's right. The next shot splintered the open shutter, and the third struck Donati in the center of his chest, directly above his silver pectoral cross.

Gabriel was unaware of precisely what happened next because he was knocked to the paving stones of the square by a tsunami of panicked faithful. When he found his footing again, he realized that Veronica was no longer at his side. He spotted her a few seconds later. She was desperately trying to pry a weapon from the grasp of a slender figure wearing a black clerical suit and raincoat. Then there was another gunshot, and she collapsed as though a trapdoor had opened beneath her.

The slender figure in a clerical suit and raincoat then leveled his gun toward Gabriel, and an instant later he heard two more shots. It would take him a moment to realize that both shots had been fired by Luca Rossetti and that he was not in fact dead. He fought his way through the fleeing crowd to the spot where Veronica lay next to the assassin in a pool of shared blood. "Please hold me," she said before losing consciousness. "The girl doesn't want to die alone."

PART FOUR

Non Finito

56

The Gemelli

It was Luca Rossetti who lifted Veronica from the blood-soaked paving stones of St. Peter's Square and Gabriel who frantically fought to clear a path through the panicked crowd. Five long minutes elapsed before they managed to reach the ambulance parked just beyond the border barrier. Two EMTs, after placing Veronica on a stretcher, immediately attempted to restart her heart. Gabriel lifted his eyes briefly toward the third-floor window on the eastern corner of the Apostolic Palace. Once again it was closed tight.

Another ten critical minutes would slide by before the ambulance reached the Agostino Gemelli University Policlinic, the renowned Rome teaching hospital located five kilometers northwest of Vatican City. By the time Gabriel and Luca Rossetti arrived—in a commandeered Carabinieri cruiser with blue lights flashing—Veronica was on the operating table. She would remain there until four o'clock that afternoon. Doctors described her condition as guarded, though for reasons never made clear they withheld her name from their public statement. The chief surgeon said the next twelve hours would likely determine whether she lived or died.

Of more immediate concern to the news media and a billion Roman Catholics around the world was the exact condition of His

Holiness Luigi Donati. Videos of the incident, recorded by professional photojournalists and thousands of faithful gathered in the square, left little doubt that he had been struck by at least one projectile, perhaps two. And yet for six long hours after the incident, the Vatican Press Office inexplicably had nothing to say about what had transpired in St. Peter's Square. Clearly, said the well-sourced American correspondent from a prominent Catholic news service, the Holy See was hiding something.

A flurry of dubiously sourced stories and social media posts only added to the confusion. A usually reliable German publication was the first to report that His Holiness had been killed in the attack. Minutes later a New York tabloid quoted "a Vatican insider" as saying the Holy Father's body was stretched out in the Sala Clementina with a rosary in its hands. An American cable news network played somber music while reporting that cardinals from around the world had been summoned to Rome for the Holy Father's funeral. A London betting parlor declared Cardinal Matteo Bertoli, the Substitute for General Affairs of the Secretariat of State, to be the odds-on favorite to emerge from the forthcoming conclave dressed in white.

By five o'clock that afternoon, even Gabriel feared that Donati might well be dead, for all attempts to reach Father Keegan or Colonel Alois Metzler had proven fruitless. Alone in a VIP waiting room at the Gemelli, he watched the live coverage on Italian television and scoured the Internet for reliable sources of information. CNN had obtained a cell phone video of Luca Rossetti killing the black-clad assassin. It was clear the gunman had been aiming his weapon at someone in the square. Someone who would now be dead, thought Gabriel, had Rossetti not fired his weapon first.

The Press Office *bollettino*, when it finally appeared, was notable for its lack of detail, stating only that the Holy Father was resting comfortably and praying for the woman who had been wounded in the incident. Shortly after 9:00 p.m., she was moved from the postsurgical critical care unit to a suite of rooms on the Gemelli's eleventh floor—rooms that were reserved for the supreme pontiff of the Roman Catholic Church. Gabriel arrived twenty minutes later to find His Holiness Luigi Donati kneeling on a simple wooden prie-dieu at the foot of her bed. There were two bullet holes in the front of his white cassock. And he was still very much alive.

———————

Body armor?" asked Gabriel.

"A lightweight vest. It's perfect for the busy pontiff on the go."

"How often do you wear it?"

"When there are specific and credible threats against my life. When I was in the United States, I never set foot in public without it."

"But you weren't wearing it yesterday in Lampedusa or Palermo."

"You noticed?"

"My hand was on your back while you were working the crowds."

"Which is why I didn't feel the need to wear the vest. You were at my side. I knew that nothing was going to happen to me."

They were alone in a small, comfortably furnished sitting room. There was a papal seal on the door and a crucifix on the wall. From the adjoining room came the occasional bleep of a respirator and the hushed voices of nurses. The muted television seemed to be playing the same thirty seconds of video on a loop. A pope under fire as he stood in an open window of the Apostolic Palace. Mayhem and bloodshed in the square below.

"What made you put on the vest today?" asked Gabriel.

"An important part of my job is to lead a life of prayer and meditation. I spend several hours a day talking to God. And on occasion God speaks to me."

"He gave you a warning?"

"A vision."

"And when the bullets hit you?"

"I felt as though I had stepped in front of a speeding train. For a minute or two, I could scarcely breathe or speak. I remained in the *appartamento* for the remainder of the afternoon until we were certain the Vatican was secure. During that time I received only one member of the Roman Curia."

"His Eminence Cardinal Bertoli?"

Donati nodded. "As you might imagine, he expressed profound relief that I had suffered only minor injuries. But I was left with the nagging sense that he was rather disappointed I was still alive."

"Was he behind it?"

"I believe the plot against me was hatched on Friday evening after our confrontation with Cardinal Bertoli. It was Don Lorenzo Di Falco of the Camorra who ordered my assassination."

"That would explain why I was the second target. Bertoli told them that I was the one who switched the paintings."

"And stole their money?"

"Rerouted it, Holiness."

"Powerful circumstantial evidence of the cardinal's guilt," said Donati. "Even so, the charges that I will soon level against Bertoli will not include conspiracy to murder a pope. There is some laundry that is far too dirty to air in public. The world must never know what really happened today."

"An act of madness by a lone gunman?"

"Why not?"

"Because it's all going to come out, Luigi. Sooner rather than later."

"And what happens when the press discovers the name of the woman who tried to disarm the gunman? Or that many years ago she had a passionate affair with the supreme pontiff of the Roman Catholic Church?"

"You will ignore the story and carry on with your important work."

"Leaving her to face the scandal alone?" Donati shook his head slowly. "I couldn't possibly do that. After all, I was the one who invited her to attend the Angelus today. I'm the reason she's lying in that bed."

"It's my fault, Luigi. I lost track of her when the shooting started. And when I saw her again, she was trying to take the gun out of the assassin's hands."

"What could have possessed her to do something like that?"

"Do you really need me to answer that question?"

Donati directed his gaze toward the television screen. A pope under fire, mayhem in the square below. "It's much different than it was in my vision."

"How?"

"There was a different pope in the window. An old man with snow-white hair." Donati rose to his feet. "How long are you planning to stay?"

"Until I'm sure she's going to make it."

"Would you like some company?"

"I would advise His Holiness to return to the Vatican."

He went into the next room instead and knelt on the wooden prie-dieu at the foot of Veronica's bed. She had been wrong about the ending of the story, thought Gabriel. If the girl died tonight, she would not die alone.

———

He remained there, hour after hour, as doctors came and went, and Veronica's vital signs steadily improved. And at half past six the next morning, when her eyes finally opened, the first face she saw was his. She stared at him as though wondering whether he was real or a dream, then began to weep. Donati wiped the tears from her cheek, and she slid once more beneath the veil of unconsciousness.

At 8:00 a.m. the doctors upgraded her condition from guarded to critical and expressed confidence that, barring an unforeseen complication, the wound to her chest would not prove fatal. Donati left the Gemelli at nine o'clock and returned to the Vatican, but Gabriel remained at Veronica's bedside until five that afternoon. He left the hospital in the back of a Carabinieri cruiser, with Luca Rossetti at his side. They stopped at the Hassler long enough for Gabriel to collect his bag, then boarded an evening train for Venice.

57

Vatican City

The great unraveling commenced at ten the following morning when Vatican and Italian police jointly released the identity of the man who attempted to assassinate the Holy Father during the Sunday Angelus prayer service. He was said to be Salvatore Alvaro, an unmarried electrician of thirty-six from Naples. Authorities declined to say how they had determined Alvaro's identity—or how he had managed to carry a loaded firearm into St. Peter's Square. Obviously, said the chief of the Vatican Gendarmerie, there had been a major breach of the city-state's security.

It therefore came as something of a surprise when later that same day the Press Office announced that the Holy See had retained three powerful international accounting firms to conduct a thorough review of the Vatican's byzantine finances. The auditors would deliver their findings to a commission of prominent Catholic laypersons, all corporate lawyers or financial services professionals, who would in turn make recommendations to the Holy Father. It was, wrote one respected commentator, the long-awaited papal shot across the bow of Vatican Incorporated.

The next unexpected turn of events came in Milan, where officers of the Carabinieri and Guardia di Finanza arrested Nico Ambrosi, a financier with close ties to the Vatican, on charges of embezzlement, fraud, and money laundering. In a move that rattled investors around the world, Swiss police simultaneously raided the headquarters of SBL PrivatBank in Lugano and froze hundreds of suspect accounts. Franco Tedeschi, the chief of SBL's asset management division, received advance warning of the raid and attempted to flee the country. He was taken into custody at Lugano Airport shortly after boarding the firm's Dassault Falcon executive jet. Swiss authorities seized the plane as well.

The following day brought shocking new details about the man who had attempted to kill the Holy Father. It emerged that Salvatore Alvaro had been arrested several times in his youth, that he had spent time in prison for armed robbery and kidnapping, that he was known to use aliases, and that he had lived for many years in France, Spain, and Morocco. Journalists who visited Alvaro's hardscrabble neighborhood in Naples were met with blank stares and slammed doors, which gave rise to speculation that he was not, in point of fact, a humble trades-man. Italy's top crime reporter pointed out that all the countries where Alvaro had lived abroad had been infiltrated by the Camorra. Alvaro, he wrote, was undoubtedly a Camorra soldier and assassin.

But why would a Camorra-linked gunman wish to kill the supreme pontiff? And why had His Holiness, only two days removed from the attempt on his life, launched an unprecedented outside review of the Vatican's finances? During the Wednesday General Audience, his first public appearance since the shooting, he had nothing to say on the subject, choosing instead to once again address the Church's obligation to help the poor and provide refuge to migrants. Against the wishes of his security detail, he circulated through the massive crowd gathered in St. Peter's Square in an open-sided popemobile. Vatican spokesman Esteban Rodríguez used the word *miracle* while attempting to explain how the Holy Father had survived the attack unscathed. The archconservative Cardinal Byrne, dispirited by the adoration shown to a pontiff he detested, acidly predicted the Holy Father would be declared a saint *before* his death.

But the video of the assassination attempt did not lie, and the questions continued unabated, especially after the Carabinieri launched a massive raid against the Camorra across the length and breadth of Campania. By the time the operation was over, more than two hundred members of the criminal organization were in custody. The top prosecutor in Naples called it the most devastating blow against the Camorra in years.

It was little wonder, then, that the Camorra made yet another attempt on the prosecutor's life, this time with a bomb planted outside his heavily defended home. His Holiness Luigi Donati condemned the attack during his next Sunday Angelus address, after which he received a preliminary report from the members of his special commission. There was no record of what was said during the session. But just twenty-four hours later, the Press Office issued a terse *bollettino* announcing the dismissal of Cardinal Matteo Bertoli, the Substitute for General Affairs of the Secretariat of State.

Missing from the *bollettino* was any reason for the abrupt firing of the third most powerful figure in the Roman Curia, which left the *Vaticanisti* no choice but to engage in unabashed speculation. The timing suggested it was somehow connected to the Holy Father's independent review of Vatican finances—a review the *sostituto* had reportedly opposed. The theory gained momentum the following day when the Holy Father stripped the Secretariat of State of billions of euros' worth of financial assets and real estate holdings and transferred them to the Vatican department known as Administration for the Patrimony of the Holy See, or APSA. Not two hours later, a beleaguered Cardinal Bertoli was evicted from his lavish apartment in the Palazzo San Carlo. He departed the Vatican that evening, a cardinal in name only, in the back of a humble Fiat 500 with no police escort. The Press Office said he was embarking on a life of prayer and penance at a remote abbey in the mountains west of Turin. "Better than being burned at the stake," remarked one anonymous Vatican insider. "But only barely."

But what sin had Bertoli committed to warrant so swift and severe a punishment? The president of APSA provided a vital clue the next morning when he announced that the Vatican would in short order liquidate its interest in a retail-and-office block located in London's New Bond Street. A more fulsome explanation appeared three days later on the front page of *La Repubblica*. Written by the paper's respected Vatican correspondent and based on a trove of internal documents, the explosive exposé detailed how Cardinal Bertoli had enriched himself while at the same time losing more than two billion euros in Church funds. Perhaps the story's most damning allegation was that Bertoli had knowingly entered into a relationship with two criminal financiers—Nico Ambrosi and Franco Tedeschi—who were in the business of laundering money for the Camorra. It all but accused the group of attempting to murder the Holy Father to prevent Bertoli's dismissal and exposure of its lucrative money laundering empire.

The story, while electrifying, was incomplete. It made no mention, for example, of an apprentice British art conservator named Penelope Radcliff. Or the renowned Leonardist Giorgio Montefiore. Or a museum guard named Ottavio Pozzi. Or a portrait of a young woman, oil on walnut panel, 78 by 56 centimeters, perhaps by Leonardo da Vinci, perhaps by a studio assistant or a later follower. Nor was there any reference to the links between the Holy Father and the woman who had suffered a near-fatal gunshot wound to the chest while trying to protect him. Three weeks to the day after the shooting, she left the Gemelli clinic and returned to her palazzo near the Via Veneto. As for the painting, it had vanished without a trace.

58

Harry's Bar

The negotiations with Antonio Calvesi were for the most part collegial, but on one point Gabriel refused to budge. He would carry out the restoration not in the conservation lab of the Vatican Museums but in his studio in Venice. He was not worried about the prospect of another theft. Having helped the Italian authorities deliver a devastating blow to the Camorra, he was now under full-time protection, as were his wife and children. The painting wasn't going anywhere.

The handover took place on the tarmac at Marco Polo Airport on the first Monday in February. Donatella Ricci had already made repairs to the walnut panel, and a noted Italian provenance researcher had commenced a quiet investigation of the painting's murky past. It was Calvesi's ambition to unveil the work in time for the summer tourist season. Gabriel, who was about to embark on the most important restoration of his career, made no promises.

The first order of business was to determine whether the portrait was in fact an autograph work by Leonardo da Vinci. It was not an attribution Gabriel could make on his own. Others more learned than he would have to examine the painting and render their verdicts, and a single dissenting opinion might doom the entire project.

But when to show the painting—and in what condition? For the sake of transparency, Gabriel decided to allow the world's top Leonardists to see the painting in a stripped state, with the damage clearly visible.

For now, it was in the condition that Gabriel had found it—hastily but competently restored. It took him the better part of a week to remove the varnish and the retouching and expose the original painting. He snapped several photographs of the panel and sent them to Antonio Calvesi at the Vatican via encrypted email. Chiara examined the painting that evening.

"Are you sure you want them to see it like this?"

"Positive."

"There's a considerable amount of damage."

"What did you expect? It's more than five hundred years old, and for the last two centuries or so it was covered by another painting."

"Could be risky."

"Perhaps. But I want the greatest Leonardo scholars in the world to examine the original brushwork with their own eyes, with no retouching or varnish."

It was Chiara, in her capacity as the managing director of the most prominent restoration firm in Venice, who placed the calls and issued the invitations. Ten days later the most respected Leonardo scholars in the world convened in Gabriel's studio. There was Santelli from Milan, Barnes from New York, Rolland from the Louvre, Kendall from Oxford, and from Leipzig University the mighty Professor Maximillian Zeller, who had once written that there were no remaining autograph works by Leonardo yet to be discovered.

Absent, of course, was Montefiore of the Uffizi. Gabriel omitted any reference to the late Leonardist during his presentation. Nor did he identify the apprentice British conservator who had found the painting slumbering beneath a Madonna and Child attributed to an eighteenth-century imitator of Raphael. The five experts examined the infrared and X-radiograph images, then took turns before the painting itself. One by one, they handed down their verdicts. There were no dissenting opinions or even equivocation. Gabriel rang Antonio Calvesi at the Vatican and gave him the news. They had their Leonardo.

———————

There were plainclothes Carabinieri officers in the streets around the palazzo, and a patrol boat was lashed to the quay. Gabriel reluctantly took to carrying his Beretta pistol again, even while standing before his easel. In the afternoons the children did their schoolwork in his studio, Raphael perched atop a stool at the worktable, Irene lying on the floor at Gabriel's feet. Bodyguards kept watch over Chiara as she shuttled between the apartment and the offices of the Tiepolo Restoration Company in San Marco.

Gabriel once again assumed Leonardo's work habits. Not the procrastinatory Leonardo who couldn't bear the sight of a paintbrush, but the Leonardo who began work each day before the sun had risen and retired when it had set again. He took a break each Wednesday afternoon to meet with his fourteen aspiring artists, and on Thursdays he always made certain to escort Raphael to the university for his weekly session with his tutor. Most nights they ate at home, but once or twice a week they ventured out with their bodyguards for dinner at one of their favorite restaurants. Afterward they would stop at Venchi in the Rialto for gelati. Irene always insisted on a supply of butter cookies for the walk home.

The Allon family's security detail increased in size in early March after the Carabinieri arrested Don Lorenzo Di Falco, leader of the

Camorra's most powerful clan. French police rounded up *camorristi* in Lyon and Marseilles, and Spanish authorities arrested a senior member of the Di Falco clan in Barcelona. SBL PrivatBank, having been abandoned by legitimate investors and depositors, closed its doors, sending shock waves through the global financial markets. Martin Landesmann snapped up the bank's elegant headquarters on the Piazza della Riforma at a bargain-basement price. A week later he took the New Bond Street building off the Holy See's hands. The loss on the original investment to Vatican Incorporated was an astonishing three hundred million euros.

Of seemingly lesser note was the story in London's *Telegraph* regarding a lawsuit filed by an ex-wife of Alexander Prokhorov, accusing the Russian oligarch of using fine art to conceal marital assets. As part of the suit, the plaintiff and her British lawyers had demanded a complete inventory of the billionaire's art collection—a collection that now included a Leonardo that was not a Leonardo. Gabriel reached the unsettling conclusion that he had no choice but to make the painting go away.

"How?" asked Chiara warily one evening while preparing dinner.

"Another extrajudicial seizure."

"You're going to steal it, you mean?"

"I couldn't possibly do it myself. I have to finish the *real* Leonardo."

Ingrid, however, was holed up at her cottage on the North Sea and bored senseless. She readily accepted the assignment but made it clear she would need a partner.

"Have you anyone in mind?" asked Gabriel.

"What about your friend from Marseilles?"

The friend was a professional thief named René Monjean. It was a wise suggestion. Monjean knew the territory and could handle himself if things went sideways.

"He won't do it pro bono," Gabriel pointed out.

"No," agreed Ingrid. "We'll need some cash."

"How much?"

"A half million, at least. A million to be on the safe side."

Gabriel killed the call, then rang Martin Landesmann in Geneva.

"Absolutely not," declared the Swiss financier.

"Thanks, Martin. I'll make it up to you somehow."

General Ferrari popped into Venice the following week. Over Bellinis at Harry's Bar, he briefed Gabriel on the escalating war against the Camorra. More than three hundred members of the Di Falco clan had been arrested, and billions in cash and other assets had been seized or frozen. The supply of cocaine on the streets of Europe had fallen precipitously. Prices had risen sharply as a result.

"All because of you and your friend the Holy Father."

"How long will I need protection?" asked Gabriel.

"Hard to say. For the moment, at least, they seem far more interested in killing one another. They're also starting to talk. One of the men in custody admitted to helping Salvatore Alvaro kidnap and murder a young British woman in Venice last September. He claimed not to know anything about her or why his superiors in the Camorra wanted her dead."

"But how did they know she was trying to make contact with Amelia March of *ARTnews*?"

"I'm not sure they did. But when Signorina Radcliff discovered that the painting was no longer in the storeroom at the Vatican Museums, she went to Florence and confronted Giorgio Montefiore."

"Says who?"

"Montefiore's secretary at the Uffizi. Apparently they had a blazing row. Montefiore told her that she had just ruined her career and threw her out of his office. Then, in all likelihood, he called his friend Cardinal Bertoli."

"And Bertoli told his investment adviser, Nico Ambrosi, that they had a problem."

General Ferrari nodded gravely. "Ambrosi and his associates in the Camorra had a solution, though. An Italian solution."

"But why was Montefiore killed?"

"It was Montefiore who oversaw the restoration of the Leonardo. When Salvatore Alvaro came to Florence to collect it, Montefiore refused to tell him where it was unless he was paid an additional five million euros. Not surprisingly, Alvaro agreed to the terms. And when he had the painting in hand . . ."

"Giorgio got three bullets in the head."

General Ferrari shrugged. "*C'est la vie.*"

"When will the Carabinieri make their findings public?"

"We are prepared to leave the two murders unsolved for the time being."

"It is essential that Penelope Radcliff receive credit for discovering the Leonardo."

"That would require us to tell the truth."

"Or a version of the truth," suggested Gabriel. "One that reveals the Art Squad's role in recovering a lost painting by Leonardo da Vinci."

"And where, exactly, did we find it?"

"I'm sure you'll think of something, Cesare."

He gave the matter a moment of thought. "There's one serious problem, you know."

"The copy of the painting I sold to Alexander Prokhorov?"

"Yes."

"I have a solution."

"Not an Italian solution, I hope."

"Danish, actually."

"In that case," said the general, "problem solved."

For nearly a month, Gabriel didn't hear from her. Then she rang one day, out of the blue, from the satellite phone on René Monjean's motor yacht. Luca Rossetti met the boat the following afternoon in the Italian resort of Ventimiglia, and by that evening both the painting and Ingrid were back in the Allon family apartment in San Polo. Somehow she had managed to spend only half of Martin's million dollars. The rest was zipped into a nylon duffel, which she returned to Gabriel—thus proving there was honor among thieves, after all.

"Any problems?" he asked.

"Candy from a baby, Mr. Allon."

"How did you pull it off?"

"It was an inside job."

"They always are."

"So they say."

"Was it one of the security guards?" asked Gabriel.

"The girlfriend, actually."

"Not the lovely Yuliana?"

"I'm afraid so."

"How much did you pay her?"

Ingrid smiled. "Nothing at all."

At the request of the children, Ingrid stayed in Venice for a few days before jetting off to her villa on Mykonos. By then it was late April and Antonio Calvesi, despite regular progress reports, was growing anxious. Gabriel assured his patron that he was hard at work, though Chiara would later attest that on some days her husband sat staring at the portrait for hours on end without so much as preparing his palette. Other days he might apply a brushstroke or two of paint and hastily depart, only to return to his studio an hour or so later and commence staring again. Chiara, having endured countless restorations, recognized the symptoms. Secretly she informed Antonio Calvesi that the Leonardo was nearly finished.

Convincing Gabriel of that fact proved far more difficult, for he was suffering from an uncharacteristic case of nerves and indecision. Chiara could scarcely blame him. The painting on his easel would soon be one of the most famous in the world, and his restoration would come under intense scrutiny. It was inevitable that not everyone in the conservation and curatorial community would agree with the choices he made. When Chiara suggested showing the painting to the five Leonardists, he refused. The five Leonardists, he said, would undoubtedly give him five different opinions. The only judgment that mattered now was his own.

And so for the rest of April he remained a prisoner of his studio. Some days he worked for twelve hours without a break, some days he applied only a brushstroke or two, some days he merely sat and stared. The beautiful young girl from Milan stared back at him over her left shoulder, with her mismatched pupils. They were, he thought, her most alluring feature.

Each Wednesday afternoon, though, he kept his appointment with his fourteen students. On the final Wednesday of the month, Dottorressa Saviano asked whether he would be willing to take on an additional student—a young boy of exceptional artistic promise. Gabriel readily agreed, despite the fact there were only a few weeks remaining in the school year. He paid the child no inordinate attention during the hourlong session but extolled the astonishing quality of his work while walking him home. The boy seemed not to hear him. His rebellious twin sister, having broken free of her Carabinieri bodyguard, was leaping in puddles left by an afternoon rain.

59

Musei Vaticani

Gabriel delivered the finished painting to Antonio Calvesi at the Vatican Museums at 2:00 p.m. on Monday. They spent the remainder of the afternoon reviewing the scientific analysis, Gabriel's extensive restoration notes, and the painting's provenance. The researcher had concluded that Leonardo probably commenced work on the portrait in the late 1490s—around the same time he was working on *The Last Supper*—and that it was with him at the time of his death in France in 1519. In all likelihood, it ended up in the hands of Salaì, Leonardo's lover and longtime assistant.

What happened to the painting next is unclear, but the provenance researcher discovered records in Milan suggesting it entered the estate of a Milanese nobleman. At some point in the mid-seventeenth century, the nobleman's descendants disposed of the painting, which by then was doubtless in a degraded condition. A hundred years later it was subjected to a restoration that left it a ruin. The walnut panel was salvageable, though, so a nameless Milanese School artist used it for a Madonna and Child, unwittingly burying a Leonardo in the process. The painting hung in the chapel of an abbey near Bergamo until the outbreak of World War I, when it entered the Vatican's collection, mistakenly attributed to Raphael's busy Florence workshop. Some years later it was demoted to an eighteenth-century imitator of Raphael and consigned to storage, where it would remain until a routine cleaning resulted in one of the most important artistic discoveries ever made.

Gabriel, after reviewing the provenance, plucked a pen from his pocket and added the name of the young British art conservator who had found the Leonardo. He then informed Antonio Calvesi that in forty-eight hours' time, General Ferrari of the Art Squad would hold a news conference and lift the veil on the entire affair.

"If he does that," said Calvesi, "it will forever tarnish the painting's reputation."

"I disagree. But I'm afraid you don't have a choice in the matter. It's all going to come out."

"In that case, tell your friend the general he can hold his news conference here at the museum."

"He was hoping you would say that."

"Will you be in attendance?" asked Calvesi.

"Why should I be there?"

"You're the one who found it."

"Not me," said Gabriel. "I'm only the restorer."

He paid a brief call on His Holiness in his rooms at the Casa Santa Marta and then walked through the soft Roman evening to Veronica Marchese's palazzo. She answered the bell wearing a stunning cream-colored pantsuit and her cat-eyed spectacles. She was a kilo or two thinner, perhaps, but Gabriel could see no evidence of damage. In fact, in his professional opinion, she had never looked more beautiful. He told her so while removing the cork from a bottle of Alteni di Brassica sauvignon blanc.

"You should see my scar," she answered.

"I'll show you mine if you show me yours."

"Your lovely wife might not appreciate that." Veronica accepted a glass of the wine and settled carefully into a brocade armchair in her elegant drawing room. "To what shall we drink this time?"

Gabriel raised his glass and said, "To life."

"I owe mine to you and your friend Luca Rossetti."

"You haven't watched the video, I hope."

"I saw it once or twice while I was at the Gemelli. The last thing I remember about that day were those green eyes of yours looking down at me after I had been shot."

"You lost consciousness very quickly."

"Did I say anything?"

"No," lied Gabriel. "You weren't able to speak."

"My doctors told me that I had to be resuscitated in the ambulance. It's a strange feeling knowing that you've been dead. Even if it was only for a moment or two."

"But you were never alone."

"I'm told you stayed at the hospital all night."

"Luigi was there too."

"That much I remember." She drank some of the wine. "At least I think I do."

"He was a wreck that night. He blamed himself for what happened."

"It wasn't his fault. In fact, I'm to blame for everything that happened."

"Why you?"

"Because I was the one who rekindled our friendship after the death of my husband. It's a miracle we were able to keep my identity a secret after I was shot. Can you imagine the scandal that would have erupted if the press had found out that the Holy Father's former lover was recuperating in his private suite at the Gemelli?"

"His Holiness managed to change the subject rather quickly. For better or worse, you were something of an afterthought."

"As were you, it seems."

"Not for long, I'm afraid."

"The Leonardo?"

He smiled.

"Am I allowed to see it?"

Gabriel handed over his phone.

"Dear God," she whispered. "You did a remarkable job."

"I had a rather good collaborator. Not to mention subject," he added. "I have no doubt the girl from Milan will soon be the most famous woman in the world."

"Better her than me." Veronica returned the phone. "Did you see His Holiness when you were at the Vatican today?"

"Briefly."

"Did he ask after me?"

"He spoke of nothing else."

She sighed. "It's rather pathetic, don't you think? This tragic tale of mine?"

"So write a new one."

"As it happens, I'm hard at work on an alternative ending."

"Anyone I know?"

"A handsome young captain who works for the Art Squad in Venice."

"Veronica . . ."

"I know, I know. He's very young."

"But?"

She smiled. "He positively adores my scar."

———

Shortly before 9:00 a.m. the following Thursday, there appeared on the website of *ARTnews* magazine a story that sent shock waves through the art world. Written by Amelia March, it detailed the reappearance, theft, and eventual recovery of a lost portrait by Leonardo da Vinci. The original discovery, according to *ARTnews*, had been made by Penelope Radcliff, the apprentice art conservator whose body had been found floating in the waters of the Venetian Lagoon the previous autumn. The source for the story was identified only as "a person connected to the project."

General Cesare Ferrari, commander of the Art Squad, provided further details later that morning at a news conference held in the lobby of the Vatican Museums. Flanked by museum officials, he alleged that the disgraced Cardinal Matteo Bertoli had played a role in the painting's theft, as had the murdered Leonardist Giorgio Montefiore and elements of the Camorra. When pressed by reporters, General Ferrari declined to say where or when the painting had been recovered. He then stepped away from the microphones while the director of the Pinacoteca—the first woman to ever lead the museum—unveiled the painting. From the four corners of the art world there arose a collective gasp.

In the days that followed, other details about the painting's rediscovery emerged, including the name of the prominent Venice-based art conservator who had conducted the restoration on behalf of the Vatican Museums. Gabriel's concerns about how his work would be received proved unfounded. Indeed, with the exception of a social media screed by a notorious art world gadfly, the reviews were overwhelmingly laudatory. The kindest words were written by Professor Maximillian Zeller from Leipzig, who declared that "Gabriel Allon had doubtless learned his craft in Leonardo's busy studio in Milan, along with Boltraffio, Luini, d'Oggiono, and the rest of the *Leonardeschi*."

When the Pinacoteca finally announced the date that the painting would go on public display, the demand for tickets repeatedly crashed the museum's website. In the first twenty-four hours alone, more than a million tickets were sold. By week's end, those wishing to see the painting could expect a wait of six months.

But on the eve of the painting's public exhibition, one thousand invited guests arrived at the Pinacoteca for a black-tie exclusive viewing—moguls and magnates, curators and collectors, prominent dealers and other assorted glitterati. Cameras flashed as Gabriel and Chiara headed up the red carpet toward the museum's entrance, accompanied by Irene and Raphael. The painting hung in Room IX of the gallery, next to Leonardo's *St. Jerome.* The museum staff tried to keep the line moving, but the girl from Milan cast a spell over everyone who gazed into her mismatched pupils.

Gabriel bade her a final farewell and escorted Chiara and the children to the museum's courtyard for the cocktail reception. There were lights in the trees and tables on the green lawn, and a chamber orchestra was playing Vivaldi. Chiara led Irene and Raphael over to the buffet, and Gabriel headed toward one of the courtesy bars in search of liquid refreshment. There were eight bars in all, but the one he chose was under British occupation. Tweedy Jeremy Crabbe from Bonhams, suntanned Simon Mendenhall from Christie's, the learned Niles Dunham from the National Gallery. Sarah Bancroft, the only American present, had somehow managed to acquire a three-olive martini. She was murmuring something into the ear of her husband, who had an arm draped over the shoulders of tubby Oliver Dimbleby. Julian Isherwood, the very picture of *sprezzatura* in an old evening jacket and carelessly knotted tie, had taken up his usual position at the end of the bar. Gabriel settled next to him and asked, "Well, Julian?"

"Well what, petal?"

"What do you think of it?"

"Think of what, darling?"

"The Leonardo, for heaven's sake."

"What bloody Leonardo?" blared Oliver Dimbleby. "We just came to Rome for the party."

It ended shortly after ten o'clock and resumed in a much smaller form in the terrace bar at the Hotel Hassler. The children wilted at midnight, so Gabriel and Chiara said their goodnights and carried them downstairs to their suite. They were late in rising and missed the noon train back to Venice, taking the one fifteen instead. Gabriel sat next to Raphael, listening to the soft scratch of a Faber-Castell pencil against a Strathmore Series 300 sketchpad. He wondered, not for the first time, why the boy had changed his mind. Surely, he thought, it had been an inside job. They always were.

Author's Note

*A*n *Inside Job* is a work of entertainment and should be read as nothing more. The names, characters, places, and incidents portrayed in the story are the product of the author's imagination or have been used fictitiously. Any resemblance to actual persons, living or dead, businesses, companies, events, or locales is entirely coincidental.

Visitors to the *sestiere* of San Polo will search in vain for the converted palazzo overlooking the Grand Canal where Gabriel Allon lives with his wife and two young children. The business office of the Tiepolo Restoration Company is likewise impossible to find, for no such enterprise exists. There is indeed a café in the Campo dei Frari called Bar Dogale, but the counterman named Paolo Caruso is fictitious, as are the security cameras. Caffè Poggi is a wonderful place to have coffee after a visit to the Gallerie dell'Accademia, and Vini da Arturo is one of our favorite restaurants in San Marco. There is no Caffè Michelangelo across the street from the Vatican Museums, no Caffè Roma on the Via Casati in Ostiense, and no Osteria Lucrezia near the Termini train station. The Brøndums Hotel was indeed a gathering spot for the Skagen painters, but to the best of my knowledge it no longer accepts finished canvases in lieu of payment.

There are several banks in Lugano's Piazza della Riforma, but fortunately SBL PrivatBank SA is not one of them, for it does not exist. Piedmont Global Capital of Milan is likewise fictitious, as is Galerie Van de Velde of Amsterdam. There is indeed an enchanting art gallery in the northeast corner of Mason's Yard in St. James's, but it is owned by Patrick Matthiesen, one of the world's most successful and respected Old Masters art dealers. The madcap menagerie of London art world figures who inhabit the pages of *An Inside Job* are invented from whole cloth, as are their sometimes questionable personal and professional antics. Deepest apologies to Wiltons for turning the renowned restaurant's elegant bar into their nightly watering hole, but I'm afraid no one else would have them.

I have visited the conservation laboratory at the Vatican Pinacoteca—in fact, I was once permitted to hold Leonardo's *St. Jerome*—but I have never set foot in the museum's storerooms and made no attempt to determine their true location. Every aspect of the theft portrayed in the novel is invented, with the exception of the premise that the overwhelming majority of museum robberies are inside jobs. Robert Wittman, one of the founding members of the FBI's Art Crime Team, estimates that 90 percent of all museum thefts have an internal component. Italy's powerful organized crime networks have on occasion dabbled in art crime. In 2016, Italian police discovered two stolen Vincent van Gogh paintings at a property linked to the violent Amato-Pagano clan of the Camorra. It is widely assumed that Caravaggio's *Nativity with St. Francis and St. Lawrence*, stolen from the Oratorio di San Lorenzo in Palermo in October 1969, ended up in the hands of the Sicilian Cosa Nostra.

The theft of the *Mona Lisa* in August 1911 was indeed an inside job; it was carried out by an Italian-born carpenter who had helped to construct the painting's protective case. Scholars agree that Leonardo began work on the portrait in 1503 after returning to Florence. The panel was fashioned from the wood of a poplar tree, which are common in Tuscany. Leonardo made his Milan portraits, however, on walnut panels. The version of *Salvator Mundi* sold by Christie's in 2017 for $450 million was likewise painted on a walnut panel, one with a large knot in the lower center. At the time of this writing, Christie's attribution of the *Salvator Mundi* to Leonardo remains controversial.

In April 1483, Leonardo accepted a commission to paint an altarpiece for the Confraternity of the Immaculate Conception in Milan's church of San Francesco Grande. While planning the work, he executed the preparatory silverpoint sketch known as *Head of a Woman* or *Study for an Angel*, which legendary art historian Bernard Berenson hailed as "one of the finest achievements in all draftsmanship." Sadly, there is no evidence that Leonardo ever made an oil painting based on the exquisite sketch. The beautiful young Milanese girl was merely the model for the archangel that appears in both versions of the *Virgin of the Rocks*, one that hangs in the Louvre and a second at the National Gallery in London. Scholars disagree over whether the archangel is Uriel or Gabriel. I chose to identify the figure as Gabriel, the celestial being for whom my protagonist is named.

I wish I could say that there was no basis in fact for the Vatican financial scandal portrayed in *An Inside Job*, but that is not the case. Indeed, nearly every aspect of my fictitious affair was suggested by actual events, beginning with the complicated London real estate deal at the heart of the story. The real building was located not on New Bond Street but on Sloane Avenue. And the powerful cardinal involved in its purchase was not Matteo Bertoli but Giovanni Angelo

Becciu, a highly regarded Vatican diplomat who once held the post of *sostituto*. A Vatican tribunal found Cardinal Becciu guilty of fraud and embezzlement in December 2023 and sentenced him to five and a half years in prison. Eight other defendants, including three Italian financiers, were convicted of related charges. All have denied wrongdoing, and at the time of this writing Cardinal Becciu was living in a grace-and-favor apartment in the Palazzo del Sant'Uffizio, awaiting the outcome of his appeal. To be clear, no one involved in the case was accused of having links to Italian organized crime.

That was not the case, however, for Michele Sindona, the high-flying Milanese banker at the center of a scandal that rocked the Church in the mid-1970s. Pope Paul VI, shortly after his election to the papacy in 1963, asked Sindona to manage the Church's finances despite the fact that His Holiness was aware of widespread speculation regarding the banker's connections to the Cosa Nostra. Sindona's fall from grace began with the 1974 collapse of New York's Franklin National Bank, in which he held a controlling interest. Franklin's failure would eventually bring down the rest of Sindona's empire, including Banca Privata Italiana. He committed suicide in an Italian prison after he was convicted of hiring three Mafia hitmen to murder Banca Privata's court-appointed liquidator. As a result of the scandal, an estimated $30 million in Vatican assets went up in smoke.

Michele Sindona's longtime business associate Roberto Calvi was at the center of the next and, arguably, worst Vatican financial scandal. Known as "God's Banker" because of his close ties to the Vatican, Calvi was the general manager of Milan's Banco Ambrosiano, which collapsed in spectacular fashion in 1982. The Vatican Bank, then led by Archbishop Paul Marcinkus, was Banco Ambrosiano's largest shareholder, and Marcinkus was the chairman of the Nassau-based holding company Ambrosiano Overseas. Calvi managed to flee Italy on a false passport and was discovered hanging from London's Blackfriars Bridge on the morning of June 18, 1982. Prosecutors in Rome would eventually conclude that he had been murdered by the Cosa Nostra. As for Marcinkus, he was briefly the target of an Italian arrest warrant. Pope John Paul II refused to comply with the warrant, leaving the Holy See in the uncomfortable position of sheltering a wanted fugitive from Italian justice. The Vatican eventually agreed to pay $224 million—approximately $700 million in 2025 dollars—to Banco Ambrosiano's creditors in "recognition of moral involvement" in the bank's collapse.

Despite the Vatican Bank's troubled history, the official newspaper of the Holy See expressed "perplexity and surprise" in September 2010 when Italian authorities froze $30 million in Vatican Bank funds as part of an investigation into money laundering. German aristocrat Ernst von Freyberg took control of the bank in February 2013, vowing to usher in a new era of transparency. But just four months into von Freyberg's tenure, yet another scandal erupted, this one prompted by the arrest of Monsignor Nunzio Scarano. Nicknamed Monsignor Cinquecento for his habit of carrying wads of €500 banknotes, Scarano was charged with fraud and corruption in a scheme to smuggle €20 million in cash from Switzerland to Italy aboard a private jet. A month before his arrest, he had been removed from his post at the Administration of the Patrimony of the Apostolic See over accusations he had laundered $750,000 in Mafia money through his personal account at the Vatican Bank. Italian prosecutors alleged that he had been acting in league with "businessmen" from Naples, home of the ruthless Camorra.

After his arrest, Scarano was held in Rome's squalid Regina Coeli prison, a far cry from the palatial 7,500-square-foot apartment he owned in the seaside city of Salerno. He once reported a theft of more than €6 million worth of art. When police asked Scarano how he could afford such treasures on his $40,000-a-year Vatican salary, the monsignor claimed that the art and the apartment had been purchased for him by wealthy benefactors. A Rome criminal court would eventually acquit Scarano of the most serious charges against him.

Before Cardinal Becciu's conviction in the London real estate debacle, the highest-ranking Vatican official to be found guilty of corruption was Angelo Caloia, who led the Vatican Bank for the two decades after the scandal-plagued term of Archbishop Marcinkus. A Vatican tribunal sentenced Caloia in January 2021 to eight years and eleven months in prison for embezzling tens of millions of euros from the Vatican Bank through corrupt real estate deals. His former lawyer was also found guilty and received an identical sentence. The court confiscated more than €38 million from the two men, and they were ordered to pay an additional €20 million in damages.

It was the late Pope Francis, not my fictitious Luigi Donati, who made a historic visit to the distant Italian island of Lampedusa to call attention to the plight of migrants. Francis also dwelled in two simple rooms in the Casa Santa Marta guesthouse rather than the ornate *appartamento pontificio* on the third floor of the Apostolic Palace. He set the tone for his papacy on the night of his election when he appeared on the balcony of St. Peter's Basilica wearing a simple white cassock, with a pewter-colored cross around his neck and scuffed orthopedic shoes on his feet. "Carnival time," he told the papal tailor, "is over."

Francis delivered a similar message to the Roman Curia regarding the issue of Vatican finances, setting in motion a titanic battle that defined his papacy. According to the *New York Times*, Cardinal Becciu was one of several powerful cardinals who attempted to scuttle

Francis's reforms. But Nicola Gratteri, a prosecutor in the southern Italian region of Calabria, warned that Francis had made an enemy of powerful forces beyond the Vatican's walls. "For many years," he told the Rome newspaper *il Fatto Quotidiano*, "the Mafia has laundered money and made investments with the complicity of the Church. But now the pope is dismantling the poles of economic power in the Vatican, and that is dangerous." Gratteri added ominously: "If the godfathers can find a way to stop him, they will seriously consider it."

Pope Francis died at 7:35 a.m. on April 21, 2025, as I was completing this novel. The 133 cardinal-electors of the conclave chose as his successor sixty-nine-year-old Robert Francis Prevost, the first American to ever serve as the supreme pontiff of the Roman Catholic Church. A former missionary who spent much of his career working in a deeply impoverished region of Peru, Prevost is expected to continue Francis's ministry, with its emphasis on creating a more open and forgiving Church dedicated to serving the needs of the poor rather than those of the rich. In my fictitious version of the Vatican, though, that vital work will be carried out by His Holiness Pope Luigi Donati, a humble street priest who preached the Gospels and built schools and hospitals for the wretched of the earth. A soldier of God on a mission of mercy.

Acknowledgments

I am forever indebted to the late David Bull for his advice on all matters related to art and restoration. Shortly before his death in December 2024, David helped me to concoct a reasonably plausible scenario for stealing a hitherto unknown painting by Leonardo da Vinci from the Vatican Museums and bringing it to market. His passion for Leonardo found its way onto the pages of *An Inside Job*, as did his charm, brilliance, humanity, and remarkable sense of humor. David was my teacher and friend, and I will miss him dearly.

My wife, Jamie Gangel, listened patiently while I worked out the plot of *An Inside Job* and skillfully edited my early drafts, all while serving as special correspondent in CNN's Washington bureau. My children, Lily and Nicholas, likewise managed to find time in their busy schedules to provide me with moral and logistical support as I struggled to meet my deadline. My debt to them is immeasurable, as is my love.

Maxwell L. Anderson, who has five times served as the director of a North American art museum, including the Whitney Museum of American Art in New York, answered all my questions, no matter how mundane. My Los Angeles superlawyer Michael Gendler was a source of wise legal counsel, and Anthony Scaramucci, Tim Collins, and my son-in-law, Kamil Sadik, provided me with financial advice. Needless to say, none of them have ever engaged in the sort of fraud and money laundering perpetrated by my fictitious SBL PrivatBank and Piedmont Global Capital.

My dear friend Louis Toscano, author of *Triple Cross* and *Mary Bloom*, made countless improvements to the novel, and my eagle-eyed personal copy editor, Kathy Crosby, made certain it was free of typographical and grammatical errors. Harper president and publisher Jonathan Burnham also serves as my editor, and *An Inside Job* was made better by his sure hand. David Koral expertly shepherded my typescript through the production process on the tightest of schedules.

I consulted hundreds of newspaper and magazine articles while writing *An Inside Job*, far too many to cite here. I owe a special debt to the reporters of the *New York Times* for their remarkable coverage of the Vatican's most recent financial scandal—and to Rachel Sanderson, formerly of the *Financial Times*, who spent nearly a year investigating the sins of the Vatican Bank. Several books were especially helpful: Martin Kemp, *Leonardo da Vinci: The 100 Milestones* and *Living with Leonardo*; Ben Lewis, *The Last Leonardo: The Secret Lives of the World's Most Expensive Painting*; Walter Isaacson, *Leonardo da Vinci*; Gianluigi Nuzzi, *Merchants in the Temple: Inside Pope Francis's Secret Battle Against Corruption Inside the Vatican*; Gerald Posner, *God's Bankers: A History of Money and Power at the Vatican*; John Cornwell, *A Thief in the Night: Life and Death in the Vatican*; and Roberto Saviano, *Gomorrah: A Personal Journey into the Violent International Empire of Naples' Organized Crime System*.

Finally, a heartfelt thanks to the rest of the team at HarperCollins, especially Brian Murray, Leah Wasielewski, Doug Jones, Leslie Cohen, Milan Bozic, Brianna Cedrone, Josh Marwell, Mark Ferguson,

Robin Bilardello, Frank Albanese, Carolyn Bodkin, Chantal Restivo-Alessi, Julianna Wojcik, Mark Meneses, Beth Silfin, Lisa Erickson, and Amy Baker. It goes without saying that *An Inside Job* could not have been published without their support and professional dedication, but I shall say it nonetheless, for they are the best in the business.

A brutal murder, a missing masterpiece, a mystery only
Gabriel Allon can solve…

When an old friend asks art restorer and legendary spy Gabriel Allon for help with a baffling murder investigation, Gabriel finds himself pursuing a powerful and dangerous new adversary.

Charlotte Blake, a celebrated art history professor, appears to be the victim of a serial killer who has been terrorizing the Cornish countryside. But there are a number of telltale inconsistencies, including a missing mobile phone. And then there is the mysterious three-letter cypher she left behind on a notepad in her study.

Professor Blake was searching for a looted Picasso worth more than a $100 million, and Gabriel takes up the chase for the painting as only he can—with six Impressionist canvases forged by his own hand and an unlikely team of operatives that includes a world-famous violinist, a beautiful master thief, and a lethal contract killer turned British spy.

A stylish and wildly entertaining mystery that moves at lightning speed from the cliffs of Cornwall to the enchanted island of Corsica and, finally, to a breathtaking climax on the very doorstep of 10 Downing Street.

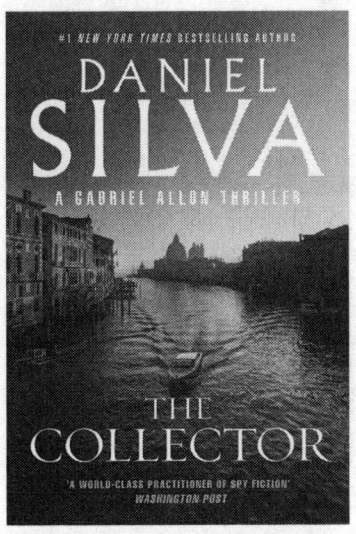

In the Amalfi villa of a murdered South African shipping tycoon, the Carabinieri have made a startling discovery—a secret vault containing an empty frame and stretcher matching the dimensions of the world's most valuable missing painting. The commander of the Art Squad asks restorer and legendary spy Gabriel Allon to quietly track down the artwork before the trail goes cold.

With the help of a most unlikely ally, a beautiful Danish computer hacker and professional thief, Gabriel follows the painting's trail to a man with close ties to the highest level of Russian power—code-named the Collector.

The missing masterpiece is the lynchpin of a conspiracy that if successful, could plunge the world into a conflict of apocalyptic proportions. To foil the plot, Gabriel must carry out a daring heist of his own, with millions of lives hanging in the balance.

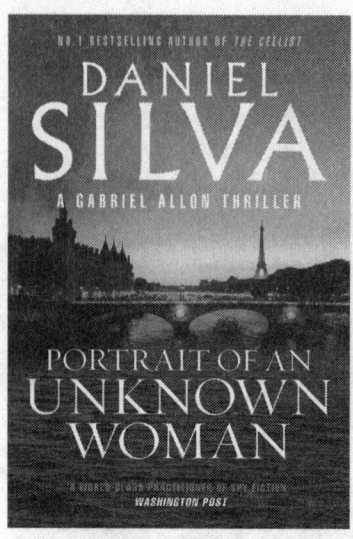

The hunt is on for the greatest art forger who ever lived ...

Legendary spy and art restorer Gabriel Allon has at long last severed ties with Israeli intelligence and settled quietly with his beautiful wife and their young twins in Venice, the only place he has ever truly known peace.

But when the eccentric London art dealer Julian Isherwood asks Gabriel to investigate the circumstances surrounding the rediscovery and lucrative sale of a centuries-old painting, he is drawn into a deadly game of cat and mouse where nothing is as it seems.

Gabriel soon discovers that the work in question, a portrait of an unidentified woman attributed to Sir Anthony van Dyck, is almost certainly a fiendishly clever fake. To find the mysterious figure who painted it—and uncover a multibillion-dollar fraud at the pinnacle of the art world—Gabriel conceives one of the most elaborate deceptions of his career. If it is to succeed, he must become the very mirror image of the man he seeks: the greatest art forger the world has ever known.